Pride Publishing books by Brian Lancaster

Single Books
Companion Required
Any Day
Salvaging Christmas
Famous Last

I0598050

FAMOUS LAST

BRIAN LANCASTER

Famous Last
ISBN # 978-1-80250-500-9
©Copyright Brian Lancaster 2022
Cover Art by Claire Siemaszkiewicz ©Copyright November 2022
Interior text design by Claire Siemaszkiewicz
Pride Publishing

FAMOUS LAST

Dedication

A huge thank-you to all the readers of my work, especially those on the Gay Authors website who have been a source of huge positivity and encouragement workshopping my stories across the years. A special callout to those who left a review for this story in its original format, which includes Raven1, G90814, Gary L, Critter Smith, Sunshine, LD Stratton, Leo 622, pvtguy, chris191070, Wesley8890, and a particular thank-you to drpaladin for coming up with the fictitious name of the country Kryszytonia. And, of course, a big thank-you as ever to Timothy M who line edited each chapter for me. Another call out to my friend, Jojit D, who has provided last minute edits for many of my books.

Thanks again to all those at TEG, especially Ann J. Léveillé, for your brilliant editing, advice and suggestions that helped me shape a better story, and to all the TEG team for your professionalism, support, helpful assistance and friendliness.

This story is set in the UK during the coronavirus pandemic and it would be remiss of me not to thank everyone at the NHS and other front-line services who worked tirelessly and selflessly to battle on during difficult times.

And last, but not least, to my husband Christopher, for his continued support as we uprooted ourselves and our two Ragdolls from Hong Kong, our home for the past twenty-four years, and returned to set up house in the south of England.

Chapter One

Rising from London's busy River Thames, the maritime metropolitan symphony combined with the constant rumble of Friday evening traffic from surrounding roads reverberated around the rooftop garden. Add to that the rapid gunfire of rotor blades from a helicopter passing overhead, and, as impossible as it may have seemed, Spencer Wyrrell overheard every perfectly enunciated word.

Bundled up on a two-seater stone bench tucked away in the corner of Muriel Moresby's penthouse roof garden, he had been alone when he'd first ventured out through the glass door some fifteen minutes before. Nobody else had been courageous enough to brave the bitterly cold weather, not even diehard smokers. Thankfully, floor-to-ceiling vertical blinds in slate grey covered the windows, closing off the toasty penthouse interior from the small garden of concrete statues and evergreen flora.

Freezing his arse off in the brutal late October air, Spencer's original sparkling masterplan had quickly begun to lose its gleam. Placed next to him, an ice bucket stacked with unmelted ice cubes, an open bottle of vintage Dom Perignon and two crystal flutes awaited the arrival of his partner in crime, colleague Bev. After two hours of helping things run smoothly in the socially distanced exhibition, she had volunteered him to smuggle out the bottle while she finished off schmoozing friends of their boss, the snooty investment banking couple with the matching Versace face masks. Initially they had approached him about three of the paintings for sale, and after he had matched them up with the artist to secure the deal, Bev had taken over. Having managed to avoid any of the other waiting guests, he thought he'd won the better part of the bargain. He was certainly grateful to be away from earnest discussions about abstract artwork that, frankly, he had no idea about or interest in.

And when the patio door had slid open – after the lenses of his glasses had finally de-misted – the person stepping through had been not Bev but someone entirely unexpected. A someone who had peered around furtively to make sure he was alone before removing his mask and pulling out his smartphone.

And there Spencer sat, slowly turning into a human ice popsicle. All he wanted now was to be somewhere else, preferably warmer – the Caribbean might be nice – instead of sitting hugging himself, scrunched up and cowering behind a tall concrete jardinière, wishing the earth would swallow him whole. Or perhaps a sudden time corridor would open up and he could be transported back thirty minutes to before he'd made the imprudent decision to step outside. And definitely before he'd inadvertently overheard the telephone conversation of the smoking-hot celebrity, Marshall J. Highlander.

"Am I speaking in foreign tongues?" came the stern but sexy voice again, a deep baritone and eminently listenable. "As I've told you already. No comment. Which of those two words are you having difficulty with?"

Unable to help himself, Spencer lowered his mask and breathed heat onto the frozen fingers of one hand before dragging down branches of the juniper bush and peering at the man's back. Standing poised and confident, with his trademark deep brown hair styled with wisps of grey drawn back from the temple, he appeared iconic, heroic almost. In real life, his height became evident. He was significantly taller than Spencer's five-seven. Dressed in beige woollen slacks and an expensive silk jacket of dark chocolate covering a caramel-coloured roll-neck sweater, he epitomised the type of model adorning the cover of any number of men's fashion magazines. As Spencer watched, mesmerised, Highlander reached his free hand behind himself, fisted the back of his trouser belt, and in doing so, lifted the bottom of his jacket to showcase his magnificent arse. Unlike many big names Spencer had met — and there had been a steady stream in and out of their magazine office — Highlander looked even more stunning in the flesh. He made an effort to take care of himself, and had cultured a calm, capable, wholly masculine persona, no doubt the result of spending many hours in front of a television camera. But unlike some of those egotistical here today, gone tomorrow personalities, Highlander's magnetism reputedly ran more than skin deep. And right now his trademark honeyed voice, which had in equal parts charmed and challenged tyrants the world over, carried a stinging warning.

"And if you print a single one, you and your newspaper will go down in flames on a Hindenburg scale, slapped with more injunctions than even your blood-sucking owner can wriggle out of. That much I promise you."

In the silence that followed, Spencer hoped Highlander had finished and would return inside. After a few moments, he peeped through the greenery and saw the man staring out over the Thames, raising the phone to his ear once again.

"Darcy. Hi. I'm good. Well, actually, no, I'm not. Look, I just had that little shit of a hack Wentworth from the *Tribute* on the phone. They have photos of Joe and me in the south of France from five years ago. Explicit, he says. Threatening to go to print Sunday. They're obviously desperate for news right now. Yes, I'm fully aware of that. No, of course I didn't, and before you ask, there is no way Joe would have... No, Darce. Joe would never do that to me. He's not like that. Because I do. Okay, okay, I'll call him. But in the meantime, what do you suggest I—? Would you? I was hoping you'd say that. You're a sweetheart. I knew I could count on you. Sorry, say that again. Oh, at some art exhibit and benefit for Mongolian orphans. Muriel Moresby's place. We're being herded around two-by-two like Noah's bloody ark. Crowd's as dull as a duchess, but I know the charity organisers personally. Probably sneak out soon. No, it's okay, I'll get a black cab. You don't need to do that. Okay then, if you're sure. A chat and a drink would be wonderful. It's on the Embankment overlooking the river. I'll text the full address. See you in an hour. Bye, Darce. And thanks again."

Spencer let the branch go, hoping Highlander had finished. But he felt intrigued at what he'd overheard. Highlander was gay? And was that common knowledge? It sounded like the poor guy had a lot on his plate right now. If only he would go inside and deal with matters. Instead, he appeared to be making another call. Spencer folded his arms across his chest to try to retain some warmth. He hadn't wanted to come to the party in the first place. Muriel, aka Her Royal Highness, had only invited her key office staff to beef up numbers and work the room. Even the word 'invited' was a stretch. Refusal or prior engagement excuses would not have been tolerated.

"Joey. Yes. No, it's not about that. Look, I need to ask. Did you sell photographs of us to the *Tribute*? From our holiday in St Cezaire in France? No, I'm not accusing you, I'm asking. Did you –? There's no need to shout! I'm just trying to figure out how they managed to get hold of –"

As Spencer watched, Highlander expelled a deep, steamy sigh and his head fell forward, his chin hitting his chest. After a few moments of silence, his voice became soft, the anguished sound tugging at Spencer's heart.

"Why? Why would you do that, Joe? Christ, what did I do to you? Did I really hurt you that –? Joe? Joey? Shit!"

Once again, a lull came from the railing. Had the call ended? When Spencer peered over, he saw the man's shoulders shaking and heard gentle sobs squeezing through the hand closed over Highlander's face. Once again, Spencer prayed hard for intervention. Maybe a member of the crew of the *USS Enterprise*'s transporter room would randomly lock onto his coordinates and beam him somewhere — anywhere — else. Or maybe if Bev would simply stumble out onto the balcony at that moment to provide the perfect comedy movie moment, Highlander would no longer consider himself alone and would leave. When everything fell silent, Spencer relaxed against the bench. Until he heard a soft scraping sound and an uncomfortable feeling nagged at him, prompting him to take another peek.

Highlander had climbed onto the concrete ledge housing the waist-high railing, stepped across, and now stood facing out to the river — and his doom. An odd sensation overcame Spencer then. A sudden rush of calm and an overwhelming emotion he had never experienced before had him jumping up from the bench. In doing so, he dislodged a glass champagne flute from the ice bucket, which shattered on the balcony floor, causing Highlander to spin around, grabbing the railing for support.

"Please don't," called Spencer gently and calmly, puzzled at the strength of his voice and suddenly aware that he had ripped off his mask entirely and stood in full view of the man.

One of Highlander's feet slipped slightly, probably due to the residual frost. Fortunately, both hands maintained their firm grasp on the railing.

"You're such an inspiration, Mr Highlander. If you're about to do what I think you're doing, it would be wrong in so many ways. Please. People look up to you. I do. And what is it you said on your show? 'No problems are insurmountable in this world. Dialogue always helps even if only to highlight and appreciate our differences.' You said those exact words to the Dalai Lama."

"I say a lot of things —"

"And people listen. I say a lot of things and people don't take the blindest bit of notice. Even my cat ignores me."

Despite the potential gravity of the situation, Highlander's shoulders shook slightly and Spencer heard a gentle chuckle.

"Tell you what, Mr Highlander —"

"Marshall."

"Tell you what, Marshall, come and share a glass of champagne with me. Talk to me. And if you still feel like doing what I think you're about to do, I'll go back inside and pretend I never saw you. Of course, I'll also never sleep through the night again, but I'm prepared to take that gamble. How does that sound?"

Highlander had gone completely still, staring out across the Thames. Spencer experienced a tremor run down his spine even though he found he had suddenly become immune to the cold.

"I must admit I never anticipated having an audience."

"You won't as long as you get down and join me now."

"And you're not going to cuff me, are you?"

"If I had handcuffs," said Spencer, his mouth working independently of his brain, "and I promise you I don't, I'd be using them to secure you to the bedposts of the metal bedframe in my bedroom, once I'd hauled you back to my flat, to cover your naked body in orange marmalade and whipped cream before having my wicked way with you."

This time Highlander turned sharply to take in Spencer, a look of disbelief on his face, before letting out loud, steamy laughter into the night. He had a nice laugh, Spencer realised, not something the public got to hear often on his high-minded programme.

"Do you talk to everyone this way?"

"Just drop-dead gorgeous celebrities," said Spencer, before placing fingers over his mouth, realising his terrible choice of adjectives given the situation.

After a few more moments of silence and after a deep heartfelt sigh, Highlander turned and began to climb back over the balcony. When Spencer moved forward to assist, Highlander held a hand palm up, warning Spencer away. Cooperating reluctantly, Spencer backed up a step.

As soon as Highlander stood on firm ground, Spencer rushed forward and threw his arms around him, held him tightly in a hug and buried his face in his chest. Without warning, sobs began to rise from inside Spencer, his body trembling, and in an odd turn of events, Highlander became the one comforting him.

"Hey, hey," came the warm voice, a hand rubbing his back. "If it's any consolation, I wouldn't have done anything. But sometimes I find an inner calm reminding myself of my impermanence. Consider it a momentary lapse in sanity."

Spencer barely listened, his head buried in the shoulder of Highlander's jacket, smelling the beautiful combination of spicy aftershave and skin.

"Who are you?" asked Highlander, gently pulling Spencer away from him and holding him at arm's length while Spencer swiped quickly at his eyes.

"People call me Squirrel."

"Why? Let me guess. Something to do with you being nuts?"

"Wow, that's original," said Spencer, straight-faced. Fortunately, he'd begun to calm down and enjoy Highlander's—Marshall's—fond scrutiny Except now he also began to feel a little self-conscious at his teary display. "Not heard that like a zillion times before."

"Now I think somewhere in your earlier appeal you promised me a glass of bubbly?"

"Okay, but can we please step away from the railing? Maybe sit down? But mind the broken glass on the floor. I dropped a champagne flute."

Spencer moved across to the bench hidden behind the large bush. Spencer waited for Marshall to join him. Without being asked, he poured champagne and handed the glass over.

"Did you want something to eat? I could pop in and grab a tray of finger food."

"I'll pass, thanks. Champagne is enough. And the food didn't look terribly appetising."

"I know, right? Even my mother could do better, and she's the world's worst cook."

"That's a tad unkind."

"It's true, though. I remember coming home from summer camp once and my dad catching me at the door and saying 'we had a lovely leg of lamb while you were away. Until your mother cooked it.'"

Marshall laughed again, and Spencer felt himself calming a little more.

"How long have you been out here?" asked Marshall, taking a good gulp then handing the champagne back to Spencer.

"About forty frozen minutes. A little before you appeared."

Spencer took a sip before topping up and raising the glass to Marshall. As he handed the glass over, he pondered the rules on sharing drinks given the pandemic but then shrugged them away. If the man sitting with him had just survived a crisis of self, he could survive a shared glass of bubbly.

"Did you catch any of my conversations?" came the famous voice.

"I did," said Spencer, feeling his face burning but keeping his eyes on the man. "Not much. I mean, don't worry. I wouldn't dare breathe a word."

"Shit," said Highlander, turning away and sighing out a cloud of steamy breath.

"No, really, Mr High — Marshall."

Marshall's attention returned, his eyes looking deep into Spencer's. After a few moments, his gaze softened and he relaxed.

"No, you wouldn't, would you? You're one of those kind souls that people in my profession rarely get to meet. So what do you do, Squirrel? Shit, I can't call you Squirrel. It doesn't feel right. What's your real name?"

"Spencer. Spencer Kenneth Wyrrell. S. K. Wyrrell. Hence, Squirrel. School was brutal. I'm not sure my parents even realised when they named me."

Once again his words made Marshall chuckle, and he felt sure, or at least hoped, his dark moment had finally passed.

"What do you do for a living, Spencer?"

"I'm a junior copy and online editor. For Muriel Moresby's magazine outfit, the Blackmore Magazine Group."

"Poor you."

"I know, right? I'm also the office gopher. But it's full-time work and pays the rent. And I'm still employed despite what's happening in the world. So I have to thank my lucky stars. Not exactly highbrow, like you, but it's a stepping stone. Even if at twenty-nine I'm still on the first step."

"To what?"

"At college I studied journalism. Once I've got enough editing experience under my belt, I'd really like to try out for one of the online dailies. Even though the competition's vicious."

"You write?"

"Not professionally. But I hope to, one day. In university I edited the student magazine and wrote articles. I even had a couple published by a local newspaper. And I did pretty well, too. Every person in this world, no matter how inconsequential they feel they are, should dream big. Isn't that right?"

"Are you quoting me again?" asked Marshall, tilting his head to grin at Spencer.

"What can I say? You're very quotable."

And very shaggable, thought Spencer but kept that to himself. As he went to top up Marshall's glass again, a mobile began to ring faintly. Marshall reached into his inside jacket pocket and pulled out his phone. He let out a soft sigh after a glance at the display and handed the champagne flute back to Spencer.

"Looks like my ride's here," he said, standing.

Spencer put the bottle back in the bucket and stood as well. "I hope everything works out okay for you, Marshall. And promise me you're going to use the lift to get to the ground floor."

Marshall appeared confused for a moment but then stared at his shoes and chuckled while shaking his head.

"You're a funny man," he said before looking up. "And, yes, I promise to use the elevator. Sorry I worried you earlier. Goodbye then, Spencer. It was an unexpected pleasure meeting you tonight."

Marshall held out his hand, and Spencer fit his own inside. Marshall's strong, warm grip closed around Squirrel's ice-cold fingers. The simple gesture of bare skin on bare skin had his heart beating faster, his cheeks heating, and even the beast in his underpants stirring. Marshall held his gaze for a moment before leaning forward and kissing a shocked Spencer firmly on the lips. When he released his grip and stood back smiling, Spencer simply stood there, his eyes wide and mouth hanging open. An amused Marshall winked once before putting on his black surgical mask and disappearing into the penthouse apartment through the patio door.

Spencer stood staring at the dark glass, wondering what had just happened. His senses returning, he knelt to the ground and had begun clearing up the broken glass when the door slid open again. A figure stepped out carrying a flute of champagne and a large plate of canapés.

Finally. Bev, his colleague.

"Sorry, sorry, sorry, Squirrel, honey," she said, flustered then freezing when she saw him on his hands and knees, picking up shards of glass.

"Oh poop. You started without me. Did I miss anything?"

Chapter Two

Five minutes late for work, Spencer marched along the office corridor, using a cardboard tray holder to balance twelve various-sized, various-coloured metal containers filled with all kinds of exotic coffee or tea permutations from Muriel's independent coffee shop of choice. Over one shoulder he had a bag containing her laptop computer and cables for hooking up her presentation. Monday morning meetings happened in the main conference room, a large boardroom space with a glitzy plaque bearing the word *Magic* on the door. Muriel started the first get-together of every week promptly at nine whether people were there or not, and very loudly named and shamed anyone who dared arrive late.

Feeling in an upbeat mood that morning, he had picked out a black shirt, black trousers and a shocking pink bow tie, with a matching pink belt and face mask—his friend who custom-made the bow ties and belts had also started a range of matching reusable masks. Together with Spencer's thick-black-framed glasses, he considered his range of colourful bow ties and shirts his personal brand. Many of his colleagues had made their approval plain.

Not Muriel, though. Except when he made the very rare mistake, he might otherwise have been invisible. She referred to their first meeting of the week as her War Council, and every Monday morning the thirty-seater conference room became known as the War Room. Not difficult to guess that her retired husband, Lord Atherton Moresby, had once been in the armed services.

Worst of all, Bev had texted him that morning while he'd grabbed Muriel's laptop, saying she was running late again and could he cover for her until she arrived.

With the tray balanced at chest height, he placed his back against the door to the conference room, took a deep breath and pushed.

Maybe the universe will be kind to me today.

"Spencer," came the condescending schoolmarm tone of Muriel, the one person in the room who chose not to wear any kind of face covering. "Nice of you to finally deign to join us. Everyone's gasping. Why is the simplest of tasks always a challenge for you?"

Or maybe not.

"Sorry, Muriel. Long queue outside the coffee shop this morning. Seems to be getting more and more popular."

A close friend of hers ran the place, and he hoped the positive comment might negate his tardiness. He placed the tall spangly black canister down in front of her first before walking around the huge conference table placing drinks in front of each of those gathered.

"Really? I find that hard to believe. At eight o'clock this morning, when my driver took me past on my way into the office, the place looked entirely empty."

Purposely not meeting her gaze, he began setting up the laptop. With the minimum of fuss, he laid the LED TV remote control and the stylish gold laser pointer next to her computer touchpad and stepped away. After tossing his switched-off smartphone into the small mesh cage in the middle of the table—one of Muriel's house rules—he made his way down to his seat and sat among his all-female colleagues. Only Beverley's seat next to his remained vacant.

"All done, Muriel. And your presentation's loaded."

Some of his colleagues questioned why Muriel had hired him. Perhaps, he told them, the head of Human Resources had suggested she redress the workforce diversity balance, although Spencer could not imagine anyone brave enough to tell Muriel what to do. Hiring someone like him, an openly gay male, would normally have ticked a few boxes. Except her son and prodigy, Blake Ulysses Moresby, had already bagged that title, even if he had never done so publicly. He had also bagged Spencer. After showing him the ropes during Spencer's first week in the company, Blake had definitely gone the extra mile to make him feel welcome. Blake, the one who got away. Or rather, the one he'd never really had in the first place, who had charmed the pants off him—literally—before shunning and finally dumping him. Working in the same office had only ever been bearable because Blake spent so much time away on assignment.

"*Finally.*"

In his messed-up way, Spencer still fantasised about Blake and tended to hide whenever the boss's charismatic son entered the premises. Blake had almost quoted him the Official Secrets Act when he cooled off their short-lived liaison. Spencer had been happy to oblige. Who wanted people knowing you had been dumped? Only Bev knew some of the story, the parts he felt less uneasy about. Muriel's dislike of Spencer had been a slow progression long after they had cooled off. Even now he had no idea why. Her disdain had become the norm, something he expected and had learnt to shrug off.

"Do you need me to —?"

"Sit. Down. Spencer."

Setting up presentations wasn't really a part of his job. Prince had asked him to fill in on Monday mornings because Prince suffered from weekend-itus, an innate aversion to Monday mornings. The third of three males in the office, Prince provided all information technology support. If Spencer had ever wondered whether Muriel was a misandrist, her open and very vocal admiration of Prince had nipped that theory in the bud. Confident bordering brash, flawless looks and built better than most of the male models who adorned the pages of their magazines — move over Tyson Beckford — and completely straight, he had a captive audience in the office. For all their tough talk, many of the women went to pieces whenever he breezed up to their desks. Spencer had watched him being ogled by the staff as he knelt to the floor to plug in cables or leant across their workspaces in his tight designer T-shirt, his firm biceps, pecs and deltoids on display, to set up additional monitors or swap out a docking station, work he really ought to be doing after office hours. With the family name of Henry, Prince Henry was fittingly treated like royalty. Spencer often overheard the girls in the staffroom talking about having had a 'royal visit' that day which had naturally resulted in them having had a 'royal flush'. From what Spencer could tell, although Prince flirted playfully with the female staff, he appeared to draw the line at dating any of them, a clear distinction between work and play. If only Spencer had consulted Prince before allowing Blake to jump his bones.

"Why is this stupid thing not working? What have you done to it?" asked Muriel, expelling a sigh after signing on and glaring at her laptop screen for a few moments while messing with the laser pointer.

Fortunately, Prince, whose older brother had married his male partner, had genuinely warmed to Spencer. As the only other male employee permanently in the office, they shared an unlikely affinity. Just as well, because Blake acted as though Spencer no longer existed.

"Point the TV remote at the screen and push the green button. If you want, I can come over—"

Somewhat clumsily, she prodded one of the buttons, and her presentation popped up on the giant flatscreen.

"Sometimes I wonder if *he* should be paying *me* to work here," she muttered, providing a scowl for the benefit of the rest of her staff.

With any other person he might have countered with something like, 'I couldn't afford you', but he knew how much she disliked backtalk, and she would only find a way to make his life that bit more difficult. Most of the women gathered grinned at the table at her remark, while a few sent sympathetic glances his way. Woe betide anyone who tried to defend him.

"And where, may I ask, is Ms Salvatore?" asked Muriel, staring pointedly at Spencer.

"Beverley will join us shortly." When Muriel said nothing, waiting for a more comprehensive explanation, he floundered while ad-libbing an excuse. "She's – uh – taking an urgent call from – uh – LMVP about their double-page advertising spread in the Christmas edition of *Collective*. Sounds like they still need reassurance."

"Advertising? Isn't that supposed to be your domain of expertise? Isn't that what I pay you to handle?"

Again with the loud voice and the laser glare.

"It's one of them, yes, but – uh – Bev has a special relationship with – "

"Is Ms Salvatore now working for you? Is that it? Are us women now relegated to clearing up your messes for you?" When Muriel's gaze took in the whole room of amused faces and soft giggles, he knew a lecture would follow. In his mind, he ran through the catalogue of wizarding spells he'd memorised from the famous books and wished he could summon to get her to stop talking. "Let me tell all of you sitting here this morning. Beverley Salvatore worked tirelessly on Friday night. She managed to secure the sale of three unique pieces of artwork to a client, while others among you were nowhere to be found." Once again, she chose the moment to stare pointedly at Spencer. "And as I hope you are all aware, twenty-five per cent of the proceeds from the sale goes to the Mongolian Orphans Fund. Beverley Salvatore is an exemplary employee, something to which you should all aspire."

Living two streets away from the office, Beverley Salvatore was probably still at home applying her makeup. How the hell she managed to get away with her laissez-faire attitude to work, he had no idea. He loved her, he really did. She was someone he confided in unconditionally and for whom he would do absolutely anything. And she could show real brilliance when she put her mind to organising events. But that did not excuse her dreadful timekeeping. Nevertheless, once again, she had managed to end up in Muriel's good books without really lifting a finger, while his impromptu excuse had landed him even higher up on Muriel's shit list.

Moreover, LMVP, who had spent a small fortune on advertising with them, was an account *he* had landed. And the truth was they were over the moon about the choice of Christmas adverts from the design consultant he had recommended. When everything went well — as he knew it would — and Muriel reached out for feedback — as he knew she would — who would get the credit?

"Beverley Salvatore is an asset to Blackmores."

Any other male employee might have considered themselves persecuted. On more than one occasion, Beverley had urged Spencer to approach their Human Resources manager and lodge a formal complaint.

But he had no need.

First of all, Spencer loved his job working in an office full of women. Even before he came out, his close friends at university had all been female, with all but a few of the male students being too vulgar or arrogant and, frankly, clueless for him to have anything in common with them. With him being gay, his office colleagues felt comfortable swapping stories about their lives and problems, especially learning his spin on the male psyche. Yes, he may have been atypical in the world of men, but the straight and oversexed older brother he had grown up with and observed objectively fitted the mould. Moreover, at work, Spencer had a game plan and had found a way to turn every crappy little thing to his advantage.

Case in point.

Buying drinks for twelve each Monday morning meant he filled a coffee shop loyalty card every time, and had never spent a single penny of his money on his own drink in the two years he'd been at Blackmores. And because of the good business he brought in, the owner often threw in a smoked salmon and cream cheese bagel.

Tick.

In order to set up Muriel's presentation, she had to provide him with her password. While running through each slide of her weekly War Room presentation, he could forewarn and forearm himself and Bev to any surprise she might be planning to spring. When he got in early, which was most Mondays, he would even have a poke around her laptop to see if he could find any interesting titbits. And she remained none the wiser.

Tick.

He excelled at his job. Without openly boasting, he knew he could do the work better than anyone in his department, and, quite frankly, he equated Muriel's constant badgering to the unrelenting persistence of an Olympic coach whose scrutiny ensures the best performance of an athlete. Never once had he dropped the ball on business-critical work. For the time being, he was paid well enough, loved the work, got along with most members of staff and worked with his friend. And when the time was right, this Olympian would find a better track to race on.

Tick, tick, boom.

Sinking back into his leather seat, he lifted the lid to his drink and stalled when he smelled milky green tea. After examining his container — metallic blue with a rainbow unicorn — he checked around the room. Three times the shop had messed up their order, and three times Spencer had been balled out about a mistake he hadn't made. A few others sipped at their drinks, but none appeared to be tasting extra-shot caffè latte instead of green tea latte. The only people who had not sampled their drinks yet were absent Bev, who unfailingly drank the same caffè latte as Spencer, and Muriel. With a hollow feeling of foreboding, he wondered if he would soon be suffering through another of Muriel's rants.

"While we're on the subject of Christmas editions, what new things are we wowing our readership with this holiday season? Tamara? What do you have in store for our hard-nosed readers of *Virago*?"

Virago was indisputably the most contentious of Muriel's four magazines. Spiked leather bodices, spiteful whips, thigh-length PVC boots and industrial chains on the cover usually indicated a softer, more romantic issue. Targeting the *Fifty Shades* generation of women, the magazine had grown in popularity over the past decade. Being available via online subscription meant an unprecedented increase in circulation and healthy revenues for the group. In her fifties, Tamara — creative director for the magazine — was dressed as usual in her powder-pink Chanel suit and pearl necklace.

Spencer tuned her out. Fortunately for him, he rarely had to contribute to the substantive content of the meeting, being the most junior in the office. Muriel would only defer to him if his boss, Clarissa, could not answer specific questions, such as details about particular articles — usually from freelance writers — and whether they had been edited within the strict deadlines and resubmitted to various editors for final sign-off. Or if she wanted a summary of readers' comments to controversial online articles, another job Spencer had been lumbered with, but one he secretly loved.

"I'm thinking we should do a piece about what modern men want?" said Clarissa, Spencer's boss, and the bane of his life. After the statement, she threw a glance Spencer's way. "*Straight* men, obviously."

Some of those in the room giggled. A Muriel clone, Clarissa didn't so much delegate responsibility as abdicate from any, especially jobs she should really be doing herself.

"Who cares what they want?" asked Muriel. Unfortunately for Clarissa, Muriel did not like having a clone of herself in the office, and the two regularly disagreed.

"Women?"

"Oh, for goodness sake, Clarissa. Do wake up. In this century, women no longer care what men want. Women take what they want without asking permission. Loretta, do we have the article on the royal engagement party by Killian yet? For the November issue of *Collective*?"

Killian Pinkerton. People did not always cotton on to Spencer's sexuality. Some people — girls mostly — still mistook his brand of bespectacled awkwardness as geek chic and, on the rare occasion, tried to hit on him. Freelance journalist and YouTube celebrity Killian Pinkerton did *not* have that problem. In all his videos, with his exaggerated gestures, heavy mascara and fluorescent suits, he purposely exaggerated his gayness. Reading and editing his fashion columns for *Swish*, another of Muriel's magazines and one that covered fashion events and celebrity gatherings, had turned out to be a highlight of Spencer's month. Nothing felt better than reading Killian's brand of beautifully worded viciousness — a cross between the eloquent satire of Stephen Fry and the scathing bitchiness of Joan Rivers.

"Not yet, Muriel. I'll chase him today."

"Spencer can do that." Muriel's frown transformed into an approving smile as the conference room door opened. "Ah, Beverley. Lovely to see you. Is everything okay?"

Along with everyone else, Spencer turned and grinned his appreciation on seeing Beverley enter stage right. Any idiot could tell she belonged in fashion. An unapologetic plus-size, his friend always dressed impeccably. Today she wore a velvet trouser suit in burnt caramel with the jacket unbuttoned, a high waistband in gold accentuating her slim waist, and a designer tangerine-and-white leaf-print silk blouse. Autumn personified. Over the weekend she had also dyed her long hair a deep burgundy, and, of course, her makeup and accessories — including an autumnal leaf-print mask — had been chosen impeccably. At Muriel's question, Beverley's expression had become anxious and she sought out Spencer, who nodded twice.

"Everything's fine, Muriel," said Beverley. "Thank you for asking. Everything's been — scheduled accordingly."

"Scheduled?" asked Muriel, concern filling her face. "With LMVP? What needed scheduling?"

Beverley said nothing as she sidestepped around the backs of her colleagues to her seat.

"Thank you for stepping in, Beverley," Spencer piped up. "Sorry, Muriel, but I've been trying to arrange a meeting with the LMVP creative team for ages. Not just to reassure them about their coverage this Christmas, but also to try and get them to commit to giving us more of their advertising revenue next year. I'm guessing Beverley finally managed to schedule a meeting with them. Am I right, Beverley?"

"Yes," said Beverley, her eyes smiling, taking her seat and her cue. "That's right, Spencer. It's this lunchtime, I'm afraid. At Fresh Off The Boat, the new seafood restaurant on the Strand. But with everything going on, it's the only time they could spare this side of Christmas—"

"Then you should go, Beverley," said Muriel. "And work your usual magic. Use your business account but make sure you submit all receipts to finance."

"The thing is, Muriel," said Beverley, opening the file in front of her, "they specifically asked to meet Spencer. Seeing as how he's been the main point of contact for their account."

"Oh, I see," said Muriel, then added reluctantly, "then, of course, Spencer should join you. But watch what you spend. And no alcohol, either of you."

While Muriel moved on to other matters, Bev removed her mask, produced a self-satisfied smile of lush burnt orange lips and reached for her drink. Before taking a sip, she stared at him quizzically.

"I thought you were going to test drive the new contact lenses today," she murmured, the metal canister frozen before her face. "Change of plan?"

For most of his life, Spencer had relied on glasses to compensate for his unique form of astigmatism — different weaknesses in each of his eyes. Bev's referral to an optometrist instead of the usual NHS optician had led to him getting specially made contact lenses, allowing him to leave his glasses at home for the first time in his life. Except not only did he find a certain comfort in the routine of wearing glasses each day, he hadn't had the balls to test his contacts out for more than five minutes.

"Running late." He shrugged and prodded a forefinger at the bridge of his glasses. "Didn't have time."

From her raised eyebrow, he knew she didn't believe him, but she let the remark go. As she went to take a sip of her drink, she froze and sniffed the lid suspiciously.

"Is this coffee latte?" she mouthed to him, as Muriel droned on while clicking through one PowerPoint slide after another.

"What did you order?"

At the end of each day the staff returned their containers to the small kitchen for him to wash up. Everyone also wrote down their orders on the paper template supplied by the shop for the following morning's order and pinned to the kitchen noticeboard.

"Green tea."

"Latte?"

"Yes."

"Thank goodness. The shop mixed up our drinks again. I have yours," he said, swapping metal holders. "It's okay, I didn't drink any. I thought Muriel had mine for a moment. That would have been another blot on my copybook."

Both of them took a sip of their drinks, both melting back into their seats. Still Muriel rattled on, showing mocked-up covers for the Christmas edition of each of their publications on the projector slide. In total, they published four magazines. *Swish* majored in the latest evening wear, celebrity dress features and fashion shows. *Virago* pandered to the bondage generation. *Hash Hag* focused on modern business alpha females and covered business wear for women of power, contained corporate gimmicks and gadgets and sports cars. Finally, their flagship magazine, *Collective*, remained a lifestyle journal aimed at upper-middle-class women with ample disposable income and featured mainstream articles and people of influence interviews, with features on eco-sensitive holiday destinations and the latest trends in housing and furniture.

"Thanks for covering." Beverley whispered from behind her canister. "Good catch, too. And just so you know, I'm doing green tea right now because I've read that it's detoxifying, low in calories, and has natural enzymes that promote weight loss even when you're sleeping. I'm trying for a seriously healthier lifestyle. I'm even considering intermittent fasting."

Spencer had read the same article in last month's edition of *Collective*. Green tea with milk had not been mentioned.

"No alcohol or French fries for lunch, then?"

"Sod that. I'm cutting down, not joining a maximum-security slimming club. Besides, Muriel's paying."

"Just you and me, though?" asked Spencer.

"Of course. But we'll have to order, eat and drink for four. And we're starting with their signature dish called Sea Spray Appetiser, a dozen oysters on an ice platter served with a glass of Moët. That way there will be no mention of alcohol on the invoice."

"Good call."

Spencer realised Muriel had stopped speaking and the darkened room had fallen quiet.

"Anything the two of you would like to share?" she asked.

"Apologies, Muriel," said Beverley. "We were just talking client strategy."

"You can do that once the meeting has finished." As soon as Spencer and Beverley nodded, Muriel continued. "Now I want to get onto some of our opportunities and challenges. Let's go around the table and hear from my talented creative team. I'll start with celebrity interview catastrophe we're facing for the December and January issues of *Collective*. As you all know, we had to pull the plug on the Sir Richard Briggs interview last week due to ongoing lawsuits, and the Hollywood bimbo—you all know who I mean—cried off at the last minute. Which has left us with a couple of gaping holes. I did my level best at Friday night's charity function, but neither Dame Penelope Lawrence nor Marshall Highlander are game to be interviewed. So, we need suggestions, with December as a matter of urgency. Let's start with Persephone. Any ideas?"

Spencer's breathing stopped on hearing the name of the cultured news reporter, Highlander, he had met on Friday night, the man who had kissed him in Muriel's rooftop garden. Another reason to be grateful for working for the Blackmore Magazine Group. Even though keeping the incident to himself had pretty much given him stomach cramps all weekend, he'd stayed true to his word and said nothing, not to

Beverley or anyone else. Because he had promised as much and, on that cold-as-hell magical night, he had been kissed by the most gorgeous man in the world. And you never jinxed an experience like that. The memory alone would keep him warm all through winter. Had he listened to his mother and applied for the position of junior copy editor at the *Bournemouth Echo* would the same opportunity have presented itself? Not on your life.

Muriel's event had eventually ended at around two, by which time nobody had wanted to carry on drinking elsewhere. Feeling exhausted and ready to crash, Spencer had headed straight home, but to pass the time on the train journey — knowing he had no Wi-Fi connection at home — he had Googled his new crush on his smartphone.

Of course Marshall Jacobsen Highlander had a Wikipedia page dedicated to him, even if it was somewhat concise. Spencer had clicked straight into the 'personal life' link. The section had given very little away. Apart from being an ambassador for three charities, including one for refugee support, no indication of his romantic life was given. In which case, who was Joey, and why was Marshall Highlander still buried deep in the closet? Then again, Wikipedia rarely told the whole story. The only mention of any relationship had been the professional one with his long-time manager, Darcy Chong.

Saturday morning, waking alone in his tiny flat and wondering for a few seconds if he had dreamt the whole thing up, he had experienced a newfound pleasure performing his weekend chores, routines he usually resented. He had changed bedclothes, washed and dried his laundry in the landlord's ancient washer-dryer, ready to be ironed on Sunday, blitzed the toilet and kitchen, vacuuming and cleaning surfaces, all the while humming and occasionally dancing along to the music playlist he had downloaded onto his phone. Even the fact he had no satellite signal and no Wi-Fi connection in the flat hadn't needled him that day. Afterwards he had gone for a late lunch downstairs at the local coffee shop where he had read his messages and checked his social media pages. He had even turned down an offer to go for drinks with old college friends on that night after searching and downloading three of Marshall's *Say What You Mean* shows from a cable news channel.

Over a margherita pizza and a couple of bottles of chilled Italian beer, he had watched the man in action from the comfort of his old two-seater black leather couch. Doing so had felt something akin to voyeurism, knowing he had tasted the man's lips and even remembering how his mother had once commented on *"what a fine-looking man is that Marshall Highlander"*. Most embarrassing of all, being as she called herself a child of the sixties, a generation who always said exactly what popped into their heads, she'd gone on to explain how she would *"let him have his way with me without a second thought"*. Fortunately, his father had not been in the room, although Spencer doubted his presence would have made the slightest difference.

The thing was, sitting there on his own, seeing the man's well-proportioned frame, observing his careful mannerisms and lithe body movement, together with that smile — *and those eyes* — Spencer had found his own body reacting in ways that generally only happened when he clicked onto one of his NSFW bookmark folders.

As the murmured updates from around the table came to an end, Muriel's commanding voice brought him out of his reverie.

"A noble suggestion, Melanie, but I think approaching the Duchess of Cambridge might be aiming a tad too high. So if that's all you have for me, it's back to the drawing board, I'm afraid," continued Muriel. "If anyone does have any ideas, let Judith know. If all else fails we have the game show host Nobby Nobson waiting in the wings for December, but quite frankly he's not really *Collective* calibre. If anyone can land a top-notch interview for the Christmas and January editions, that person will get an additional twenty per cent incentive on top of their usual Christmas bonus. Now, where's Evelyn?"

"Not feeling well and working from home, Muriel."

"Again?" huffed Muriel, followed by a world-weary roll of the eyes. "Can somebody from HR please give her a call after this meeting and see when she'll be back in the office? I don't suppose, in the absence of our event planner, that anyone else can give us an update on the main event of the calendar year, the Blackmore Magazine Group Client Christmas Party? And how on earth is this going to work, given current restrictions?"

"As far as I know," said Beverley, who had always been friendly with Evelyn, "email invites were sent out a month ago and online responses are already starting to come back. Evelyn booked the same venue as last year and the deposit has been paid, but if things get worse, the money is refundable. The venue owners are organising the catering, too, as far as I'm aware. Although I heard the quartet Evelyn booked cancelled due to illness. As for the finer details of the night, such as who the speakers are going to be and the actual programme running order, I'm afraid I have no idea."

Muriel's gaze went dramatically heavenwards once again, as though the whole world was collapsing around her. In his favour, Blake had not inherited the same dramatic facial expressions. Understandable for Muriel, because the Christmas party for clients tended to be the firm's most important media event of the year.

"If things get worse, will you consider cancelling?" said someone from around the table.

"Don't be ridiculous! We rely on the client party to generate interest and sponsorship for the forthcoming year. Without that we may as well close our doors."

"I'll call Evelyn and find out what she knows," said Bev.

"Thank you, Beverley. In which case, I think we should all get back to work. Unless there's anything else?"

Maybe Spencer should have picked a better moment, but his inner voice had already started working his mouth.

"What's happening about the staff Christmas party? I mean, are we still having one? And what's the budget this year? I'm happy to help organise again, if you want."

"Apart from the fact that nobody really cares, Spencer, social gatherings are discouraged," said Muriel. The thing was, people did care, especially knowing the client event would most likely go ahead. Members of the team had already approached him about the staff event, something they could enjoy without having the pressure of networking politely with clients. "There are more important issues at stake. I'll be providing mulled wine and mince pies at lunch on the Wednesday before we break for the Christmas holidays. Whatever you decide to do, leave me out of the loop. And the finance department will be able to let you know if we have any budget. Now, if there's nothing of *real* importance, let's get back to our desks."

As everyone started to rise and everyday chatter settled around the room, Spencer stayed back, waiting to head to the front of the room and unplug Muriel's laptop, but noticed Prince standing in the doorway. He winked at Spencer and pointed to himself with his thumb, before moving over to where Muriel packed her bag. As Spencer left the room, he heard Muriel's voice rise with pleasure.

"There you are, Prince," she cooed. "You are such a dear for doing this."

"No problem, Muriel. That's me job."

"Yes, but I do hope you know how much we all appreciate you around here."

Spencer let out a soft sigh as he squeezed past them and headed for his desk. He decided not to let any minor irritations get to him today. After all, he had managed to get a free lunch out of the dreadful woman.

Chapter Three

"You're not going anywhere, Spencer," said Clarissa, his boss, tapping her long scarlet fingernail on the sheets of paper in front of him. "Beverley will have to find someone else. The deadline for these is three o'clock today, after which you'll need to do a final review of *Hash Hag* online, which, as you know, goes live after midnight, tonight. I'm sorry but you'll have to work through your lunch break."

Like Muriel, Clarissa's apologies were as hollow as her occasional praise, but she, too, had to be obeyed. To do otherwise might mean being deprived of the good stuff, like being the first to read and, on the rare occasion, give feedback and suggested edits for the latest column by Killian Pinkerton, or being given an afternoon to sift through and collate comments for specific hot topics in *Virago*. Despite what people might think, he loved his job, loved tightening stories to make them eminently readable and, although nobody except Bev had ever said so, he knew he was bloody good at what he did.

What irked him was that he had seen the stories Clarissa wanted him to edit sitting in her in-tray the previous week. Of all the team at Blackmore, she printed off paper copies of articles for editing — so much for being environmentally friendly — and manually marked them up. The previous Friday, having pondered whether she would find the time to complete them, he was going to offer to help her out. But then everybody had been scooped up in the rush to get things ready for Muriel's socially distanced charity event.

"Are you sure, Squirrel?" said Bev, turning up just before eleven-thirty in her tan Burberry overcoat. Prince stood silently a few paces behind her, peering over her shoulder at Spencer. "Do you want me to have a word with Muriel?"

"What's the point. She'll only side with Clarissa. She always does."

"That's so unfair. They're Clarissa's deadlines, not yours."

"I know, but with no interruptions I'll get them done in no time. You're still going for the lunch though, aren't you?"

"I'm taking Prince."

"You're taking our IT guy to a client meeting?" said Spencer, grinning at Prince.

"Oi, mate! That's Regional Head of IT to you," said Prince, unhooking his mask and grinning with an impressive set of pearly whites.

"Nice title considering we don't have a region, and you're the only person in the office who deals with IT," said Spencer, enjoying the banter.

"Muriel said it's fine to bring Prince. Said he'd make a good replacement," said Bev, giving him her sympathetic smile.

"Yeah, I bet she did," said Spencer, remembering Muriel's words to Prince only that morning. Then again, none of this was their fault. "Go on, you two. Go and enjoy. Maybe we can pop to the Cork and Bottle for a drink after work."

"Sounds good to me, Squirrel," said Beverley. "Long as they're open."

"Can't, I'm afraid, Spence," said Prince. "I got me pirates session after work."

"Pirates? Does he mean Pilates?" Spencer said to Bev, carefully enunciating the word as 'purr-lah-tees'. Beverley offered up a shrug.

"No, mate, pirates. I'm in the local church production of *Treasure Island* at Christmas. We're rehearsing all the pirate scenes tonight, trying to make sure we're all safely distanced from each other."

"Are people actually booking tickets? Bearing in mind what's going on out there?"

"They had been. Now? I've no idea. Guess we'll find out tonight."

Spencer cracked on as the office slowly emptied of colleagues. Without any interruptions, he knew he could knock out the work quickly. By one-fifty, he had everything but the website review completed and placed back on Clarissa's desk, so he donned his mask and decided to grab something to eat. Lunchtimes tended to be flexible on the side of generous at the magazine, and he wasn't surprised to note the empty office. While waiting for the lift, he chatted to Kimberley, the pretty young newbie on reception, because most people ignored her.

After waiting in line for over fifteen minutes at the ground floor food stall, playing a mindless app game to distract himself, he picked out a rather tired-looking tomato and mozzarella baguette and a lukewarm seasonal mushroom soup. As the lift doors to his floor opened, Kimberley stood up from behind her desk, her eyes beaming at him.

"So romantic," she said cryptically, her hands clasped beneath her pink-masked chin.

"I'm sorry?" said Spencer, looking at the contents in his hands. "It's only soup and a sandwich, Kim."

"Not saying another word," she said, folding her arms and using a frankly sickly-sweet tone. "Except to say that she must love you loads."

Did she mean Clarissa? Because he felt anything but love from his boss, especially after she had robbed him of a champagne lunch. Not stopping to talk, he smiled back sweetly from behind his mask. At some point he would need to get around to telling Kim about his orientation, but not today. Maybe when she was in a more stable mood. Spencer's puzzlement seemed to amuse her even more, as her adoring gaze trailed him all the way to the frosted office door. Shaking his head, he flashed his access card at the panel and re-entered. And turned the corner towards his open-plan desk.

"What. The. *Fuck*."

A vast arrangement of long-stemmed roses — around three dozen — in pink and classic red sat to one side of his desk, the blooms artistically arranged inside an elegant glass vase. Propped against the front, in a wrapping of golden foil tied with a scarlet ribbon, someone had positioned an enormous box of chocolates.

When he got closer, the sound of the mechanical click of the office door startled him. Other staff members were returning from lunch. Checking closer, he saw a small white envelope buried among the blooms, something he plucked out and stuffed into his trouser pocket. He had a pretty good idea which bastard had hijacked him with this embarrassing display but wanted to check first.

He snatched up his desk phone and called reception. Before he could say a word, the giggling voice of Kimberley answered immediately.

"Told you, Spencer. So romantic."

"Um, Kim," he asked, "who brought these?"

"A delivery boy, of course, silly. From the florists, I suppose."

"Yes, but," he asked, trying to remain calm, "who are they from?"

"You don't know? The boy gave your name. Isn't there a card with them?"

Behind him, a couple of 'oohs' and 'aahs' and other mortifying noises began to fill the air. Someone had been evil enough to turn him into a Hallmark moment on a day that was neither his birthday nor Valentine's Day. Shaming him at work could be the ploy of only one or two people – his older brother, Garrett, who was frankly too cheap to fork out on a stunt like this, or his ex, Blake.

"No, there's not. Did you see one when they were delivered?"

"No, I can't say I did," she said. "But surely you know who they're from?"

Spencer breathed a sigh of relief. If she hadn't seen a card, then he could pretend someone had sent them anonymously. This was the kind of embarrassing stunt Blake might pull in an attempt at an apology for his appalling behaviour. Had he done so eighteen months ago, then the gesture might have meant something.

Bastard.

"I have no idea who they're from," said Spencer, louder than he needed to for the sake of the gathering, then pretended to look for a card. "And I'm looking right now, but I definitely can't see a card. Thanks anyway, Kim."

After he had taken a few breaths and put the phone down, people immediately began asking questions. Somewhat theatrically, he inspected the chocolate box thoroughly, turned the vase around and even checked on the bottom, all the time shaking his head. By now the small crowd had grown, holding out phones, taking photos of him with his prize, probably posting straight onto social media sites. Fortunately he only usually socialised with Bev outside work, so he would not see any of their posts. Nonetheless, he began to feel overwhelmed with the attention and excused himself to use the bathroom.

Blakemore Group rented the whole of the eighteenth floor, which meant they had exclusive use of the bathrooms. For Spencer, Prince and Blake—and any occasional male visitor to their office—having their own dedicated, always clean male bathroom had become a company perk. After work once, he had given Blake a blow job in one of the cubicles. Happier times. As soon as he had used his key to get inside, Spencer felt tempted to rip the small greeting card in half and flush the remains away. Instead he locked himself in a cubicle, sat on the toilet lid and pulled out the small envelope. After all, with his long dry spell, any attention felt good. Slipping a fingernail beneath the flap, he took a steadying breath before prising out the card and reading the neat handwriting.

To my bushy-tailed superhero,
Thank you for saving me with kind words, a big heart, and a warm hug on Friday night, a day when I was feeling at my lowest.
MJH xxx

Marshall Highlander. And just like that, warmth rose in his cheeks. The welcome surprise melted his pissed-off mood. When he reread the words, pleasure curled in his stomach. Of its own volition, a smile pushed its way to the surface and fixed itself on his face. Looking into space, he fanned himself with the card.

Of course. Chocolate-covered nuts. Nuts for the squirrel. How had he not made the connection? Twisting around, he flushed the toilet and began to stand, wanting to rush to find Beverley and tell her. But when his hand touched the cold lock of the cubicle door, he froze, remembering he had told her nothing. What would she think if he confided now? Besides, what parts could he reveal without betraying Marshall's trust? Perhaps he could edit out some details. He would have to think of something fast because he needed someone to confide in and, when she saw the display, she would hound him relentlessly until he confessed.

When he got back to his desk there she stood, her face planted in the buds as though searching for something. When she pulled back and turned around, her hands went straight to the golden belt around her hips.

"Been having fun while I've been gone?" she asked.

"Not really. While I popped out to get a sandwich, these landed on my desk."

When she looked again then returned his gaze, her mouth turned down in dismay.

"These had better not be from him," she said. Firmly on his side after 'the Blake incident', she barely tolerated his ex's presence in the office. Spencer noticed her cheeks appeared a little flushed, and not from too much rouge, he guessed. Even her eyes had the slightly glazed look he knew all too well after she'd had a couple of drinks. "Because if they are, I will stuff them into the bin at his desk and make sure you Instagram the moment. And then I will personally go round to his penthouse flat and ball him out."

"They're not from him, Bev," said Spencer, keeping his voice low. "Calm down. The truth is…well, it's a little more complicated."

Spencer looked around to see if one of the small soundproofed cubicles was unoccupied. Fortunately, he spotted one in the centre of the room.

"I have a confession to make," he said, standing and leading her away. As an afterthought, he grabbed his sandwich and soup, although his appetite had all but evaporated. The moment he had closed the door and they had each taken a seat, she pounced on him.

"Before you say anything, I need you to come to a Halloween party this Saturday as my plus-one. My friend tells me there'll be some of your people going. And I'm not going alone. So you'd better have a costume in that closet of yours."

"Parties are banned. Surely you've seen the news about social gatherings?"

"This is different, Spence. The house is in the middle of nowhere and provides digs for a bunch of medical students who all live together. It's all fine. And more importantly, I need you to accompany me because there's someone special I need to meet."

"I'm not sure, Bev —"

"It's not optional, Squirrel. You can't stay at home sulking forever. You're coming, end of story. You are never going to shake off Blake the Flake until you put yourself out there." Spencer had no reason not to go, but he hadn't felt sociable for months. "Now, what's that lovey-dovey delivery all about? I know you didn't meet someone over the weekend, because you would have called me. Tell me you didn't send them to yourself to make Blake jealous."

"No! They're from a person I met on Friday night. At Muriel's party."

He plucked the card from his pocket and showed her. She read the words and smiled to herself but then her expression became understandably baffled. He took a deep breath because he needed to confess to somebody before he exploded. And he knew Bev well enough to know that if he asked her to say nothing, the way he'd done during his clandestine affair with Blake, he could rely on her complete discretion. Closing his eyes for courage, he began to explain.

"While I was waiting for you in Muriel's rooftop garden, Marshall Highlander — MJH," he said, tapping the card, "came outside to take a private call. Except he didn't know I was sitting there. The long and the short of it is that he was not terribly happy with the caller. When he'd finished, he realised I'd been there the whole time. We had a long chat and, in my usual clumsy way, I think I must have helped because he laughed, and then gave me a hug. After that, we shared a glass of bubbly before he left. End of story."

Not quite the whole story, but enough to sound believable. Bev sat there, waiting, staring at him, her mouth hanging open.

"Marshall Highlander? *The* Marshall Highlander?"

"It depends. How many Marshall Highlanders do you know —"

"Spencer!" said Bev.

"Yes, then," said Spencer. "*The* Marshall Highlander. He was there at the event —"

"I *know* he was there. I opened the door to him. It was me who said hello to him and welcomed him in. Are you telling me he's sending you flowers?" Right then, she did a very Beverley thing and slapped manicured fingers across her shiny lips before pulling them away and asking. "Tell me you did not try to jump his bones —"

"What? No! We chatted, that's all. He's just a really nice man —"

"Who is sending you roses and chocolates. That kind of gift is not a thank you for chatting, Squirrel. That's so much more than a thank you. How could I think they were from Blake? His idea of a romantic gesture is kissing a mirror. So how did you leave things? With Marshall Highlander, the sex god, whose homosexuality is the world's worst-kept secret. Let me guess. He's your fairytailicious ending, isn't he?"

Spencer put his head in his hands. Bev had coined the phrase after almost meeting Harry Styles at one of Muriel's charity events. He and his entourage had left five minutes before Bev had arrived. For months afterwards she had stalked him on social media, convinced they would eventually end up together.

"Bev," he said, looking back up, "please don't blow this out of proportion. On the night in question, I said a few kind words and I'm sure this is simply Marshall's grown-up way of saying thank you. Don't read anything more into it, because I'm not. But you need to help me come up with a plausible story to tell our colleagues. With red roses and chocolates on display, they're circling like sharks around chum."

Beverly sat back and put her chin in her hand. Making up stories had always been her forte, and he could see the wheels turning.

"From your mum? An early Christmas present?"

"Why would she? It's not even Halloween. On top of that, roses and chocolates? From my *mother*? Sorry, but that's just plain icky and gross."

"Good point. Okay, why don't we go with my first assumption and tell people they're from a lying, cheating, sack-of-shit, ex-boyfriend in a pathetic attempt to win you back."

"You really don't like him, do you? But no, that won't float. One, because I don't want anyone else to know about us being a thing, and two, because if he deigns to pop into the office this week, he will naturally deny everything. More importantly, the few who do know would expect to see me ramming the bouquet into the paper shredder stem by stem. And I truly want to take them home with me."

"Good point. And on that subject, a quick word of warning. The little prick is rumoured to be gracing everyone with his presence on Saturday night—"

"Blake?" said Spencer, a shiver running through him. "At the Halloween party?"

Until then, Spencer had been pondering ways to get out of going. Now the sick and twisted part of his psyche that had kept him awake at night, imagining a sobbing Blake on his knees—naked, of course—begging to get back together with Spencer, had wormed its way into his head.

"Possibly, which most likely means he won't turn up. And anyway, don't worry. It'll be Halloween so if he does show up I can legitimately Jamie Lee Curtis him if he tries anything. Now, where was I?"

"Roses and chocolates."

"Oh yes. Path of least resistance. Let's stick as close to the truth as possible. You were at a private party over the weekend where you were introduced to a group of guys and happened to mention where you work.

Somebody must have taken a shine to you and sent the gift. But you've no idea who. Trust me, everyone loves a mystery like that. Of the secret admirer variety. Up until they have to slap a restraining order on the stalking bastard."

Spencer pondered the idea for a moment. As explanations went, that was a reasonably good one and didn't even feel like a lie.

"Great, let's run with that. If anyone asks, say I've been racking my brains trying to figure out who the person might be. Now I'd better get back before Clarissa—"

"Hang on. I have a question. How do you plan on saying thank you?"

"How about a glass of bubbly after work?"

Bev stared at him for a second, before closing her eyes and shaking her head.

"Not to me, idiot. To him?"

"Oh. *Oh.* I hadn't thought about that. I suppose he must have a social media page. When I get a minute free, I'll browse and check. Leave him a note."

"Want me to get you his private number? So you can send him a message?"

"You have Marshall Highlander's private number?"

"Of course not. But Muriel's PA, Alice, will have. Leave it with me. Meet me outside the Cork and Bottle at six-thirty. And bring those flowers and chocolates with you. You know how I love to see you squirm, dear heart."

Chapter Four

Ten-thirty Saturday evening, Spencer sat beneath the sallow light of a standing lamp, balanced on the arm of a rickety navy or black corduroy-covered couch. Crammed against one damp wall of a room off the kitchen, the sofa provided the only remaining perching point far enough away from the noisy bodies leaping around in the living room. Depressing as the thought might be, he had to admit to having outgrown these kinds of parties offering cheap booze and a buffet of variously flavoured potato chips.

Just as well Bev had offered to buy him dinner at her favourite Italian place. When they arrived at nine-thirty, the party was well and truly in full swing. Her genuine persuasiveness — she'd wanted to meet up with someone in particular but would not say who — and her insistence that he accompany her had outweighed his concern about attending an illegal gathering. And in truth, she had been right. He had needed to get out of the house more.

After seeking out the party connection — Bev's college friend whose brother shared a rented, detached house with five other medical students in a rundown part of town — they dumped their bottles of drink off in the kitchen. The fact that everyone wore surgical masks seemed fitting given the students' training and the current precautions. Bev had managed to recognise eyes behind the masks of old college friends and stopped to chat. After the third time this happened, Spencer had told her he would find himself a seat, which was how he had ended up on the arm of the small sofa.

With a deep sigh, he looked around the room. If the excited eyes were anything to go by, most of those attending — probably friends of the host's younger brother — seemed to revel in the loud noise and the crowds and the squalor. Spencer sat alone observing everything, realising he had finally stooped to the level of sad, voyeuristic wallflower.

Next to him, a pair of mummies covered from head to toe in bandages — medical students, bearing in mind the considerable amount, complexity, and skill of the bandaging — made out with wild and passionate abandon. Spencer could not even determine their gender, whether they were a pair of men or women, or one of each. At first the sight made him squirm, until he saw the funny side and realised how delightful was the whole notion of two gender-indecipherable embalmed corpses making out in the present age. What he did know was that if they decided to take things to the next level, there might be considerable passion-dampening unwrapping involved.

When he stretched a leg out to reach for the phone in his trouser pocket, somebody stepped on his foot.

"Sorry," he said, the unnecessary apology coming from him automatically.

With a wince of pain, he tried to tuck his feet out of the way. Random drunken people — most appeared to be in their late teens and early twenties — had been staggering past all evening, some falling onto him or the swathed couple.

When he checked his phone, his brother Garrett had just sent a message. With nothing better to do, Spencer decided to start a message dialogue.

Garrotte: How's your week going?
Spence: Next question.

His week had been dreadful. Not only had Muriel and Clarissa dumped a shit ton of work on him, causing him to work until ten most nights, but his landlord had sent him a letter saying he was selling the flat and would not be renewing his rental agreement. Spencer would need to find somewhere else to live by the end of February when the lease ended. Everything seemed to be falling to pieces around him.

Garrotte: You better be coming home next weekend. For Guy Fawkes. Mum's expecting you. She's making sure there's extra food.

Spence: Mum's cooking? Are you trying to scare me off?
Garrotte: Dad says they're ordering takeaway from the new Chinese.
Spence: <sweating man emoji> Maybe I will come then. I'll text dad so he can pick me up from the station.
Garrotte: You bringing anyone?

Spence: So you can torture them and mum can poison them? I'll pass. You?

Garrotte: Maybe. Met this v sweet babe thru work.

Spence: Cool. Try not to break up with her before Friday.

Garrotte: <middle finger emoji>

He put his phone away as a couple of girls in party dresses made their way past. Besides Bev, few had made an effort. Dressed as the Queen of Hearts from *Alice in Wonderland*, her colourful costume hugged her in all the right places, showcasing her impressive cleavage. At the same time, her makeup varied slightly from the film queen's, with a dark shade of blue for her eyeshadow and a flowing hairpiece of blood-red curls.

Hers had been the best costume he had seen, no competition. Far better than his shabby, black-masked Count Dracula ensemble. But even he had made more of an effort than most of the males, which confirmed his suspicion that everyone else was straight. In the thirty minutes he had been sitting there, the only decent costumes he had seen had been a Wonder Woman, a very passable Daenerys Targaryen wearing a dragon face mask, and two black fishnet-stockinged naughty nurses. They had been the exceptions to the continuous line of mediocre wandering in search of the bathroom.

Spencer fidgeted with his phone again to check the time. Ten-forty. Another twenty minutes and he would be gone, whether Bev joined him or not. He hated Halloween. Growing up, his family hadn't even acknowledged let alone celebrated the occasion, deferring to the hot dogs and funfairs, the bonfires and fireworks of Guy Fawkes Night. But these days having trick-or-treaters show up on the doorstep happened more often than carol singers on the lead-up to Christmas.

He took a sip of his watery wine and looked around to see if he could locate his queen, but she had been at her social butterfly best that evening. Leaning back, he thought about the week just gone.

Marshall Highlander had not responded to his text message. As promised, Bev had managed to get the man's personal number, something Spencer had saved into his contacts. Over a week ago now, they had spoken, and Highlander had kissed him in Muriel's rooftop garden, an event now branded forever into his memory.

After deliberating on Monday evening — refusing point-blank to send anything with Bev leaning over him — Spencer had defaulted to a simple thank you for the flowers and chocolates, a line about being too generous and signed off with his name followed by a squirrel emoji.

After that, nothing.

Then again, what did he expect? Bev had demanded an update every day at work and seemed almost more disappointed than him when he had nothing to report. Maybe because she knew Spencer too well, but on Thursday she told him that Marshall had been on assignment the whole week in one of the stans — Afghanistan or Kazakhstan or Tajikistan, and might even have been Istanbul — and would probably not be able to use his personal phone.

Spencer pushed his own phone beneath his black cape into his trouser pocket and decided he would do a quick search of the house to see if he could find Bev. If not, he would fire off a phone message and head out. As he leant forward to place his half-full plastic tumbler of wine down on the floor by his feet, someone spoke directly to him.

"Spencer?"

The voice sounded all-too-familiar. There in front of him, in open sandals, dressed in a shining gold and brown headdress, bare-chested with defined pecs and six-pack, and exposed muscular legs on full display, stood a very sexy pharaoh.

"Blake," he choked.

Shit, shit, shit.

Spencer did his level best not to slip off the arm of the couch onto the bandaged lovers. Even before Blake had asked him out, he had found himself getting tongue-tied around the man. Something about Blake's stony-faced confidence had initially attracted him until he'd begun to understand the difference between confidence and arrogance. In the three months they had been together, the change had been subtle but there nonetheless. Sex had been energetic for the most part, often one-sided with Blake being the only one to get off and sometimes physically rough bordering on brutal. But the feeling of having someone wanting him and turning up to his flat had drowned out all the other niggling voices, even the fact they never kissed or ventured outside the four walls of Spencer's flat when they were together. Now, whenever he saw Blake, he had to remind himself how wretched he had felt at the end when Blake had dumped him via a direct message on Twitter. *A fucking tweet.* Who did that? So he did his best to avoid the man — and here he was again at the most inopportune moment with Spencer feeling at his most vulnerable.

Where the hell was Bev when he needed her?

"Nice outfit," said Blake, his annoyingly handsome smile slipping into place. Not wearing any face covering had been Blake's trademark protest. "You always did rock the whole faux-vampire look. Might have worked better with contacts instead of glasses. But I love the white face paint."

Spencer had not painted his face, his pasty complexion wholly natural and probably accentuated by the pale lamplight. Knowing Blake, he already knew that and the comment had been a lame attempt at humour.

"Thanks, I think. Yours is very impressive. Egyptian nobility meets *Magic Mike*. Looks like someone's been working out. Is that mascara?"

Each of Blake's eyes had been outlined in thick black makeup culminating with an upward flourish at each side. The whole effect made his naturally intense gaze — a lot like his mother's — feel positively denuding. Unusual for Blake, whose sense of fun had remained hidden when they were together. Spencer noted that Blake's humour had not perished entirely, from the slight smirk lifting one side of his mouth.

"Been to a Halloween dinner before this. But one has to make the effort for a party, doesn't one?"

"Shame they didn't state that in the invitation. Who do you know here? The host?"

"No, I was invited by a friend of a friend. Nobody you would know."

And there it was, the real Blake surfacing, as snobbishly class conscious and dismissive as ever. No doubt if there were any other single gay men at the party with flawless skin, a beautiful bone structure and breeding, also looking for a one-night stand, they would have scoped out this perfect male specimen by now. Blake epitomised a particular Instagram genus of hard-bodied flawless looks and utter superficiality. Spencer had lost count of the number of times he had bailed Blake out at work, completely rewriting his jumbled mess to make the article shine. Blake might look like a demigod, but he couldn't write for shit.

"Are you here to escort these two back home?" asked Spencer, pointing at the two mummies who appeared to have fallen asleep, tangled together. "The embalmed escapees from Giza?"

Blake's smile faltered and his eyebrows knotted slightly. Another obvious tell on their incompatibility had been Blake's rudimentary humour, not to mention his irritation whenever Spencer and Bev had got together and laughed all night about one topical reference or another. Maybe he should have read the signs better.

"Pharaoh," said Spencer, pointing to Blake, before indicating the slumbering duo. "Mummies. Get it?"

Breaking down jokes for Blake had long ago become a tiresome process.

"Ah. Yes. Funny," said Blake, clearly not amused. "Are you here with anybody?"

For a second, Spencer wondered why Blake wanted to know, and considered making something up. But then what was the point? Blake always did have a way of seeing straight through him.

"I came with Beverley, but she's disappeared on me. Don't suppose you've seen her? We're going to share a cab home and, to be honest, I'm about ready to go."

"Salvatore? What is she dressed as tonight? Let me guess. Something from *Cats*? Rebel Williams, perhaps?"

Spencer was almost impressed.

"It's Wilson. Rebel Wilson. And Salva — *Beverley* — is dressed as the Queen of Hearts."

"Of course she is. No, I haven't seen her. Do you need a lift home?"

The question caught Spencer off guard, and his mind started to reel. In his heart of hearts, Spencer knew Blake wouldn't want anything more substantial than a shag if he did take him home. But would that be enough for Spencer? Could he separate his already dented heart from the physical act? He already knew the answer.

"I'm fine, thanks."

"Don't be daft, Spence. It's a bugger of a journey, Ilford to Morden," said Blake, until his eyes betrayed his uncertainty. Spencer doubted Blake had ever ridden public transport. "Isn't it? Besides, surely you're not chancing the Tube this time of night, are you? And an Uber's going to cost you an arm and a leg."

"I'll figure something out. And anyway, I thought you didn't drive. Or did your mother let you have her driver for the evening?"

"Ambika drove us here."

Right then, as though waiting for a cue, an astonishingly good-looking South Asian girl appeared. Dressed as a cowgirl complete with an authentic-looking suede skirt and thigh-length boots, she wore an impressive Stetson and had a red bandana tied around her face. Ambika's long dark hair spilt down from beneath the hat and out across the shoulders of her gingham shirt. Similar to Blake, she wore no mask.

She leant forward and offered her impeccably manicured hand in greeting. Spencer was welcomed by a firm handshake and a genuine smile.

"Are they a part of your costume, Blake?" asked Ambika, nodding to the slumbering mummies. Spencer liked her, someone he thought he could happily get to know. Perhaps she was a family friend. "And are they both drunk, or have you had them embalmed?"

Despite himself, Spencer hissed out a chuckle.

"How do you know my Blake?" asked Ambika.

My Blake? Spencer stared hard at his ex. Beverley had once asked him if the rumours about Blake being bisexual were true. Right now he appeared unwilling or unable to offer an explanation. Spencer wondered how he should reply but then went for the easy out.

"We're work colleagues," said Spencer, who wasn't surprised Blake hadn't mentioned him. "Well, we work in the same office on occasion."

"Oh, really?" said Ambika, smiling. She had a friendly smile of bright white teeth, a smile that seemed entirely authentic. "Blake doesn't talk about his work."

"Probably because it's not that interesting. Everyone thinks working in the magazine business is glamorous, but we spend most of our time bored to tears staring at computer screens, like everyone else in the world."

"You can say that again," added Blake.

"Are we inviting Spencer? To the party?" asked Ambika to Blake.

"Firstly, I'm not sure if we'll be able to go ahead, Bika, given everything that's going on. And I certainly hadn't considered inviting work colleague — "

"But you must. I want to meet all the people who are a part of your life. Look, Spencer, Blake and I are hoping to host an engagement party in December. If you're free, we would love for you to come."

"Engagement party? Who's getting engaged?" asked Spencer, not quite catching on.

"We are, of course," said Ambika happily. "Blake and I."

Spencer swung his gaze to Blake for his reaction and saw only a blank expression before the terrible truth sank in. Almost two years ago they had been in the same bed pretty much every weekend, with Blake pummelling him into the mattress and both dissolving into a pool of sweat. Spencer had been blissfully unaware that Blake had wanted something different. Once again—a personality flaw perhaps—he had realigned everything to absorb Blake into his life, only to have been left with nothing over a tweet. And in the months that followed, he had consoled himself with the thought that Blake was simply not long-term relationship material. To hear now that he planned to marry this woman had Spencer momentarily lost for words.

"That's fantastic. I'm really pleased for you," Spencer heard himself say, unable to look directly at Blake. Peripherally, at least, Blake had the decency to look slightly abashed.

"I'll—uh—give you the details of the party next week at work. Now where is it you live, Ambika?" asked Blake. "I keep forgetting. I told Spencer we might be able to drop him off on the way to your house. Wasn't it somewhere in Surrey?"

"Epping, silly. I live in Essex."

"Nowhere near Morden, then?"

If he hadn't felt as though someone had ripped out his stomach, he might have laughed. Typical Blake, always being driven around by his mother's driver or by friends. The man probably got lost in his own back garden.

"Epping is in the opposite direction," said Spencer, grateful for the mix-up. "Look, it's no problem. Thank you anyway, but I can quite easily find my way home. Congratulations on your engagement."

A sense of relief escaped him once he had said goodbye and made a beeline for the front door. He didn't even bother looking for Beverley, who had probably hooked up. Even before they'd arrived, he'd had the feeling she was seeking someone in particular. As soon as he hit the pavement and the chill air, feeling utterly clearheaded after only two glasses of watery wine, he dug out his phone and checked directions to the nearest station.

Somewhere in the universe, a celestial being must have finally noticed his plight and felt a sprinkling of compassion because the TfL line train for Stratford came almost immediately. As soon as he seated himself in the nearly empty carriage, he texted Beverley to say he had departed. After that, he switched his phone to silent mode and glared at his vampiric reflection in the dark glass of the train window while mulling over his life.

Was he going to spend the rest of his days alone? Because as dating track records went, his was appalling. Why could he never hold on to anybody? Why was he never enough? Before Blake, his previous relationship had been four years ago. And that had ended the same way — except the brush-off had been in person, not by a tweet. Was there a stamp on his forehead that read 'reject'?

At midnight, after a couple of connections, the train finally pulled into the Tube terminus at Morden.

Spencer felt tired, empty, and ready to fall into bed. As he used his travel card to pass through the barrier, the phone in his pocket buzzed urgently with an incoming call. Not difficult to guess who that would be, probably to berate him for deserting her at the party.

Except when he bought out his phone the name on the display read Marshall.

"Hello?" said Spencer tentatively.

"Spencer? Is that you?" came the distinctive baritone voice.

So maybe the celestial being hadn't finished with him entirely.

"*Yes!* I mean yes, it's me. How are you?"

"I'm fine. Well, I landed back this afternoon and I'm now settled at home. I know it's late. Is this a good time to talk, or should I call back tomorrow?"

Spencer stepped out onto the freezing street where a gust of arctic wind nudged a couple of fast-food cartons along the pavement. Pulling up his collar, he headed for the pedestrian crossing with the phone clamped to his ear. Just after midnight and the roads were deserted, with only a huddle of people around the minicab stand.

"Actually, this is a perfect time to talk. I'm just leaving Morden station and I've got a fifteen-minute walk to my front door. I live in a flat above a pizza shop, so you can talk to me and keep me company on the way, if you like?"

Marshall's deep chuckle came down the phone, lifting Spencer's spirits.

"Where have you been tonight?" asked Marshall. Before beginning his tale of woe, Spencer let out an overly dramatic sigh.

"Let's just say that I'm coming home from the absolute worst Halloween party ever, full of unimaginative costumes worn by straight, horny students, where they served watered down booze. And during which I lost my best friend, bumped into my ex-boyfriend of six months, who in turn introduced me to his girlfriend slash soon-to-be fiancée before inviting me to their upcoming engagement party and, to add insult to injury, I had to make my own way home from the other side of the universe. Bet you can't beat that?"

"Well, let's see. I've just returned from Afghanistan where me and the film crew narrowly escaped an attack by the Taliban. If we'd hit the checkpoint ten minutes later, we'd have been caught right in the middle of the gunfire and I doubt we'd be talking right now."

And just like that, Spencer's woes of the night paled into insignificance.

"Marshall. Are you okay?"

"I'm fine. Comes with the job. Heaven knows what will happen if the US ever decides to pull out of Afghanistan like they've been threatening to. Anyway, I think you had things a lot worse. This ex of yours doesn't sound like a particularly nice person. Did you know he dated women as well as men?"

"No. But then I'm not surprised. Blake was never one for sharing."

"Blake? As in Blake Moresby, Muriel's son?"

Spencer stumbled to a halt.

"Oops. Maybe I shouldn't have said anything. I keep forgetting you know people."

"*Come on*, Spencer. You know a lot more about me than I do about you. But I had heard from a very close friend that Muriel's son is a self-absorbed, egotistical prick."

"Hoi! That's my bastard ex-boyfriend who dumped me by tweet you're dissing," said Spencer, chuckling.

"Not my words," said Marshall, laughing along. "But those of a good friend. Who is now living in Papua, New Guinea. And no, before you ask. The two things are not related."

"What were you doing in Afghanistan to almost get killed? I didn't think people could travel right now."

"Strictly speaking, they can't. But, let's just say, our producer managed to pull a few strings. Officially we were there to cover a human-interest story about the Afghanistan national cricket team, how they're persevering and succeeding in spite of adversity. And all of this against the backdrop of strained peace talks."

Spencer strolled down the lamplit pavement towards home and looked at the darkened windows of the terraced houses that lined the way. Maybe the bitterly cold weather was to blame, but nobody else had braved the streets that night.

"Tell me about this cricket team. And when will the programme be aired?"

From the lighter tone of his voice, Marshall appeared to enjoy talking about his trip, about chatting to the captain and most of the players, asking about their lives in the sport and how they coped at home. Many of them had experienced hardships and lost loved ones in various conflicts. Absently, Spencer wondered why they couldn't have simply done the interviews via an online conferencing system, why they'd needed to actually be there in person, which would have been much safer. But he didn't voice the concern.

"We take so much for granted in this country, don't we?" said Spencer instead, when Marshall paused.

"Things like the relative peace, safety and security. I imagine that kind of experience grounds you every time you land back from a hot spot."

"In a way, it does. But I still love what I do and I wouldn't have it any other way."

"Just as well. Because you're bloody brilliant at what you do."

Once again Marshall's deep laughter came down the phone.

"Thanks for those flowers and chocolates, by the way," said Spencer. "Caused quite a stir in the office."

"Yes, I did worry a little about that. But I needed to say thank you and the only thing I knew about you was your name and the fact you worked for Muriel's magazine company. What did they say when they found out I'd sent them?"

"They didn't, because I didn't tell them. Only my best friend, Bev, knows the truth. Everyone else thinks they were sent to me by a secret admirer."

"Which is a fairly accurate assessment, actually."

Spencer smiled into the phone. Marshall's voice was doing all sorts of wonderful things to his insides.

"Hey, look," Marshall continued. "I'm sorry it's taken so long to get back to you. It's because of the phones I use. I have a personal number that I keep constant track of, one I only give to a few people, like family and Darcy. But I have another that I use for business contacts, the number I would have given to Muriel Moresby. When I'm away on an assignment, I rarely check that phone, so I'm really sorry I missed your message. But as you'll see, I'm sending you my private number."

And just like that, a message with a contact file popped up on his screen.

"I'm honoured."

"And I wondered if you might want to grab dinner with me sometime. I'm going to be flat-out next week, recording a couple of shows, but wondered how you're fixed next weekend."

Spencer stopped walking.

"You want to have dinner with me?"

"Yes."

"You want to have dinner with *me*?"

Marshall laughed, and Spencer grinned into his phone.

"You sound surprised."

"No. Well, yes. I am, I suppose."

He began walking again, taking the long way around the main road instead of the shortcut through the darkened alleyway, the one he would happily take in daylight. On a night when things had finally begun to look up, he was not about to tempt fate.

"You shouldn't be. You're a really nice chap, Spencer. And I like that you treated me as an ordinary person, and the fact I knew I could trust you — "

"You can."

"I know. I also like your sense of humour and the sound of your voice. So what do you say about dinner?"

"Next weekend?"

"If you're free."

Something nagged at Spencer. An earlier text message from his brother.

"Bugger. It's Guy Fawkes Night next weekend, isn't it? I have to do the dutiful son thing and stay at my parents' place in Bournemouth. Guy Fawkes is kind of a family tradition."

"Is your mother cooking?"

Spencer puffed out steamy laughter into the early morning air.

"You remembered. That's the first thing I asked. My brother tells me they're planning to order takeaway from the local Chinese restaurant on Friday night. And on the Saturday, traditionally, my dad takes us all out to a decent restaurant for lunch or dinner. So I think I should be safe. And I'll be home Sunday evening. Could we do dinner the weekend after? Or any weekday after next weekend?"

"Absolutely. Let me check my schedule and text you. Do you mind if I pick the venue?"

"Of course not. Hey, how is everything else? That problem you were having? Did your friend Darcy manage to get everything resolved?"

"If you're talking about that bloody newspaper hack, then yes. We threatened them with court action. I'm just hoping they know what's good for them."

Spencer approached the row of shops where he lived. To the right of the darkened window of Romano's Pizzeria stood the chipped black door that led up to his flat.

"Well, I'm home," said Spencer, fishing the keys out of his pocket with one hand. "Thank you for keeping me company and cheering up an otherwise dreadful evening."

"You're welcome," said Marshall, his warm voice making Spencer tremble with pleasure. "I just wish I was there with you right now."

"Yeah, me too."

"Goodnight, Spencer. Sleep well. And I hope you know how special you are."

By the time Spencer reached the top step to his flat, he had almost forgotten about his depressing night out.

Until he unlocked the upstairs door because there, sitting beside an empty bowl and amid a box of ripped-up jasmine-scented tissues knocked down from his kitchen table, sat his ginger tabby, Tiger, glaring with feline petulance.

Chapter Five

On the two-hour rail journey from Waterloo to Bournemouth station, where his father waited to pick him up, Spencer had plenty of time to reflect on the week just gone. As soon as he had stowed his luggage and taken his seat, he removed today's choice of navy bow tie with white polka dots — but left his matching mask on — and undid the top button of his light blue shirt. With many commuters still working from home, he was happy to get a seat by the window, plug in his ear pods, and settle in for the ride.

Work had been strangely less manic than usual, but Spencer guessed the lull to be the quiet before the Christmas snowstorm. Clarissa had been as lax as ever with her work, because he'd noticed a pile of deadlines as he left to get his train, editorial columns she needed to review and complete before the Monday afternoon deadline. No doubt they would end up getting dumped on his desk Monday morning and he would have to work through lunch again to make sure they met the cut-off point.

Being able to text Marshall's private line a couple of times had been a highlight, although he had received only the occasional response, very formal and usually apologising because being the show host, he had been confined to the studio where use of mobile devices was strictly controlled. On the upside, they had agreed to have dinner the following Friday, the venue a surprise but with them meeting in a small private bar around the back of Liverpool Street station. At least Spencer had something to look forward to the following week.

At Bournemouth station, he met his father at the agreed meeting point. They performed their usual greeting ritual of an awkward hug followed by his dad insisting on carrying his small wheelie luggage, and as usual, Spencer refusing, telling him he could manage.

Right now, he relaxed in the passenger seat of his dad's toasty-warm Volvo, his head lolling against the cold window as they wove their way through the lamplit streets from the station to their home near the seafront. The radio played soft American acoustic rock. What with the gentle tunes and the overheated interior, Spencer almost dropped off. Except he couldn't help noticing that something had changed about his father, something he could not determine at first. Only when he glanced sideways at his father's profile did he spot the diamond stud in his left ear and his long brown and grey hair — salt and pepper, his mother called it — tied back by what appeared to be a couple of black hair bands. During a phone call a few weeks ago, his mother had mentioned his father going through the male menopause.

"How's Garrett doing?" asked Spencer, causing his father to smile.

"While the rest of the world is falling to pieces, your brother's website development business has had a bumper year. Three hundred per cent up on last. Don't know how he does it. He always seems to fall on his feet."

"So can you now—finally and legitimately—kick him out of the house?" asked Spencer.

His father's shoulders rose and fell in silent laughter. They had the same conversation every time Spencer came to visit.

"That boy knows when he's onto a good thing."

"That *boy* is thirty-three years old next February. You and Mum had already had both of us by that age."

"True enough. He's been courting a new lady. Penny. Or Jenny. Could be Jodie, I wasn't really paying attention. She's coming over for dinner tonight, so you'll get to meet her. Maybe this one'll stick around longer than summer. Although I wouldn't, you know—"

"Hold my breath."

"Precisely. He tends to shy away from commitment and responsibility. Talking of which, who's looking after the mog while you're here?"

"Gino's wife again. She helps run the pizza shop downstairs, if you remember. They have the flat next to mine. She's going to pop in and check up on Her Royal Highness a couple of times over the weekend."

"That's a nice little flat you got there."

"Which the landlord wants back next Feb," said Spencer, letting out a tired sigh.

"Seriously?" said his father, turning briefly to check him. "Maybe it's time to think about buying, son. You know your mother and I are more than happy to stump up a deposit."

Spencer's parents constantly fretted about him living in London, and had offered the deposit for him to buy somewhere a number of times. The problem was that Spencer wanted to feel more settled before he made that kind of commitment.

"I know, Dad. And that's really kind of you both. But I still haven't decided what I'm doing with my life."

Once again a comfortable calm descended.

"And on the subject of my sons' dating lives, how about you?" said his father. "Any new fellow on the horizon? Would be nice to hear that at least one of my sons is settling down."

When Spencer had come out at eighteen, his parents had been totally cool about having a gay son, especially as their oldest appeared to be on a mission to inseminate the whole fertile female population of Southern England. Even so, Spencer cringed whenever his father asked if he had a boyfriend. For a brief moment he wondered whether to mention Blake getting engaged—they knew about him and Blake, even though they'd never met him—but then decided to keep the news to himself.

"Not much going on out there right now, Dad."

"Not even on that phone app? Grumblr, isn't it?"

Spencer couldn't help sniggering.

"Grindr. Not my style."

"Really? I thought all the gay boys hooked up through those online dating apps these days. Your brother used to have a waiting list courtesy of his straight one, Tinkler."

"*Tinder!*" said Spencer, horrified at the thought of an app by the name his father supplied.

"That's the one."

Sometimes he wondered if his father made the verbal faux pas deliberately. But his brother's Tinder adventures had been the talk of the family. In fact, Spencer had told Bev that if his brother had not been among one of the first twenty members clambering to sign up to the launch of the dating app, he would be shocked stupid. His father had once likened Garrett's carefully orchestrated dating life to the precision of a traffic police officer at a busy intersection when the traffic lights had failed, sometimes with two or three dates lined up back-to-back in a single evening.

"My brother is a gigolo. End of subject. How are you and Mum doing? Made any new friends down here yet?"

Long before he had taken early retirement from the police force, Spencer's father had made clear his dream for them to retire to Bournemouth. And six months after his last day, they had sold the Merton Park home Spencer and his brother had known since childhood and moved to a bungalow on the south coast. But, as with all things in life, the fantasy had not lived up to the reality, and, five years later, they had made very few new friends.

"Not really. We joined the Bournemouth Conservative Club briefly. Your mother found them all a bit uppity. Not really our sort of people. But your Aunt Kathleen's only down the road in Southampton and our old neighbours, Bill and Mandy Sampson, came down to stay for a week. So we're never short of company."

His father had spent the first couple of years working on the bungalow, gutting the interior and getting the overgrown garden up to snuff, so he had been happily occupied. Now, with only the exterior paintwork needing some serious reconsideration, he had more time on his hands. But whereas the Wyrrells of Merton Park had tended to be social magnets with their neighbours – largely because the family home had belonged to Spencer's grandfather and great grandfather – the retirees of their Bournemouth neighbourhood tended to keep themselves to themselves.

Finally the Volvo slowed in front of their bungalow. In the daylight, with its powder-pink walls, hot-pink front door, white-painted trimmings and white window boxes, the single-storey, three-bedroom abode looked like a doll's house. All of the men in the family detested the colour scheme, but apparently a woman's opinion trumped them all. Only Garrett's motorcycles lent the property a semblance of masculinity. He had acquired another since Spencer had last been home, a new black Triumph standing next to his sleek scarlet Ducati Monster 1200S, both lit up by the home security lighting and parked in the driveway.

"Go say hello to your mother. I'm going to pick up the nosh."

"Don't they deliver?"

"They do, but I want to give the old girl a longer run in this cold weather, while I've got her warm. There's your mother now."

Spencer grinned at seeing a warm light and a familiar silhouette fill the front door. While his father kept the engine running, Spencer got out and grabbed his bag from the back seat. As usual, his mum waited to give him a hug. She was a congenital hugger and always had been, even when he'd brought friends home from school. Tonight she had on grey tracksuit bottoms and a pale lemon crew neck sweater, which showcased her red curly hair. While his father could happily project manage all the structural changes to their new home including digging up the garden, Coleen Wyrrell provided the interior design and the pretty flowerbed arrangements. Which was why the interior of their home would not look out of place in a home design magazine or on a lifestyle television show. Figuring he'd better get the greeting out of the way, he walked into her waiting arms and had the life squeezed out of him.

"How *are* you, darling?"

Where Garrett had inherited their father's flinty-coloured irises and mother's tightly curled, ginger hair, Spencer had lucked out with his father's thick brown locks and his mother's sea green eyes.

"Grmph. Mmm'okay."

"Where's your father?" she asked, letting him breathe again and peering over his shoulder.

"What? The Karl Lagerfeld wannabe, you mean?" he said, causing his mother to snicker and slap him gently on the shoulder. "I bet that look went down like a string vest and a knotted hanky hat at the Conservative Club."

"Oh, honestly, darling. Those people. You'd think they were descended from royalty, the way they looked at us over their true blue surgical masks. Have you eaten? You're looking a little malnourished."

"Had a quick sandwich on the train, but not really anything much since lunch. Dad's giving the car a bit of a run and gone to pick up the takeaway."

"I was going to do one of my lovely casseroles, but Garrett insisted on Chinese."

Thank you, Garrett, thought Spencer. He remembered the last casserole his mother had conjured containing beef chunks, barley wine — she'd run out of red wine — prunes with the stones still in, mostly shelled walnuts and the plastic top of a spice jar of dried chillies which had somehow found its way into the pot.

"Is he here?"

"Watching American rugby. Go on through."

After he had stepped past her, he stopped and turned.

"American what?"

"You know, rugby. The kind they play in America. Except they wear those crash helmets, and stuntman padding, and knee-length trousers. And everything happens in fits and starts. No idea what he sees in the game."

"It's football, Mum. American football."

"Pointless, dear, is what it is. At least in rugby they have scrums and you get to see those tight bums, hairy legs and chiselled faces — even if some do have broken noses and more than a few teeth missing."

"Okay, so on that score, I am totally with you."

Whenever the family watched a rugby game together, his father and brother would lower their faces into their hands and groan every time Spencer and his mother dissected the better-looking, put-together players, and especially when they started pointing out key physical 'attributes', including which one had the tightest arse or the player who was packing the most.

Spencer headed into the living room, to witness his brother sprawled lengthwise on the family couch, watching the flatscreen television.

"Ho-bro," said Spencer, in greeting.

"Mo-bro," replied Garrett, without taking his gaze from the sports programme.

Spencer left his weekend luggage by the door and went over and perched on the arm of the chair. After staring at the screen for a couple of seconds, he scrutinised his brother. Unusually for him, he wore decent jeans and what looked like a stylish long-sleeved Paul Smith fitted shirt in black and purple. As usual, his wild red hair had lost sight of its comb.

"Dad says you've got some new squeeze coming over."

"Peony. She's this hot babe from work I've been seeing since before August. Bringing her cousin, too. Friday night, so we're going to eat here together, then ditch the wrinklies and head for Propaganda," said Garrett before finally giving Spencer a once-over. "You'd better have brought something badder than what you're wearing."

"You want *me* to come?"

"It's Friday night, Spence. And it's a mixed club, so they'll—you know—have some of your tribe there, too," he said, by way of explanation.

"Why do you always rope me in? You know I'm too old for all that shit. I'd rather stay home and watch *The Chase* with Mum and Dad," said Spencer, trying hard not to sound whingy. The Halloween party had taught him that he had long passed the age of endurance for hot, noisy and sweaty parties. Moreover, he knew Garrett would try to get him drunk.

"Tough. You're coming."

"We'll see. I'm going to dump my bag. And then I need a shower," said Spencer, jumping up but then stopping. "And why exactly do you need two motorcycles? I saw the new Triumph in the driveway."

Garrett sat upright then, his eyes widening dramatically and his voice lowering, his full attention on Spencer.

"That's not mine," he said. "It's Dad's. Mum's furious. Whatever you do, don't mention it in front of her."

"Is Dad okay in the head?"

"Of course he is. Just not used to sitting around doing nothing."

Garrett had a point. Their father had spent most of his forty years working for the Metropolitan Police out in the field. On the rare occasion when he talked about his experiences, Spencer saw him get truly animated and learnt just how much of the grim side of society his father had witnessed.

"Maybe you should be taking *him* to Propaganda."

"Go and get showered."

Spencer had never gotten used to the bungalow, the fact that all the bedrooms led off from the main hallway. All of his time living at home with his parents in Merton Park, he had 'gone up to bed' using stairs, something this single-storey home didn't have or need. Even in his Morden flat, he had to go up a flight of stairs to get to the open living room-cum-kitchen.

One of the modifications his father had made in the bungalow was to add a second bathroom — a shower room, to be more precise — and link the original bathroom exclusively to the master bedroom. That way his mother and father had all their own facilities on one side of the hallway when guests came to stay, something that had been lacking in their one-family-bathroom home back in London.

After taking his shower and dressing in a pair of comfortable denims, a white tee and a navy woollen jumper, he found the family at the dining table. An interesting young woman sat at the end of the table, facing him, as he entered. She wore a tight white V-neck sweater with her ample cleavage showing and the distinct beginnings of a tattoo on her left boob. With a nose stud and multiple ear piercings, she was definitely Garrett's wild-child type.

Interestingly, to her right, there sat a guy around Spencer's age with shaggy, boy-band blond hair and the rosy, flawless complexion of a twelve-year-old. More worryingly for Spencer, he had on a few layers of long-sleeved T-shirts to ward against the weather, but the bright yellow one he chose to wear on top had the words 'Gay As F**k' sitting inside a rainbow across the front.

"Come on, bromo. We're all waiting to start eating," said Garrett, opening up a tub of noodles. Across the tabletop sat around ten assorted containers of food. Their father always over-ordered.

"Shall we do paper plates and plastic cutlery?" said his mother, opening a cupboard in the kitchen. "Save on the washing up?"

"No," said Spencer adamantly, heading to another cupboard and pulling out china plates. "Since when have we become the Gallaghers from *Shameless*? And what about saving the planet? Don't worry, I'll wash up, if that's what you're worried about."

"It's not that," she said, hands on hips now. "I've got all these paper plates left over from the house-warming barbecue we had in the back garden two years ago, that only a couple of our neighbours bothered to attend. You don't need to wash up, I can put the plates in the dishwasher easily enough, if that's what you want."

<header>Brian Lancaster</header>

"I'll help. Save the paper and plastic pollution for your next barbecue."

Spencer threw down a handful of stainless steel cutlery then passed the plates around before plonking himself down next to his father, who sat checking through the invoice from the shop.

"As my brother is too rude to introduce me," said Spencer, "I'm his younger brother, Spencer."

"Garrett," growled their father, without looking up from the receipt. "Manners."

"And I'm Peony," said the girl, after giggling silently as Garrett gave Spencer the middle finger. "And this is my cousin, Lyle."

"Charmed," said Lyle, with a pout and tiny royal wave from across the table. Spencer hoped the smile he returned seemed authentic. But if Garrett had been thinking the two of them might be compatible, he could not have been more mistaken. Lyle was painfully thin, pale skinned, and had a preciousness about him, one of the *ne-me-touche-pas* gays Spencer had met in the past, even in the way he stabbed at the plate then glared with disgust at the food on his fork, as though he found the prawns or noodles personally offensive and not worthy of his digestive system.

"Hope you don't mind, Mum," said Garrett, as everyone slowed to grazing at the end of the meal, "but I'm dragging Spencer out tonight. To Propaganda with me and Peony. Lyle's planned to meet up with his boyfriend, and I thought you and Dad could have the house to yourselves."

Spencer wondered if anyone heard the barely restrained sigh of relief issuing from him at hearing that Lyle already had a boyfriend.

<footer>81</footer>

"Poor Spencer's only just got here," said his mother, hands on hips, and Spencer almost agreed with her. "Give him a chance to relax."

"You'll have him all day tomorrow, Mum. Tonight he's free, single and he's ours."

All too often he wished he no longer had the single label. He knew how tonight would end and how tomorrow would begin. Alone in bed, with still-ringing eardrums from the deafening music, thumping headache from too much alcohol, and his mother's burnt breakfast to try to keep down.

"Is this nightclub far?" he asked, a sudden idea coming to him. There was one sure way to make sure he stayed sober.

"About fifteen to twenty minutes by cab. Why?"

"Dad, can I borrow the Volvo?"

"Of course you can."

"Don't you want to drink?" asked his brother.

"I'm on antihistamines. Can't drink," lied Spencer.

"You've got hay fever? In November? Who has hay fever in November?"

"They're not just for hay fever, Gar," said Peony, giving Spencer a sympathetic smile. "My sister has to take them because she's allergic to animals."

"He has a cat!" said Garrett, not buying the excuse one bit.

"Look, come on. I've already taken them, so I can't drink. And it's going to be problematic getting a cab on Friday night. Dad's already warmed up the engine, so I'll drive us there in the toasty warmth—because it's pretty chilly out there right now, isn't it, Dad?"

"Cold as a nun's bum," said my father, now reading a car magazine.

"See? That way, if you guys decide to go on until late, I'll bring the car home and you can get a cab back."

Spencer knew his brother well enough to know he intended to party hard. Usually they would arrive together, Garrett would buy beers and shots, then disappear into the crowd hunting and gathering—but probably not tonight with Peony by his side—and Spencer would eventually be left to find his own way home.

Sometimes, he thought, *the simplest plans are the best.*

Chapter Six

Spencer awoke disorientated Saturday morning, in a warm but preternaturally darkened bedroom that was not his own, to the growl of thunder and arbitrary lightning flashes behind thick heavy curtains. As he lay there, bleached light flooded the room followed by a flurry of raindrops pummelling his window. When he sat up and checked the phone, the time read eight-forty-five. He'd still had no response from Marshall to his text message on Friday. He wouldn't send another, conscious of his new friend's time and work pressures and, moreover, he didn't want to come off as a phone stalker.

Dropping the device onto the duvet cover, he stretched out his arms and yawned. Most Saturday mornings he was woken by cat breath and a wet cat nose being pushed into his ear, and by the pizza shop owners downstairs moving around and getting ready for the weekend. Fortunately this morning he had met the new day without a hangover, thanks to his quick thinking the night before.

In the end, he had managed to ditch his brother and friends after only two hours. Lyle's boyfriend, Tate, had been insanely good-looking. Tall, muscular, great hair, deep sexy voice — a solid ten in Spencer's hotness rating scale. And yet Lyle had treated him with disdain, looking bored and pushing away from any affection, allowing only the occasional peck on the cheek and only enduring a protective arm around the shoulders. Forty-five minutes in and Spencer had wanted to slap Lyle. Or Tate. Or both of them. Peony must have sensed his annoyance, because she had sidled up to him while Garrett had gone for more drinks.

"*So what do you make of the sugar babes?*"

"*Sugar babes?*"

"*Tate and Lyle.*"

Spencer had choked on his lime soda. He hadn't made the connection between their names and the sugar company.

"*Honestly? I don't get it. What do they see in each other? Lyle is about as interesting and welcoming as a colon scan — I know he's your cousin, Peony, but you did ask. He could teach Mona Lisa a thing or two about how to look bored. Tate, on the other hand, is a total hunk who is clearly smitten with Lyle, and I have absolutely no idea why.*"

"*Join the club, sweetie. Takes all sorts. My cousin always has attracted total hotties.*"

"*Maybe I should try losing fifty pounds, bleaching my hair blond, wearing T-shirts with inappropriate slogans and adopting an air of aloof tiresomeness. Perhaps then I'd have more luck snaring someone like Tate.*"

At least Peony had found him funny.

"*You and Tate? I'd give it two weeks before you got bored. After the hot sex had worn off. Yes, he's good-looking in a* subjective kind of way, but he has nothing to say for himself, no opinions or interests."

"Might be worthwhile just for the fortnight of hot sex. It's been a long dry spell."

Peony had chuckled into her ice-filled virgin mojito. Another surprise for Spencer was that Garrett had chosen a girlfriend who had a personality, and one who didn't appear to drink alcohol. Finally his brother had struck gold. He also wondered—maybe a little unkindly—how long it would be before Garrett fucked everything up.

"Your brother said you were funny. He and your parents think you're too fussy."

Spencer hadn't been surprised to hear his brother had been talking about him.

"Now I've finally met you, I disagree," she had continued. "I said to him tonight, you wait, he's just biding his time. One day he'll shock the hell out of the lot of you."

One pleasant surprise from the night before was how much he had enjoyed chatting with Peony, even if he didn't agree with her prediction about him. She knew what she wanted and recognised what she had in Garrett, rough edges and all. And even a fool could see that, right now at least, she was as besotted with him as he was with her. And in Spencer's book that had to be a win-win all round.

After showering, he wandered into the kitchen diner where his father perched on a bar stool at the kitchen island wearing his tartan dressing gown, his earbuds in, totally immersed in a news channel on his tablet. Behind the counter, his mother scowled at their swish new coffee machine, which appeared to have been designed to look like the control panel on the flight deck of an airliner.

"Any chance that contraption makes cappuccinos?" asked Spencer.

"It does. Usually," she replied, clearly flustered. "If only I could find how to switch the stupid thing on. I used this button on the side yesterday, but nothing's happening. Surely it can't be broken already. We've only had the thing a couple of weeks."

Spencer walked over, put a plug into the wall socket and flicked the on switch. Instantly the machine whirred to life. His mother turned and shook her head at him with exasperation.

"Honestly, I don't know why your father finds it necessary to unplug things at the wall socket at night. It's so annoying."

"You know how safety conscious he is. Doesn't want the place to burn down while everyone's sleeping. And as long as he doesn't touch the fridge or the freezer, I'd say you're okay. Any chance of that coffee?"

Even though she'd had no idea to check the wall plug, his mother appeared to handle the coffee machine with the expertise of a barista. Within minutes she had produced a generous mug of foaming cappuccino with a sprinkling of chocolate on top. His father, no doubt getting a whiff of coffee, removed his earbuds and smiled at his wife.

"Ah, there he is, my husband. Back from the outer reaches of the Interweb."

"I'd love a coffee, thanks, dear."

"Where is this Guy Fawkes event tonight?" asked Spencer. "In a park, I'm guessing. Will they still be going ahead?"

"Let's see what the weather does," said his father, peering out at the garden through the floor-to-ceiling sliding doors that provided a perfect panorama of the ongoing thunderstorm. "They usually put on a display along the seafront, off the pier, but if this keeps up maybe they'll cancel. We'll see."

"Emergency triple espresso, mother," came a croak from the door. If Garrett's carrot-coloured mop had appeared unruly the day before, this morning it had taken on a life of its own, like a ginger mushroom cloud.

"I'm not even going to ask what time you got in," said his mother, standing guard at the coffee machine. "How come Spencer doesn't look like an extra from *The Walking Dead*?"

"I left them to it," said Spencer. "There are only so many lime sodas a boy can take."

"Are you permanently off alcohol?" asked Garrett, scraping out a stool and taking a seat next to him. Once installed, he grabbed Spencer's mug and took a mouthful of his coffee.

"No, of course not. But you know I've never been one for getting wasted."

"Which probably explains your abysmal batting average."

"He's being sensible. A person shouldn't rely on Dutch courage to chat up people. That's how accidents happen. Ask your Auntie Julie," said his mother, about her single parent sister, before turning towards the window. "Oh my goodness. Will you listen to that."

His mother's words had been partially drowned out by a loud clap of thunder, rattling the patio doors.

"Alcohol helps get your foot in the door," said Garrett before turning to Spencer. "What's Mum knocking up for breakfast?"

"Mum's not knocking up anything," said his mother, back to them, slamming down a mug of coffee in front of Garrett. "If you want toast, you know where the toaster is. Your father's treating us to brunch at Hunters at midday, a restaurant along the seafront that we both adore. They have a special set-price brunch which comes with freshly caught lobster cooked to your liking. Tonight we'll grab hot dogs or fish and chips from one of the stalls along the front while we watch the firework display."

"What firework display?" asked Garrett. "The event got cancelled two weeks ago because of the dreaded plague. Along with everything else."

"Seriously?" said Spencer, clunking his mug down on the countertop. "You mean I've been dragged all the way down here under false pretences?"

"Why didn't you tell us?" asked their mother.

"I thought you knew. And I assumed Dad would be doing fireworks in the back garden instead. Like he did when we were kids. Anyway, what's the big deal?"

His mother sighed and shook her head.

"In which case, we'll take a family stroll along the seafront after brunch, to make up for the lack of fireworks. And don't worry, Spencer darling, this weather is just like the coronavirus. It'll soon blow over."

* * * *

The weather did not blow over.

Fortunately for Spencer, his parents knew how to pick a restaurant. Hunters turned out to be exceptional and, considering the time of year, only half full, probably due either to the weather or to the health concerns across the nation. Six courses served over three hours complemented by sparkling wine, and

Spencer lounged back in a hazy buzz of too much fresh seafood and bubbles.

Sometimes he simply loved to observe his family interacting with one another, surrounding him with warmth like one of his mother's hugs. His parents might disagree over some things but not very often. In fact, they seemed to appreciate each other more now they'd both retired, appreciated each other's strengths in their union.

Five of them shared a table overlooking the seafront — Peony gamely agreeing to join them — as the foul-weathered light show playing out over the English Channel occasionally dragged their attention away from conversation. His brother sat with his arm protectively around Peony the whole time as she sipped on her pomegranate mocktail while Garrett followed suit with his father and ordered beer.

"Would you hate me if I said that I'm glad there's no firework display tonight?" said Spencer. "This is much more fun, all the family together."

"Oh, Spencer, you are such a sweetie to say that," said his mother. "But we've been to a firework display ever since you were small boys. Such a lovely tradition."

"Tradition? My arse. More like British sordidness at its worst," said Garrett. "What other culture celebrates some poor sod getting hanged, drawn and quartered — cut into four pieces and each part sent to the four corners of the country — for attempting to blow up the Houses of Parliament? You'd get a medal for doing the same thing these days — "

"I don't think that's quite right, son," said their father, ever the policeman. "You'd get banged up for a considerable number of years, in case you're getting any treasonable ideas."

"And how do we celebrate?" continued Garrett. "By creating a scarecrow we call a 'guy', clothed and stuffed with straw, then sitting the poor sod on a mound of wood piled ten feet high before setting light to the whole bloody thing. More like a horror movie or publicly sanctioned arson."

"Any public bonfire needs to be authorised, carefully prepared, and managed to meet local fire safety codes," added their father. Spencer's family had all learnt to tune him out.

"You know," continued Garrett, "a lot of historians reckon the introduction of Guy Fawkes Night celebrations was a ploy by the church to erase an old pagan festival."

"Samhain," said Spencer. "Or All Hallows' Eve. You're right. Probably the former." One of the magazines Spencer worked on had run an article about the Gaelic celebration that signalled the harvest season coming to an end and the beginning of the darkest, coldest stages of winter. "In times gone by, they constructed huge bonfires not only to keep people warm, but to scare away wild animals and evil spirits."

Only Peony seemed to be paying any attention to what he was saying.

"And did you know there's apparently somewhere in the country that refuses to celebrate Guy Fawkes Night?" continued Spencer. "The place where Guy Fawkes went to school. They don't allow his image to be burnt out of respect for their former pupil."

"God, no wonder you're single," said Garrett. "Spouting crap like that."

"Don't say that about your brother, Garrett," said their mother, before turning to Spencer, her cheeks rouged from one too many glasses of bubbly. Spencer, who shared his mother's complexion, imagined that he looked similarly flushed. "When are you going to bring someone home, Spencer? You know your father and I will be fine."

"We've had that conversation, dear," said their father.

"As I told Dad, it's not exactly the best time to meet new people, Mum. The atmosphere out there isn't exactly conducive to dating right now."

"Is anyone having dessert?" asked their father.

"And anyway," said Garrett, after downing his pint and thumping his glass down on the table. "Mum's going to have her hands full soon. Being a grandmother, and all."

"Do you think we could order two?" asked his mother, to the menu. "There are so many. And I can't decide between the chocolate soufflé and the Eton mess."

"Have both, love," said their father, also staring at the menu but absently reaching across to pat her hand. "I can share with you."

Spencer stared between Garett and Peony—both looking down at the menu Garrett held—the sudden realisation of what had been said washing over him as though he stood outside in the pouring rain. Had Garrett spoken the words he'd thought he'd heard? Did his parents already know and had taken the news in their stride? But surely they would never have kept something like that from him. He tilted his head to one side and looked quizzically at Peony. Eventually she looked up, giggled, and nodded.

"Mum! Dad!" said Spencer loudly. "Are you paying attention? Your son, Garrett, has just made a monumental announcement."

Peony laughed aloud now and Garrett pulled her across and kissed the top of her head.

"Peony and I are having a baby," he said.

Finally, he managed to get their parents' attention.

"What? How did that happen?" Spencer's mother's features had frozen in shock, the dessert menu dropping from her fingers.

"Usual way, Mum."

"And you're both okay with this?" asked their father.

"How long have you known?" said their mother at the same time.

"I'm over the moon. We both are. And we've known for about three weeks."

"Why didn't you say anything before?" asked their mother.

"Because I wanted to have the whole family together," said Garrett, grinning at Spencer. "Seeing as you're all going to be on child-minding duties."

"Yes," said Spencer, "I don't think that's going to happen."

"Not you, of course. I wouldn't trust you to look after my pet tarantula," said Garrett, before supplementing the comment because of the horrified look his father gave him, "if I ever had a pet tarantula."

"What do your parents think, Peony?" asked Spencer's mother.

"Peony's mother passed away four years ago," said Garrett. "And she never met her father."

"Oh, heavens. I'm so sorry."

"It's fine," said Peony. "Well, it's not fine, of course. I wish Mum was still around. But there's no point wishing for the impossible, is there? At least the child will have you both as grandparents. And Spencer as an uncle, of course."

"I think it's brilliant. I'm going to be cool, gay Uncle Spencer. And I am going to spoil your kid rotten, bro."

Peony giggled again and snuggled into Garrett.

"I'm going to pick out dresses and accessories and makeup," added Spencer.

"We don't know the sex yet," said Garrett.

"And your point being?" said Spencer, enjoying watching the smile drain from his brother's face while Peony tipped back her head and laughed aloud. "Does this mean you'll finally be getting your own place?"

"It's early days," said Garrett, giving Spencer the stink eye before talking to his parents. "The baby's not due until April or May. And we haven't really discussed—"

"Of course you're not, Garrett. Not yet, anyway," said his mother. "Peony will need someone around to help with the baby. You'll stay with us, of course you will. We'll be happy to have you, won't we, Colin?"

For the first time that weekend, Spencer's father stepped out of his mental man cave and really joined the party. After studying Garrett then Peony, making a careful assessment, he turned to Spencer's mother.

"We'd be delighted," he said, before kissing her on the cheek. "*Grandma*."

This single word instantly got Spencer's mother's attention.

"Okay. House rules. This child will *not* be calling me either Granny or Grandma."

Everyone but Spencer's mother laughed. She had made the fact clear on other occasions when they talked about the possibility of her sons having children — either or both of them.

"How about Nanna?" asked Spencer.

"I guess that might work."

"Shame, I had my heart set on Glamma."

"Don't push your luck, Garrett," said their mother.

"Thank you both," said Peony, directly to Spencer's mother and father. She appeared almost relieved, but then she had only just met the big-hearted Wyrrell family.

"This calls for a celebration," said Spencer's father, beckoning the waiter. "Hello there. Can we get everyone a glass of bubbly so we can make a toast? Oh, except for the mother-to-be over there. She'll have a glass of sparkling lemonade."

A good sport, the waiter smiled at Peony and gave a thumbs up, then stayed to take their dessert orders before heading to the kitchen.

"Surely you can have one glass of champagne," said Spencer.

"I could. But I'm not taking any chances," said Peony.

Spencer's mother nodded her approval before folding her napkin onto the table, and insisting on swapping places with Garrett. Finally their mother had a project she could get her teeth into — a new grandchild on the way. Spencer felt happy for her. With the three men of the house sitting together, Garrett got the grilling he thoroughly deserved.

"You know the saying, Garrett?" said Spencer, enjoying his brother's discomfort. "A baby is for life, not just for Christmas. You're going to have to step up your game."

"I know that," said Garrett, scowling at Spencer.

"And are you going to make an honest woman of her before the baby arrives?" asked their father. "Or are you happy to bring your child into this world without—"

"Dad! Please!" said Garrett, looking over his father's shoulder. "We haven't thought that far ahead. Where's that bloody champagne?"

"Well, you'd better *start* thinking ahead. April is just around the corner. Now I've got something really important I need to ask. Are you paying attention?"

Poor Garrett squeezed his eyes closed and, while pinching the bridge of his nose, bobbed his head twice.

"How would you feel about me going ahead with that roof extension? Give you both your own double bedroom and private bathroom, as well as a small adjacent room you can use as a nursery?"

Garrett's eyes shot open and even Spencer felt the sting of tears. Maybe their father didn't speak very often, but when he did, he usually had something huge to say.

"You would do that for us?"

"I've been wanting to do the extension for ages. But your mother quite rightly said we didn't need the extra space with only you at home and Spencer living in London. Now I have a legitimate excuse and I think your mother will be completely on board."

"I would love that. But let me contribute this time, Dad."

"Don't be ridiculous. I'll be using you boys' inheritance to pay for the renovations, so consider this payment in advance. Honestly, in all the time we've lived down here, I've never seen your mother look so happy. And you know how I am when I've got a project on the go. Ah, here are the drinks. Let's have that toast."

* * * *

Without a break in the weather, they spent the rest of the day at home. Peony and Spencer's mother sat in the kitchen talking about all things babies, while the men watched replays of football matches — football without padding — on one of Garrett's many sports channels. His father lasted all of an hour before he fell asleep in an armchair.

Spencer sat back and marvelled at his family. Life in the Wyrrell family usually cruised along on smooth waters, but when surprises came they were often showstoppers, like their parents' move to the coast. And now his brother, someone he had fairly — or unfairly — considered too immature to hold down a relationship, was about to bring a child into the world. In a strange way, he felt jealous of the change Garrett and Peony would have in their lives, of the love and hugs the child would receive from his parents.

Only Spencer appeared immune to the Wyrrell good fortune, although he could hardly complain. After a dinner of grilled cheese on toast and a mug of tea, he lay awake in his room, contemplating the day and wondering when the universe would finally wake up and include him in its plan.

He didn't have long to wait.

Chapter Seven

On Sunday morning, he awoke to a quiet house with only the distant thrum of traffic outside the bedroom window. Unsurprisingly, considering their choice of supper the night before, he'd had nightmares and had woken startled a couple of times. Garrett had insisted on an evening of toasted cheese sandwiches and horror flicks to accompany the continued stormy weather. The evening had culminated in an old classic called *Don't Look Now*, about a married couple who travelled to Venice after the husband was commissioned to supervise the restoration work on a Venetian church. Spencer had seen the film before, but had still managed to get hooked into the suspense, particularly on the husband's sightings of his dead daughter in the red cloak, which had made his skin prickle. And every time he had gasped aloud in shock at one scene or another, he'd turned to find Peony and Garrett staring at him, trying hard to stifle their giggles.

Right now he felt tired and brittle from broken sleep. After using the bathroom, he packed up his weekend bag then headed into the breakfast area. His bespectacled mother sat at the kitchen island reading newspapers, one hand cradling her head, the other wrapped around a coffee mug. The sight made him smile.

Nice and quiet, business as usual after yesterday's earth-shattering announcement. With both his parents avid newspaper readers, Sunday mornings had always felt like a safe haven of calm in their household.

"Where are the boys?" he asked. "Still sleeping?"

"They decided to go for a bike ride," she said, still scanning the newspaper. "Seeing as the weather's improved."

"Oh. I see," said Spencer. He had tried to avoid mention of his father's motorcycle purchase. For some reason, she didn't seem annoyed and picked up on his response.

"I know," she said, looking up and giving him a knowing look. "I don't really approve, darling, but if it means your father and Garrett having male bonding time together, who am I to complain?"

"I suppose. As long as they're careful. I wonder how Peony feels about the father-to-be of her child out on his bike after a day of heavy rain."

"Exactly," said his mother, staring away from her paper for a split second and more than likely storing away that little remark for later. In Peony, she had a new ally.

"Anything newsworthy in the papers?" he asked, heading to the coffee machine.

"Looks like another national lockdown on the horizon. Probably the end of next week. Not that we'll be affected much, with us both retired and Garrett able to work from the living room table. Will they let you work from home?"

"Even if they do, I can't. I don't have internet, do I?"

"How will you manage to work, then?" she asked absently, still scanning the paper.

"They'll still allow minimal staffing. If I've got a lot to do I'll mask up and brave a Tube train or splash out on an Uber into the office. Otherwise I'll work from the coffee shop downstairs as long as they're open. I'll figure something out."

Unaided, he had made himself a mug of cappuccino—pretty straightforward, as he'd found out—and a slice of toast. He perched the other side of the counter, where a more substantial pile of newspapers sat, and pulled out a colourful magazine poking out from one of the papers.

While tucking into dry toast, he scanned the entertainment section, one of his favourite parts, impressed to see a few plays continuing to run in the West End. A review caught his attention, of a new play called *The Right Side of the Family*, adapted from a well-known author's acclaimed novel.

The story centred on the family of a prestigious Conservative politician in the sixties coming to terms with the tragic death of their much-loved eldest son in a boating accident while at Cambridge university. With a celebrated cast of actors performing in a time of difficulty, Spencer felt sure the reviewer would be generous. But even though some of the performances received a lukewarm mention, the review was nothing short of vitriolic. Somewhere around London, he mused, people who had sweated over the production would be waking to this nasty review, one that barely touched on the premise of the play and had only a passing mention to the author's original work.

He sat back for a moment, drained his coffee, and considered the kind of treatment he would have given the review. Of course, he would have insisted on seeing the play first off — at least once — but in his favour, he already knew the book intimately.

Just as he returned from the coffee machine with a refill, his mother turned over the newspaper she had been reading, slapped her hand down on top and let out a loud cry.

"Oh no, not him," she exclaimed. Looking like a wise old owl with her huge glasses perched on her nose, she picked up and tossed one of the Sunday tabloids across the counter to him. "Will you look at that? Marshall Highlander is gay. Which is perfectly fine, of course, and not completely unexpected. I mean, with those eyes and bone structure he must have had dozens of women queuing up to date him in his time. And now here he is, splashed all over the Sundays, caught making a complete fool of himself on the French Riviera with some boy young enough to be his grandson."

Shock followed by dismay washed through Spencer as he stared down at the paper.

"I wouldn't believe everything you read, Mum."

"I don't. But those pictures provide pretty damning evidence."

With the mug cradled to his chest, Spencer picked up the paper, went over to the dining room table and fell into one of the chairs. After taking a deep gulp, he faltered momentarily before turning to the front page of the *Tribute*.

Jumping out at him, the scandalous headline sat above a photograph of two men sunbathing by a swimming pool—a private pool in a villa with high walls—with the younger man naked and lying on his front with his backside on full display, his face smiling up into the sun and the camera lens. Next to him, the unmistakably delicious figure of Marshall Highlander lounged on a sunbed, his body bronzed and decked out in tight white swimwear.

MARSHALL HIGHLANDER IN GAY SEX SCANDAL WITH JOE HOLLINGBROKE
by TOBY WENTWORTH

Journalist and political television host of the talk show Say What You Mean *Marshall Highlander is at the centre of a sex scandal today after photographs surfaced of him and a former gay lover, the once popular celebrity Joe Hollingbroke, better known for his role of Donkey in the long-running soap opera* Waterloo Lane.

Highlander, the son of film producer Leyton Highlander and socialite Gloria Ann Shelley, is said to have begun the affair while Hollingbroke had been a minor.

Shot at a holiday villa in St Cezaire sur Siagne on the French Rivera, the photographs show the tan and naked couple cavorting around a swimming pool.

Highlander, 41, a bachelor, has repeatedly avoided the subject of his sexuality. He is a close friend of actor and gay activist Charles Pollard and a champion of many causes including AIDS foundations and gay support groups.

See centre pages for more on this breaking story.

Spencer hated himself for reading the story, which took up the centre pages of the tawdry rag, but he wanted to understand the extent of the damage. Surely in this day and age someone being outed by a newspaper was no longer a headline, but the insinuation that his love interest had been under the age of consent would have definitely sold papers. Although nowhere did they imply that the police were involved. By the end of the badly written, poorly edited — French *Rivera*, for goodness' sake? — and highly speculative article, what was patently obvious to Spencer was that Marshall's ex-boyfriend, Joseph 'Joey' Hollingbroke, had royally fucked him over. Spencer wondered how much money he would be getting from the exclusive, and whether he was using the media attention to resurrect his flagging popularity.

After finishing the story and gulping down his coffee, he excused himself to go to his bedroom. He pulled out his phone and sat there for a full five minutes, staring at Marshall's text number, not knowing what words to write. In the end, he texted the simple line — *If you need to talk, I'm here for you.*

* * * *

By the time he'd readied to leave for the station, he had still not heard back from Marshall. Naturally, the poor man would be keeping a low profile somewhere, probably at his manager's place. Spencer would still have liked to know how Marshall was coping. He also wondered — a little selfishly — whether their planned dinner out the next week would be affected, then chastised himself because he knew, beyond any doubt, that it would. Marshall would have far more pressing concerns.

"Are you okay?" said his mother, fussing with the collar of his jacket the way she used to when he was a boy about to head off to school. "You've been very quiet today. Is this about your brother's announcement?"

Garrett had escaped to Peony's bedsit in the afternoon, after their light lunch together, probably for some private time or to discuss the future. Or maybe Spencer had scared him away. He had, after all, ribbed Garrett relentlessly about the responsibilities of fatherhood.

"Not everything's about Garrett, Mum. I'm mulling over things I've got on my plate at work next week."

He loved both his parents and rarely filtered anything when he spoke to them, but right now was not the time to tell them about his encounter with the tabloid's latest prey.

"Oh, sorry, dear. I haven't asked you. How are things going in the wonderful world of magazine publishing? You remember we have a local paper down here, don't you? *The Bournemouth Echo*. They're bound to be interested in a serious journalist with your talents, ones that are honestly being wasted right now."

She didn't bother to mask her contempt for Spencer's employer. His mother had never been a magazine person.

"I love my job. And I'm bloody good at what I do. I just wish they'd see me as more than an office boy, someone to fetch and carry and clean up after people's messes. I take great pride in what I do."

"You're conscientious to a fault, darling. You get that from me. Those people neither appreciate nor deserve you."

Like all mothers, Coleen Wyrrell thought her sons had been born to lead, not to follow or to be managed. At least Garrett ran his own company.

"And you're coming back for Christmas, aren't you?" said his mother, standing with him on the front doorstep while Spencer's father revved the car's engine. They usually timed everything to the second so that Spencer would be on the platform five to ten minutes before the train's departure. If all went well, he would arrive at his front door in Morden between seven and seven-thirty.

"Of course. If I'm allowed."

"What do you mean, if you're allowed?" she asked, looking aghast.

"If the government are talking about a national lockdown, about introducing a tier system, then they'll soon start restricting the number of people for any kind of gathering."

"To six, according to your father. So even if Penny joins us this year — which I would love — that's only five of us. And I promise to let your father cook the turkey this year."

Folding her into his arms, he gave his mother the kind of oversized hug she gave others.

"I promise to move heaven and earth to make sure I get home, Mum. Who else does Christmas like the Wyrrells?"

"Exactly. And you know you can bring someone, if you want to," she said, giving him one last squeeze then pushing him away before he could respond. "Go on with you, now. Your father's waiting."

* * * *

Whenever he visited his parents or came home from work midweek during the summer months, Spencer enjoyed the short walk back from Morden station. With the daylight on his skin, the quick burst of exercise and the fresh air — he even took the shortcut through the park some days — he savoured the remains of the day before arriving home. But during the dark winter months, he put his head down and marched beneath the row of streetlights.

At seven in the evening, seeing groups of people huddled around the grimy station entrance was not unusual. Some waited for taxis or connecting buses to head to their homes while others met up with friends. But there always seemed to be enough random groups of people hanging around not to worry too much.

Except tonight, for some reason, Spencer singled out a tall man in a dark overcoat. He lounged against the wall with the collar up, a black woollen ski hat dragged down over the ears, wearing dark glasses and a black surgical mask covering his mouth. Dressed like an assassin, he peeled away from the wall beside the station convenience store the moment Spencer exited the station. Shaking his head at his overactive imagination, Spencer wrapped the ridiculously long brown and mustard scarf around his neck — a Doctor Who scarf, his father called the gift — before beginning the hike for home.

Somebody had once told him that intuition is real and that we should never ignore the signs, then went on to impart a cautionary fable about Welsh miners sensing wrongness in the air of a mineshaft and escaping just before the roof of the mine collapsed. Spencer felt nothing like that, but without even thinking, he turned a couple of times to see if he was being followed. Both times he saw nobody. Both times he cursed his brother and his insistence on last night's television horrorfest.

When he reached the familiar row of shops, with the cheerful green, yellow and red lights of Romano's Pizzeria, he felt the tension drain from him. With one hand on the handle of his luggage, he pushed open the front door to the empty shop. Instantly, the owner's head popped up from behind the counter.

"Hi, Gino," he said. "How's business?"

"Hey, Spencer. Bloody crazy until half an hour ago. How's family?"

"Same as ever, mad as a box of frogs."

"All families are the same. Mine are all back in Milan, thank goodness. You want to order your usual?"

"Let me check upstairs first. Let Tiger know I'm back then see what I've got in the fridge that needs finishing. I'll pop down if I need to order."

"Okay. And don't worry. Your cat, she is still alive. My wife has been spoiling her with fresh fish and cat treats. Think she wants to kidnap her."

"Good luck with that. But please thank Mrs R for taking care of her. No doubt the little princess will still give me attitude for being away the whole weekend."

"That's females for you."

Spencer laughed. "I'll take your word for that."

Before he opened the downstairs door, he acted the dutiful son and texted his mother to tell her he had arrived home safely, a ritual he had agreed to and would probably continue for as long as they were both alive.

Tiger met him as he opened the top door to his apartment. As always, after parking his luggage and kicking his shoes off, he spent a few minutes kneeling and petting her until she eventually provided her 'all-is-forgiven' purr, made better when he poured dried food into her bowl. With her cared for, he set about unpacking his bag and heading to his small bedroom wardrobe to choose an outfit for work the next day. Once done, he switched on the Bluetooth speaker on his coffee table and put on some soft jazz music, then checked the fridge for an evening meal. Gino's wife had left him some fresh milk, but he had little else apart from a half loaf of bread, a couple of eggs and some butter. In the freezer, he had stocked up with store-bought frozen meals for the week ahead but decided he might treat himself to one of Gino's pizzas. As he readied to pop downstairs, his front-door buzzer sounded.

Out of necessity, Spencer had personally invested in a video phone so he didn't have to hike all the way downstairs and use the spyhole every time someone called on him. Too many times — back when Romano's could open late — they'd had drunks falling out of the pizza shop in the early hours and ringing his doorbell for fun. Right now, on checking the monitor, he let out an audible gasp on seeing the silhouette of a tall figure in a dark ski cap and sunglasses standing outside his door. After a pause, curiosity got the better of him, and he pressed the answer button.

"Hello? Who is it?"

"It's me," came the hesitant, yet vaguely familiar, voice.

"Sorry. Who's me?"

"Marshall. Marshall Highlander," said the man, before looking up into the camera lens while pulling down his mask and removing the shades. "Can I — um — can I come in?"

Spencer gaped for a moment, unable to believe his eyes. Marshall Highlander stood on his doorstep, had come to see Spencer in his hour of need. Without a moment of hesitation, he pushed the intercom button.

"Hang on a minute. I'll come down and let you in."

Chapter Eight

When Spencer yanked open the door, Marshall stood there, a large black bag over one shoulder. Even in the wan light of the pizza shop, he appeared hesitant, scared almost.

"Is it okay if I come in? I know we don't know each other that well. And I didn't even return your text yesterday, although, to be honest, things have been a little manic. But I'm — well — I've run out of options of places to go and people who I can trust. I suppose I could hole up in a small hotel somewhere, but even then the bastards can still find —"

"For goodness' sake, Marshall, get in here."

Spencer opened the door wide and pulled him by the arm over the threshold. Before closing the door, he leant outside and checked the pavement. Everything appeared as usual. A masked couple entered the pizza shop arm in arm chatting, happily absorbed in each other's company, but the street was otherwise empty. Satisfied, Spencer closed and bolted the door before turning round.

Marshall had perched on a lower step of the staircase. He looked utterly defeated, his scarf lowered, his mask and glasses now removed. A large holdall sat next to him. Spencer watched him rub his hands up and down his face and through his hair, as though to wash away what must have been a nightmare of a weekend. When he stopped and looked up at Spencer, dark circles beneath his eyes spoke of sleepless nights, and his skin stretched taut with anxiety. Did he think Spencer might turn him away? The man looked not so much hounded as hunted. At the thought, Spencer's heart wrenched, and he did exactly what his mother would have done in the same situation—he scooped Marshall up from the step into a tight hug.

Held close, he could feel Marshall's body trembling, maybe with tension, maybe with relief, but quivering nonetheless.

"Hey, don't worry," said Spencer, rubbing Marshall's back. "You're safe here."

"Am I?"

"Of course you are."

After a few moments, feeling Marshall's body relax, Spencer let go.

"You'd think I would be immune to this." Marshall appeared embarrassed at showing weakness. "Or at least understand the score. I work alongside the paparazzi much of the time, don't necessarily agree with their principles, but we've always had a mutual understanding. Being their target is not pleasant. Not pleasant at all. I knew they would be waiting for me outside my flat in South Kensington, so I asked the taxi driver to take me past Darcy's place in Chelsea, and saw the bastards had set up camp there, too. I realised then they would be hanging around anyone I'm connected to. That's when I thought of you. I got him to drop me at the Tube station here. I remembered you saying you'd be coming home from your parents' place on Sunday evening. I would have called or texted you, but my phone died on me."

"Come on, let's get you upstairs," said Spencer, leading the way. He wondered how long Marshall had waited around for him to appear, deciding there and then not to bring up the newspaper story. "That was you outside the Tube station mini market?"

"I'm afraid so." Spencer heard Marshall following behind. "I was going to ask the cabbie to drive around the area and find a pizza shop — I remember you telling me you lived above one — but then worried the guy might recognise me and notify someone. Apparently parancia comes with the territory."

"Just good sense, if you ask me. The driver probably thinks you're catching the Tube back into town. Now be careful in here. I have a cat who thinks she's the most important living creature on the planet. You will either be ignored as unimportant or hissed at as an intruder, and hopefully not clawed."

When Spencer unlocked the door, Tiger sat in the doorway to the bedroom, nosey as ever, eyeing them both. As Marshall stepped into the room, she came straight over and brushed herself against his leg, her tail in the air. Spencer's mouth dropped open.

"I have never, ever, seen her do that to another human being," said Spencer, watching Marshall reach down and scratch her head, and more incredulously, watching her not only allow him but positively purr her enjoyment at the attention. "I kid you not, my brother is scared of her. She's even been known to *bite* him."

"She's a beauty. What's her name?"

"Tiger," said Spencer. "Tiger Neon."

"After the Killers song?"

"You see? With that kind of taste in music, of course you're welcome here. Now, sit yourself down and let me get you something to drink. I've only got tea or coffee, I'm afraid. Nothing stronger."

"Tea would be lovely, thanks. Can I charge my phone?"

"Of course. There's a power socket just behind the sofa."

While Spencer set about making mugs of tea, he kept an eye on Marshall watching him make his way over to the sofa and plugging in his phone charger. When he finally dropped onto the sofa, he let out a deep, heartfelt sigh. Seconds later, Tiger jumped into his lap and curled up. Spencer laughed in amazement and shook his head. He had never known his cat to be a people person, not even with her owner. While Marshall massaged his cat's head with one hand, he switched on his phone with the other and checked the display.

"Oh, heck, Marshall," said Spencer. "There's something I need to tell you. You won't get a phone signal anywhere in the flat, in case you need to call somebody or you're waiting for a call. You'll have to go downstairs into the street. And the landlord never put in a landline or Wi-Fi, so we're pretty much stuck on a desert island in here."

Instead of being put out, Marshall appeared relieved.

"I knew there was a good reason for coming. Apart from being here with you. This is the perfect choice, my Last Homely House East of the Sea."

Spencer smiled as he held the carton of milk in the air and waited for Marshall to nod.

"A Tolkien fan, too," said Spencer, bringing the drinks over and placing them down on the coffee table. "You know, I might never let you leave."

"Right now, that sounds absolutely perfect. And I bought you some marmalade, too. From the convenience store at the station."

"Marmalade? Okay, that's very kind of you," said Spencer, a little baffled, as he took the seat next to Marshall.

"Marmalade and canned whipped cream, if my memory serves me correctly."

"Oh, heavens," said Spencer, putting his hands over his eyes and feeling his cheeks burning. Next to him, he heard Marshall laughing softly, the shoulder touching Spencer's shaking with humour.

"It's okay," said Marshall, placing a warm hand on Spencer's shoulder. "I'm only kidding. But you should know I have a solid memory for facts and figures, and especially for things people say."

"Noted."

Apart from Tiger's loud purr and the soft music from Spencer's speaker, they sat unspeaking in companionable silence, nursing their drinks, Marshall using a hand to massage the top of Tiger's head.

"Thank you for doing this," said Marshall eventually.

"My house is your house. And apparently, my cat is all yours, too."

"Would it be really awkward if I asked to stay the night?"

Spencer's heart started to speed up then until he reminded himself that Marshall needed to stay off the radar and Spencer's flat had proven the perfect haven.

"Of course you can. I'd be honoured to have you stay. You can take my bed and I'll sleep on the sofa—"

"Spencer, I can't ask you—"

"It's fine. I often fall asleep out here. And you clearly won't fit on this old thing. Your legs would be dangling off the end. Now before you argue any more, do you want to grab a hot bath? Or you can use the attachment over the tub to have a shower, if you'd prefer."

Marshall pushed his head back into the leather sofa and let out a deep sigh.

"You know, the mere thought of a hot bath is making me feel better already."

"Done, then. I'll run a bath for you. Have you eaten?"

"No, but you don't have to—"

"I'm hungry, too. While you have a bath, I'm going to run downstairs and order us an extra-large pepperoni and chilli pizza. Hope that's okay?"

"Sounds perfect. I'm really sorry to do this—"

"Right, that's it. Stop now. If you apologise one more time, I will confiscate my cat. Just let somebody do something nice for you. Let's start with a fresh towel and I'll run you a bath while you entertain Tiger. And when you've finished your bath, go and change in the bedroom. I'll dig out some casuals for you to wear and leave them on the bed, a sweatshirt and tracksuit bottoms. The track bottoms may be a little short, but they're the best I can muster. Hopefully, by the time you've bathed and changed into those, I'll be back with the food. Something to note. Because of the ovens downstairs, the floor to the flat might be toasty-warm right now, but it gets cold during the night. I'll leave out some thick woollen socks, long ones, for you to wear to bed."

Without another word, Spencer headed to the bathroom, stopping for a quick look back over his shoulder as he reached the door. Marshall had been checking him out as he walked away. The realisation sent a thrill through him. The truth was, he enjoyed taking care of Marshall, loved seeing his smiled appreciation at the small kindnesses. Without a second thought, he pulled out his expensive bubble bath and plopped a generous amount into the running water while steam filled his tiny bathroom. Once he had the tub filled, he went back into the living area.

"Couple of things. It's an old flat, so there's no fancy bathroom fixtures. But the plumbing works and the place is heated, so you won't freeze to death. And more importantly the flat comes with — "

"You, Spencer," said Marshall, reaching out and grabbing his hand. "The place comes with you. Honestly, you have no idea how much this means to me. And remind me to show you photos on my phone of some of the far-from-fancy places I've stayed around the world while reporting on one situation or another. Your flat is five-star luxury accommodation by comparison."

"That's nice of you to say, and I actually love living here. But I was going to mention the easy-to-reach shops." Spencer took his hand back and reached for his wallet and keys. "Now, I'm going to take some money, leave my phone on the table so you can still listen to the music while you're soaking — Bluetooth still works without the internet, thank goodness — and pop down to the pizza shop. Put Her Royal Highness onto the floor when you're ready. Jump in the bath while the water's nice and hot. Don't leave it too long."

"Yes, Mother."

Grinning, Spencer bounced down the stairs, two at a time. Gino was already serving another customer at the counter, and he waited to place his order, which included a six-pack of bottled Italian beers. While he waited, he realised he hadn't asked Marshall whether he drank beer, but he was sure alcohol of any kind would not go amiss, bearing in mind the weekend he had endured.

Around twenty minutes later, when he pushed open the upstairs door to his apartment, Marshall was sat cross-legged on the sofa in grey sweats and white socks, watching television with Tiger installed again on his lap. Spencer went to the kitchen counter and placed everything down.

"Hope you don't mind. I used your hairdryer in the bedroom. Not a big fan of wet hair on a cold night."

While pulling out plates, cutlery and his small bottle of hot sauce, Spencer continued chatting with Marshall.

"Me either. You look better, refreshed."

"I feel better. Much better, thank you."

"My pleasure. I bought us some beers to go with the pizza. Thought you might like something more fortifying to drink than tea or coffee."

"Good call," said Marshall.

Spencer searched his kitchen drawers for a bottle opener. He rarely drank at home but had brought a corkscrew combined with a bottle opener with him when he moved in. Once he'd popped the tops off a couple of beers, he took one over to Marshall, finding him flipping through news channels on Spencer's flatscreen.

"Are you okay to watch the news?" asked Spencer.

"Damage is done now, isn't it?"

Spencer couldn't help but notice the resigned tone in Marshall's voice. On all the programmes of Marshall's that Spencer had watched, the man had never backed down from asking hard questions. Now the tables had been turned and Marshall was the one having to answer them. Spencer went back to the kitchenette and brought the pizza box and plates over to the coffee table. He placed a slice on each plate before handing one to Marshall. Without thinking, he picked up the remote and clicked off the television.

"You know, sometimes you begin to wonder if you can trust anyone," said Marshall, staring at the plate.

"There must be people you can still lean on, surely? Like Darcy?"

"There are. Not many, though. Not entirely," said Marshall, becoming reflective. "I usually go and stay with my mother if I need space from life and work. She lives in a small village outside Oxford. But she's in the Bahamas right now."

"Very nice."

"Can I trust *you*, Spencer?"

When Spencer met Marshall's sincere gaze and felt his vulnerability, his heart wrenched. Of course Marshall felt betrayed, after being exposed publicly by somebody he thought beyond scrutiny. He wanted to say yes, that he could trust him with his life, but those words would be easy to say and maybe Marshall needed — deserved — more.

"That's a question you need to answer for yourself. I can only tell you that I would never do what Joey did to you, that seeing you like this breaks my heart and I would punch anyone in the nose who tried to hurt you right now. But then, you don't really know me. I could say anything. The point is whether you believe me."

Marshall fell quiet and nodded solemnly.

"I can only give you my word. And if it helps, I've suffered humiliation at the hands of a partner — not as publicly as you — but I know the number that kind of thing does on your self-esteem. Only you can help yourself bounce back from something like that. You also know for a fact there's no internet access or phone connection here, so I'm not about to call anyone. I truly want this to be a safe space for you, Marshall."

Once again Marshall processed Spencer's words, and eventually, he returned a sympathetic smile.

"Poor Spencer. Both times we've met, you've seen me at my lowest ebb. You must be wondering what a mess I am, this man who's dropped into your life twice."

"Just to clarify, I happen to like this man."

Marshall smiled.

"Is that so?"

"It is."

Marshall began asking Spencer about his weekend with the family — probably a ploy to distract them both from Marshall's melancholy — and before long both of them were laughing. By the time they had finished the pizza and managed two beers each, and when Spencer noticed Marshall try to stifle a yawn a couple of times, he realised the time had slipped away from them.

"It's already ten-thirty," said Spencer, standing up from the sofa. "Maybe it's time for bed. I'd better grab a pillow and quilt cover for the sofa —"

Before he could move off, Marshall grabbed his hand.

"Spencer. The bed's plenty big enough for two. And I promise to be a gentleman if you lie next to me. To be honest, I'm not sure I can even sleep. Not for long, anyway. My brain won't stay quiet."

"Are you sure, Marshall? I don't want you thinking I've lured you—"

"I brought myself here. There was no *luring* involved. And honestly, it would be good to have your company tonight. Even if we're just lying next to each other, keeping each other company and chatting."

Once again a frisson of excitement shot through Spencer at Marshall's words, and the fact he still had hold of Spencer's hand. Blake had been the last person to share his bed, and that felt like an eternity ago. At any other time he might have found himself giving off seductive signals or maybe even returning a flirty comment, but doing so when the man was so vulnerable would be a low move. Instead he squeezed Marshall's hand and smiled his encouragement.

"In which case, I would love to join you. It's going to be another cold night and we can keep each other warm. And I have a feeling we might be joined by her ladyship, who usually hogs the sofa at night."

"'Marshall Highlander,'" said Marshall, in his best television reporter voice, "caught in scandalous menage-a-trois with cute magazine editor and his cat.'"

"Cute?" said Spencer, smiling at Marshall's light-heartedness and hauling him up from the sofa.

"As you said yourself, I say it like it is."

Spencer grinned as he pushed Marshall towards the bedroom, towards his bed, which was barely a double.

"Which side should I take?" asked Marshall, standing at the foot of the bed.

"I usually sleep in the middle, so take your pick."

Marshall went to the far side, correctly interpreting that side as the one Spencer rarely used. Both sides had a small table, but on Spencer's side there stood a small lamp he left switched on until sleep. He set about turning off lights in the flat, and when he returned Marshall was sitting on the edge of the bed, removing his watch. When Spencer stretched his arms in the air, yawning on tiptoe, he turned to find Marshall staring at his backside before looking quickly away.

"This is a bonus to my otherwise boring Sunday evenings," said Spencer, deflecting as he slid beneath the cover. Marshall got in too and laid on his side to face Spencer.

"I guess we both usually go to bed alone. If you need to sleep, turn the light off. I'll be fine in the dark."

"Are you not tired?"

"Not really," said Marshall, even though he looked exhausted. "But I don't want to keep you awake."

"We can talk for a bit, if you like? Maybe you can tell me about yourself."

"What do you want to know?"

"Tell me about your family. Your mother and father. There's not much on your Wikipedia page. And although I am not normally an iStalker, I did look you up."

"Did you now? Then you know who my parents are?"

"I think so. But tell me anyway."

Marshall flipped onto his back and appeared to seek out something on the ceiling before he began talking.

"My father's the film producer Leyton Highlander and my mother is Gloria Ann Shelley. That's the name she still goes by, now they're divorced. Before she met my father, she was at the start of a promising modelling career, but eventually planning to start her own fashion house, like Stella McCartney. But then, as she says herself, she made the mistake of falling for my father. She was the daughter of one of his wealthier financial backers, a natural platinum blonde and stunning. They had me late in the game. Mum would have been thirty-three, ten years younger than Dad. He already had a mistress by then. Although she has never said as much, I have a strong suspicion I wasn't planned. Probably the result of make-up sex after one of their infamous fights. I didn't hear many of them growing up. I mostly read about them in the papers. Just like all the men in my father's family, I had a private nanny until I was old enough to be shipped off to an all-boys preparatory boarding school in Edinburgh, and then on to Eton at thirteen to study for my exams."

"That's brutal. You never saw your parents?"

"During the holidays. Every summer we'd fly off to the sun somewhere exclusive. Stay in the finest hotels and eat the most expensive food. Dad spent most of his time in the room on his phone, but Mother liked to get acquainted with the local neighbourhood. By the end of the holiday she'd be on first-name terms with all the shopkeepers. I think that's where I get my love of talking to strangers."

"She sounds lovely."

"She is. She was my rock. Still is."

"And what about you?"

"What about me?" asked Marshall, turning to Spencer.

"Tell me about the real you, not the television version."

Marshall gave Spencer a withering smile.

"For all the celebrity bullshit that goes with the job, I'm a private person. Don't get me wrong, I'm not complaining. I love the job, but I also cherish my privacy. Funny, really—when I was a news correspondent, I only got recognised in public now and then, which, at the time, was quite nice. Now with the regular television slot airing here and the US, I can't go many places without being identified. I live in a flat in South Ken, which is my London base for when I'm working, and I own a converted coach house in the countryside on the outskirts of Cambridge. No doubt the bastards will be staking out both places. But if I'm going to be completely honest—and I feel I can be around you—I'm actually lonely a lot of the time. People say nice things about what I do and I get my fair share of fan mail, but none of it's real. Sometimes I think my amazing job and being personally happy are different sides of the same coin, and you can only flip one, not both. My father definitely felt that way about his marriage."

"That's harsh," said Spencer, nodding his understanding, even though he knew of many celebrities across the world who had found a perfect balance between the two. When he turned to check on Marshall, he found him lost in thought, staring blankly at the ceiling. "Don't give up hope, Marshall."

Marshall kept staring up but smiled at the words.

"Does your mother know about you?"

"That I'm gay?" Marshall laughed as though Spencer had said something hilarious—or naïve. "Of course she does. I think she suspected before I did, before I'd hit puberty. She never admitted as much, but I think she made the mistake of saying something to my father when I was around eight. That summer, instead of going abroad with them, my father shipped me off early to summer camp in the north of England. They ran the place like a military school with morning drills and assault courses and survival classes. And cold showers. Worst of all, the place was full of bullies. Not just among the other students, but the faculty members, too."

"Sounds dreadful."

"You have no idea. But I'm not the kind of person to back down from hard work, or to shy away from bullies. In fact I loved the outdoor activities, and quickly made friends. But, as usual, the few spoiled the stay for the many, constantly picking on us to do the tasks nobody else wanted, like cleaning the toilet block, or being on table kitchen duties after meals. They'd clearly singled out all of the new kids, the ones who hadn't been there before. When my mother called to ask how things were going, I gave her a detailed account about what was happening. My father had booked me to stay for four weeks, but the next morning she came to pick me up. Honestly, I think she was more upset than me. Should have heard her screaming at the duty manager and then down the phone at my father."

"Will she have read the papers?"

Marshall heaved out a deep sigh at that remark

"Not sure they would have reached her yet. She will eventually, though. But she's used to public scrutiny. My parents' messy divorce was splashed all over the tabloids. I just hope I haven't let her down."

"Of course you haven't. From what you tell me about her, she'll see the article for the bullshit that it is."

Marshall released a small laugh, then reached over and squeezed Spencer's hand. Spencer held his breath and savoured the brief touch, and only breathed again when Marshall started talking.

"I should be used to this. In my field of work, I've been bombed, sworn at, shot at, spat at, hidden out in a school in Syria while a gang of terrorists passed nearby. You'd think I'd be immune to a bit of gutter press tittle-tattle."

"None of those other things were personal."

Marshall smiled gently again and softly shook his head.

"You can turn the light out now. I think I might be able to sleep."

Spencer did as asked.

"I think I'm in good hands here. Although I want you to know the incredible restraint I'm exercising right at this moment, having you within such easy reach," came the humoured voice in the darkness. Spencer almost rolled over and fell into his arms. He knew that one word from him and they would be doing things he had recently dreamt about. But apart from not wanting to be a rebound fling, Marshall deserved to be taken care of, deserved some rest.

And while over the next half-hour Spencer tried to keep his eyes closed, tried to slow his heartbeat despite having the world's sexiest man next to him in his bed, he heard Marshall's breathing slow to a soft, steady purr.

Finally, the poor guy had found some peace.

Chapter Nine

Around six, both of them finally gave up trying to sleep any longer and decided to get up and get dressed. Of the three times Spencer had awoken during the night, twice Marshall had lain awake beside him, and both times Spencer had reached out to give his hand a squeeze before falling back to sleep again. On the third, not only had Marshall slotted his body in behind Spencer's, along the length of his spine—a wholly wonderful and warming experience—but his soft, even breathing could only have meant that he was sleeping. Add to that the arm slung protectively across Spencer's waist, and he had soon fallen back into a deep slumber. Most embarrassing of all, he had awoken roasting hot, with a rock-hard stiffie poking into his backside, and his own tenting the front of his sweatpants. Gently lifting Marshall's arm, Spencer had leapt out of bed and run into the bathroom.

* * * *

"Here. Put these on," said Spencer, much later. Marshall had returned from a shower in a fresh change of clothing, except for the tracksuit bottoms, which he had donned again, and the thick white socks he had sensibly chosen to keep wearing. Spencer handed over a pair of light-brown-framed glasses with a slight tint in the lens.

"Are they prescription?"

"No," said Spencer. "They're kind of fake specs. Well, *designer* fake specs."

Blake had left the frames behind after his last visit, and Spencer had never gotten around to returning them. Typical of Blake, he didn't need glasses, the lenses being made of clear glass, but he thought the look made him appear more sophisticated in business meetings. Even at the time Spencer had found the oddity more pretentious than professional but had not voiced his opinion. Worst of all, Blake's nose from bridge to tip was so thin the glasses always slipped down, and he was forever pushing them back up with his forefinger like a latter-day Clark Kent. Marshall, by comparison, rocked the look.

"Now put on your face mask and ski hat."

Spencer enjoyed making Marshall do his bidding and with the hat, the glasses and the black mask, Marshall was pretty much unrecognisable.

"Go and look in the mirror."

Marshall did as asked and chuckled at his reflection.

"The shades you wore yesterday were a bit much, by the way," said Spencer. "Rather than make you look invisible, you came across as sinister, as though you were about to rob a bank or murder someone. But these make you look normal, and as the mask is mandatory right now, you're not only being socially responsible, you're also incognito and pretty hot."

"Okay," said Marshall, removing his mask and smiling at the last comment, but turning quizzically to Spencer. "What's happening right now? Are you throwing me out?"

"Of course not. But at the end of the arcade of shops downstairs," said Spencer, "there's a locally run artisan coffee shop which also serves food. It's doubtful anyone would recognise you in the twenty yards from here to there, but let's not take any chances. They open at six-thirty, but I'm told the morning rush doesn't start until around seven-thirty to eight. I'm usually gone by then. Dressed like this, both of us in glasses, we look like a couple of nerdy friends, or at a push you could be my older brother. I suggest we go down, get some decent coffee and a muffin or bagel while you check your phone and let Darcy know where you are. And I can phone in sick."

Marshall turned quickly at that comment.

"You're not going to work today?"

"You know what, Marshall? I have never taken a sickie in the two years I've worked for Blackmores. I think I'm due a bit of latitude to spend the day taking care of a special friend in need. I think they can do without me for just one day, don't you?"

Marshall's generous smile lit up his face, and Spencer felt his stomach turn to jelly.

"I do. And can I say how nice it feels to have you looking after me. Are we ready to go, best geek friend?"

As soon as he pushed open the door to the Morden Bean Sanctuary, pungent aromas enveloped them both. Spencer visited the place very occasionally, on Saturday or Sunday mornings to check his phone, and recognised neither of the young servers behind the counter. Monday morning and only two tables out of around twenty were occupied, probably by other insomniacs.

Spencer took Marshall's order then pointed to the empty table at the far end of the shop, a private corner where two armchairs of battered brown leather sat around a low circular coffee table. As Marshall, quite rightly, took the seat with his back to the room, Spencer noticed him fish in his jacket pocket for his phone and make a call. Some minutes later he joined Marshall with a tray of drinks — an Americano and a caffè mocha for Marshall, and an extra-shot caffè latte for himself — together with a plate of assorted muffins. He'd also bought a couple of croissants, and slices of quiche and pies to take away, for lunch, and had packed those into his bag.

"Have you checked in?" asked Spencer, lowering the tray onto the table. Marshall had removed his mask but kept the hat and glasses on. Although Spencer would have still recognised him by his handsome smile, nobody from the road or the door could see his face.

"Just spoke with Darcy. Things are much as we expected. She's been flooded with calls from the press and she's handling them with her usual hard-nosed professionalism. But we're going to need to talk later today. At least she knows where I am now, and she's going to pick me up around seven this evening. Fortunately I'm not needed in the studio this week, but Darcy is adamant that I don't stay off the radar for too long, doesn't want me to appear as though I've got anything to hide. Look, Spence, if you need to go in to work today — "

"Marshall. I'm staying home with you," said Spencer, ripping away his mask. "In fact, I'm going to call our HR team right now — they won't be in the office yet, but I'll leave a message — and then I'll text Bev and my boss. Neither will be up yet, but for a change *they* can both cover for *me*."

Without a moment of hesitation, Spencer made the calls. As anticipated the one to HR went straight to the department voicemail, so he left a message saying he'd woken with a fever — which wasn't far from the truth — and thought he should be a good corporate citizen and stay home. After that he texted both Clarissa and Bev, saying he was unwell, knowing both of them checked their respective phones for messages first thing. In a final act of defiance and with a self-satisfied sigh, he thumbed the power off button on his device.

"Done. Now I'm all yours for the day, without fear of getting any disturbances."

"I'm honoured. Thank you, Spence."

Spencer had begun to enjoy Marshall using his shortened name.

"Have you checked any of the online tabloids yet?"

"Yes," said Marshall, turning his phone around and showing Spencer the same photo on the homepage of a morning tabloid internet site. "The article has obviously spilled onto the dailies. The cheap rags are having a field day at my expense."

Spencer's stomach curdled when he read the headline, not so much at Marshall being gay, but at the insinuation about him being involved in underaged sex. Once again Spencer decided to digress to save Marshall's feelings.

"I have to say that resort looks amazing. Private, I'm guessing?"

"It was — or should have been. Don't know if you read the whole article, but that photograph was taken in St Cezaire sur Siagne on the French Riviera. I hired a villa with a tennis court and swimming pool for the two of us. About five years ago. It had been a busy year. Joey had a few weeks off from shooting the soap, and he'd bought this new camera drone he liked playing around with. Which is how he managed to get photos of him starkers with his backside on full view and the one with me leaning over to kiss him. Thank goodness I chose to maintain my modesty."

"Have to say, you rock those Speedos."

"Thank you. Maybe I can model them for you one day."

Spencer enjoyed the gentle flirting.

"Maybe you can. What do they mean by the heading? How old was he?"

Marshall stopped drinking his coffee and sat back.

"In the photo? He'd have been around thirty, I guess."

"Okay, so when did the law change?"

"I'm not with you?"

"Well, the last time I checked, the age of consent to any form of sexual activity in this country was sixteen for both men and women. How is Joey considered a minor?"

Marshall heaved a huge sigh.

"They're selling newspapers, Spence, so they need a juicy headline. If you'd read the whole article, you'll know the reporter goes on to say that I first met Joey when he was fourteen and I was twenty-one, which is correct. I was at university with his brother, Alex, and over the summer went to visit them in their family home in Dorset. What I don't like is the insinuation that anything happened between us back then."

"The tabloids love their fake news."

"Don't they just. On that brief visit, I barely said a word to Joey apart from a formal hello. They have a large family, six of them, Joey being the youngest and Alex the oldest."

"Is Alex gay?"

"God, no. Single-mindedly heterosexual. Back in our uni days, he was intent on seducing as many of the world's female population as he could, if you know the type."

"You just described my brother."

"He's a changed man now he's married, a doting husband and father of three."

"Maybe there's hope for Garrett, then. Are you still in touch?"

"Yes. But I'm not sure how he's going to take all this. Or his parents, come to that. We used to get on so well together. I hope they don't believe the underage sex inference."

Marshall looked away, clearly lost in thought. Spencer noticed customers arriving in the cafe and looked about to check nobody was settling nearby before continuing the conversation.

"When did you and Joey get together?"

"Not until much later. We met again a few years after that first meeting, when Joey turned seventeen and came out to his parents. Knowing about me, they asked if I would have a chat with him — provide some wisdom, so to speak — about what it means to be gay."

"And that's what brought you together?"

"No, not at all. In fact, I think Joey didn't particularly like me. It was years later that we met at the television studio Christmas party. He'd have been twenty-seven and had just landed his role in *Waterloo Lane*. Back then, my career was beginning to take off as well, so I spent a lot of time working abroad. But we managed to make things work and a couple of years later he'd moved. We were together around five years."

"When did you break up, if you don't mind me asking?"

"A year after those photos were taken. I can't say I blame him. I spent most of my time travelling the world, so he was left alone far too much. Those were heady days for him, too. His first taste of the spotlight. Got invited to a lot of parties while I was away. And whenever I returned from anywhere, we spent the first couple of days fighting. He said I treated him like a fisherman's wife, left at home to wait for the husband to return to port. But the heated arguments felt a lot like what my parents had gone through and I could feel him slipping away. I used to say there would always be collateral damage being in a relationship with someone who spends so much time away and often in combat zones. He used to tell me I'm a rank outsider bet in the love and relationship stakes."

The admission sent a wave of sadness through Spencer, but then his natural optimism bounded back.

"Don't sell yourself short, handsome. People have been known to win big on rank outsiders."

For all of his melancholy mood, Marshall grinned at Spencer and even laughed a little.

"What are you planning to do about the article?" asked Spencer. "Did Darcy say?"

"That's the first question I asked, one of the reasons she wants us to meet up later. There's not much we can do about the *Tribute* now —"

"How about suing the bastards for every penny they have?"

"That's not going to make the article disappear, is it? It's already out there."

"Might feel good though. So what's the plan, then?"

"Sometimes the best line of defence is attack. Darcy has a strategy. I think she's going to arrange for me to do an exclusive with a more reputable Sunday paper, through a sympathetic journalist, and tell them my story, the real story. Let them take the *Tribute* to pieces for their shoddy journalism. And in the meantime, our legal team are working on getting the editor to publish an apology and take down the online photos."

"But if you do another story, won't you have to come out publicly?"

"Which is honestly such a joke. I've been out of the closet since the age of twenty. Everyone at university knew and so does everyone I work with. And I haven't exactly been a monk since I graduated. There are plenty of men who can and will support my story, if I ask them."

"Not Joey, though."

"No, not Joey," said Marshall a little harshly.

Spencer wanted to ask more about Joey, but sensed Marshall's deep sadness and disappointment when he spoke about his ex. He did not understand how somebody could betray a person as pleasant and as genuine as Marshall.

"How will they cope without you there today?" asked Marshall.

"They'll manage. But I know they'll all be shitting bricks at the meeting this morning, what with no special entertainment slot for the client Christmas bash and the lack of a decent showpiece for the magazines during the holiday season. Muriel Moresby is on a mission to get a top-notch celebrity interview for the December issue of *Collective*. She's even offering an incentive bonus to anyone who can land someone decent. Desperate or what? I think she approached you already at the charity event, the one where we first met."

"I said no."

"Of course you did. Quite right, too. Those interview articles tend to be a combination of fluff and personal intrusion, and that's about the last thing you need right now. Somebody ought to bloody well interview her. Give her a taste of her own medicine."

Spencer took another sip of his caffè latte and savoured another warm hit to his bloodstream. With a soft snort, he wondered who would sort out the coffee order for the morning meeting, but then shrugged the thought away. Somehow they would manage without him. Or not, he didn't care.

"Wait," said Marshall, his voice grabbing Spencer's full attention. "Back up a moment. That's actually a brilliant idea. How about you suggest to Muriel that I interview her and her husband live on stage at the client event? And they can get the whole thing filmed. As long as she's happy to have me involved, what with everything that's going on. That would be a great platform for people to get to know the couple, warts and all. And then they can use the material for the Christmas edition of *Collective*? We might even be able to get the station to air something, if Moresby will allow our crew in to record. That way I stay in the spotlight and Muriel gets her interview."

Spencer sat stunned. An interview with the Moresbys, warts and all? What would the world make of the real Muriel Moresby? With Marshall asking the questions, no punches would be pulled. But would she even buy into the idea? After a few moments, he came back down to earth.

"I'm not sure how she would feel about that," said Spencer.

"Not a good idea, then?"

"Are you kidding me! It's a *fantastic* idea. But would you really do that?"

"Why not? Okay, so she's not the usual kind of high-profile subject I might interview, but like I said, as long as she's onboard, everybody wins. Muriel gets her interview, and I remain visible—"

"And I get a bonus."

"And you get a bonus," said Marshall, chuckling. "I'll need to square things off with Darcy and the network, but I'm sure she'll be up for the idea. I'll ask her when she drops by to pick me up later."

"Just so we're clear, that's not why I invited you in yesterday. To take advantage of your celebrity status."

"I know that," said Marshall, before becoming pensive. "But out of interest, why did you let me in? I wasn't completely sure you would."

Spencer's words died in his mouth. How much should he tell Marshall about how much he liked him, *really* liked him? And how he only wanted the best for him. When Spencer looked up into his eyes to answer, he noticed the coffee shop had filled noticeably.

"You're a complete arse if you need to ask. Have you finished yet? This place is beginning to get busy."

Marshall smirked at Spencer before draining the last of his coffee. Readying to leave, he pulled his ski hat down around his ears and put on his black mask.

"How do I look?"

"Like a tourist who's lost his way in the French Alps. Now, is there anyone you need to text or call before we leave? Remember we're off the grid upstairs."

"Nope, I'm good."

"Excellent. I've bought pastries for lunch so we don't go hungry. We need to walk back past my door, so I'll give you the key and my phone and I'll see you back upstairs. I'm going to stock up with extra food from the convenience store. It'll be open by now."

"You don't need to give me your phone, Spence. I do trust you."

"I know that," said Spencer, handing over the items as they headed for the coffee shop door. "But I'll have my hands full, so you'll be doing me a favour."

When Marshall stepped in front and opened the door, Spencer's lenses immediately steamed up from the waft of icy air hitting his face. Removing them for a second to wipe them, he popped them back on and stepped out into the cold morning.

"Oh my God, it's you, isn't it?" came the shrill voice of a girl standing outside, her eyes wide, as Marshall followed him through the door. She stood across the pavement by a litter bin, a cigarette in one hand and her cardboard coffee cup in the other.

Spencer and Marshall froze, both staring at her. Spencer wondered if they could make a run for his front door. But then he noticed her attention was not on Marshall at all, but on him.

"I'm sorry, I think you've got mixed up—" began Spencer.

"Shut up, I know it's you. Tom Holland. Spider-Man. The hair totally gives you away."

"Actually, I'm not," said Spencer, as Marshall moved behind him. To make his point, Spencer once again removed his mask and glasses, even though the girl became little more than a blur.

"Oh," she said, the disappointment in her voice plain. "No. You're not."

"Don't worry, he gets that all the time," said Marshall, clearly enjoying himself.

"Yeah, no. My mistake," said the girl, turning away to take a puff on her cigarette.

Spencer grabbed a chuckling Marshall's arm and hauled him along the road.

"Not funny, Marshall."

"I beg to differ."

"Get up those stairs," said Spencer, laughing along, enjoying the light-hearted camaraderie. "I'll deal with you later."

"Promises, promises," said Marshall, stopping at the front door and winking at Spencer.

Chapter Ten

Figuring they would be spending time sitting around talking, Spencer stocked up on tea bags, instant coffee, bread, milk, butter, and a pack of assorted biscuits — including custard creams, bourbons, chocolate digestives and Jammie Dodgers — as well as buying a selection of canned soups he could heat up to go with the baked goods.

When he got upstairs, Marshall had already made himself at home on the sofa, his socked feet stretched out in front and crossed at the ankle, and Tiger once again curled up in his lap. One of the white socks had almost come off and hung limply over the right foot, while the left leg of his track bottoms rode up and showed a hairy shin. His gaze was focused in concentration, his head resting back against the sofa with his hair — freshly released from the hat he had been wearing — taking on an adorable life of its own, clumps sticking up at random. Apart from scratching the top of Tiger's head with one hand, he waved the remote at the television with the other, changing stations until he reached a news channel.

Spencer understood the rare moment he was observing, an utterly relaxed version of Marshall Highlander that few people got to see, and the realisation filled him with an oddly potent mix of affection and desire.

"Making yourself at home?"

"I have to say, Spence, it's a very comfortable flat. A bit chilly right now, but comfy."

"Convenient for the commute to work, too," said Spencer, putting things away into the fridge. "I always get a seat on the train into town, with Morden being the southbound Northern Line terminus. And the landlord is okay. Apart from redecorating the place before I moved in, he fitted out the bathroom and kitchen and put in a new bed. Many of the appliances are new. Shame he wants the place back in February."

"Oh dear," said Marshall.

"It's fine. Not sure I'll be able to get anywhere for the same price, but at least he's given me plenty of notice. And the reason it's so cold right now is because the ovens downstairs aren't turned on until around ten. I've cranked up the central heating but I might drag in the cover from the bed."

And that was how they spent their morning, sitting together beneath the bed quilt on the sofa, watching daytime television, avoiding any news channels and occasionally making hot drinks. At lunchtime, when Spencer went to use the bathroom, he came back into the room to find Marshall standing at his bookcase. Somehow he had found Spencer's journalism portfolio tucked away in the corner.

"These are really good, Spencer," he said without looking up.

"Thank you. Finally got a friend to help me create a website in my name and put them up online along with my CV – although not much has happened since. My mother thinks I need someone to kick my backside to get me moving. Some of them are from university, but others are pieces I sent off to various publications and managed to get published. I'm rather proud of my letter to the *Guardian* about the implications of leaving the European Union and about the misinformation going around at the time. They published that around three weeks before the Brexit vote. Fat lot of good it did."

"Doesn't matter, Spence. You stated your case. I'm sure there were plenty of others who took an educated, factual, but opposing view who also got published. And I take my hat off to them, too. The important thing is that you made your voice heard. The downfall of any democracy will be the day when apathy outweighs people needing their voices to be heard, when a tyrant gains power due to majority abstention."

"Did you write that?"

"I don't think so. But I'm sure I heard it somewhere."

"In which case, I might steal it."

They continued chatting while Spencer set about getting lunch for them. They decided on piping-hot chicken soup, a small slice of quiche each, and a mini chicken and leek pie to share, followed off by half a croissant each with marmalade and whipped cream – the filling courtesy of Marshall.

"What's in these croissants?" asked Marshall. "I don't usually do sweet, but these are delicious."

"Marmalade, of course. But the Bean Sanctuary bakes their own chocolate croissants. I have a seriously sweet tooth and I've never found better."

"They're amazing. I'm usually a savoury person."

"Come on! What about ice cream?"

"Yes, I like some ice cream."

"Favourite flavour?"

"I'm a traditionalist. I prefer good old dependable vanilla."

"Sacrilege. When there is such a huge range of flavours available. Including some unusual ones like avocado, red chilli, and even lobster."

"Sounds awful," said Marshall, pulling a face.

"Don't knock what you've never tried."

"Go on then. What's your favourite?"

"As I said, I have a sweet tooth, and there are lots of runners-up. Salted caramel with cookie dough, Rocky Road, Cookies and Cream. But my all-time favourite?"

"Go on. I'm on the edge of my seat."

"Strawberry cheesecake ice cream. I could happily sit here and eat a tub to myself."

"Heavens. Sounds a little sickly for my taste."

"Don't be too quick to judge. I bet you'd have turned your nose up at chocolate croissants before today, wouldn't you?"

"Point taken. They are darned good."

* * * *

In the afternoon, back on the sofa, the apartment became noticeably warmer and, still beneath the quilt, Spencer fell asleep with his head on Marshall's shoulder. Sometime later he woke to find Marshall gazing fondly down at him, his arm around Spencer's shoulders. Up so close, he could see his irises were not merely a deep dark brown, as he had assumed, but predominantly cocoa-coloured, darkly rimmed around the outside edge, and with flecks of caramel and gold.

Beautiful.

"Hey, little fella. You nodded off there."

"In your arms. Not sure if I ever want to wake up."

Marshall drew his hand to the back of Spencer's neck.

"Maybe I can persuade you?"

Before Spencer realised what was happening, Marshall had leant in farther. With a soft gasp at what was about to happen, Spencer closed his eyes and felt the light pressure from Marshall's wonderfully soft lips. During those first few tentative moments, Spencer wasn't sure whether to respond, or to sit still and allow Marshall to control the kiss. But then something inside him kicked in, molten lava rising from the depths, taking over his body's responses and silencing all thought. He pushed into the kiss, deepening the embrace, tilting his head to one side to get a better taste and connection. Marshall's body responded in kind and he pushed back, his hands cradling Spencer's face. Their kissing became more frantic, more erratic and heated, hands travelling over bodies until Spencer switched positions and straddled Marshall's lap. Only then did Spencer's irritating common sense awaken and he pulled them apart.

"No, Marshall. This isn't fair on you."

"You don't want to — ?" came Marshall's breathless response.

"Of *course* I want to," said Spencer, pushing his hardened groin into Marshall's. "I just don't think, given everything that's happened to you recently, that this is a good idea right now. I'm just being honest with you."

Marshall's dark gaze became unfocused as he stared past Spencer's shoulder. After a few moments, he let out a deep, defeated sigh and nodded.

"Yes, you're right. Of course you are. However much I want this."

Spencer climbed out of his lap, adjusting himself and sitting back down next to him.

"Me too," said Spencer. "And if you feel the same way when everything's blown over, I'll still be here."

Marshall chuckled fondly and nudged Spencer's shoulder.

"I will. Feel the same way. I just hope you will, too."

Spencer had no doubt in his mind and smiled happily. As he watched the television, he noticed Marshall turn and observe him for a few moments before speaking up.

"You remember I told you I'd been in Afghanistan to interview the cricket team?"

"A human-interest story? Yes, of course I remember."

"Well, that wasn't the whole story. The reason we flew there rather than arrange a telephone interview was because—and I can't give you specific details here—one of the officials who had been opposed to any peace deal had requested an interview to announce a change of heart. But in order to do so, this official insisted that the interview be in person, at a secret location in the Helmand Province, and that they would only speak to me. In order for our team to go, we needed agreements from our government, the UN and, of course, assurances from the Afghan National Security Services."

Spencer shuddered to think of the kind of dangerous situations Marshall had to face in his line of work.

"And everything went okay?"

"We were in and out in four days. And everything was fine. More than fine."

"Apart from almost getting killed in an attack at a checkpoint?"

"Well, yes. But we weren't the target."

"Not much comfort when the bullets are flying. But I'm glad you got what you wanted. And even happier that you're here and in one piece."

Spencer had begun to feel more than a simple friendship with Marshall, but this new piece of information niggled at him, bringing home the often dangerous nature of Marshall's chosen profession. Once again, he kept the concern to himself.

* * * *

At just after six-thirty, there came an urgent buzzing on Spencer's intercom. Both Spencer and Marshall looked quizzically at each other before Spencer jumped up to check the video panel.

"Is Darcy usually early?"

"Sometimes," said Marshall, going to the bedroom to collect his things. "But not often."

Meanwhile, Spencer picked up the phone and checked the display.

"Oh. My. God!" He didn't mean to sound dramatic, but the sight had him all kinds of excited. Marshall must have heard his tone because he hurried in from the bedroom.

"Is it the press?"

"No, it's my colleague Bev. And she's holding a bottle of champagne up to the camera. Not sure what's happened, but this must be worth hearing."

"Are you going to let her in?" Marshall sounded hesitant.

"She knows I met you, Marshall. But she has no idea that you're here right now. How could she? But she's not going to be a problem, trust me. Can I let her in?"

"Go ahead. You know I trust you, otherwise I wouldn't be here."

When Spencer answered the front door, he barely managed to get out a hello before Beverley pushed past, swiping him with the large bag she clutched under her arm, and heading straight for the stairs.

"You are not going to be-*lieve* my day," she muttered as she stomped out each syllable on the steps. When he looked up, he realised Marshall stood framed in the upstairs doorway, holding the door open. Bev must have been looking down because when she finally lifted her gaze, she clunked to a stop.

"Fudge me. Marshall Highlander. What the heck are you doing...*oooh*?"

"It's not what you're thinking," said Spencer, coming up the stairs behind her.

"You don't know what I'm thinking."

"Maybe not, but I can hazard a pretty good guess."

"He's wearing your clothes. What am I supposed to think?"

"That he's keeping a low profile in my flat."

"With your clothes on."

"In comfort."

"And he's the reason you pulled your first ever sickie?"

"He—he needed somewhere to stay for the night—"

"For the *night*? He slept here? In your bed?"

"Yes, but we didn't—it wasn't—"

By now, Marshall, standing with Tiger between his legs, had begun to chuckle at the back-and-forth between them.

"You two are like an old married couple," he said eventually.

"He wishes," said Bev, a quip he had heard many times before, as she stopped at the entrance and held out her free hand. "Beverley Salvatore. We met at Muriel Moresby's charity event, but you probably don't remember me. An honour to meet you again, Mr Highlander."

"Marshall, please. And I do remember you, Beverley. Although Spencer has told me a lot more about you since."

"Don't believe a word. He's got a very creative mind. I'm guessing you're not going to say no to a glass of bubbly? Bearing in mind the media shitstorm you've been dodging?"

Spencer followed Bev into the flat, and a bemused Marshall shut the door behind them. She had already thrown down her bag and coat onto the table, and went over to Spencer's cupboards, opening one after the other, obviously looking for glasses. He only had tumblers, but she already knew that.

"Top shelf, above the sink. What are we celebrating?"

Once she had the glasses lined up on a countertop, she took a moment to compose herself before turning her full attention to Spencer.

"Hell in a handbag, Spence. Everything went to the dogs today. No coffee for the Monday morning meeting, and lots of frayed tempers. I wasn't there at the beginning, but I heard that Muriel blamed you, blamed the fact that you didn't have a contingency plan in place for when you might be sick. Apparently she said something like 'we have a plan in place for Covid, why don't we have one for morning coffee?' I didn't get there until almost nine-thirty and by then they'd sent Kimberley out to get the drinks. Also, Prince wasn't there at the beginning of the meeting—he said he sent you a text message at eight, but you didn't respond—so they had to figure out the laptop setup themselves. And Muriel announced during the meeting that Evelyn, the events manager, is on long-term sick leave and won't be returning to the office this side of Christmas, so the client party is hanging by a thread. She wants me to take over, as if I haven't got enough to do already. Surely she realises that getting something decent arranged with such a short deadline is virtually impossible—"

"Or virtually possible," said Marshall cryptically, which tripped Bev up for a second before she ignored him and carried on.

"On the plus side, Killian finally sent through his December article—hot off the press—which is apparently awesome. But he adamantly refuses to let anyone but you touch it, because, according to him and much to Muriel's annoyance, 'Spencer is the only one who understands the subtleties of my prose and my blend of humour—'"

"You get to proofread Killian's work?" asked Marshall. "That's pretty impressive."

"Do you know him?" asked Spencer.

"We've met at a couple of benefits. He's very particular."

"Excuse me, I'm holding the talking stick!" said Bev, asserting herself, apparently wholly over the fact that *the* Marshall Highlander stood next to her. "You two have had all day to talk and I am pretty much bursting at the seams. So, final thing, Spence, just so you know, Clarissa missed three important deadlines today, something she attributed to you. Told Muriel she'd asked you to finish them up on Friday before you left for your parents' — "

"That's a barefaced lie!"

"Yes, and Clarissa knows that. I tried to back you up, told Muriel you wouldn't sit on something that important, but I've no idea if she believed me or not. If only you'd been there to defend yourself."

"If I'd been there, none of that would have happened. I'd have ended up doing Clarissa's work over lunch as usual and no deadlines would have been missed. For fuck's sake, I take one day off. *One.*"

"Spence, I'm so sorry —" began Marshall, who appeared crestfallen.

"No, Marshall. You have nothing to apologise for. This has nothing to do with you. I told you, I'm tired of being treated like the office whipping boy. It's time I took my mother's advice and started looking around for another job. Well past time, actually."

"Which is exactly what I thought you might say, Spence," said Bev. "But I came because I wanted you to be forewarned. Are you coming back to work tomorrow?"

"I am. And I appreciate the heads-up. At least I won't be blindsided."

"And a glass of bubbly can't do any harm, can it?"

Spencer mugged at her and was about to reply when his front-door buzzer went off again.

"Bloody hell," said Beverley as Spencer headed for the intercom "It's like Paddington station in here. Did you invite someone else to the party?"

When he stared at the video, he only saw a pair of beautifully painted Asian eyes poking out from beneath a fur-lined hood, the rest of the face covered by a black scarf like a ninja assassin. The woman peered around herself as though she expected to be attacked at any moment.

"Hello?"

"Good evening. This is Darcy Fraser-Chong. Not sure if I have the right address, but is Marshall Highlander there, by any chance?" came a clipped, flawless British middle-class voice that oozed expensive elocution lessons.

"Marshall," said Spencer, wanting to make sure. "Can you check before I let her in?"

Marshall came over, peered at the intercom display, and nodded.

"Hang on a moment, Darcy," said Spencer. "I'll need to come down and let you in."

"Hurry up, then. I'm freezing my fucking tits off out here. Much longer and I swear, my nipples will fall off from frostbite."

"Yes," said Marshall, grinning at Bev's shocked face. "That's definitely Darcy."

Standing inside, assessing his flat, Darcy Fraser-Chong looked like one of the fashionable side characters in the movie *Crazy Rich Asians*. Tall, slim, immaculately turned out, and with her Eurasian features and confidence, she could easily have been mistaken for a high fashion model or a refined movie star.

Until she opened her mouth.

"Well, isn't this fucking cosy? Very cloak and dagger, Marshall, darling," said Darcy, starting at the device in her hand. "And why the fuck, may I ask, is my phone not working?"

"We're in a big black hole here," said Spencer. "No Wi-Fi, no satellite coverage —"

"And no champagne flutes, I see," she asked, staring at the bottle and the waiting tumblers. "This reminds me of my bastard father recalling his life in the eighties. So what's the score? Is the lack of facilities by design?"

"I'm sorry?"

"I mean, is this some kind of halfway house for those who wish to stay off the grid? Criminals, spies, terrorists? Fallen-from-grace royalty?"

"This is Spencer's home, Darcy. He lives here."

Eventually, Darcy's full attention came to rest on Spencer.

"Ah, yes. And here he is at last, Marshall's elusive protector —"

"Darce, be nice," said Marshall. "Spencer's been absolutely incredible."

"If you say so, dear," she said, then brought her attention back to the kitchenette. "Is anyone going to open that Perrier fucking Jouët? And, if so, what are we celebrating?"

Bev, who had been staring open-mouthed at Darcy, suddenly sprang to life. She dashed over to the counter and put her considerable skills to use popping open the bottle, pouring glasses of bubbly and handing them to Spencer.

"We're celebrating the fact that I'm probably going to get the sack tomorrow —" began Spencer, handing the first tumbler to Darcy.

"For having a sick day?" asked Darcy after taking an appreciative sip.

"Spencer," said Marshall, placing a warm hand on Spencer's shoulder, "if you want me to call Muriel and explain to her why you weren't in—"

"Don't you dare!" said Spencer, handing the next drink to him.

"No fucking way," said Darcy, at the same time.

Both of them chuckled at their similar responses, while Marshall rolled his eyes.

"I guess that's decided, then," he said.

For the next hour, they chatted like old friends. When pushed, Darcy spoke sparingly about developments over the weekend. Spencer felt sure she heavily edited the truth. Even so, she gave them a pretty harrowing picture of the pandemonium the story had caused, especially for the people close to Marshall.

Marshall inspired Bev when he elaborated on his earlier comment—*virtually* possible—about holding the client event virtually, not with guests in a room but with them attending online. At first Spencer doubted whether an online event could generate the same interest or fun as its physical equivalent, but Marshall enthused about a hugely successful virtual client event he had attended in September. The party for the launch of a new car by a world-class manufacturer had been organised by a company catering virtual parties and had included a link to a screen interface made to look like a racing track. Pavilions bordering the racetrack had represented different aspects of the launch, such as talks about engine specifications, video demonstrations and even computer driving games, all things happening simultaneously. Bev listened without speaking or interrupting—which Spencer had rarely seen—and guessed the seeds of an idea had already been sown.

Eventually Darcy checked the time and announced they had to leave. Beverley offered to wash glasses, while Marshall expressed his need to use the bathroom before they departed. Darcy invited Spencer to show her around the rest of the flat, an odd request and not difficult bearing in mind the single-bedroom affair. Once inside the bedroom, however, her real intention became clear.

"Okay, Spencer K Wyrrell," she said in a lowered voice. "I want the truth. Are you playing him? Do you have an angle here?"

"An angle?"

"Don't act dumb, dear. Are you playing Marshall? Are you snuggling up because you want an exclusive for one of Moresby's magazines? Because if that's the reason you've taken him in and why you're being so nice, you had better be well-armed. *Capiche*? I play a mean fucking game, and I take no prisoners."

"No, I—I just like him. There's no ulterior motive, no angle, I promise. I don't want an interview or a story. I'm a junior copy editor at the magazine, nobody important."

"In which case, what's this he just whispered to me about interviewing Muriel Moresby? At her magazine's client event?"

Spencer's mouth dropped open.

"That was *his* idea, not mine. If you'd rather he didn't do it, that's fine by me. As long as he's okay. And honestly, if you need me to sign an NDA or something about him being here today, then I would be more than happy to do so."

"You'd really do that?"

"If it makes you both feel more comfortable, then yes."

She studied him for a long moment before visibly relaxing. Without taking her eyes from him, she unclasped her bag and put a slender hand inside.

"I'm sorry for being a bitch, but he's been let down a lot lately. By people he thought he could trust. You're the one on the roof, aren't you?" she said, handing over her business card. "The one who talked sense into him that night?"

"I'm not sure you'd call it sense, but I did make him laugh."

"Whatever you did, he's a little smitten. But be careful with him. He has a fragile heart."

"Something we have in common."

Darcy appeared to be warming to him. She didn't apologise again for her harsh words, but her tone softened. He didn't blame her. Somebody needed to be firmly in Marshall's corner.

"He needs his friends around him right now, Spencer."

"I know, and I'm glad he has you. I'm also here, Darcy. Whenever he needs me. No angles, I promise."

"Yes, I think I believe you. And, trust me, that does not happen often. There are a lot of ruthless bastards out there. That's my personal number on the card. If you need to call me, for any reason, do so."

"Thank you."

"Not from inside this cave, of course."

"Of course," said Spencer, grinning.

When they returned to the main room, Beverley was putting on her coat just as Marshall emerged from the bathroom.

"Okay, Beverley," said Darcy. "Where do you live?"

"Mornington Crescent. But you can drop me at the Tube station. I'll take the train."

"Not in this weather, you won't. We'll drop you home. I told my driver to pick me up at seven-thirty from outside here. We'll drop you off first, and then I'm bringing Marshall back to my place. Don't worry, Marshall, we can avoid the bastards by going in through the underground car park."

They descended the stairs in single file to the front door, with Spencer bringing up the rear. A gust of frozen air wafted in when Beverley opened the door. Since they had arrived, the weather had become noticeably colder, signs of frost already on the pavement, and while Darcy and Beverley waved a quick farewell before running to get into the waiting car, Marshall stayed back.

"Good luck tomorrow morning, Spence. Don't let Muriel give you any shit. You're worth far more than they're giving you credit for. I can tell that from your portfolio, and the fact that Killian trusts you. And don't forget about my offer to do the client-party interview for Muriel. Darcy is completely on board. Use those things as leverage if you have to, and, if push comes to shove, just call me and I *will* talk to Muriel—"

"You don't have to do that, Marshall. I can look after myself."

"I'm sure you can, but the offer's still there. And is it okay if I ask you to keep Friday free?" asked Marshall. "I hope things might have improved by then and I would love to see you again, to say thank you. I'll send you details via a text message, if that's okay?"

"I would love that."

Spencer felt sure he would turn away then to avoid being seen outside. But instead, he pulled down his mask, leant forward and kissed Spencer full on the lips before grinning and turning away, heading towards the waiting Tesla.

Spencer remained there in the doorway, grinning despite the freezing air, the kiss fresh on his lips, feeling weatherproofed against any coming storms.

Chapter Eleven

Spencer read the same line for the third time. His brain would not take a step back and view the words on the page objectively. Thorough editing required objectivity. Even from the first hasty read-through, he knew Killian's article was good. No, scratch that, brilliant. Savagely witty and beautifully observed, he had managed to paint the various royal engagement guests as vividly as characters from a novel by Dickens, complete with colourful descriptions of the more outrageous fashion faux pas, together with the unique quirks and mannerisms of some in attendance. That he had also eavesdropped on various conversations and peppered the column with wonderful malapropisms had been a masterstroke — The Right Honourable Lady Jenkins talking about her brother's battle with 'prostrate cancer' or a former Tory minister decrying the Chinese authorities for banning the people of Hong Kong from enjoying 'universal suffering' like the rest of the civilised world.

Eventually, he put his head in his hands. Arriving early to the office had seemed propitious, but all he had succeeded in doing was to sit there waiting for the hammer to fall. In anticipation, he had worn a funereal ensemble of black trousers, white shirt, black mask, and black- and mauve-striped bow tie. The idea had been to arrive before anyone else, and keep his head down, keep himself busy with emails and other admin items, before getting stuck into the article by Killian. And when, by ten, Clarissa had still not arrived for work, Spencer had started to think that maybe he'd had a reprieve — until his phone rang and Alice's name popped up on the display. Alice was Muriel's personal assistant.

A shimmer of coldness passed through him. After letting the phone ring three times, he picked up.

"Hello, Alice."

"Morning, Spencer. Hope you're feeling better. Muriel wants to see you in her office at ten-thirty. Is that going to be a problem?"

Alice always asked if the meeting time would be okay, even though nobody ever dared decline. Spencer liked Alice. Everyone did. Being so close to her tyrannical boss, she let people know what kind of mood Muriel was in, and, where possible, gave them a heads-up about why she wanted to see them.

"That's fine. Did she say what it's about?" he asked.

"Not exactly. But I think it may be about what happened yesterday."

"I see."

"For what it's worth, she doesn't appear to be in a bad mood this morning."

"I'm sure I can fix that," he replied.

Alice giggled.

Of course, the next twenty minutes dragged like the run-up to an election. After restarting Killian's piece, he finally threw in the towel and decided to wait until after the meeting — if there was going to be an 'after'.

Alice gave a sympathetic smile before ushering him in.

Muriel's corner office took up a big chunk of the southern side of the floor and, during the winter months, saw the brief rising and sinking of the sun. A line of award plaques sat pride of place above a long settee of plum-coloured leather, adorned with small throw cushions in pink and violet. In front, a crystal coffee table — gifted by a renowned furniture designer — sat on a jet-black sheepskin rug. On the few occasions he had visited Muriel's office, he had come to hate the colour combination, which would not have looked out of place in the garden outside his parents' bungalow. Only a piece of modernist artwork appeared new, fixed to the inside of the square column separating the floor-to-ceiling windows and breaking the panorama outside the office.

"Sit down, Spencer. You're making the room look untidy."

Spencer's attention swung to Muriel behind her desk as she snapped shut the lid of her large metallic purple laptop. Maybe fitting the occasion, she, too, wore black — a high-necked dress in charcoal cotton with a mauve silk scarf around her shoulders. He took the leather seat across from her, which appeared to sink three or four inches as his weight took hold until his eyes drew level with the top of her coffee mug.

"Do you want to explain to me what happened yesterday?"

She had the usual Muriel intimidation glare as she stared disapprovingly at him.

"I was sick—"

"Remove the mask. I feel like I'm talking to a highwayman."

Spencer did as told and folded the black mask into his trouser pocket.

"I had a slight fever and thought it best to stay home. But I followed procedure, contacted the HR team and left a voice message. I also texted Clarissa."

"I see."

Spencer offered nothing more. In the past, he would have filled one of Muriel's silences with a flustered explanation, and probably given away far too much. But not today. If Muriel wanted to see him, she could jolly well explain why. He wasn't about to volunteer any information.

"Everybody knows you weren't in. What I want to know is whether you're aware of what happened here yesterday? In the office. Did anyone explain to you?"

"Clarissa's not in yet."

Another of Muriel's silences while she processed his answer.

"Do you know why I chose to employ you, Spencer?"

"I have my suspicions," he replied, without missing a beat.

Muriel narrowed her eyes at him. His heart started to speed up.

"And?"

A whole speech flashed up on autocue in his mind about her attempt to redress the male-to-female workforce ratio. If he got onto the fact that she had employed one of those, her son Blake, and segued into the subject of nepotism, there would be no stopping him.

"I heard other candidates turned the job down. I suppose I was sort of Hobson's Choice."

"Where did you hear that?"

Blake had told him about two other candidates being far better qualified for the role, both women. One had decided to pull her application, and the other had been offered a better-paid position at a rival magazine.

"I can't remember who told me."

"You shouldn't listen to office tittle-tattle. You were chosen out of all the other candidates because I needed someone competent, reliable, and well-organised to assist Clarissa. I put a lot of pressure on her, and unfortunately, she doesn't work well with other women."

"I see."

He didn't see, at all. If that was indeed the case, why hadn't anyone told him at the interview, or at least during his onboarding? And why would Blake have lied to him? In the two years he had worked with Clarissa, she'd appeared to take the job for granted — the kind of person his brother referred to as a vocational skiver — and relied on him to do the bulk of her tasks. Maybe a female colleague would have been less accommodating. Bev certainly wouldn't have put up with the unequal distribution of work.

"Do you? A lot of things went wrong yesterday, and on each occasion the cause appeared to involve you — or, rather, your absence. To begin with, there was a complete lack of morning beverages and nobody to assist with the conference room equipment. During the day, apart from an important legal document going missing, and water damage in the small meeting room, your absence caused missed deadlines, and the icing on the slowly crumbling cake was Killian Pinkerton believing that you are the only person competent and trustworthy enough to give the final sign-off to his pieces of fluff. I would dearly like to hear what you think about all of this, to get your perspective."

"Do you really want to hear what I think?"

"I encourage all of my staff to speak their minds. If you have something to say, I would like to hear it. And then I will tell you what I would like to happen in future."

If Spencer had felt damned before, Muriel's last remark pretty much sealed his fate. If she didn't get rid of him during the meeting and expected him to continue being the office punch bag, he would walk anyway. Was there any point in stating his case? But then he thought back to Marshall's parting words to him and decided to speak his mind.

"Okay, this is what I think. But let's get a few things straight to begin with. Apart from taking my statutory annual holiday and public holidays, I haven't had a day off sick in the two years that I've worked for you. I could point out a large number of your employees who have had more sick days than the annual leave allowance you grant them. And yet the first thing you want to whinge to me about is coffee and why there was none because I was sick for a day. Here's a thought. Why don't you invest in a coffee machine in the conference room? Or better still, if it's a matter of cost savings, get those attending to buy their own beverages on the way into the office. I offered to get drinks once, because the receptionist whose job it was had resigned. What I did back then was a gesture of goodwill, something everyone has subsequently taken for granted."

Muriel had begun to pout, her expression turning waspish, but once the dam walls had been breached, there was no stopping Spencer.

"As for the conference room setup. This is something you employ a perfectly competent IT person to deal with. Even then, in my opinion, it's not really something that someone as highly qualified technically as Prince should have to deal with. Plugging a cable into a wall socket, for goodness' sake. How difficult can it be? Prince spends evenings here sometimes, doing tests and making sure the network is working stably. That's what you pay him to do. Once again, I made the mistake of helping out on one occasion when he had a problem getting here on time. Now the burden seems to have been transferred to me. What else was it? Oh yes, missed deadlines. If you had bothered to check, you'd have found those deadlines belonged to Clarissa, not to me. And if she had asked me to complete them for her on Friday, I would have done so before I left the office for the weekend, the way I always do, even if that had meant forfeiting my lunch break. She did not. I have no idea about the lost legal document or the water-damaged meeting room, and would suggest you get Alice to check with your legal team and the buildings technicians respectively. On a final note, because, after all, you're encouraging me to speak my mind, I ask you to stop using me as an office lackey in future. Use me for the professional skills for which you employed me, such as editing other people's work. And I include proofreading the pieces by Killian Pinkerton in that. His stories bring in a whole new raft of recognition and readership to *Collective*."

Spencer sat back in his seat and folded his arms, feeling the heat that had risen in his cheeks. Muriel sat staring at him, her eyes wide.

"Do you have anything else to add?" she asked.

"Yes. Although you may not be aware, Marshall Highlander is a close friend of mine. I know he is going through some public difficulties at the moment, but he has offered to help us — help *you* — to kill two birds with one stone, so to speak. And he — "

"I have no idea how someone like you knows Marshall. But if this has anything to do with the *Collective* interview, I have already approached — "

"For goodness' sake, Muriel, will you just let me *finish* for once?"

Now the blood had truly drained from her face and, to top everything, her hands came together beneath her chin as though she were Mother Superior praying for him to be struck by a carefully aimed bolt of lightning.

"Go on."

"Marshall has offered to provide his services to formally interview you and Lord Moresby at our client Christmas party in early December. He said that a lot of what you do — privately and professionally — goes unnoticed, and having a candid interview with you both onstage would be a highlight of the evening. Following the interview, you could consider using selective material — maybe have some exclusive sections not used during the live interview — to fill the celebrity interview page of the Christmas edition of *Collective*. He feels the readers of *Collective* would be delighted to learn more about the lives of the owner and her husband, and I completely agree with him."

As he watched Muriel process his words, he sat stiffly in his chair, and mulled over the idea of being fired and grovelling for a job working for Marshall. When she'd finally processed what he had said, and composed herself to declare her final judgement, he prepared himself for the worst.

"Clarissa called me at home last night to resign her position with immediate effect," she said, taking him completely by surprise. "Were you aware?"

"No, I was not."

"Well, I'm going to need you to step into her shoes."

"You're giving me her job?"

"Let's not get ahead of ourselves, shall we? I'm asking you to take over the role while I decide how we are going to deal with the void she has left and consider her replacement. But if you do a good enough job, I see no reason not to offer you an opportunity to interview for the position."

His mind tried to catch up with what was happening. Had Muriel hoodwinked him? He'd thought he had been brought there to defend his position in the company, only to find he was being expected to step up and replace Clarissa.

"How long?" he asked.

"I beg your pardon?"

"How long am I going to be filling the senior role? Is this going to mean an adjustment to my salary? And will I have anyone to assist me, in the same way that I assisted Clarissa?"

"This is all new, Spencer. I need to consult HR and talk this situation through with them. Right now we don't have any spare resources to give you. But from what you say, you've been taking on her work in the past anyway, so it shouldn't be too much of an adjustment, should it? In the meantime, I'll make sure the menial duties you mentioned are redistributed. How does that sound?"

Spencer turned his head to look out of the window. Dirty grey clouds meant a possibility of rain, maybe even sleet or snow. Should he accept the chance to shine in Clarissa's role? Or should he tell her to get somebody else? He needed somebody he trusted to talk to, someone impartial, outside the confines of the company.

"Can I think about it?"

"Why would you need to think about it?"

"You're asking me to take on a lot of extra responsibilities that are above my pay grade. As you say there is no guarantee of a permanent position in the future, and very probably no monetary incentive, bearing in mind the cost-cutting we've been through recently. I would like some time to think about this."

Muriel released a deep, world-weary sigh as though listening to the bellyaching of a twelve-year-old.

"Apart from the Friday deadlines, which Tamara's team took over and completed, I don't see that there's anything urgent Clarissa was dealing with, so I'll give you until tomorrow. As for the interview by Marshall – I will need to consult our office publicist to run the idea past her and decide whether this is good for us right now. I'll call Marshall and let him know my decision. Although I do find him difficult to contact."

"Once you've made a decision, you can let me know. He and I are in direct contact with each other."

"Are you?"

"Yes," he replied, staring back at her. "Now, if that's all, I have work to do."

"Indeed you do, Spencer," said Muriel. "Indeed you do."

When Spencer left the office, he had no idea who had come out on top. He had an uneasy feeling Muriel had managed to get exactly what she wanted.

He needed to talk to Marshall.

Chapter Twelve

Late Thursday night, as the southbound Tube train pulled out of Colliers Wood station, Spencer was one of the few remaining passengers in the carriage. In the pocket of his duffle coat, his phone vibrated with a call. He pulled out the device and stared at the display.

Marshall.

With a snort, he thumbed the green accept button.

"Hey, you," came the soft baritone voice before Spencer could speak. "It's me."

Spencer felt his grin stretch across his face. He had grown to enjoy Marshall's voice and his gently teasing tone.

"Hello, me. How are things?"

Down the phone, Marshall breathed out a deep sigh.

"Oh, dear," said Spencer, his smile slipping. "That bad?"

"Actually, no. Things are going unexpectedly well. I've just been horribly busy this week. Sorry I haven't been able to phone since Tuesday, but Darcy's had me running in circles all over town."

"I know. Your televised statement to the press yesterday was brilliant, by the way. I've watched it about twenty times on YouTube. And there are some wonderfully supportive comments on Twitter, in case you haven't seen them yet. A couple of trolls, too, but nobody pays them any heed."

"Thanks for saying that, Spence. It means a lot. I've had thousands of messages from people — family, friends, colleagues, and people I don't even know, offering words of support. We've also got a full-page story coming out at the end of this week in the *Sunday Chronicle* by Damien Littlejohn. Does your mother read the *Chronicle?*"

"She does now. I'll make sure my brother buys a copy."

"Are you on a train?"

"Congratulations. You have not lost any of your powers of perception."

"Bit late for a school night, isn't it? Where are you heading?"

"Home."

"At ten-thirty? Don't tell me you're just getting back from work?"

"I'm doing two jobs now, Marshall, and have a ton of extra responsibilities. I need to put in the hours. And I can't take work home with me, partly because of the lack of connectivity in the flat, but also in part due to the attention demands of a feline demon who is giving me a hard time since her new best friend abandoned her."

Spencer had texted Marshall Tuesday lunchtime after he'd met with Muriel and he had phoned back almost immediately. They'd spoken for around an hour, initially about Spencer's new position and Muriel deciding whether to go ahead with the interview. After that, Spencer had asked Marshall how he was coping and his strategy for dealing with the press. Even before the call ended, Spencer had decided to try the job out, to make his mark until Muriel decided who to appoint as Clarissa's replacement. Marshall had essentially agreed with the idea as a stopgap until something better turned up.

"Tell the little princess that when things settle down this end, I promise to come over with some TLC."

"Tender loving care?"

"Tasty little chewbits. They're these cat treats I saw at the supermarket."

"Funny man."

"Hey, the reason for calling is to see if you're still free tomorrow night?"

Spencer's heart gave a tug of delight. He'd been hoping Marshall would ask him but hadn't wanted to presume anything, especially with everything going on.

"Hold the line, caller. I need to check my insanely busy social calendar," said Spencer, before pulling the phone away from his ear and, under his breath, counting to five. "Yes, I'm still free. I kept the evening blocked out in the hope you might be off the hook."

"I am, and I'd like to see you. I'll send you the address for a private bar around the back of Liverpool Street where we can meet. You'll need to quote my membership number, so I'll send that by text along with the address. Can you be there for six-thirty?"

"I can. I was going to work late again, but I'm sure a night off is in order."

"Good. And would it be presumptuous if I asked you to bring an overnight bag?"

Now Spencer's stomach joined his heart as a nest of wasps escaped inside.

"Not one bit."

"Can you get someone to cat-sit?"

"We're pulling into Morden station right now. I'll ask Gino's wife while I'm ordering tonight's dinner."

"Pizza again?"

"It's been a long day and I can't be bothered to cook."

"And the pizza is damn fine. I can vouch for that."

Spencer laughed as the doors to the train clanged open and a waft of icy air invaded the carriage.

"Just arrived at Morden. I'll see you tomorrow, Marshall. Six-thirty."

"Until then, Spence."

* * * *

For all the time Spencer had spent working in Central London, he had only occasionally ventured out around the vicinity of his office and rarely into the heart of London. He was wholly unfamiliar with the streets around Liverpool Street station. Fortunately, the journey took only half an hour, and ten minutes later he found himself in the spider's web of small streets around Spitalfields Market. With the help of the app on his mobile phone, he found the innocuous road with the recessed but otherwise unremarkable black front door Marshall had indicated in his text message.

A simple aluminium buzzer panel with a video screen was fixed to the right-hand side and, as instructed, Spencer punched in a four-digit code. After a few seconds, a man's face appeared on the screen, the voice pleasantly professional, clearly a member of staff.

"Good evening, sir. May I have your name, please?"

"Oh, yes. It's — uh — Spencer Wyrrell. W-Y-R — "

Immediately, a loud, continuous buzzing sounded, followed by a soft clunk.

"Please come in."

Once he had checked his coat, bag and mobile phone, a young attendant led the way unhurriedly up a low rise of stairs with Spencer following sheepishly behind.

On the top landing, the building opened into an elegant foyer with pastel frescos on the walls. A long polished table housed a colossal vase in the centre filled with a beautiful arrangement of milky peach, purple and burgundy flowers, perfectly complementing the décor. Spencer peered around and noticed rooms leading off either side of the table. He almost lost the attendant, who had turned into a room on the right.

After weaving around several groups of men and women in clusters around low tables — a few he thought he recognised from the pages of one of Muriel's magazines — he stopped at two high-back chairs in worn brown leather placed in a bay window overlooking a courtyard. Marshall had been sitting facing them but stood, smiling happily, as Spencer approached. Once again a little twist of pleasure filled Spencer's chest at the fond gaze and smile, and the promise of an evening together.

"Mr Highlander. May I present your guest, Mr Wyrrell."

"Thank you, Barnaby."

"You're welcome, sir. A waiter will be with you shortly, once your guest is settled."

As soon as the steward left, Marshall stepped around the small table and pulled Spencer into a tight hug. Spencer's head fitted snugly beneath Marshall's neck, and he wanted nothing more than to stay there. From the lingering hold, he guessed Marshall needed the embrace as much as he did. After taking a deep breath of Marshall's faint but pleasant scent of cinnamon and sandalwood, he prised himself away and took a seat.

"I hope you don't mind meeting here," said Marshall. "I know the club might come across as a little snobbish and exclusive but at least I can be confident we won't be plagued by the press or any curious punters. There are strict rules about privacy, which means we can drink and chat together without being disturbed."

"Fine by me," said Spencer.

"You look good," said Marshall, sitting back down and waiting for Spencer to do the same. "I know it's only been a couple of days in the new job but how are you coping?"

"Honestly, I'm probably overcompensating. The late nights are largely to get myself up to speed with things I've never been involved with before. But tonight is a welcome and much-needed relief. Otherwise I might have stayed in the office. I'm terrified of letting anything fall through the cracks."

"Of course you are. But you're enjoying the challenge?"

"It's — you know — good to be in control. But there's this nagging voice telling me that no matter how hard I work and how well I do, the job will never be mine."

Something moved across Marshall's face, something bordering annoyance, but he appeared to let it pass.

"Darcy spoke to Muriel's publicist. The interview's on for the magazine client event."

"That was fast. I'm amazed Muriel agreed. Surprised she didn't insist on taking control of the whole thing."

"Oh, she did. Said I would be provided with a list of sanctioned questions from their legal team, a list I would need to sign and agree to use on the night. But we're familiar with those kinds of demands. Most politicians and celebrities want to control their interviews, to paint themselves in the best possible light. But at the end of the day the interview is aimed at the audience and they are the only ones that matter. If they feel an interviewer is being too lenient, or is being overtly partisan or siding with a person, there will be floods of complaints. I've seen it happen. Not to me, thank goodness. Fortunately we have a clause in our contracts about respecting the professionalism and integrity of the interviewer, which essentially overrides their demands and gives me carte blanche to ask whatever I want."

"Good to know. And thank you again."

"No, thank you, Spence. Darcy made sure to let the publicist know that the whole thing was your idea. If you don't get the credit, you need to let me know."

"Yes, boss."

Marshall chuckled fondly until his attention was drawn elsewhere. A waiter in the club's uniform and a white apron appeared at their table.

"What would you like to drink, Spence?" asked Marshall before the man could speak. "I am reliably informed they have bottled Peroni, if that's your preference."

"No, it's Friday night," said Spencer, noticing Marshall had a long drink of clear liquid. "And I'm in a good mood. Let's have a gin and tonic."

"Ah. Are you really sure?" said Marshall, a pained look on his face.

"Yes," said Spencer, but beginning to doubt himself. "Why?"

"Godfrey?" asked Marshall, his attention on the waiter.

"Sir," said the young man, with a suppressed smile. "We have over one hundred varieties of gin, from over twenty different countries. It's one of our club's specialities. Do you have a particular preference, or would you like me to run through them with you?"

"All one hundred?"

"Yes, sir."

"Do you have original Hendrick's?"

"Naturally, sir."

"Then I'll have that. With whatever tonic water you think goes best. And a slice of cucumber, if you can."

"Good choice, sir."

Before leaving, the waiter pulled out a coaster from his apron and placed the item on the table. When Spencer looked up, he saw Marshall grinning and nodding appreciatively.

"Well played, Spence."

"Are you kidding? I feel like a dork. I didn't realise places like this still existed."

"I still don't believe people live above high street pizza parlours."

Spencer chuckled and relaxed back in his seat. When he looked farther down the room, he noticed a doorway into what appeared to be a restaurant.

"Are we eating here?" he asked.

"Would you want to? I mean, I booked us into my favourite Bangladeshi restaurant on Brick Line, somewhere I've been going for the past twenty years.

The food is sensational. I asked for a semi-private room upstairs so we're not disturbed. But I could always cancel—"

"No. If it's your favourite, then I want to try."

"Can you take spicy food?"

"I'm not going to lie and embarrass myself. I can take mild to medium."

"Me, too. That's settled then. Let's finish our drinks then head over under cover of darkness. No rush, and no pressure tonight. Just the two of us."

"Just the two of us. Sounds perfect," said Spencer.

* * * *

On the busy lane, the entrance to Dhaka Street Food appeared daunting and very public, announced by neon lights in vibrant colours and bright illumination from inside. Walking next to each other, Spencer faltered a step. Marshall must have sensed his hesitation, because he linked arms with Spencer and leant into him.

"Don't worry. We'll be using the side door. I phoned ahead and they're waiting for us."

Without hesitating, Marshall pushed open the door to the side of the entrance and entered, letting Spencer slip in behind him. Immediately, pungent spices hit Spencer's senses, making his mouth water. A man introduced himself as Arnab, the owner, and led them upstairs to a simple but comfortable room with four small tables of four seats.

"Just you in here tonight, Mr Highlander. Another small party had booked, but they cancelled because of the lockdown next week."

"Must be playing havoc with your business."

Arnab shrugged, the resigned gesture of a man who had no control over external circumstances.

"What can you do? I am fortunate to have a very busy delivery service. But many other people in the food industry are having difficult times. Can I get you anything to start?"

"We'll have a couple of beers."

"Kingfisher?"

"Perfect."

After Spencer had taken a seat opposite Marshall, he relaxed and peered around the room. Pictures he assumed to be of famous sites in Bangladesh lined the walls—a lush green tea plantation, distinctive fishing boats like Aladdin's lamp lined up along a wide beach, an impressive stepped Buddhist monastery of red bricks, a floating market of hundreds of boats on a busy river selling all manner of produce, a red-brick mosque.

"Thank you for this," he said, noticing Marshall grinning at him.

"That's okay. You can make it up to me later."

Spencer grinned, his cheeks growing hot.

"Arnab will serve us whatever he thinks is good today. But I usually start with *haleem*, a type of lentil soup, and *fuchka*, a street food in Bangladesh. Arnab's version is a hollowed-out crispy puri filled with tamarind chutney, chilli, chaat masala, potato, onion or chickpeas. Delicious. And I also love his *hilsha* curry. *Hilsha* is a fish, a type of herring that's used in Bangladeshi cuisine. It's marinated in chilli paste and turmeric and then fried and served with vegetables and spices."

"Sounds wonderful. I'm in your hands, Marshall, and happy to let you order."

"To be honest, Arnab does the ordering. Him and his family do the cooking. We just have to do the eating and paying."

If Spencer was honest, he worried about having spicy food, in case things got more intimate later on. Spicy food and lovemaking had never worked well together in the past. But Marshall appeared so chilled and happy to share his favourite place with Spencer that he stopped worrying and relaxed into the evening.

"You know, I always thought Bangladeshi cuisine was the same as Indian."

"India alone is a huge country with regional variations in cuisine. It would be like using the term Southern European cuisine to sum up Portuguese, Italian and Spanish food. They're each very different. And although you might recognise some of the names of Bangladeshi dishes, there are many you won't."

"I suppose you've visited Bangladesh."

"Many times. A beautiful country. I was there most recently for the general election. Not sure if you're familiar with Bangladeshi politics, but the election saw a landslide victory for the ruling party. Except there were doubts about the legitimacy of the result and claims the elections were not free and fair."

"You do like your hotspots, don't you?"

"It's my job."

"And you clearly love what you do. I really admire that about you."

Marshall reached across the table and took Spencer's hand in his own.

"You'll get there one day, Spence. Just be patient."

"I am. I will. To be honest," said Spencer, looking down at their joined hands, "I'm just enjoying this right now. You and me. I really like you, Marshall."

177

Marshall smiled fondly while stroking his thumb across the back of Spencer's hand.

"I really like you, too. And I'm looking forward to having you in my bed tonight."

"Yeah, I *thought* you might be up here," came a loud, harsh voice from the doorway. Marshall instantly pulled his hand away, leaving Spencer surprised at the absence of warmth.

Across the room, the young man in the newspaper photographed with Marshall, Joey Hollingbroke, glared with disgust at them. He appeared thin and drawn, dishevelled in dirty jeans and a parka jacket that had seen better days. His dark eyes glowered at Spencer for a second before returning to Marshall. "Didn't waste any time replacing me, did you?"

"I am very sorry, Mr Highlander," said Arnab, who had appeared behind Joey, looking mortified. "He asked if you are here and I remember he is your friend."

Spencer noticed the blood had drained from Marshall's face.

"It's fine, Arnab. He'll only be a minute," said Marshall, and Arnab took that as his cue to leave. Marshall's eyes came to rest on Spencer. "I'm sorry about this, Spence."

"Yeah, he's *sorry* about this, *Spence*. Sorry about his fucked-up ex-boyfriend showing up, embarrassing him in public again."

"What do you want, Joe?" asked Marshall patiently.

"Respect. Loyalty. A little attention would be nice. The usual things. I saw you on the box, by the way. Heard what you said."

Spencer noticed Joey's unsteady stance in the doorway, his left hand shaking noticeably. What with that and the ashen complexion and bloodshot eyes,

Spencer wondered if Joey might be drunk or might have taken something.

"I was simply defending myself, Joe."

"Yeah, you're good at that, aren't you? Not good at defending other people, though, are you? You should bear that in mind, *Spence*, for when your time comes."

"Are you using again, Joe?" asked Marshall.

"None of your fucking business. Why haven't you called?"

"I've called you countless times. But you either don't answer, or you hang up."

Joe stared hard at Marshall then, as though trying to process the words.

"Were you trying to ruin me, Joe? Trying to destroy my career, my reputation? Was that your intention? Because that's what all this felt like."

Joe's face crumpled then, and he began to sob uncontrollably. A seat scraping out from the table caught Spencer's attention as Marshall strode across the room and took Joe in his arms. Joe tried to push him away, but Spencer had been in that embrace before, and — with a tinge of jealousy — knew its strength and comfort. After a few moments, Spencer began to feel awkward, sitting and observing the spectacle. Marshall must have sensed the same thing because, still holding Joe, he turned to Spencer.

"Spence, I can't leave him like this. I need to get him home. I'm really sorry. Can we take a rain check?"

Joe was hurting. He could see that clearly. And Marshall had a big heart. Even if he wanted to, what else could he say?

"Of course."

"Should I ask Arnab to pack the food for you?"

Spencer had forgotten entirely about the food but felt accepting the offer might make Marshall feel better.

"That would be great."

In truth, Spencer's appetite had all but evaporated. With a sinking feeling, he realised the evening he had been anticipating, had been looking forward to with excitement all day — all *week* — had just been pulled out from under him.

"I'm going to get an Uber," said Marshall, waving his phone at Spencer. "Want me to order you one?"

"It's okay. I can find my own way home."

"Come on, Spence. I insist. At least let me send you home safely."

"Sure. Fine."

As Spencer sat there, watching Marshall turn away to make his calls, he felt an almost voyeuristic discomfort, seeing Marshall cradling his ex in his arms. Suddenly ashamed at his behaviour, he began to look away. Until he noticed the two of them start moving out of the door. Once again, he peered up just in time to see Joe lift his head from Marshall's shoulder, and aim his gaze directly at Spencer.

And smile.

Chapter Thirteen

Over the following weekend, Spencer received a couple of apologetic texts from Marshall and a heads-up that he would be busy with work the whole week, but nothing more substantial. The notion that Marshall's ex — he couldn't bring himself to say his name now — had been using him would not go away. Every time he thought back to that night, he remembered the calculated smile the ex had thrown Spencer's way, the gloating expression that meant 'I win and you lose'.

The kind of smug smile a person gives you when they manage to snag the last seat on the train home when you feel ready to drop from an exhausting day at work. Or when the person in front of you in the coffee queue, one you've been waiting in for ages, invites their friends to join them, then turns to smile at you without offering a word of apology. That horrible quirk of human nature that some relish, of getting one over on someone else.

Maybe he should have been angrier, but he felt for Marshall and understood why he would desire to deal with things on his own. Not only did they have history, but Marshall knew the family and would want them involved if his ex had, as Spencer suspected, been high on drugs that night.

Even understanding all of that, he still moped around the flat all weekend, trying to take his mind off things by immersing himself in mundane housework, rattling around the place like a melancholy ghost haunting the four walls. Even getting a hard copy of the *Sunday Chronicle* and reading the excellent article by Littlejohn three times about the life and times of Marshall Highlander, the real man, had only succeeded in making him feel lonelier. Above all else, he wanted to have the man there to talk with, to kiss and cuddle and soothe.

With very few people coming to the office all the next week, and still no phone call from Marshall, Spencer buried himself in his work. He tried to call Marshall a couple of times, but on each occasion the call had gone to voicemail. Finally, his injured pride and insecurities had taken over, telling him that he had every right to be angry, telling him they were over before they had begun. Marshall had decided to get back with his ex, however much Spencer hated the thought.

Friday morning, when Spencer stepped out of the lift into the overheated office foyer trying to cheer himself up dressed in a frivolous Friday combination of a hot-pink shirt, floral bow tie, and cobalt blue suit, finished off by a black mask and belt, young Kimberley's eyes smiled with approval from above her pale yellow mask. Instead of nodding and heading straight into the office, he had made a conscious habit during the week of making conversation. She was a sweet girl, harmless and a little naïve, and each day that week he had learnt a little more about her life. On Thursday she had insisted on him calling her Kim, not Kimberley. Twenty-four, engaged, and living in a small flat with a guy called Grant who swore too much and played football on Sundays but otherwise adored her

"Morning, Kim. Anything special happening this weekend?"

"Nothing planned. Probably stuck indoors, binge-watching cable television series. The odd thing is that last year we'd have probably done the same thing, what with this awful weather. But it's the fact we're told to stay in that makes me want to rip off my mask and run out into the streets naked."

Spencer stopped, shocked, letting out a guffaw.

"I'd probably clear that with Grant before you do. And please, no streaking in the office, at least not during office hours."

Kim placed an unnecessary hand over her mask and giggled.

"Nobody would notice, anyway," she said. "There's barely anyone in today."

"Is Muriel coming in?"

Muriel had been locked in her office all week but had flitted in and out from time to time without talking to anyone. Even though she'd agreed to go ahead with the idea, she'd mentioned nothing about the interview with Marshall at the Monday meeting and he wondered if she was having second thoughts. For the first time, the Monday morning War Council had been conducted virtually, with even Spencer dialling in from his office desktop computer. Beverley had been nowhere to be seen all week, and he had missed catching up with her, but they still kept in touch by text messaging. He had yet to tell her about his disastrous night out with Marshall.

"Muriel's not going to be in today or all next week. She phoned and said she's going to be working out of her place on the Embankment."

"Thank heavens. In which case, if you do decide to strip off today, let me know and I might join you."

Once again, Kim snickered.

"Beverley's here, though."

"She is? Excellent. Haven't seen her all week."

Spencer's mood instantly brightened. Texts were fine, but he could do with a dose of Bev in the flesh. As he was about to go, Kimberley lifted a pink Post-It note and read the message.

"Oh, and Blake phoned to say he'll be here mid-morning. Said he needs to talk to you."

And just like that, Spencer's mood deflated.

"Did he say what about?"

"No."

"Okay, well. He knows where to find me."

Spencer got straight down to work. Every evening before he headed home, he left himself a list of prioritised tasks for the next day, usually putting the one he knew he'd have to spend most time completing on the top. One of the things he had always found satisfying was in breaking down huge tasks into smaller ones, listing them down, then crossing items out as he completed them. Doing so, he felt a sense of accomplishment at the day's end, even if some essential tasks had not been fully completed. Prince had tried to get him to use an electronic to-do list — to save paper — but his manual system had always worked fine.

"Hello, stranger," came a familiar female voice from behind him. "Fancy taking a few minutes out for a coffee, a blueberry muffin and a chat with your bestie?"

Spencer had been so absorbed in his work he'd barely registered the time of day. He immediately stopped what he was doing, checked the clock on his computer — already ten-thirty — then swivelled around in his seat and jumped up.

"Sorry, Bev. I meant to come and find you an hour ago. Lead the way."

Living nearby, Bev had discovered a tiny coffee shop hidden down one of the small lanes around the back of the office. None of the office staff knew about the place where Bev was considered a regular. They took a booth by the window with their muffins while waiting for their drinks.

"I suppose you read the interview in the *Chronicle* about your boyfriend?" she began.

"Not my boyfriend, Bev," he said then proceeded to give her a download about Friday night. Talking out loud brought up feelings he had been trying to suppress, and he felt tears begin to sting his eyes.

"Oh, Squirrel, baby," she said, reaching a perfectly manicured hand across the table and squeezing his fingers. "Why didn't you call me over the weekend?"

"I know. I should have. But I didn't want to bother you."

"Always phone me, Squirrel. Always. Especially as I can't phone you, living in that cave of yours. That's what friends are for."

"Thank you. I will in future. It's been a miserable week."

"Poor you. Don't lose hope, baby. Sounds to me like he's dealing with a lot of crap at the moment. Maybe you need to be a little patient for him, for you both, while he sorts things out."

"I've never been very good at patient."

"Yeah," smirked Bev, as their coffees arrived. "Me neither. But apparently, it's a virtue. Apart from Marshall, what other gossip do you have? You go first, and then I'll tell you mine."

"Where do I start? My brother is going to be a dad. Clarissa resigned and Muriel asked me to take over her role." That week, he had received an email from the Human Resources department about awarding him a compensatory one per cent raise on his salary each month for taking on extra responsibilities and a change of title to Acting Senior Editor. Spencer did not dare share the news with his mother. He knew exactly what she would say. "I'm sure you've heard already, but she has also agreed to let Marshall interview her and the hubby for the client Christmas party. Oh yes, and be careful. Kim in reception is so bored she's threatening to streak through the office."

"Wait, what? Slow down. Go back to the start."

* * * *

Half an hour later, caught up on everything in his life, and Spencer began to feel more normal. When he'd pushed her about her own gossip, Bev had held her hands up and refused to try to match his. They finished up their drinks and strolled back to the office arm in arm, both togged up against the cold weather. As they came out of the lift and into reception, Blake stood there talking to Prince, both leaning back against the counter, observing them. As always, Blake tried to look elegant but came off as uptight, too stiff and condescending in his silver-grey Italian designer suit, but he still managed the clean-cut handsomeness and confidence that had ensnared Spencer. Prince, on the other hand, far outshone Blake in the attraction stakes as he grinned and winked at them.

"Well, well," said Blake, a thin smile forming. "Talk of the devil, and in walk Tweedledum and Tweedledee. I was just looking for you."

"Oh, yes," said Bev, staunchly immune to his charm. "Which one of us?"

"Both, actually. Can we take this to a conference room? They're all empty right now. You too, Prince."

Prince shrugged his bewilderment at them as Blake led them into the empty office and across the floor to the largest conference room.

"As I'm sure you all know, Ambika and I are having a private engagement celebration for close friends and younger family members at my parents' place in Beaconsfield. Around sixty guests. My fiancée is insisting that I invite a sample of my work colleagues, so I'm inviting you three. It's tomorrow afternoon and I need you to arrive no earlier than one-thirty."

"Hang on. Tomorrow? That's a bit short notice, isn't it?" asked Bev.

"My mother would be *deeply grateful* if you accept the invitation."

"What if I have other plans?" asked Spencer.

"Cancel them."

"In other words, we have no choice," said Bev.

"Let's just say that your presence would be greatly appreciated. Now, as social gatherings are discouraged at the moment, you'll need to keep this under wraps. And I mean no telling your friends or family. We're recommending people come in cars of no more than four and make sure everyone is masked up. It all sounds a bit cloak and dagger, I know, because it's not strictly above board, but my parents have managed to pull some strings—"

"You are not serious?" asked Bev.

"Completely serious. We'll issue you with a letter saying you are all required as support volunteers for a charitable event. We're rarely disturbed by the police, being so far out of town—but in case you do get stopped and questioned on your way, show them the letter. You'll also need to say you're carpooling with fellow volunteers, people you know, and if they need to check, ask them to call the number on the letter. The contact at that number will confirm your names."

"This is like a covert military operation," said Bev, echoing Spencer's thoughts. "Did your father come up with these plans?"

Blake ignored her.

"I'll also give you a map of the location because, as I say, we're out in the sticks and satnav doesn't always work. It does mean you'll need a designated driver for the day, someone who doesn't drink and can drive you home. But I'm sure you can arrange that. Any questions?"

"Yeah. I have my cousin living with me," said Prince. "I'm supposed to be staying at home keeping him company this weekend. My mother's an NHS nurse and has to work."

"How old is he?"

"Twenty-two."

"And he can't look after himself?"

"That's not the point. He's our guest. It would be rude and inhospitable to leave him on his own, and we're not that kind of family."

"Bring him, then. Email me his details and I'll make sure he's added to the letter. Anything else?"

"Is Muriel paying us overtime for this?" asked Prince.

"And for the new party dress I'll need to buy?' added Bev.

"Any other questions?" asked Blake, ignoring them both. When nothing else came, he pushed his backside off the conference room table and headed for the door. "I'll see you all tomorrow. Wait here for a minute, and I'll get the sheet with the directions."

The moment the door thumped softly closed behind him, Bev began to rant.

"What a fucking cheek," she said, unusually angry. "I had a nice weekend planned. Now I've got to put myself at risk of being fined, or at worst, arrested, just to entertain that fuckwit's whims and wishes."

"Come on, Bev," said Prince. "It'll be a laugh. I don't drink anyway, so I'll drive as long as we share the cost of petrol. Can you meet outside Tooting Broadway station, Spencer?"

"Of course. What about Bev? Are you going to pick her up from home?"

"I haven't said I'm going yet," she said, folding her arms.

"You're going," said Prince.

"You're definitely going, if I have to go," said Spencer at the same time.

All three of them laughed together.

"Okay, but no way are you picking me up," she said, mugging at Prince. "I'm a big girl, and don't want you coming all the way up here. That would be a waste of time and petrol. But I'm going to need a trip to the hair salon and I really am buying a new dress. Actually, we should order an Uber and charge the company —"

"He's coming back," said Prince, staring out through the conference room glass.

Blake returned and handed out the instructions, a copy to each of them.

"Before you all go, I need you to give me your word you'll say nothing to any of the guests, and especially to Ambika's family, about Spencer and me, and our little dalliance —"

"Blake," said Spencer, stunned at Blake's words. "Prince has no idea."

"Oh, please," said Prince, rolling his eyes. "Your office romance? Has to be the world's worst-kept secret."

"Careful, Prince," said Blake, raising an eyebrow. "People in glass houses and all that."

Spencer had no idea what he meant, but Prince quietened instantly.

"We promise not to say a thing, okay?" said Bev, not bothering to hide her irritation. "Now can I go? I've got a ton of work to do, especially now my weekend has been hijacked."

"Yes, of course. Thank you for agreeing to this. Uh, Spencer," said Blake, as the others filed out. "Can you stay back, please? I need a private word."

Spencer had a feeling Blake wanted to address their short affair, or whatever the hell it had been. God forbid anyone should cast any doubt on Blake's perfect heterosexual record. Anger bubbled inside Spencer, something he pulled quickly under control. Having survived intact, he no longer wanted any feelings for Blake. And, over time, that had begun to happen.

Without waiting for Blake to speak, Spencer asked a question.

"Did you hear I've taken over from Clarissa?"

"My mother told me. Although I think she used the expression 'caretaking the role'."

"Did she?"

"I believe she's looking at the opportunity to bring new blood into the organisation."

Out of the mouths of babes spills the truth. Spencer should have guessed as much. Muriel had never had any intention of offering him the job.

"So, what did you want, Blake?"

Blake fell quiet for a moment and appeared to be considering his words.

"What did you think of Ambika? You only met her briefly at the Halloween party."

The question took Spencer by surprise. He thought back to the smart, attractive and genuine woman he had met and how she had made him laugh.

"I like her. She's sexy and smart. And I love her sense of humour."

"Her humour?" said Blake, his eyes not meeting Spencer's. "Yes, she has your kind of humour. She liked you."

"There you go, then. She's a good judge of character, too. What's the problem?"

Blake's eyes swung back to Spencer's, his face as unsmiling as ever.

"Look, I know we had that—*thing*—some months back. But I hope everything between us is still cordial—"

"You don't need to worry, Blake," he said calmly. "I promise you I'm not about to make a scene in front of your fiancée or her family. Or anyone else, come to that.

What happened between us, happened. Past tense. And what's past is past, dead and buried. Agreed?"

"It's not that I didn't — that we didn't — have fun, but — "

"We've both moved on. Yes, I understand completely. You don't need to worry, Blake. That water is so far under the bridge it's pretty much reached the ocean by now."

And with those parting words, Spencer walked out of the conference room. When he looked back, Blake still leant against the conference room table, staring at him, an unfathomable look on his face.

Chapter Fourteen

As agreed, Spencer met Prince at Tooting Broadway Tube station around Saturday lunchtime. Sitting shotgun in Prince's black Mini Cooper Countryman, he had been tasked with navigating using his mobile phone routefinder app and the hand-drawn map Blake had provided to get them to the remote venue. Bev already sat in the back with Prince's good-looking cousin Nile, who had his earbuds in and nodded a sullen welcome to Spencer without removing them. Bev shook her head slightly, a silent communication to leave him be.

"Who has a playlist?" asked Spencer, trying to lighten the mood. "For the journey. To get us in the mood?"

"I made one dedicated to Blake and this whole day," said Prince, grinning in the rear-view mirror. "It's got *Anywhere But Here* by Easton. *Road to Nowhere* by Talking Heads. *Creep* by Radiohead and sung by Briar Justin Crum. Lady Gaga and Bradley Cooper singing *Shallow*, and Billie Eilish with *Bad Guy* —"

"How about Katy Perry singing *Ur So Gay*?" asked Bev.

Prince leant forward and barked out a laugh, his breath misting the windscreen.

"Bev!" said Spencer sternly, turning in his seat. He felt bad admonishing them about him and Blake, but they had been sworn to secrecy. He'd always assumed nobody he worked with knew about them. Prince's comment had been a shock revelation and he hadn't had a chance to talk to him since Friday about how many other people knew or suspected.

"Relax, Squirrel," said Bev from behind. "We'll both behave. And if you're worried about Nile, he's not even listening."

"She's right," said Prince, grinning. "Mind you, Spencer, don't you think Blake comes across as a bit gay at times? I'm sure he was hitting on me at one of our staff drinks."

"Well, he's getting engaged to a girl now," said Spencer. "Case closed."

"Closet case, you mean," said Prince, roaring with laughter and setting Bev off.

"Prince!" said Spencer.

"What are you laughing about?" asked Nile, who had removed his earbuds.

"Nothing," said Bev and Prince in unison, before falling into fits of giggles again.

Spencer leant forward and put his head in his hands.

* * * *

Fortunately, nobody stopped them along their journey. Prince had opted to head southwest before joining the M25 heading north, guessing that traffic would not be heavy. Once they'd left the motorway the roads to the north of Beaconsfield shrank seamlessly from broad metropolitan to narrow rustic, into a confusing maze of tight B-roads. Right now they hurtled down a serpentine country lane.

"Slow down, Prince," said Spencer, checking the paper map. "There should be a left turn up ahead, but it's not showing on my phone app."

"How close are we?" asked Prince. He was a good driver, kept his eyes fixed to the road and generally drove at a speed that ensured the comfort of his passengers.

"According to the satnav? Eight minutes. Although we're also currently driving through a field according to the device. Good job Blake gave us these typed-up directions."

They almost missed the lane, which was concealed by overhanging bushes. Bev managed to spot the flaky signpost nailed to a tree trunk for the New Horizons Rehabilitation Centre.

A ten-minute crawl down the lane and the Moresbys' country residence came into view, a vast modern farmhouse set in the middle of acres of farmlands. Accessed by another private route, itself virtually hidden by overhanging trees and towering hedgerows, the Moresbys' home stood isolated and secluded.

As instructed, they parked up farther along the lane in a covered car park designated for rehabilitation centre staff and visitors, where other cars were already parked. Once out of their Mini, they followed Blake's instructions along a covered pathway leading them back towards the farmhouse, but stopped before they reached the home. A sign pointed them to the end of a massive old barn.

"The fuck?" said Prince, staring up at the place while Spencer reread the instructions.

"Are you sure this is it? Blake would never allow this. I know it's Christmas, but surely they can't be holding the party in their bloody stables!" said Bev, pulling a face.

He couldn't blame her. She had splashed out on a new outfit, a scarlet strapless cocktail dress that she had on beneath her black raincoat. Her matching slingbacks sat in the small carrier bag dangling from her hand. Spencer had seen a picture she'd sent him from her phone — from what must have been the shop — and she had pushed the boat out today, even having her red hair styled for the occasion. As usual, she looked amazing.

"The instructions point to the entrance on the south side," said Nile, taking the lead.

When Spencer looked back and studied the whole arrangement, he realised what the Moresbys had done. If a police helicopter were to pass overhead there would be no sign of any untoward activity. The cars sat concealed beneath coverings, the path to the barn was under a covered walkway. Only the short walk along a concrete way skirting the building was exposed to the elements.

A vestibule with large double doors had been built onto the awning on the south side of the barn, and inside someone met them and took their temperatures followed by their names. Once this had been done, and after confirming they had all arrived in the same car, they were given a rectangular number tag in red plastic for their coat and phone check. The woman also pointed out the digits on the reverse – eighteen and fifteen.

"We will come and notify you ten minutes before but you will need to leave at this time. We want to make sure large groups of people don't depart together and potentially draw attention to the location. If you need to leave earlier, please inform us at the door."

"I thought the party finishes at ten," said Prince.

"For close guests of the couple only. Others are politely requested to leave earlier, at their allotted time," said the woman, stony-faced.

"Nice. Really nice," said Beverley, glaring at the woman. "Do you know how much I spent on this dress?"

"Please feel free to take the matter up with Mr Moresby junior."

Once inside, and just beyond the threshold, all of them stood frozen to the spot, gaping at the wonderland. The whole A-frame interior had been decorated beautifully with simple white lights and silver pennants hanging from exposed beams. More white lights mixed with silver had been wrapped around the barn's columns, a theme continued onto each of the tables. Ten round tables with white tablecloths and white seats spaced generously apart from one another filled the central space. At the same time, one of the aisles contained tables crammed with chafing dishes, the other housing a long bar already staffed by white-jacketed waiters. Even the floor of polished teak must have been laid specially for the event, and Spencer noticed with a smirk how all windows had been covered with thick blackout curtains. Unsurprisingly, the Moresbys had thought of everything.

"Follow me, please, and I'll show you to your table," said one of the attending staff.

Spencer's group was led towards a table containing other staff and partners from the magazine, including Muriel's personal assistant, Alice, and her husband.

"Is this the naughty table?" asked Spencer as he took the seat next to her.

"Because if it wasn't before, I think it probably is now," said Bev, sitting on the other side of him and making Alice's husband laugh.

Spencer looked to the head table of six where Blake and his fiancée sat in the middle, with Blake's sister Beatrice and someone who appeared to be the youngest of Ambika's brothers at the end. To Ambika's right sat someone he assumed to be her sister followed by the older brother. Blake — as unsmiling as ever — caught his eye and nodded, something Spencer returned equally formally.

"He's molten hot," said Bev, leaning into Spencer and following his gaze. "Ambika's brother, I mean."

"Which one? They both are," whispered Spencer.

"Yes, but the younger one has that brooding Mr Darcy look about him."

"Steady, kitten. We haven't even had a drink yet."

"I was checking him out for you, not me."

Drinks soon came, along with an introductory speech by Ambika's older brother once most of the guests had arrived. After he finished, a band started playing gentle music while, one by one, each table was invited to collect a food tray from the buffet table.

Before Spencer knew what had happened, the hour pushed five.

"Spence. Keep Nile company, will you?" said Prince as he dragged Bev out onto the dance floor. "He's being a miserable little gay boy."

"Fuck you," said his cousin, flipping Prince off. Prince simply grinned and moved into the crowd of revellers, dragging Bev behind him. Spencer could see the slight family resemblance, although Nile's face had softer edges than Prince's and a gold hoop through the left nostril. But both looked after their bodies, and both had muscled chests and pecs even though Nile's frame was slighter, leaner. Both fitted into their trousers nicely, although Nile had a tattoo on his dark skin peeking up from the collar of his tight white shirt.

"How do you know my cousin, then?" asked Nile. He hadn't spoken a word during the journey, or the whole time they'd been in the barn, except to his cousin. Spencer assumed he didn't want to be there.

"We work together."

"Bit of a wanker, in't he?"

"Prince? No, he's all right, actually. One of the good ones."

Nile appeared to like the answer and turned to smile at Spencer, whose heart did a little happy dance at the intensity of his perfect rows of white teeth.

"Sound like you know his bird really well."

"His bird? I didn't know he had one."

"The one we came with. The one in the car? Thought she worked with you too."

"Beverley? They're not—" began Spencer, beginning to chuckle until the penny dropping was more like a comet hitting the ocean. "Wait. She's his *girlfriend*?"

"They've been going at it for a couple of months now."

Of course. How had Spencer missed that? Probably because he was so caught up in his own world that he'd missed everything else going on around him. But everything made sense now. Bev late on Monday mornings then Prince showing up half an hour later, Bev choosing Prince as her lunch date when Spencer had to work over lunch. Prince knowing about him and Blake. Blake's comment about people in glass houses. Everything made perfect sense now.

"Bloody hell. I thought they were just work mates."

"Yeah. Work mates with benefits. Who apparently go at it like rabbits, if what he tells me is true. She stayed over at our place last night."

No wonder Beverley had already been in the car that morning. If she had taken the Tube down to Tooting, there was no way on earth that she would have been on time, let alone early. Why hadn't she said anything?

"Fuck. She's my best friend at work. And I never even knew."

Spencer took a tug on his beer and tried to spot her across the dance floor. The band was playing a ballad, and couples now slow-danced together.

"Anyone in your life?" asked Spencer. "Good-looking bloke like you?"

"Split up with my boyfriend a month or so ago."

"I'm sorry. Just before Christmas. That's tough."

"Together three years. All men are bastards."

Spencer chuckled and Nile turned to smile.

"He dumped you?"

"Other way around."

"Oh. So that makes *you* the bastard."

Nile shrugged. He leant forward in his chair, his head hanging down, his arms on his knees and hands clasped together.

"He wanted marriage and babies, you know? The whole nine miles."

"Yards. And you didn't?"

Nile sat up and used both hands to indicate his upper body.

"I didn't go through all this to end up with stretch marks."

Spencer burst into laughter. Nile didn't.

"It's not a joke. I'm trans."

"Shit," said Spencer, feeling mortified at his insensitivity. "I'm sorry, I had no idea. Prince didn't say anything."

An uncomfortable silence fell, during which Spencer floundered around for something to say. He liked Nile, found him easy company and didn't want to offend him.

"Couldn't you have fostered or adopted instead?" he said, then wished he hadn't said anything.

Nile scrunched his eyebrows together, considering his words.

"I never thought about alternatives. But yeah I suppose we could have discussed other options. The problem is I have a bit of a temper, and once the subject was brought up, I shut it straight down. Prince says I have no filter and prefer to tell it like it is. And I don't tend to be good at listening, either. Once the topic was out there, I knew it would never be far from Tommy's mind, his wanting to be a father. Tommy's my ex. In the end, I walked away."

Spencer understood all too well. He had seen healthy relationships break down because one partner refused to compromise or negotiate their personal agenda and in doing so had ended up losing their soulmate. He hoped Nile and Tommy had not been too quick to judge each other.

"How about you? Any boyfriend or ex?" asked Nile.

"An ex. But just like your boyfriend, I got dumped. Almost two years ago. So I know how that feels. My ex is sitting on the top table right now, the one getting married."

"Blake?" exclaimed Nile, clearly shocked. "Fuck off!"

"Okay. Shit. I didn't know you knew him. Forget I said anything, and for goodness' sake, don't tell anyone. I am not in the habit of outing people, even bastards like him."

"Seriously, though?" said Nile, his voice a fierce whisper now. "Blake is *bi*?"

"Actually, when I first met him, I thought he was gay. But, yeah, I suppose he's bi. Or pan. Or whatever. But I think he passes as straight these days."

Nile pulled a disgusted face.

"Does his fiancée know?"

"I don't know. I don't think so. And please, don't go outing him at his own engagement party. Apart from his sexuality being none of our business, I work for his mother and she'd probably kick me out of the company."

"Don't worry. My lips are sealed. What happened, then? You're a kinda cute-looking guy. Why'd he dump you?"

"Cute? I'm cute? Do you know how offensive that is?"

"Told you, I tell it like it is. Come and have a dance."
"What?"

"Dance with me. Or are you too stuck up to dance with —"

Spencer shot up from his seat, almost knocking his bottle of beer over.

"Bring it on."

Out on the dance floor, he spotted Prince and Bev slow-dancing close together, laughing at a joke. The look they shared made their intimacy so obvious. Once again, Spencer groaned inside at how he had missed something as unmistakable.

"Kiss me," said Nile, bringing Spencer's attention sharply back to him.

"What? I'm not kissing you. I've only just met you."

"You don't think I'm hot?"

"Of course I think you're hot. I think you know that already."

"So it's because I'm trans?"

"No!" said Spencer, flustered now. "I mean, maybe. I don't know."

"What do you have to lose? Indulge me."

In the middle of the dance floor, Spencer stared at Nile for a few seconds, but could see he was serious. *What the heck*, he thought, *the man is seriously good-looking*. He brought their lips together, closed his eyes and kissed. Maybe he was dreaming, but as he closed his eyes, there seemed to be a quick burst of light. But that was all. The kiss did absolutely nothing, a little like when his grandmother had pecked him on the lips as a small child. When he opened his eyes again, Nile was grinning at him.

"Nothing from this side. How 'bout you?"

"Not really," said Spencer. "I mean, no offence. I'm sure you're a good kisser."

"The first time I kissed Tommy, he got a boner. Rock-hard. And my insides turned to jelly. I wanted to fuck him right there and then. All bets were off after that. You ever had that happen to you?"

Spencer thought back to Marshall kissing him and smiled. When he closed his eyes, he was right there in the moment with Marshall again, feeling his heat and smelling his body.

"Yeah, I have."

"And?"

Spencer opened his eyes.

"It's complicated."

Nile's gaze shot out across the room.

"Blake?"

"No! God, no. Not Blake. Blake didn't like kissing."

"You never told me why he dumped you."

Spencer huffed out a sigh. He tried not to autopsy their time together, especially after how low he had sunk. Only later, hearing gossip from Bev and others around the office, had he learnt that Blake rarely stayed around long. Hopefully Ambika would be a turning point.

"I think he got bored with me. And honestly, there wasn't much to keep us together. Not really. Not like you and Tommy. Sounds to me like you two were made for each other."

Nile pulled away to gape at Spencer, who simply shrugged. As far as he was concerned, if Nile could dish it out, then he could take it.

"Rub it in, why don't you?" said Nile.

"I, too, tell it like it is."

Nile chuckled, but then fell quiet and looked down the floor.

"I fucked up, didn't I?"

"Not my place to say. But from what you tell me, he sounds perfect."

"Yeah," said Nile, nodding. "Yeah, I need to do something about that. He's stuck in Dublin right now with his family. He went to see them in November and now he can't come back until things get better here. I need to reach out to him, though, to see how he is. See if there's anything worth salvaging."

"Your call."

"It is, yeah," said Nile. "Thanks for being honest."

"It's a specialty of mine."

"Listen. You're in Morden. I'm stuck in Tooting for the foreseeable future. We're only four stops from each other on the Northern Line. How about we catch up sometimes? For drinks or a meal, once things open up? I could do with someone other than Prince for conversation, who only ever talks about computers and Beverley. Neither of which interest me. And I promise never to ask you to kiss me again."

Spencer laughed. In truth, he could do with more friends. He enjoyed Nile's frankness and welcomed the idea of having someone fun to see outside of work, someone to entice him out from the sanctuary of his flat at the weekend.

"I'd love that."

Spencer noticed Bev and Prince approaching, leaving a safe platonic distance between each other Prince waved the red plastic tag in front of them.

"We've just had our fifteen-minute call. We need to get going soon," said Prince.

"Are you getting your thang on with Nile?" asked Bev, grinning wickedly and winking at Spencer.

"No, we're not," said Spencer, raising an eyebrow at Bev. "Unlike you and Prince, we're just friends."

Bev's grin melted from her face, while Prince grinned and looked away.

"I told him," said Nile. "Sorry, cuz. I didn't realise you two were still under cover."

"Not much of a cover," said Spencer. "Dancing and kissing at the boss' son's engagement party for all to see. Why didn't you say anything, Bev?"

"Because she was worried about you," said Prince, chipping in. "Worried about the relationship crap you've been through lately. She's happy — we both are — and she didn't want to rub that in your face."

"It's true," said Bev, looking sheepish. "I was going to say something when I came to your place on the day you were sick, but you had company. And then, when we had coffee yesterday and you told me about Marshall, and then about your brother, I decided to put off telling you until later. Are you mad at me?"

How could he be mad at her? She was one of the few people who cared about him. Instead of answering, he pulled her into a tight hug.

"Of course not. I'm really happy for you both. You make a fantastic couple."

"We do, don't we?" said Prince. "Now get your arses in gear, before they throw us out."

Leaving through the main doors with the party still going strong, Spencer and his group emerged into darkness. Frost had begun to pepper the ground. As they ambled back to the car, Spencer looked around and listened, but could only hear the sounds of the night.

He had to hand it to Blake and his deviousness. Nobody passing would ever be able to tell that an illegal party was in full swing inside the darkened barn.

Chapter Fifteen

On Monday morning, when Spencer stepped out of the farthest of four lifts, the first thing that hit him was the appearance over the weekend of a giant artificial Christmas tree in hot-pink twinkling with snowy white lights and silver baubles, and a huge matching pink garland hung up behind the reception desk. He stopped in his tracks at the sight and chuckled, already feeling better about his day. As he moved forward unnoticed, he spotted Bev standing behind the reception desk, looming over Kim, talking loudly and clearly.

On the ride home from the party he had sat in the back with her while she talked about her and Prince being a couple. Prince had chipped in occasionally. They had spoken again more privately on Sunday over the phone when Spencer had popped down to the local café for a coffee. Listening to her enthuse happily about her relationship with Prince had been infectious, and he had even ended up feeling better about himself.

Today she appeared to be dishing out instructions to Kim, but the moment she looked up and saw him, her face transformed with a mischievous excitement he knew only too well.

"Squirrel!" she said, her voice a high-pitched squeal. "Did you hear what happened? After we left the party?"

"Happened where?" asked Kim, looking up from her screen.

"Nothing," said Bev. "Spencer and I went to the same party on Saturday."

"Blake's engagement party?" said Kim, rolling her eyes. "World's worst-kept secret. I had calls from his friends all day Friday, asking to confirm directions. And if you're talking about the newspaper article, then I imagine the whole office knows about the secret party by now."

"Newspaper article?" asked Spencer, before wondering how many 'worst-kept secrets' the office was cultivating.

"Come with me," said Bev, leading him through the office to her desk, where she had a copy of a free newspaper open to the centre pages. One side read *Lord Moresby's Son Flouts Lockdown Rules*. Four photographs in full colour sat around the story. One that jumped out at him was of random people crowding the dance floor. But, when he looked carefully, he could make out himself and Nile at the very moment they had kissed. Who the hell had taken that?

"After we left on Saturday, the barn got raided. There were around thirty-five people left. Blake and Ambika had asked close friends and family to stay behind and party on. Until — wait for it — at around eight o'clock, the police and the press turned up. After they eventually found him, Blake got charged. Under the current lockdown regulations any illegal gathering of over thirty people and the police can issue a fine of ten thousand pounds."

"Shit!"

"I know, right? He knew he should never have held the party. Thank goodness we left early, otherwise we'd have been complicit. No idea how your picture got in there. Prince thinks someone must have snuck their phone into the party. Probably the same person who was the whistleblower."

"Blake must be so pissed off."

"Yes, but not about the fine, which no doubt Mummy and Daddy will take care of," said Bev, grinning, then tapping her forefinger lower down the page. "Read the second-to-last paragraph. Out loud, please."

"'Clearly eschewing social distancing rules but keeping things in the family, the husband-to-be, Blake Moresby II, was found outside the venue among the bushes by police officers—'"

"'—having fellatio performed on him by the bride-to-be's youngest brother,'" finished Bev with a flourish, trying hard to stifle a laugh. "Yes, darling. Your ex royally fucked up."

"Poor Ambika," said Spencer quietly. She didn't deserve that kind of embarrassment. Then again, maybe finding out now was better than after they were married. "What has Muriel had to say? Is she in the office?"

"No, she's off all this week. Supposedly preparing for the client-party interview. Not sure if that's even going to happen now after having the family name splashed all over the paper. Do you think Marshall will walk away?"

Spencer hadn't thought about Marshall all weekend. After hearing nothing back from him, Spencer had decided to beat a dignified retreat.

"Actually, no. I think Marshall's interview would be the perfect antidote. Let's face it, he's had a fair amount of public shit to deal with himself recently. I reckon he might make a good ally."

"Are you going to talk to him, to Marshall?"

"I've tried, Bev. He's not returning my calls."

"Oh, babe. I'm so sorry."

Just then, Bev's phone rang.

"Oh shoot. I need to answer this and it's going to be a long one. Can you take the paper? There's something on page two you might be interested in."

Back at his desk, he switched on his computer and took off his coat, readying for the day ahead. The story on page two centred around Hollingbroke, who had walked away from yet another television show due to 'artistic differences' with the producers. The article went on to analyse Hollingbroke's recent outing of ex-lover, Marshall Highlander, his spats with television executives, his fading career, and his rapidly declining popularity among viewers. Rightly or wrongly, Spencer thought there might be a comment about the actor being checked into rehab, after what he had seen at the restaurant. But the article mentioned nothing.

Once again Spencer lost himself in his work and only came up for air at around eleven, when his phone rang with an external call.

"Hello, can I speak to Spencer Wyrrell."

Spencer thought he recognised the voice, female and professional. But the name temporarily escaped him.

"Speaking."

"This Madeleine Morrison from Peerpoint Consultancy. Do you have a moment?"

Spencer knew about Peerpoint. They specialised in recruiting journalists and other professional editorial staff. Blackmore Magazine Group rarely used them, Peerpoint's specialism aimed more at serious-minded journalism. Not surprisingly, Muriel despised them. But sometimes senior members of staff at Blackmore were called upon to provide references for juniors going on to better things, something Clarissa would have dealt with in the past. Spencer would need to become familiar with this side of the role if he was going to fight for the promotion.

"I have a few minutes. Please go ahead."

"Can I call you Spencer?"

"Yes, of course," said Spencer, chuckling while continuing to work on the article on his screen.

"Can I ask, Spencer, have you heard of Ed Coleman?"

Ed Coleman headed up the *National Herald*. Spencer only knew him by reputation. A hard-nosed, hard-working journalist, he had fought his way up through the ranks of the national newspaper industry to become the editor-in-chief at one of the most respected British newspapers in the country. Whoever had snagged a job with him, in no matter what capacity, was one lucky so-and-so.

"Of course. But by reputation only, not personally. What's this about, Madeleine?"

"Ed looked over your online portfolio of work, and he was impressed — which, let me tell you, happens very rarely. He wants to meet with you. But with the current chaos and Christmas deadlines looming, he wanted to do so sooner rather than later. How's your schedule fixed tomorrow? Would you be able to meet him for a chat? Maybe for an hour?"

Spencer had not been paying full attention and the words sank in slowly, the full realisation hitting him hard.

"Wait. *What?* Ed Coleman wants to talk to *me*?"

This time Madeleine laughed politely.

"Yes. Like I said, he was impressed with your work. Would you be able to find your way to their offices? They're in London Bridge. I can send you the location details. You're in Mornington Crescent, aren't you?"

"I—uh—yes, I am."

"Okay. It shouldn't be more than forty-five minutes by Tube. And then it's a five-minute walk from London Bridge station. Or you could get a taxi, if you're feeling flush. Can you make ten o'clock tomorrow morning?"

"Yes, I can—I'm sure I can. What do I need to bring?"

"Just yourself, Spencer."

"But—uh—surely he doesn't want to see me just for a chat?"

"Well, put it this way. I work for a recruitment agency that specialises in placements in the media sector. He's a legend in the newspaper business who is always on the lookout for fresh young talent. He'd rather go through the professional channels than approach you directly, so that's why I'm calling you and doing him this favour. After that? Well, I think you're smart enough to join the dots, don't you?"

"I'll be there. Ten tomorrow. In fact, I'll get there fifteen minutes before. Can you send the details to my personal email account? Do I need to wear a suit? Does he—?"

"Spencer, relax," said Madeleine, chuckling again "You've already done the hard part by getting his attention. Just relax tomorrow and be yourself. Okay?"

"Yes, yes. Okay. Thank you so much, Madeleine You've absolutely made my day."

"I'm glad. Now give me your mobile phone number and I'll text the details."

Spencer rattled off his number, and they both waited until the information pinged onto his phone.

"All the best for tomorrow, Spencer. And just a small piece of advice. Ed is not a fan of Muriel Moresby, not a fan at all. I don't know exactly what happened, but I think they came to blows a while ago. I don't know how you feel about her, but I would steer clear of singing her praises. Are you okay with that?"

"Oh, heavens. More than fine. You really don't have to worry about that."

Madeleine laughed aloud this time.

"Okay, then. You've got my personal number now. Will you give me a call and let me know how it went?"

"I will. And thank you again."

When Spencer ended the call, he threw himself back in his chair and sat staring at his phone for a full five minutes. Already anxiousness had begun to fill his stomach. Questions crowded his head. How had Ed found his way to Spencer's portfolio? Had somebody told him to take a look? Someone like Marshall? More than anything, he wanted to call Marshall and hear his voice, even if he hadn't been the one. But then who else? And did Madeleine mean that Ed was already preparing to offer Spencer a job? A real job, at the *National* goddamn *Herald*?

After tilting his head to the ceiling and taking a deep, steadying breath, he looked around at his colleagues in the almost empty office. None of them realised the world had just shifted on its axis for him. Spencer wanted to run into Bev's office and tell her the news, but knowing she was busy, decided to send her a message and promise to get in touch with her after the interview. He also phoned Kim to let her know he would be working from home the next day.

* * * *

That evening, still pumped up with nervous excitement, he tried in vain to calm himself. Three times he considered calling Marshall's number but backed down each time. What if Marshall hadn't been the one who had talked to Ed? Although if not, then who? And what if he had decided to get back with Hollingbroke? Spencer didn't want any upset tainting his upbeat mood.

Eventually he settled for a long hot bath and tried to relax, still unable to concentrate on anything but Marshall. Finally he let the inevitable happen, and used the fingers of one hand to stimulate himself while using the other to jerk himself to a shuddering climax. The release and diversion seemed to do the trick, and he managed to calm down.

Once dressed in sweats, he pulled a frozen meal of Thai chicken curry from his freezer and, while waiting for the microwave to do its job, tried watching television.

When his front doorbell sounded at eight, he put down his plate and leapt off the sofa, only to see a bunch of young kids dressed in scarves and bobble hats — with two grown-ups behind — standing ready and holding out hymn sheets. The Christmas season had already begun. Scooping up three one-pound coins and some leftover candies from Halloween, he bounced down the stairs. He tried to smile through a cute but painful rendition of *Ding Dong Merrily on High*, where the chorus of Gloria sounded a little like a kindle of kittens on a runaway rollercoaster.

Racing back upstairs to the warmth of his flat, he settled into the detective drama on the television and had just finished his meal when the doorbell sounded again.

Another group of carollers stood outside. This time, he released a heavy sigh and considered ignoring them. Except he didn't want to jinx his run of luck by being miserly. Once again he scooped up coins and sweets. When he opened the front door, a group of adult singers greeted him, and their version of *O Holy Night* was well-rehearsed with beautiful harmonies. People stopped on the street and came out of shops to listen. Luckily, Spencer had his wallet in his pocket and, at the end of the performance, handed over a crisp ten-pound note.

Coming back to his apartment, still smiling to himself, he went to his bedroom and scanned the clothes in his wardrobe, wondering what to wear for his interview. Would his usual combination of shirt and bow tie come across as too flamboyant? But then he remembered that Madeleine had told him to be himself, so he pulled out his cobalt blue suit, white shirt, and electric blue bow tie, and hung everything on the back of the wardrobe door, ready for the morning. Just after he had brought out his matching brown shoes and belt, the doorbell sounded again.

"What the fuck."

Three sets of carol singers in one night? Too much. This time, he ignored the caller. Very carefully, he placed the accessories onto his bedside cabinet and sat on the side of the bed, just as the doorbell sounded again.

Beep. Beep. Bip-bip-bip. Beep. Beep. Beeeeeeeeeeeeep.

Either somebody urgently needed to get his attention or they were trying to contact him by morse code. He jumped up from the bed to check the video display, still unsure whether he wanted people to know he was at home. However, this time, the person whose nose almost pressed into the camera was instantly familiar.

"Hi, Darcy."

"Are you going to open this fucking door or not?"

"Coming."

As soon as Spencer unlocked the front door, Darcy rushed past him without a word and began to hurry up the staircase.

"You'd better have something to fucking drink," she said as she thumped up the stairs as though wearing heavy Dr Martens.

"Lovely to see you, too, Darcy."

"Fuck off."

Inside the flat, Spencer went straight to the fridge and pulled out a bottle of pinot grigio. Gino's wife had left the wine when she had volunteered to cat-sit for Spencer the night of the aborted Bangladeshi meal. All the while, Darcy stood next to him, making him feel slightly uncomfortable. Before handing one of the tumblers to her, he had a quick sip to make sure the wine was still fresh.

Darcy grabbed the glass tumbler and swallowed a mouthful. When she thumped the glass down on the countertop, Spencer jumped.

"Something you probably don't know, Spencer. Joseph 'Joey' Hollingbroke used to be a client of mine. I was the one who succeeded in getting him the audition and negotiating the original gig on *Waterloo Lane*. Ungrateful little shit. Typical of some of these soap stars, as soon as they gain popularity, they want bigger and better. Eventually Joey got bored with the show and wanted to break into Hollywood, and I didn't have the connections. So he fired me. What many don't realise is that films are a whole different ball game. Some make the transition. More become casualties along the way. Joey never really made the grade. All he picked up was a coke habit. Now he's pretty much doing anything that comes his way just to stay in the public eye. I'm ashamed to say that I encouraged his relationship with Marshall. Not because of any publicity, you understand, but because I thought they would be good for each other, that Marshall would be a calming influence. Fucked that one up big time, didn't I? All I succeeded in doing was making Marshall miserable. And then you come along."

"Darcy, I'm—"

"No. You don't get to speak yet. I need you to hear me out, Spencer. Marshall has no idea I'm here. Consider this an intervention. Because I get the impression you're both waiting for the other one to reach out—"

"I did call him, Darcy. A number of times but—"

"I know, I know. I am fully aware of what happened at the curry house. And then radio silence while Joey manipulated him again, playing on his sympathies. Every time Marshall seems to get back on an even keel, there Joey is, entering stage left to fuck with him."

"Joey looked terrible. Looked as though he was on something—"

"Two years ago, maybe. But he's been clean and sober since. The only thing he's addicted to is publicity. But he's really good at acting the victim, playing the role of the desperate ex-boyfriend. And poor Marshall still buys it, every *fucking* time."

The smile. Spencer remembered Hollingbroke smiling at him at the restaurant. Had everything else that evening been a performance, too? Apparently so.

"Anyway, I need you to sit down for me. Now," she said, and waited until he had plopped down on the sofa before joining him and pulling out her smartphone. "Yes, I know you're in a cave here. But I recorded this onto my phone yesterday, a message from my answering machine. Seems like he's okay to say these things to me, when he should really be saying them to you. Now will you please shut up and listen."

Darcy pressed a finger on the screen and placed the phone on his coffee table.

"...the thing is, I really like him, Darce," came Marshall's deep baritone, with a vulnerability in his voice that made Spencer's heart squeeze. "And I'm in trouble right now, because I don't know how to tell him. I've already let him down a couple of times, and I'm not sure I deserve another chance. But he's different. Every time he walks into the room, I feel lighter. I feel as though there's somebody in this world who sees the real me, someone who's on my side. And I honestly don't believe I've ever had that before, not with anyone. You know me, I give all or nothing, and I fear my heart has already decided—but that I've already lost him. I know things are difficult because I'm constantly in the public eye, and have to spend time away often in dangerous places, and even when I'm back, I'm buried in work for weeks on end in the studio I know that if we do spend time in public together, I'm going to get recognised and he will, by association become recognised, too. And I'm not sure it's even fair to ask him to suffer the kind of invasion of privacy that comes with celebrity. I know I never asked for it for myself, but in the whole grand scheme of things, Darce I hope Spencer realises that I'm just an ordinary man first. And famous last."

Famous last.

Spencer's eyes burned. Nobody had even talked about him that way before. And in that moment, he knew he had never given up on Marshall, knew he owed him a second chance.

"Is he at home?" asked Spencer quietly.

"Are you going to call him?"

"No. I want to go and see him."

"Now?" asked Darcy, her eyes wide.

"Yes, right now."

"Fuck my sexy slingbacks. He's so right about you Come on, I'll give you a lift. And on the way there, I'll let you have his address and the front-door code. After that, you're on your own. But I'll alert the doorman that you're coming. That'll get you all the way up to his front door. How does that sound?"

"Perfect."

"The rest is in your hands."

"Let's go."

"Hang on. Before we go, do you need to bring anything? You know, just in case—?"

Spencer remembered his interview. Did he dare bring his suit with him? Or would that be presumptuous? But then again, he was owed a sleepover. Maybe he needed to take a chance. He jotted something down on a notepad sitting on the coffee table.

"Can you do me a favour?"

"I thought I already was. What do you need?"

"I'm going to pack a bag with work clothes. But can you nip to the coffee shop along the way? There's something I need you to get for me."

Darcy snatched the piece of paper from his hand and let out a huff.

"Honestly, the things I do. I'll see you downstairs at the car in five."

"You're a star."

"Yeah. And don't you fucking forget it."

Chapter Sixteen

Darcy's driver pulled the Mercedes up outside a stylish Victorian terraced block of flats down a road between Kensington Park and South Kensington Underground station. Spencer yanked the black hoodie over his head and climbed out into the freezing night. As he made his way up the three stone stairs to the double doors of brass and glass, his overnight carryall and suit holder over his shoulder, his anxiousness grew. But before he had a chance to key in the door code Darcy had given him, the door buzzed loudly. When he looked around, a grinning Darcy waved at him from the back seat of the car, her phone clamped to her ear, before turning and giving the driver instructions to drive on.

Spencer pushed the heavy door and entered the overly bright foyer. Ornate antique sofas upholstered in gold and brown stripes sat stiffly opposite a mirrored wall, while all around white pedestals housed slender black onyx vases filled with arrangements of white lilies. The concierge met Spencer along the hallway and led him over to the waist-high reception desk.

"Sir, I'll need to check your bag before activating the lift. Would you mind?"

Although a little puzzled, Spencer did as asked and allowed the older man to rummage through his clothes. He wondered absently if the concierge had acted as a buffer between what must have been the recent spate of press members trying to gain access, or whether other residents insisted on this kind of security. In less than a minute, the man had finished.

"Fifth floor, sir," he said, activating a button from his seat hidden behind the reception desk. "Lift's at the end on your left. When you come out on the fifth, turn right and go to the far end."

"Does he know I'm here?"

"Not unless someone called him," said the man with a knowing grin. "And I had my instructions from her ladyship out there not to breathe a word."

Spencer grinned at the 'ladyship' reference, of Darcy being somebody who needed to be obeyed. That much he was beginning to understand. But she was also somebody to have on your side.

Stepping out into the corridor on the fifth floor – the top floor – he noticed the opulent theme continued. At the end of the hall stood only one door. Spencer dropped his bag, taking a deep breath before ringing the doorbell. While he waited for an answer, he bent down to unzip his bag's side pocket and pull out the brown paper bag. Just as he was zipping the gear back up, a voice came from behind the door.

"Who is it?"

Marshall's voice sounded strained and guarded. Of course, he might still be cautious about opening the door to uninvited guests, especially if he thought the paparazzi might confront him.

"Hi, Marshall. Sorry, I should have called ahead. It's me, Spence—"

The door flew open and Spencer, still kneeling, was confronted with a pair of black trousers and beautiful bare feet. As Spencer straightened, Marshall's mouth dropped open in surprise. He looked as though he had not long arrived home, still in a crisp white shirt with the sleeves rolled up and collar undone. Spencer had never seen him lost for words but enjoyed the moment.

"Delivery for Mr Highlander," said Spencer, grinning broadly and holding out a brown paper bag. "Chocolate croissants. Apparently his new favourite. Consider these a peace—"

Before Spencer had a chance to finish, Marshall had scooped him up into his arms and pulled him close, his arms tightening around him, his head thrust against Spencer's neck.

"Spencer," he murmured in his ear. "I thought I'd lost you."

Spencer put his arms around Marshall and tightened the embrace, inhaling the man. Both hung on like that for a long moment, Spencer's feet almost off the ground. After a second, Spencer felt one of Marshall's hands caress his back and land on his backside, squeezing gently. With Marshall's body crushed against his own, Spencer's heart began to race, blood flowing straight to his cock.

"Marshall," whispered Spencer, barely able to breathe. "Hate to spoil the moment, but you're crushing my croissants."

Marshall began to chuckle and loosened his grip, allowing Spencer to regain his feet.

"What's with the holdall? Are you moving in?"

"That's my work suit and clothes. Am I being presumptuous this time?" said Spencer, peering hopefully at Marshall. "Or is that going to be okay?"

"As if you need to ask," said Marshall, reaching down and taking the bag. "Follow me."

Along a short, blue Oriental-carpeted corridor, Marshall's apartment opened into a spacious lounge. Three matching sofas in soft shades of light and dark blue surrounded a predominantly white marble fireplace with gold flecks. A large flatscreen television fixed to the wall showed a news channel. All the walls, curtains, cushions and vases followed a blue-and-white theme. Everything sat perfectly in place. Even the large paintings of ships and seascapes complemented the colour scheme, and Spencer felt as though he had just walked into an interior design set befitting an edition of *Collective*.

"Do you rent this place?"

"Sort of," said Marshall, reaching for the remote on the gold-topped coffee table and silencing the programme. Only the pink mug on the table and the various newspapers strewn across one settee implied someone in residence.

"Furnished?" asked Spencer.

"Yes," said Marshall with a chuckle, dropping Spencer's holdall and suit holder onto one sofa. "Why do you ask?"

"Because, if you don't mind me saying — and even though the place is classy and toasty-warm — the décor's a little cold. Doesn't match what I know about you. I would have expected at the very least wooden bookcases stuffed with all manner of literary classics, biographies and journals. And maybe photos and souvenirs scattered around from your travels. Although, in all honesty, I don't know you that well —'

"You tagged me perfectly, actually," said Marshall, who had already begun laughing as Spencer talked Grinning still, he sat down and patted the seat cushion next to him. "You've just described the living room in my house outside Cambridge. The truth is that my father owns this place and has asked me to stay here while he's looking for a buyer. I usually spend my evenings here after work and there's no point in personalising the space. And, yes, you're quite right. It is a little cold and formal — a lot like my father. But now you're here maybe you could help me warm the place up."

Spencer didn't hesitate. After dropping the brown bag onto the coffee table, he unzipped and removed his hoodie before hurrying across the room to stand over a seated Marshall. Lowering himself down so that his knees went either side of Marshall's waist, Spencer squeezed his arms along the back of the sofa behind Marshall's neck and brought their foreheads together. Warm hands clamped onto and caressed Spencer's backside.

"I've missed you," said Spencer, staring into fathomless brown eyes.

"I'm so sorry, Spencer, I —"

"No," said Spencer, placing a forefinger over Marshall's lips. "No apologies. Not in words, anyway. If you've missed me, too, you can show me how much."

They had only kissed a couple of times before, and only tentatively, but the memories had been scorched into Spencer's brain. This time neither held back. Hunger met hunger, lips pressing together, mouths opening and tongues dancing to an urgent rhythm.

Deep inside Marshall, a groan erupted, and his arms tightened around Spencer's waist, pulling him closer. Their bodies moulded together, Spencer's knees crushed into the back of the couch, not that he cared because his solid hard-on collided with Marshall's equally stiff and substantial cock. Spencer removed one of his hands from around Marshall's neck and reached between them, rubbing his palm the length of Marshall's erection and receiving a deep growl in reply.

"Spencer, I need you," Marshall whispered hoarsely.

"That's kind of why I'm here."

"Tell me what you want."

"I want you inside me."

Marshall breathed out a hot, relieved sigh into Spencer's neckline.

"Thank God. Hang onto my neck."

Spencer did as asked and Marshall rose from the sofa carrying him. Spencer couldn't help letting out a small yelp of delight as they crossed the room and entered through a doorway. Just inside, Marshall leant forward and lowered Spencer gently onto a huge mattress. When Spencer turned his head, he saw a mound of plush pillows and throw cushions aligned perfectly at the headboard. But his attention came straight back when hands began expertly pulling down his sweatpants and underwear. Cool air invaded his midsection — but not for long. Marshall had lowered himself down between Spencer's legs and now eyed his erection with feral hunger.

"God, Spencer. Every single thing about you is beautiful."

Spencer pulled his top off completely, before dragging a pillow over and placing the soft fabric under his head so he could watch Marshall take him apart. Every action, every moment of concentration — when Marshall maintained eye contact while caressing him — had Spencer's heart racing with desire and other parts of his body catching up to respond.

Hot kisses and breath on Spencer's genitals had his cock straining with anticipation, gooseflesh springing up on his arms and legs, but the subsequent tongue smoothing wetly up the underside of his shaft brought him very close to orgasm.

"No," he heard himself say.

Marshall stopped and appeared adorably startled.

"I'm stark naked," said Spencer, stating the obvious. "And you're dressed like you're ready for a game of poker."

"I don't play poker — "

"Can you lose some of the clothes, maybe?"

With a humoured shake of the head, Marshall rose carefully from the carpet and stood over Spencer. Already the pronounced bulge in his trousers had Spencer's mouth watering. Far better than any erotic dream Spencer could have imagined, Marshall began to undress. First he removed his belt, slowly, purposefully, dropping the item onto the floor, the celebrated news correspondent far sexier than a professional stripper. Then began the unclasping of his shirt, button by delicious button, revealing his well-defined, hairy chest. With the shirttails lifted out, Spencer's eyes were drawn to the treasure trail of hair leading down from Marshall's chest, disappearing beneath the waistline, pointing the way to future promise. Once Marshall had dropped the shirt to the floor, he moved his hands to the trouser button before unzipping the fly and slowly, very slowly, easing down his clothing. Spencer held his breath, watching as Marshall smoothed the fabric down, inch by inch, revealing the beginnings of a mound of dark pubic hair. Still with his hungry gaze on Spencer, who could have sworn he had stopped breathing, Marshall slid his trousers and underpants farther down until his thick uncut cock sprang into view, bobbing a couple of times. Even when Marshall had stepped out of the trousers, revealing his thick muscular thighs, and gravity had stopped the bouncing, Marshall's cock repeatedly twitched, probably in anticipation of having Spencer laid out before him.

Without a word, he dropped back between Spencer's legs, this time eliciting a groan from Spencer when his large hands landed at the top of either thigh, massaging gently, and his warm, moist mouth swallowed Spencer's cock. Spencer squeezed his eyes shut, lost in sensory overload, and his heart almost stopped when he felt the fingers of one of Marshall's hands smooth into his crack. Instantly, when one fingertip probed inside, the groan became a whimper.

Both mouth and fingers withdrew, leaving Spencer empty, and he was about to open his eyes when he heard a drawer slide open and shut. After a sharp snapping sound, Marshall's mouth returned to work on his erection with a vengeance, and a lube-covered finger returned to loosen him up. A couple of times he squirmed in spasms on the bed, one hand grabbing a mound of the duvet cover, the other tugging on Marshall's hair as the expert mouth continued dismantling him and the probing finger finally reaching the pot of gold inside, causing him to arch his back.

Soon after, his barely held together restraint dissolved, a disembodied groan of ecstasy issuing from him, his body surrendering to the powerful orgasm that ripped through him. Electricity lit up every nerve-ending, his body shuddering at the intensity, as Marshall swallowed everything he had, turning his bones to liquid.

As he lay back panting, black spots floating across his eyes, a shadow moved over him, a hot mouth clamping hungrily onto his own as the mattress continued to shake. Warm liquid landed on his stomach and chest from Marshall's own orgasm, the kiss becoming a deep guttural moan, sexy as hell. Marshall collapsed heavily next to him.

Both lay panting for a few moments. Spencer enjoying the way his body gradually came down from a high he had rarely experienced. Once he heard Marshall's breath calm beside him, he turned to speak.

"Wow."

"Good?" asked an amused Marshall.

"Incredible. How about you?"

"Better than anything I'd imagined," said Marshall, turning his head in Spencer's direction. "And I have a pretty good imagination when it comes to you."

Spencer warmed inside at hearing that Marshall had dreamt about them being together.

"But I thought we were going to—" began Spencer.

"You're not going anywhere tonight, are you? We've got all evening, Spence. But I thought maybe we could have a breather first."

"In which case, I might need a multivitamin. If later is going to be anywhere near as good as that."

"Later is going to be much better," said Marshall, grinning and nuzzling Spencer's ear. "Much, much better."

"Better make that a defibrillator then."

Marshall laughed aloud before rolling over and kissing Spencer. After that, he leant across and plucked some conveniently placed tissues from the bedside cabinet and cleaned Spencer up as best he could. When he fell back, they lay there both lost in thought, staring up at the ceiling.

"Darcy dropped me here tonight," said Spencer eventually.

"I'd guessed as much. She's the only one I talked to about the two of us."

"She really cares about you."

"I know. I put too much on her. But she knows how much I like you."

"She played me the message you left on her phone."

"Oh no, she didn't. I'm so sorry —"

"Don't you *dare* apologise. It was the kick up the bum I needed to get up the guts to come over here. As soon as I heard what you said, everything suddenly made sense."

Marshall turned to him and smiled, then pushed his arm beneath Spencer's neck before leaning forward to kiss him. Spencer loved the intimacy, the proximity and warmth of Marshall's body. He noticed Marshall thinking as he rested his head back on the pillow and stared into the air above them.

"Joe was playing me at the restaurant. On the way to his parents' place in the Uber, he suddenly announced he felt fine and could we ask the driver to come here instead. I was so furious for wrecking what was otherwise turning out to be a perfect evening. I'm so sorry, Spencer. I feel as though I'm constantly weighing you down with my baggage. And I fell for his bullshit again. But honestly, it wouldn't have been the first time I'd rushed him to emergency or taken him to rehab for an intervention."

Spencer had already guessed as much but felt validated to have had his suspicions confirmed. Marshall's ex was trouble, and Spencer would be more cautious if ever he ran into him again.

"What did you do in the end?"

"I made the driver take us to his parents' place in Chelmsford. He became crazy, of course. He's used to getting his own way. But I was just as furious by then. Fortunately it wasn't late and his parents were up. We had a long chat together, all of us, well into the early hours. I got Joey to admit the lies written in the paper about us both. His parents are decent folk. Oddly enough, it was his father who talked about me taking out a restraining order on Joe, after I'd explained him barging into the restaurant. Joe couldn't believe what he was hearing from his own father's mouth, but the man meant every word. I didn't take one out, in case you're asking, and despite Darcy calling me a soft-hearted fool."

"Why didn't you call me?"

Marshall looked away then, clearly pained.

"I should have. But I had a moment of doubt, wondering if I was putting too much on you. Thought I'd give you a few days or a week of calm without all my bullshit. I genuinely was busy, but I still should have called. And then I saw that freebie newspaper with you kissing another man at Blake's party and I told myself I was being a fool, that you'd moved on. Told myself I should let you live your life."

"Well, just so you know, that guy is called Nile. He's the cousin of a work colleague and although he's a friend, there's nothing between us. And the kiss was an experiment he instigated, to see if there could be anything between us. I never told Nile this, but it felt like getting kissed by my grandmother. Besides, as I hope you can tell from my appearance tonight, I still have unrequited amorous feelings concerning a sexy news correspondent I met recently."

"You do?"

"I do. Although that was a good start."

"Wait here," said Marshall, jumping from the bed, his tight backside heading for the bedroom door. A few moments later he returned, unashamedly naked with a tub of ice cream and a spoon. When he neared the bed, he turned the label to face Spencer.

"Strawberry cheesecake," said Spencer, sitting cross-legged as Marshall joined him and did the same. "Were you expecting me?"

"Let's just say I hoped you might be here one day. And after your enthusiastic recommendation, I thought I'd give the flavour a go. But with you being here now, it seems only proper that I feed you a spoonful or two."

"You're really making things up to me, aren't you?"

Marshall removed the lid, then ripped the plastic cover from the inside. Whenever Spencer bought the ice cream, the top would be off within minutes of him bringing the carton home, and probably half the tub would have been devoured by now. As promised, Marshall fed him first, a small taste, and Spencer let out a suitably wanton moan of pleasure. Marshall simply stared at him.

"Would you have preferred this to a blow job?"

Spencer stared back, horrified, ice cream still on his tongue.

"Are you serious? No way. Although this makes for a nice carnal dessert course."

Marshall poked his tongue at a dab of ice cream still on the spoon but pulled a face.

"Mmm, no. Too sweet for me. Honestly, if pushed I'd skip the dessert buffet and go straight to the savoury stuff, like the cold cuts and selection of cheeses."

Spence remembered Marshall had said the same thing before but wasn't about to let him off the hook.

"Heathen!"

Marshall laughed aloud and handed the spoon and tub to Spencer, leaning in to kiss him and dip his tongue in Spencer's mouth. When he pulled his head away, he was still grinning as he nodded and reached across to wipe something from the side of Spencer's mouth with his thumb.

"Although, I must say, the ice cream tastes much better from inside your mouth. Maybe it's an acquired taste."

The kiss fuelled something inside Spencer, and, placing the carton down onto the bedside cabinet, he leant forward and brought their mouths together again. Instead of pulling back, he deepened the kiss, allowing their tongues to dance and warm each other, while his icy hands cradled Marshall's face. Moments later, Marshall's fingers traced the bare contours of Spencer's chest, making him shiver, especially where the thumbs brushed over his collarbone and down across his nipples. Unexpectedly, Marshall pulled his hot mouth away.

"Sorry, my hands are cold —"

Spencer pushed Marshall's right hand down between his legs, in an attempt to warm the fingers. Marshall's eyes opened wide before his lips met Spencer's. Marshall's breath deepened and his generous cock took notice, already beginning to rise from its slumber. After a few moments, Marshall withdrew his fingers and pushed Spencer down onto the bedclothes. Once again their mouths crushed together, Marshall instigating a hungry embrace, his hand smoothing into the many creases of Spencer's body. This time around, Spencer had been so immersed in the sensation, in the writhe of their bodies, that he gasped aloud when a new coat of cooling lube pressed into him. Marshall's intention became clear, switching to a couple of fingers to loosen him up, gently but firmly twisting and probing before adding another, all the while maintaining the eager kissing until Spencer felt ready to come unglued.

"Now, Marshall," he said, pulling his mouth away. "Please."

Marshall needed no more encouragement. Kneeling over Spencer, his eyes dark with lust, his cock straining erect, he slicked some lube onto his shaft before rolling on a condom and adding more. Without losing eye contact, he grabbed a pillow, lifted Spencer's legs and placed the soft cushion beneath his lower back. With that, he fell forward until his face hovered over Spencer's. Without asking for permission, Marshall crushed their mouths together and at the same moment the tip of his cock touched Spencer's hole. Pushing firmly but still in control, Marshall began to enter him, to stretch him, a little painfully at first, but expertly taking his time, listening to Spencer's body.

"That's all of me," said Marshall. "Now tell me what you want?"

"I think you can probably work that one out," said Spencer, a sheen of sweat on his brow.

"Right at this moment, if you could have anything in the world from me, Spence, tell me what that would — "

Spencer's patience gave out.

"Stop teasing me! I want *you*. I just want *you*. Please. *Now*."

With a grunt, Marshall began the slow writhing dance of bodies. Spencer found the pain and pressure subsiding, replaced by a slow build of pleasure. Marshall moved purposely slowly, too carefully, until Spencer wrapped his legs around his lower back and began to push against him, encouraging him and wanting more.

Inevitably — and far too soon — his body began the delicious but irreversible headlong rush towards orgasm. Marshall drove into him, exactly where he needed him, wanted him, until he grabbed for his own cock and pulled a couple of times, issuing a wanton moan as his muscles clenched tightly, his legs wrapping firmly around Marshall as he spurted warm liquid onto his chest and stomach. And as the muscled strength in his legs subsided along with his twice-spent body, he felt Marshall thrusting erratically and shuddering on top of him, felt sure he sensed the condom inside him filling with warmth.

Spencer blinked his eyes, blissed out and sublime, unable to move. He barely noticed Marshall rise from the bed and disappear for a moment before returning with a warm damp cloth and dry towel. Spencer opened his eyes again to watch as Marshall gently cleaned him then lay back down again, their heads touching on the bedclothes. Spencer reached down to knit his fingers with Marshall's.

"Hey, I've got an interview tomorrow with Ed Coleman, editor-in-chief of the *National Herald*. Did you happen to have anything to do with that?"

"I'm not going to lie. We met up last week about some other things and I might have mentioned you. But just so you know, someone else already put him onto you. He likes your work, Spence, and he's been meaning to contact you, but I think I might have given him the nudge he needed."

Someone else had recommended him? Spencer wondered who else knew about his work and also knew Ed.

"Well, anyway, thank you for that. I'm seeing him at ten tomorrow. What's he like?"

Marshall admired Ed, who he described as a no-nonsense, hard-working journalist, someone who had made his way to the top in an undeniably tough and cut-throat industry. Marshall talked about hotspots around the world they had visited together, adding anecdotes of their time in the field.

"By the way, I need to leave very early tomorrow morning for a prior commitment. Hope you understand?"

"Of course," said Spencer, staring up at the ceiling. He had been hoping they might have breakfast together before he headed for his interview. "That's fine."

"Oh, heavens, Spencer," said Marshall, pulling Spencer into his arms. "You think I wouldn't rather be here with you? Of course I would. But I'm helping pack and deliver food parcels and Christmas presents for the homeless, something we do every Christmas. It's a UK-based charitable organisation I've supported for many years. But we're having to do it in shifts this year and I happen to have picked the early morning shift. Originally they said they only needed my face as an ambassador, but I prefer to get stuck in and help with the heavy lifting, so to speak. What they're doing is vital, especially this year with the virus taking away a lot of people's livelihoods. We're not the only country in the world where the number of homeless has risen at a time of year when people should be preparing to celebrate the festive season with their families and loved ones. So I want to help where I can. What I'm doing is a drop in the ocean, but I like to think that every tiny bit helps."

"Now I feel dreadful. If I didn't have an interview to stress over, I'd join you."

"Tell you what," said Marshall. "Come back here tomorrow night and I'll cook you dinner. I'd like to hear about your interview. And I want to pamper you for a change. Deal?"

"Definitely. I'll head home after the interview, feed her ladyship, and pack a bag. What time shall I come back?"

"Six too early?"

Spencer leaned in and kissed Marshall.

"Six is perfect."

Chapter Seventeen

The second time Spencer awoke he was alone.

Much earlier that morning, he had sensed Marshall trying to slip quietly out of bed, but the man had not been able to resist leaning over and kissing a bleary, half-awake Spencer. After which, they'd made out until Marshall had pushed his body gently away and insisted he go back to sleep and wake refreshed for his interview. At first Spencer had complained, wanting to spend the precious few morning moments in the shower with Marshall — until being reminded that they would be together again later that evening.

Right now, everything in Marshall's huge bed felt soft and comfortable and excessive. He pulled one of the fine cotton pillows from the other side of the bed and pressed his face into the softness, the scent of Marshall still lingering in the fabric. Certain parts of his body ached, but not in an unpleasant way. If Marshall had remained in bed with him, he would have happily instigated another round of lovemaking. Pushing the pillow away, he stretched his arms out across the mattress and grinned at the ceiling before pulling his knees up to his chest.

Rather than lying naked, overthinking things, he swung his legs to the side of the mattress and sat up. After pushing his hands through his hair, he noticed the blurry outline of a blue Post-It note stuck to the bedside clock. He snatched up his glasses and read the words.

Morning, Sleepyhead. Follow the Post-It trail. Next stop, kitchen.

Spencer laughed softly to himself. Even though the clock read seven-thirty, and he felt sure no house staff would enter the apartment without knocking, he pulled on a pair of track pants and a white tee before jumping onto the carpeted floor.

In the kitchen, he spied a yellow note affixed to an impressive stainless steel coffee machine, not dissimilar to his parents' new purchase. Beneath the spout sat an empty white mug with the red logo of a news television channel.

Press the caffè latte button and wait. Next stop, living room.

After doing as instructed and waiting as the machine churned to life, he peered around Marshall's kitchen. Brand-new appliances filled a room more spacious than Spencer's living room. With a shake of his head, he wondered how many of the devices ever got used. When the machine began to slow, and the smell of coffee reached his nose, he let out an involuntary carnal moan and grabbed the mug.

With the vessel beneath his nose, he ambled into the living room. There on the coffee table a plastic covering sat over a dinner plate with a Post-It, this time in pink, stuck to the top.

Eat me. Next stop bathroom.

Beneath the plastic covering, Spencer found one of the chocolate croissants and some freshly cut fruit — watermelon, honeydew melon, orange, mango, and pineapple slices. Not unexpectedly, a pile of the day's newspapers sat on the sofa, already scanned by the looks of the ruffled front pages. Spencer plonked himself down, grinning at the little windows into Marshall's life, into his daily routine. While enjoying the light breakfast, he flicked through the papers, noticing Marshall had ordered pretty much all the dailies. With pleasure, he dug out the *National Herald* so he could swot up on the paper's main stories before his meeting. After reading from cover to cover, then checking messages on his phone — none from Marshall — he yawned into the morning and headed for the bathroom.

There, hanging from the door of a bathroom wardrobe, he found his freshly pressed suit and shirt. Marshall had even brought his socks, underwear and newly shined shoes into the room and placed them on a wicker bench. Two green Post-Its were pinned to the jacket pocket.

Suit, shirt and shoes ready. Rock the interview. Enjoy the shower and use anything you want. Fresh towel left out for you. Next stop second bedroom.

By the time he had finished his shower and dressed, checking himself in the mirror to assess his suitability and deciding he looked as good as he ever would, he returned to the kitchen to refill his coffee cup. While the coffee brewed, he headed to the spare bedroom, which appeared made up but empty. This time an orange note sat on the duvet cover.

Unless my mother stays, this room rarely gets used. But I'm giving you the virtual tour anyway. Now go and be fabulous like I know you can be. MJHx

Smiling to himself in the hall mirror, and feeling happy at what he saw, he made sure he had everything before closing the apartment door behind him. Downstairs, as the lift door opened, a new, younger concierge smiled a welcome then went back to working on his computer. On his way to the door, Spencer plucked out his phone and used the map app to find his way to the nearest Tube station.

Leaving at eight-thirty, he knew he could be at the newspaper offices at just after nine, find a nearby coffee shop and hang out until around nine-forty. That way, when he turned up at the reception ten minutes early, he wouldn't seem too desperate and more importantly, would not be late. Had he been like Bev, he would have left everything to the last minute, trusted there would be no delays or obstructions, and — not in Bev's case, of course — he would have turned up not only a sweaty wreck but a bag of jangling nerves. In his book, the extra time and caution was simply a fallback in case things did not go to plan.

As he marched along the road towards Herald Towers, his phone began to ring.

"Squirrel," said Bev, her cheerful voice instantly putting a smile on his face. "Good luck today, baby. Tried to call you yesterday night but I got your voicemail, so I guess you were at home. How are you feeling?"

"Terrified."

"Do you want me to courier you a Valium?"

Spencer laughed aloud.

"Do people actually do that kind of thing?" he asked.

"All the time."

"Thanks anyway, but I'll manage. And I'll let you know how it goes later."

"Are you coming in afterwards?"

"No, I have the day off today —" Right then, his phone buzzed with another call. Marshall. "Bev, can I call you back? Marshall's on the other —"

"Speak to you later. Break a leg."

Spencer thumbed the button for the new call.

"Marsh. How's it going?"

"This manual work thing is entirely overrated. We haven't stopped packing boxes and loading them into vans all morning and we're only just stopping for a cuppa."

"Poor you. But keep in mind the good you're doing. I bet there aren't many in your profession who would roll up their sleeves and muck in. I'm proud of you."

"Thank you, Spence."

Spencer could tell from Marshall's tone that he appreciated the compliment.

"More importantly, how are you doing?" asked Marshall.

"Nervous. But I'm about to hit the coffee shop."

"You didn't get coffee this morning?"

"During my guided Post-It tour of your apartment, you mean? Yes, I did get coffee. But I'm very early and it'll give me time to settle down and calm my nerves. Thanks for ironing my suit and shirt, by the way."

"All part of the service. You can make it up to me later. Hey, I'm phoning to ask what you fancy for dinner tonight. Any thoughts?"

"Many. But I'm in public and most them are pretty indecent, so best not to say them out loud. But, just so you know, one of them involves that easy chair you have in the corner of your bedroom—"

"Uh, Spence," came Marshall's lowered voice. "I'm sitting here with a group of volunteers, people I don't know. And I have to stand up and carry on working in five minutes, so could you maybe save the lurid descriptions—"

Spencer burst out laughing.

"Sorry. I'm really sorry, Marsh," said Spencer, still chuckling. "I should have realised. As for tonight. Your choice of takeout. Although not South Asian, please."

"Takeout? Who said anything about takeout? I'm cooking at home for you tonight. See you at six. Are you still heading home first?"

"I'd planned to. Why?"

"Pick up another change of clothing. I'm driving tomorrow, so I'll drop you into work."

Spencer had visited Herald Towers a couple of times over the years. The first three floors constituted a vast shopping mall with a large cinema complex on the third floor, and shops and restaurants scattered around the other two. Being in the Tier Two restriction zone, the area was considered high alert for the coronavirus, and he expected most shops to be closed for the day. Luckily enough, he found an open coffee shop inside the ground floor, probably catering to office staff. Although he couldn't sit in the premises, he still purchased a takeaway coffee, then went outside the building and found a small concrete garden area with wooden seating.

After checking messages, he brought up a browser and mugged up on basics about the newspaper group, such as how they employed around three to four thousand people globally. By comparison, Muriel's Blackmore Group had at most seventy to eighty staff. Estimated daily circulation figures for the *National Herald* came in at just under one and a half million, which did not include online subscriptions. Blackmore Group, a wholly different beast with primarily monthly publications, had a circulation of under two hundred thousand. Not that a person could fairly compare like for like.

After what seemed like an eternity, he finished his coffee, waited in the newspaper reception area, and stared at the neat row of clocks above the familiar newspaper logo, announcing the time in five different time zones.

Through a glass dividing wall, Spencer observed Ed Coleman finishing up on his computer. He could not even hazard a guess as to the man's age. Sporting a grey ginger comb-over, combined with being overweight, Ed appeared younger than someone in his fifties, but then Spencer had never been good at guessing people's ages. On the surface the man's whole face appeared to be a perpetual frown as he glared at his monitor, from the troughs across his forehead, the fixed furrowed brow, the deep parentheses around his mouth to the stubbornly neutral mouth giving nothing away. And he typed brutally with only the forefingers of each hand as though he were trying to kill some annoying insect running across his keyboard.

When Spencer was eventually ushered in, Ed relaxed and looked up, his face transforming into a smile.

"Mr Wyrrell. Thanks for coming in at such short notice."

Spencer liked him from the first words out of his mouth — an unapologetic cockney.

"My pleasure. And you can call me Spencer, if that's easier."

"Sounds good. Why don't you begin by telling me about the work you do at Blackmore."

Spencer had been prepared and talked up his role, making sure he explained about recently stepping into his boss' shoes following her departure. After Spencer answered a few questions as briefly as possible, and asked a few, Ed seemed satisfied and changed tack.

"I suppose what I should have asked was whether you actually read the *Herald*?"

"From cover to cover. And I'm not just saying that because I'm sitting here. If you check your records you'll find I've had four letters published in your reader's section over the years. Without sounding too sycophantic, I'd say the *Herald* is my daily of choice."

"Favourite parts?"

"The editorials. I'm Jonathan Mycroft's number-one fan."

Spencer went on to dissect the daily version, which he knew by heart. He knew enough about the industry to understand how different newspapers appealed to their readers, what kind of front pages demanded attention. But he also knew Ed would need to have a handle on each of the sections and how they attempted to provide something for everyone.

"And I love the *Sunday Herald* the best, mostly because I get a quiet day to read from cover to cover, but also because there's the arts and literature section—"

"You read the arts and lit reviews?"

"Are you serious? Avidly."

"Good to know someone does," said Ed, with a chuckle.

"It's the first thing I turn to in the Sunday supplement, for the book, film, and theatre reviews. Especially theatre, which I love. People often think reviews are simply a reviewer's personal opinion about a production, which, in fairness, is what they generally are. But a true theatre review is created to guide somebody who is considering seeing a play, to give them background and substance. Things like an outline of the plot, the historical setting, cultural significance, and relevance, and about some of the characters. Criticism should form only a small part of the review and, in my opinion, be wholly substantiated. I read a review at the weekend in another newspaper—yes, I read other papers, too—of the stage version of *The Right Side of the Family*. Have you read the book?"

"Why don't you tell me about it?"

Spencer couldn't tell if Ed was humouring him, but he didn't mind because he loved the novel, had read the novel at least three times.

"Well, I was excited to read the review and find out how the story was being staged. *The Right Side of the Family* is set in the eighties, long before I was born, a fictional story about a highly respected Conservative MP in Margaret Thatcher's cabinet whose son dies in a boating accident during his last year at Cambridge.

While the MP pulls a few strings with the local police and eventually resorts to using a private investigator to find out more, he discovers that his son had been in a clandestine gay relationship with a Pakistani national, a freshman in the same college. This happens during the era when AIDS really came to the fore in the UK. The discovery rocks the family and, at the funeral, where immediate family members have been ordered to bury the truth, the secret pretty much tears them apart. It's a cutting insight into British middle-class attitudes of the time and the hypocrisy surrounding family, race, and sexuality."

"Sounds like a laugh a minute."

"Anyway, the reviewer in this other daily dove straight in and made a big deal about the performances of the actors—he didn't seem to like them at all—but made no reference to the plot, the background, or the main characters from the original work. If I hadn't read the book, I'd have been left wondering what the play was actually about. To be perfectly honest, reading the piece felt more like listening to the rants of a bad-tempered reviewer with an axe to grind, essentially warning potential theatregoers away from the performance rather than trying to enlighten them. And I don't know about you, but when a reviewer tells me not to do something without a valid reason or justification, I'm likely to do exactly the opposite."

Spencer explained that when he read something like that, he guessed the critic's only consideration was self-interest, in getting readers to admire his or her writing. He was often left wondering if the person had been slighted at some point in time by one of the cast members or someone in the production team. Moreover, he questioned whether anyone critiqued the critic and his or her body of work to see if there was any method or rationale behind their reviewing, or if they regularly panned public works because in doing so they knew the uninitiated public would be more likely to read their articles.

As a writer himself, he wanted people to connect with what he wrote, know he had truly researched the topic and that they could trust his viewpoint and integrity as a writer. Maybe, he said, that might seem a little naïve because he understood that the newspaper's main concern was selling news.

Ed sat listening the whole time, without comment, smiling at Spencer's explanation. When Spencer finished speaking, Ed nodded once before speaking.

"If I were to take off me editor-in-chief hat for a mo', I'd tell you honestly the arts and lit section don't exactly float my boat. I'm more a current affairs and sports bloke. Not that I don't appreciate what they do, but I leave all the artsy stuff to my executive editor. I'm a believer in playing to strengths and mine are national and international news, and sports."

"You sound like my dad."

"Yeah, how about your folks? What papers do they read?"

"My parents?" asked Spencer, wondering what was behind the question.

"I only ask 'cause in most surveys we find kids tend to continue to read the same papers as their parents into adulthood. Did your parents influence your reading habits?"

Spencer laughed at the question.

"Mum and Dad are at opposite poles of the political spectrum, and both love their newspapers. Our house is always filled with every daily imaginable. Dad spent his whole life in the police force and his affiliation has always been with the Conservative Party. Even today he speaks with reverence about Maggie Thatcher. You can probably guess which papers he reads. Mum, for most of her working life, worked for the NHS, and is a Labour party supporter through and through. She idolised Tony Benn, loved listening to him speaking, but I know she also admired Cherie Booth, Tony Blaire's wife, when New Labour led the country. My parents have a healthy respect for each other's political opinions, always listening to each other, even if they don't always agree. I heard recently that my mother consented to joining the local Conservative Club in Bournemouth just to keep my dad happy. Although, if I know her, she probably agreed to do so just to cause mayhem from within."

Ed surprised Spencer by tilting back his head and guffawing into the air. Funny how those small revelations, idiosyncrasies about his parents he rarely explored with anyone, about just how well they worked together, made him love them even more. After a moment, Ed thumped the palms of both hands on his desk.

"Okay, look," he said, once he'd settled back. "Let's not beat around the bush. I like you and I like what I've read of yours. I've no idea why you've been wasting your time in the fluff market but it's good you've kept your editing skills tuned. More importantly, you come highly recommended by some people I hold in high regard, and let me tell you, there ain't many in the world. So I'm going to go out on a limb here and offer you a starting position as an assistant reporter. We have a vacancy open right now. You'd be helping our senior team to begin with but I'm sure you'll soon step into your own. I don't know what they're paying you at Blackmore, but I'm sure we can better anything they're offering. And you'll get all the perks, too. Does any of that sound of interest?"

"Very much so."

"Marion at reception will get you to fill out a form with your details and we'll email the offer to you. What's your notice period?"

"One month."

"Brilliant. If we can get something out to you by the end of next week — our recruitment team is a little hard-pushed right now what with people being out — and as long as everything adds up, we can get you on board mid-January. That would work perfectly for us. One question, though. Are you okay to let Muriel Moresby know — only if you decide to accept the formal offer — or would you prefer me to phone her on your behalf? I'm happy to do that as a matter of professional courtesy, even though me and Moresby are not otherwise on polite speaking terms — "

"No!" said Spencer, a little vehemently, then more calmly. "No, I want to tell her myself. I definitely want that pleasure."

"Oh, I see," said Ed, smirking. "Not a fan either? I'm guessing you're not one of those in her famous little clique of favourites?"

"If her clique is the sun, then think of me as Pluto."

Once again Ed rolled his chair back and laughed at the ceiling.

"Right. Enough. Get out! I've got work to do. Marion will sort you out. Reckon you're going to fit in perfectly around here, Spencer. Now go and have a great Christmas."

"You too, Ed. And thanks for the opportunity. I reckon we've both made a good choice here today."

After completing the personal details form, Spencer walked out of the office with a spring in his step. For the first time in as long as he could remember, he didn't need a starship engineer to beam him anywhere.

Chapter Eighteen

Winter daylight had gone to bed by the time Spencer called Marshall from the road leading to his South Kensington apartment. Two minutes out of the Tube station and his ears had turned blue from the cold. As instructed, he had been home to pack a bag, given Tiger some pampering and plenty of food, then made his way to Marshall's place. On the Tube he had tried calling Bev a couple of times, but on each occasion the call had gone straight to her voice message. For a change, Marshall was the one person in his life answering his calls.

"Hello, you," came the warm voice in his ear, much needed on that sub-zero night.

"I'm about five minutes away."

"Perfect. I'm just warming a couple of mince pies and mulling wine. Should help to warm your cockles on this frozen night before the main course. Are you okay with that?"

"Can you hear my mind working overtime trying to think of a suitably salacious retort to having my cockles warmed by you? But honestly, all I can really think about right now is getting some life back in my cold, numb hands and feet. And that sounds like just the job. I'll see you in five."

"See you in five. Looking forward to hearing all about your day."

Spencer didn't want to overthink what it meant when the concierge buzzed him in before he had even reached the front the door. Or the fact he greeted him in the overheated reception by name, Mr Wyrrell, with a genuinely friendly smile, told him he didn't need to check his bag this time and that Mr Highlander was expecting him. He had only been there once, the day before, but already everything felt familiar. When he stepped out of the lift on the fifth floor, the door to Marshall's apartment stood slightly ajar. Spencer pushed his way in, closed the door behind him, and called out a welcome.

"In the kitchen, Spence," came Marshall's voice, as a waft of something amazing assaulted his nose and made his mouth water. "I'm reducing the red wine jus. Put your bag in the bedroom, kick your shoes off, then come and join me."

When Spencer entered the bedroom to drop his bag and remove his coat and shoes, he noticed a couple of things. Since the morning, the bed had been remade immaculately, all the throw cushions and pillows now arranged meticulously back in place. On the corner of the bed, Marshall had left a pack of cat treats for Spencer's princess, a small gesture that made him smile. And on the far bedside cabinet, now in full bold view, sat a pack of condoms and a tube of lubricant. Spencer's grin grew wider in the confidence of knowing that later on in the evening they would be enjoying each other's bodies.

In the kitchen, pungent garlic, onion and other indistinguishable but equally delicious odours filled the air, along with Christmas music blasting from a standalone speaker. Installed at the stove, Marshall — wearing a pair of navy chinos, a light blue polo shirt and a white kitchen apron — swayed his hips along to Slade's ancient Christmas classic, *Merry Xmas Everybody*. Without making a sound, Spencer crept up behind him and pressed his body into the back of Marshall's, his arms snaking around his waist, matching his dance movements. Even with the strong smells of cooking in the air, Marshall's skin smelled of a mix of lavender and pine. With Spencer's cheek resting against Marshall's upper back, he felt a deep chuckle rumble through Marshall.

"I don't care if the world is falling to pieces," sighed Spencer. "I love this time of year."

"You're a big old softie at heart, aren't you?" said Marshall, pivoting his upper body around until he could tip his face down to smile at Spencer.

"What if I am?"

"Absolutely fine by me," said Marshall, kissing him softly but quickly pulling away. "Oh my goodness, you really are cold, aren't you? Like kissing an icicle."

"But I'm feeling better by the second."

Spencer continued to hug Marshall from behind for a few moments until Marshall pushed him gently away using his backside.

"Go on with you, before I burn something. There's a mince pie and a glass mug of mulled wine on the table. Can you top me up from the saucepan?"

Spencer grinned when he saw the mess Marshall was making, the tabletop covered with dirty saucepans and used bowls. Spencer's father cooked enthusiastically on the rare occasion the inspiration took him, but his mother always complained about him using every bowl, every utensil and saucepan in the kitchen. Marshall, by comparison, appeared to be oblivious of the mess he was creating around him. Spencer poured them both mulled wine then placed a glass next to Marshall. After taking a sip of his own, he went over to the kitchen sink and began cleaning up.

"You don't have to do that. You're my guest."

"I need something to do. Anyway, if I don't clear space on the table, there will be nowhere to eat, will there?"

"You know, there's a dishwasher to your left. Just rinse the pans and put them inside. I'll do a full load later, once we've eaten."

They worked around each other seamlessly, Marshall busying himself at the cooker and Spencer clearing up after him as well as laying the table for their dinner. While working, he took a sip of the wine, but found the mix a little too potent and aromatic, and, when Marshall wasn't looking, poured the contents into the sink.

"How did the day go, Marsh? With the charity?"

"Really well, but the job was unbelievably strenuous. Manual labour is not something my body is used to. Thank goodness I have that huge bath, which I filled with spa salts and hot water, and wallowed in for an hour to try to get out all the kinks in my muscles."

"Sounds like you deserved it.

"And how about you? You got the job," said Marshall, his back still to Spencer. The final words had been a statement, not a question.

"Did Ed phone you?" asked Spencer, frozen to the spot.

"No, but I can tell by the spring in your step. And the fact that he'd be an idiot not to employ you while he had the chance. It went well then?"

"I think so. We had a good chat and he ended up offering me a position starting in the new year. Once I've received the offer, I'll need to talk to Muriel."

"That will be fun."

"You know, funnily enough, I'm looking forward to it. Next year's going to be interesting, what with moving out of my place and starting a new job. And I can't help thinking the latter is, in a large part, thanks to you."

"Hey, don't sell yourself short. You're a talent, Spence, and you're finally getting what you deserve."

On the tip of Spencer's tongue was to ask whether that included Marshall, but he decided not to tempt fate.

"Hey, I haven't asked you," said Spencer. "How are things coming along with our client Christmas event? I can't believe it's a week from tomorrow. Is everything okay at your end?"

"You haven't spoken to your friend Beverley?"

"She's not been answering my calls. But, in her defence, she seems to have been swamped with work recently."

"I imagine she's been tied up working on the event. Probably spending time going through the finer details with the events company, Virtually Integrated Parties. From what I understand though, it sounds pretty impressive. VIP will be operating all the technical aspects from their own premises, but the control centre will be in your office where Beverley's team will be coordinating everything. That way, if clients need to phone in with questions or problems, they just use your standard office numbers. From our end, everything's arranged. Our studio's providing the live link-up for the formal interview. Muriel's publicist provided us with the sanctioned set of questions at the weekend. I'll use those as a guideline, as always, and then just run with my gut instinct."

"Just hearing you say that makes me want to tune in. Sounds like a lot of work is going on behind the scenes"

"At the moment, I only know about the interview I'm conducting. But Darcy tells me email invitations with links have been sent out to clients, because she's one of them. They've been requested to dial in from seven-thirty, thirty minutes before the show begins. Of course, you know Darcy. She immediately clicked on the hyperlink, never does what she's told, and the link took her to a Blackmore Magazine Group Client Party holding page telling her she had arrived too early. And that's pretty much all I know. Where are you going to be?"

"I was hoping to be with you in the studio. But I suppose that will be up to Muriel."

"Well, I already told her I wanted you with me as this was your brainchild. And I think Darcy is going to insist, too, so I don't think there will be any issue. I just wondered if you would prefer to support Bev."

"Honestly, I think I'd only be in the way," said Spencer, the thought of talking to Muriel unsettling his stomach momentarily. He decided to change tack. "Goodness, whatever you're concocting smells delicious."

"I'm almost finished. How do you take your steak?"

"Medium, please."

"Me, too. Good choice."

"How did you know I wasn't a vegetarian?"

"We haven't known each other long but there were clues, Spence. The extra pepperoni pizza we ate together and the beef and onion pies from the coffee shop kind of gave you away."

"You did tell me you were observant. And thank you. It's not often I have people cook for me. I'd have eaten anything you put in front of me."

Marshall froze momentarily and became pensive.

"You make a good point though. We don't really know much about each other, do we?"

"Isn't that the best part? The fact that we're getting to know each other from scratch?"

Marshall laughed as he forked their steaks onto plates.

"You're right. I really am enjoying this, Spence. Go and take a seat."

And once again, as he did what he was told, Spencer's heart did a little happy dance at hearing his nickname. Marshall finished putting fried onions, mushrooms, sautéed potatoes and grilled tomatoes onto their plates, then brought them to the table.

"In the three small bowls there's Dijon mustard, creamy horseradish, and some of my mother's homemade English mustard, which should come with a health warning. It's like eating a mix of raw chillies, wasabi and molten lava. What do you want to drink, beer or wine?" he asked, putting a plate down in front of Spencer.

"What are you having?" asked Spencer.

"I was going to have a glass of red."

"Can I join you?"

"Of course."

They sat eating in companionable silence, Spencer tucking into the excellent meal. Marshall had uncorked a French claret, the exact name of which — beautifully pronounced by Marshall-- had already escaped Spencer, but he agreed that the wine complemented the meal perfectly. Eventually Marshall began talking about his limited cooking skills, explaining how he had learnt them by carefully spying on his grandmother as he sat at her kitchen table. Ten minutes into the meal, the intercom phone on Marshall's kitchen wall rang. For a second he appeared annoyed, in two minds whether to answer the call, but then he shook his head and went to the video display.

"Good evening, Finn."

"Good evening, Mr Highlander," came the voice from the device. "There's a Ms Corbett here to see you. Said you would know what it's about. I told her you had a guest. Shall I send her up?"

"No, It's okay, Finn. She's just dropping something off. Get her to take a seat in the foyer and I'll come right down."

"Righty-ho, sir."

Marshall replaced the phone then began removing his apron.

"It's Lindy, one of our television assistants. She's dropping off some important papers for me to sign. I'll only be a second. Help yourself to more vegetables."

With Marshall gone, Spencer got up from the table and cleared the rest of the used pans from the stove, bringing the pot of vegetables over to the table. Marshall returned not long after, carrying a large manilla envelope, which he tossed onto the countertop.

Spencer wanted to ask what the call was about, but thought he'd wait for Marshall to offer an explanation.

Marshall took his seat and returned to his food without a word.

"Do you want to heat that up?" asked Spencer.

"No, it's still warm enough," said Marshall with a chuckle. "When I'm overseas, working to tight deadlines, we tend to live on lukewarm food. That's what the papers are about, actually. Some legal stuff I needed to sign and get out of the way for my final overseas assignment of the year. Those are my copies in the envelope."

"Oh yes?" asked Spencer as Marshall forked a chuck of steak into his mouth then sipped his wine. "Where to this time?"

"Monday after the client event, a small team of us are flying to Eastern Europe to cover the presidential inauguration in Kryszytonia. Chairman Tobias Karimov is being sworn in as the new president, and he's not only a good friend of mine — I've interviewed him twice on my programme — but something of an inspiration. His reforms are going to transform their country. Because of the state of things globally, few governments are sending dignitaries to the ceremony, but I've been invited to attend personally to witness and record the historic moment for posterity with others from the press corps."

"Sounds like a great honour."

"It is, it really is. And probably my last overseas assignment for many months. My other news is that I'm pushing back on my workload. If my recent run-in with the press has taught me anything, it's that I need to put more time aside for myself. The latest series of *Say What You Mean* doesn't air until March, and another series isn't scheduled at the moment. However Darcy's been working her magic behind the scenes, and the television network has commissioned a new programme with me as the host and voiceover, shooting in the third quarter, where we examine landmark legal cases in Britain and around the world and how they changed the course of history. They want to call the show *Marshall's Law*, and it means I'll be spending a lot more time here at home."

Spencer really liked hearing Marshall would be around more, but simply smiled down at his plate. Spencer took his time eating, waiting until they finished their meals together. Both sat back in their seats, grinning at each other.

"What are you doing for Christmas?" asked Spencer, taking a sip of the wine.

"Good question. I'd usually stay with Mother, but it looks as though she's going to remain in the Bahamas. Can't say I blame her, with everything going on here. As for me, I don't know. I'll probably invite myself to Darcy's—"

"Come with me," blurted Spencer. "To my family's place in Bournemouth. I'm heading down on Christmas Eve. I mean, only if you want to. But I'd love to have you there. The whole family would."

"They know about me?" asked Marshall, more humoured than curious.

"No, but I'm sure they'd be fine. In fact, I *know* they would. But only if you want to come. I don't mean to pressure you into—"

"Hey, slow down a bit. I would be honoured to join you, Spence. I want to meet the lovely people who brought such a sweet guy into the world."

"Seriously? You'd really come?"

"Would we have separate bedrooms?"

"No. I mean, I could check to see if Garrett's going to be there. But I've got my own decent-sized bedroom with a double bed. Well, it's not as huge as yours, but it's comfortable and, at a squeeze, big enough for the two of us."

"This is sounding better by the minute."

"And my father promised to cook the turkey this year, in case you're worried about food poisoning."

Marshall laughed out loud.

"Okay. Well, I really need to meet this poor, put-upon mother of yours whose culinary skills you're constantly disparaging. And I would be more than happy if you introduced me as your new boyfriend."

"Really?" asked Spencer, his eyes wide.

"Yeah, really," answered Marshall, his fond gaze dropping to Spencer's mouth before his smile slipped away and he met Spencer's gaze. "Just one thing."

Spencer fully expected him to beg off the idea.

"I'm volunteering again on Christmas Eve. Only in the afternoon, from three until six. Me and some others are helping to work a soup kitchen around the back of King's Cross station. Would it be okay if we leave after that?"

"Depends," said Spencer, hoping he didn't sound as relieved as he felt. "Can I come and help? In the background, of course?"

"Of course you can. The more the merrier."

"In which case, you've got a deal. I'm not sure what kind of rail service they'll be running Christmas week, but there's bound to be a fast train from Waterloo after six, which will get us in at around eight-thirty. I can't wait to see my parents' faces."

"Or, instead of relying on trains, I might give my Beamer sports a run, if you don't have any objections. There's a secure municipal car park not far from the kitchens."

Spencer couldn't help grinning. Christmas was going to be the best ever. Although he didn't know much about cars, he could only imagine the look on Garrett's face when he not only turned up with Marshall, but in a BMW sports car.

"Are you tired?" asked Marshall, breaking the silence.

"No," said Spencer through the grin he could not keep from his face. "Not in the slightest. But I'm definitely ready for bed. Can I grab a quick shower first?"

Marshall's fond gaze and smile transformed into something different altogether. Instantly, he pushed his chair away from the table and stood up.

"Tell you what. You shower while I tidy up in here. I'll meet you in the bedroom in ten minutes, where your dessert will be waiting. Deal?"

"Sounds curious," said Spencer, rising from the table. "And what exactly is for dessert?"

Spencer's eyes opened wide when *the* Marshall Highlander pushed a hand into his waistband, down inside the front of his own trousers, and squeezed.

"Me, Spence. Dessert is me."

Chapter Nineteen

Lying awake next to a deeply sleeping Marshall, Spencer realised the truth. He was in deep trouble. Not only had he fallen totally in love with this man, but he had done so weeks ago. Everything added up. Because since then, he had felt different, lighter, more optimistic about his future. Too many good things had happened to him, so surely somewhere in the universe, cosmic forces had combined and aligned to pave the way. And the all-encompassing wave of affection that had overcome him the evening before, walking into the kitchen and seeing a relaxed Marshall jigging his hips to a Christmas song at the stove, had confirmed his suspicions beyond any possible doubt.

He had fallen hopelessly in love.

Not the fleeting infatuation he had sampled with Blake, nor the sexual companionship he'd resigned himself to with a few others, but something overwhelming and complete, as though he and Marshall were the missing pieces to a jigsaw puzzle that finally made sense as a beautiful picture.

But as much as the knowledge made him more concrete, grounded and three-dimensional, it also filled him with a foreboding. What if he did something to mess things up? Or what if Marshall didn't feel the same way? His heart might be floating in the stratosphere right now, seeing the moon and the whole glorious world below for the first time in his life, but that was also a long way to fall. Moreover, how did he broach the topic with Marshall? It would destroy him if he confessed his feelings and Marshall didn't feel the same. Maybe it would be best to keep the words to himself until the right time, or in the hope that Marshall might say them first.

After his shower that night, he had walked into the bedroom with just a towel wrapped around his waist, only to find an empty bed—until he'd turned to see Marshall naked in the easy chair, ready and eager, a condom already on his lube-slicked hard-on. Where the old Spencer might have faltered a moment, wondering if he could possibly live up to expectations, not a single moment of doubt had surfaced. Instead, he had walked straight over to Marshall and wrapped himself around his body as if doing so were the most natural thing in the world. That night their lovemaking had cemented what he'd already known, that together they simply *worked*. The night's sessions had been prolonged and effortless, each giving and selfless, each taking time to ensure the other's pleasure. Marshall turned out to be a generous lover, constantly surprising gasps out of Spencer, and only losing his perfect rhythm and control as his own orgasm roared down the runway and took flight.

Spencer leant over to the bedside cabinet, popped on his glasses and checked his phone. Five-forty. He noticed a couple of missed calls from Bev. Not that he would have answered, not if doing so would have meant breaking the magical chemistry of the evening.

With a sigh, he swung his legs over the side of the bed, pulled on track bottoms and took his phone to the kitchen. In pride of place against the kitchen's mirrored splashguard, Marshall's state-of-the-art coffee machine beckoned. He knew himself well enough to know that he would not return to sleep if he drank coffee now. On the other hand, in an hour they would be getting up anyway, so he shoved a mug under the machine's nozzle and pushed the button for a double dose of latte. No gurgling, guzzling noises came from the device, which was as sleek and silent as a Tesla. While he waited, he looked around for a teaspoon, then opened the freezer door and, standing there grinning, helped himself to a couple of teaspoons of ice cream. *Make yourself at home, Spencer*, he said to himself, unable to stop from smiling. Securing the carton back inside the freezer, he collected the mug then perched on a stool and checked messages on his phone.

There was something to be said for having connectivity at home. Spencer fired off a text message to Bev explaining how he had been 'otherwise engaged' then another to his brother telling him to let everyone know that he would be bringing a guest home for Christmas, with details to follow. Midway through he heard a soft thump at the front door and went to check the spyhole. The back of a concierge's uniform moved away and turned into the lift. Spencer opened the door to find a neat stack of newspapers on the outside mat. Without a second thought, he scooped them up and brought them to the kitchen island.

Halfway through the third newspaper and his second coffee, he was engulfed in a hug from behind. Warmth enclosed his whole back, a cool nose poking him beneath the ear.

"You make less noise than my cat," said Spencer as Marshall kissed him hotly beneath the right ear.

"I'm in stealth mode. Why are you up so early? Couldn't sleep?"

Almost mimicking Spencer's earlier movements, Marshall—in only black briefs—moved over to the coffee machine, plucking a mug from a cupboard above before setting the device in motion.

"I slept like a baby, actually. It's just that when I'm awake, I'm fully awake, if you know what I mean?"

"Sadly, I know exactly what you mean," said Marshall, stifling a yawn. "Thanks for fetching the papers. Anything worth looking at?"

Spencer drank in the muscled back, arms and hairy, powerful legs of his lover.

"There is now."

Marshall rotated around and smiled at Spencer. With a small sigh, he picked up his mug and leant back against the countertop, assessing Spencer.

"I could get used to this. To us. I'm usually alone in the mornings."

Spencer didn't want to overthink the remark, so quickly deflected with a joke.

"Whereas I am usually awoken by cat breath."

"Yes, we really ought to remedy that. Should I come for a sleepover with you and the princess tonight?"

"As if you need to ask."

* * * *

Exactly a fortnight before Christmas, the Friday of the client party came around all too quickly. Anticipating being needed, Spencer had managed to get the bulk of his work done before Friday, and whatever was left could wait until the following week. Not that he had needed to bother. Bev appeared to have everything under control, and Spencer had been scratching around for work that morning. As instructed by Marshall — they had not been out of each other's company since the weekend — he had worn a dark ensemble that morning, of black jeans, black shirt, and black-and-white polka dot bow tie, to blend in with the technicians behind the scenes at the television studio. More worryingly, he hadn't heard anything from the *Herald* since the interview and had started to worry until a personal call from Ed the day before had reassured him that something would soon be on its way, just slightly delayed because of staffing issues at the paper.

"Do you need me for anything before I head off?" asked Spencer in the early afternoon to a slightly frazzled Bev. Still dressed impeccably, she clutched a large tablet computer under one arm and had perfected marching between offices.

"Did you get your Covid test results?"

"Yes, Mother. Negative, same as you. I wouldn't be here, otherwise."

One of the stipulations of being present at the studio during the recording was that everyone had to test negative for the coronavirus before being admitted. In an unusual show of collaboration, Muriel had extended the testing to anyone choosing to work in the office rather than from home, even if not involved in the event.

"Then just go," she said, walking backwards away from him. "The driver's waiting for you downstairs. And honestly, there's nothing you can do here. Bugger off to the studio. Suck up to Muriel and his lordship."

Had he been asked to go and suck off Marshall, he might have relished the instruction.

"Yeah," said Spencer, pleased to be dismissed. "You know that's not going to happen."

"Just promise you're not going to rush the stage and announce your resignation," she said, grinning. Spencer looked around at that remark to make sure nobody else had heard, before giving her the stink eye.

"Don't worry," he replied. "I'm not saying a word until I get the offer in my hands."

With a final wave, he made his way out and heaved a sigh of relief as he stood in the lift and the doors closed.

As they opened on the ground floor, a black-suited, black-masked man stood in the foyer holding a sign with Spencer's name. Marshall's doing. He had insisted that Spencer should be driven to the studios, even though Elstree—not more than forty minutes' drive away—was just as easy to get to by train.

Once he had installed himself in the plush black leather seats of the Tesla, he pulled out his phone and texted Marshall to let him know he was on his way, then sent one to Bev to wish her luck. Her true talents had undoubtedly come to the fore this particular year.

Every email invitation for the Blackmore Group Virtual Christmas Party had provided clients with a secure link that allowed them to log into the virtual-conferencing application with a landing page, a snow-covered Blackmore Christmas Village. Different cottages and houses represented the four magazines, and two music halls had various bands playing non-stop music, one modern, another more Christmassy. In the centre of the screen, the town hall held the main event. They even had a library, where people could reference archived copies of magazines. A countdown in the top left-hand corner let clients know when certain crucial events would occur, such as the welcome speech and the primary interview of the Moresbys by Marshall J Highlander, with the promised appearance of some special guests.

With little traffic on the roads, Spencer found himself arriving at the studio in good time and was ushered through by security staff, once he had been issued him with a unique guest identity tag.

"Are you Spencer Wyrrell?" said a youngish woman, who met him as the car door opened. Like others, she was clad in black tee and jeans, and a tell-tale wireless headset.

"I am," said Spencer, caught up in the wonder of the moment.

"Follow me, please. Mr Highlander has been asking for you."

"Has he?" said Spencer, warmed inside.

"Says you have something for him."

"I do?" said Spencer, suddenly worried he had forgotten something.

Inside the cavernous belly of the building, Spencer wanted to stand and take in the scene. He had never seen the inner workings of a real, live studio before. As vast as a warehouse, the building had a few bodies dotted around, dressed in black and almost invisible, busying themselves in the darkened periphery. Free-standing cameras stood idle but would work independently, computer-operated from what he guessed to be a hidden control room. All attention and lighting focused on the small red-covered stage with three modern chairs, adequately spaced apart, one side for Marshall and the other for Muriel and her husband. Either side of a giant screen, equally colossal photographs of the couple on a mocked-up cover of *Collective* had been staged.

"He usually insists on private alone time before a show," continued the woman. "But he's been laughing, joking, and upbeat with everyone today. Puts the team in such a good mood when he's like this."

"Maybe it's because this isn't an officially planned programme," offered Spencer.

"Maybe." she said, grinning. "He's certainly looking forward to running with this new kind of format. I hope he warned you that it's going to be a stop-start affair this afternoon. Can get a little boring for visitors. I'll get you set up with headphones, and if you could just lose the bow tie, you'll blend in perfectly."

Marshall had explained to Spencer how they would run the Moresby interview along the lines of an old UK television show called *This Is Your Life*, and how guests would not appear in person in the studio, but on the large screen.

Leaving the stage behind, he followed the woman and entered the shadowy depths of the studio. Eventually she stopped outside an unmarked black door, lifted one side of her headphones and placed her ear against the surface before rapping her knuckle a couple of times. After turning to him, she opened the door with her shoulder and waved him in.

Marshall sat in a leather chair facing a huge mirror, a towel around his neck. As Spencer entered, he spun the whole seat around towards him. The thin woman standing over him with jet back hair and an ear full of earrings holding a powder brush — clearly the makeup person — jumped back as the chair rotated. A couple of black-T-shirt-wearing staff lounged on an old brown leather sofa.

"Team, this is Spencer," said Marshall, while they all studied him. From their knowing smiles, he had the distinct impression Marshall had been talking about him. Spencer faltered for a moment, unsure of how much people knew about them both.

But Marshall leapt up from his seat, ripped off the towel and moved forward to Spencer. Without hesitating, he placed his hands on either of Spencer's shoulders and planted a kiss on his lips.

"Spencer's my boyfriend," came the words, loud and proud, warming Spencer to the core.

"And now I'm going to need to reapply," said the makeup woman in a stern voice, but grinning nonetheless. "Will you please sit down and hold still, Marshall?"

"Spence, the grumpy prima donna here is Chase. And over there on the settee are Kerry-Anne, our OB producer, and Colm, our cameraman, who are both coming to Kryszytonia with me. We've just been having a briefing to finalise arrangements. Guys, do you think you could give me a few minutes alone with Spence?"

Still grinning, the two on the settee jumped up and headed out. Chase stood back, threw the brush into a bag on the tabletop, then thrust her hands onto her hips.

"Five minutes, Marshall. I still have a lot of work to do and you're on in thirty. So no nookie while I'm gone. Nothing that's going to mess up your hair, anyway."

As soon as Chase had closed the door behind her, Marshall pulled Spencer against his body, their foreheads touching. Spencer savoured a combination of faintly perfumed powder and breath mints.

"Boyfriend?" said Spencer, unable to stop his grin.

"Do you mind?" asked Marshall.

"Are you kidding," answered Spencer, sure his gaze had already answered for him. "Hey, was I supposed to bring something? You told the woman who brought me here that I have something for you."

Marshall chuckled before squeezing a hand down between their bodies, down in between Spencer's legs.

"Yes, and you can give it to me later tonight, after Darcy's."

Spencer chuckled before kissing Marshall, but then pulled his head away, puzzled.

"Darcy's?"

"She's having a private after-show cocktail party tonight. Naturally, you and I are invited. After which we'll head back to yours as agreed, and you can show me just how much you appreciate me doing this gig. Then we'll enjoy a leisurely Saturday morning lying in bed, with whipped cream and marmalade on croissants, pots of fresh coffee and the daily papers. How does that sound?"

"Sounds absolutely perfect."

"How about a preview?"

Spencer had begun to enjoy this needy side of Marshall. He marvelled at how easily they could lose themselves in each other, bodies pressed tightly together, Spencer deepening their kiss and Marshall's hands roaming down his body and clamping tightly onto his backside.

Neither heard the door open.

"Mr Highland — ?"

Even as he came back to earth, Spencer would have recognised that voice anywhere.

Muriel Moresby.

"Yes, Muriel," said Marshall, turning to her but without releasing their embrace. Spencer placed the back of his hand across his mouth, and turned away, unable to stop the grin tugging at his face.

"I — uh — I just wondered if there were any last-minute items we needed to go over. And I wanted to check to see if you'd received the Blackmore hamper, or if there was anything else we could get you."

"No, I think everything is covered. And thank you, Blackmore has certainly gone the extra mile," said Marshall, his arms tightening around Spencer. This time Spencer could not resist turning to look at Muriel. As expected, the usual pinched moue tightened her lips as she met his gaze, but after a moment, she managed to squeeze out a stiff smile.

"Spencer."

"Muriel."

"Looking after our guest?" she asked, the smile at odds with the annoyance in her eyes.

"Doing my best, Muriel."

"Good. Well. Carry on."

As soon as the doorway emptied, Spencer and Marshall dissolved into giggles like teenagers until they returned to their passionate embrace. Moments later, Marshall sighed and pulled his head away, staring into Spencer's eyes.

"Don't ever ask me to hide you, Spence. You're the best thing that's happened to me in years, and I don't care who knows it."

"I'm not — I would never — "

"I just hope you realise how much I — "

"Okay, you two. Time out!" called Chase, standing in the doorway, hands on hips, with the woman who had brought Spencer into the building. "Really sorry, Spence, but I need to work my magic on this man before the show begins. My reputation is on the line here."

Marshall released Spencer but held him at arm's length.

"It's going to be a long afternoon, Spence. A lot of stopping and starting, which can get very boring, very quickly. Darcy suggested you go on to hers early, at around five. We should be done here by around six and the show airs at seven-thirty. The Moresbys have asked me to stay back for an informal drink after the show to watch the half-hour screening. Of course, you're more than welcome to stick around and join me, but Darcy's invite means I've got a legitimate excuse to slip away and join you. And Beverley and Prince will be heading to Darcy's once they've finished."

"I'm happy either way, Marsh."

"Then I think you should head to Darcy's. I'll text her driver, arrange for him to pick you up. Now before I give Chase my full attention, I'll get someone to take you to the sound booth."

* * * *

Marshall had been right. Recording the show turned out to be long and arduous, but far worse for the host and his guests, who had to spend long stretches of silence beneath the hot studio lights. By four-thirty, after the third comfort break, Spencer had almost dropped asleep in the sound booth.

Not that the content had been boring. Marshall had been brilliant, beginning gently with questions around how the Moresbys had met—at the Henley Royal Regatta, a rowing event held annually on the River Thames by the town of Henley-on-Thames, England—then talking about their early life together. Screen guests included Muriel's younger sister, Erica Blackmore, celebrated author and winner of various book awards; ninety-year-old retired General Sir Reginald Cumberland, Lord Moresby's first commanding officer; as well as several other well-known celebrities. Much to everyone's surprise, there was even an appearance by a lesser—but still well-known—member of the royal family.

Everyone had rehearsed anecdotes about one or both of the Moresbys, who'd sat enjoying themselves and occasionally chipping in. At first, Spencer had wondered if the whole section would be as tame as the original *This Is Your Life* show—until Marshall started to ask more pointed questions.

"Many in the publishing world regard your magazines as superficial and frivolous, Mrs Moresby. Eleanor Finnigan at *News Speak*, for example, once referred to *Virago* as 'onanistic tripe'. How do you respond to this kind of criticism from your peers?"

Muriel must have been prepared for this question because she provided a suitably upbeat response, citing some of the celebrated articles her magazines had published over the years and the contemporary inclusion of Killian Pinkerton's column among her successful additions.

Marshall had also singled out Lord Moresby's military career in an era when British strength and influence across the world had all but fizzled out.

"Lord Moresby, not many people are aware that you were a senior officer on active duty aboard the HMS Somerset, a British battleship deployed during the Falklands conflict. Tell us about your memories of that time."

Once again Marshall followed up with some hard-hitting questions about the validity and cost to the nation of the conflict, about the waste of human lives and whether Lord Moresby thought things could have been handled differently by the then incumbent Thatcher government.

"To coin a cliché, Marshall, hindsight is a wonderful thing. Yes, there are things I wish we had taken time to consider more in the moment, such as listening to other nations about extending diplomatic talks before resorting to conflict. I'm sure our present government wishes they had listened more acutely to the advice being doled out to them by South Korean and Italian medical authorities about the seriousness of the current pandemic. And if they had, maybe this country would not be in such a dreadful state right now. But as a nation, we have never been terribly good at listening to other nations, have we?"

Spencer liked Lord Moresby. In conversation he talked openly, candidly and without any apparent hidden agenda. Throughout the interview, the man never became flustered, always pausing to consider the meaning of Marshall's words and always providing a level-headed response, never evading the question. Spencer wondered how he managed to put up with Muriel, but they appeared tight, very much together and on the same wavelength. His mother had a theory that the best partnerships were often between opposites. The Moresbys certainly bore out that theory.

Before the final break, Marshall brought up the Moresbys' recent party, a question that clearly took Muriel by surprise.

"We have both been subject to media scrutiny recently, Muriel. In your case, Blake Moresby, your son, held an illicit engagement party on the grounds of your estate. How much were you aware of what he had planned?"

Muriel managed to answer the question well enough, but as soon as the cameras stopped recording for a break, her face transformed with an annoyance Spencer had personally experienced frequently. She demanded that the question not be included in the main feed. Spencer didn't wait to hear the response, because he took that opportunity to use the restroom and find Marshall. The man himself had been heading Spencer's way, and they met along the passage behind the set.

"I was coming to find you," said Marshall, looking dapper and grinning.

"Ditto. And I'm trying to find where they keep the good coffee."

"You and your coffee. Follow me."

Marshall led them back to a large room set aside, full of people dressed in black—like an after-funeral gathering—and other people taking advantage of the break. Marshall had only a minute to chat over bottled water, happy with how things were going, before one of the staff came to usher him back. Before going, he openly planted a kiss on Spencer's lips as the crew members looked on. As soon as he had gone, Spencer got himself a large latte and a sandwich before finding a space against the wall.

Until someone came to join him.

Ambika, Blake's fiancée. Dressed in pure black, she looked as stylish as he remembered her, wearing designer jeans, a silk blouse and pashmina scarf wrapped around her neck.

"Is Blake here?" asked Spencer, looking around the room.

"He was earlier. His mother asked him to go back to the office, to check on things there. Rather than both of us going — and me getting in the way — he asked me to stay."

Spencer grinned. Blake's bossy presence would undoubtedly please Bev. After sharing a few awkward pleasantries about the weather and how well they felt the show was going, Ambika put her drink down and confronted Spencer.

"How long were you together? You and Blake?"

Spencer almost choked on his coffee and looked away. He floundered for words for a moment, and what to tell her, but then met her sad gaze, deciding she needed to hear the truth.

"Three months. But if it's any consolation, what we had was over almost as soon as it started. This all happened long before he met you. And what we had felt sordid and superficial, if I'm going to be completely honest. Stolen moments at weekends, clandestine hook-ups. Which, honestly, is not my style. I'm surprised he even told you."

"He didn't. I guessed. Both times I met you, at Halloween and then our engagement party, he would always avoid talking about you when I pressed him. And after what happened with my brother, I put two and two together."

"I didn't even know he was into girls when we first met. I'd just started with the company and I was a little starstruck and flattered by the attention."

Ambika smiled sadly but nodded her understanding.

"Do you think I should give him a chance, Spencer?"

"Have you spoken to him? About what happened?"

"Not enough. Everything is so fresh right now. And I wanted to give myself time to process how I felt. We've been treading on eggshells around each other. At the time, he insisted he still loves me and, the truth is I still love him, too. He claims my brother did the instigating, and, with my brother, I can truly believe that. But you know, it still takes two."

"The fundamental question is, knowing what you now know about Blake, can you still accept him? Or has that knowledge become a deal-breaker?"

"I don't know. What do you think I should do?"

Spencer could never accept that kind of arrangement, constantly living in fear of a partner finding comfort in the arms of another.

"I can't answer that for you. You need to do what you feel is the right thing for you. Do you trust him?"

"Ah, now that's the clincher, isn't it? *Do* I trust him?"

"Like I said, nobody can answer that for you."

But Spencer already had his own opinion. Blake cared only for himself. When Spencer had been with Blake, they had never gone out or seen other people. But to go behind Ambika's back at their engagement party and perform sexual favours with a member of her family right under her nose was beyond despicable. How could you trust anybody who would even consider doing something like that? He noticed she had fallen silent, and Spencer felt an overwhelming sense of compassion for her. He liked her, but he meant what he had said, that only she could decide.

"I'm still wondering what bastard snitched on you at the party. I hope you don't think it was me or any of the work people I came with. "

"Of course not," she said, managing a weak smile. "It was one of my aunties. We could only invite a few, and mostly younger family members due to restricted numbers. But the reality is that my extended family is massive. Some people's noses were naturally put out of joint when they didn't get an invite. When one of my idiot cousins who I did invite smuggled their phone in and fired off a couple of photos, this particular aunt—known for causing trouble—got hold of them and forwarded them instantly to friends in the press. They, in turn, called the police. The rest you know."

"Well, if it's any consolation, we had a great time."

"And now you're dating Marshall Highlander, you lucky thing. I saw him kiss you. Absolutely adorable."

Spencer felt his jaw drop. Dating? A month ago he might have denied the claim, but now? Instead he began to smile with pride. He would never refuse Marshall to anyone.

"I have no idea what he sees in me."

"Yes, you do," she said, squeezing his arm. "Doesn't take a woman to see he's smitten. You make the perfect couple. Good for you, Spencer."

"Thank you. And I truly hope you work out what's best for you."

Only as Spencer settled back in the booth for the final half-hour did he realise that both Ambika and Muriel had publicly spied him together with Marshall, and would probably tell Blake what they'd seen.

Not that it mattered, but he wondered how Blake might take the news.

Chapter Twenty

Poor Marshall.

He arrived at Darcy's party much later than expected. Despite being upbeat and chatty, Spencer could tell by the way he continually pinched the bridge of his nose that he was tired. After greeting Spencer and his colleagues, Darcy had whisked him off for an hour to meet various important guests.

By the time he climbed the stairs to Spencer's flat and dropped onto the sofa, he looked thoroughly exhausted. And in between Tiger climbing into his lap and getting the attention she had been craving, and Spencer coming back from the toilet, Marshall had fallen asleep. Spencer managed to get him to the bedroom, undress him and put him to bed, accepting that nothing would happen that night. But how could he be annoyed? Marshall had worked his arse off during the day. Just being in bed together was enough.

Fortunately, the man had woken refreshed and ready for action the next morning. They finally left the apartment for decent coffee – takeaway only – and a stroll just after midday, and spent the whole weekend together with most of that in each other's arms.

* * * *

Wednesday afternoon, Bev perched on the side of Spencer's desk, her enigmatic smile beaming. As usual, she dressed to perfection in a warm burgundy-and-beige trouser suit. She had good reason to be happy, and Spencer could never resist wallowing in her good vibrations. Still riding the high of the virtual Blackmore Christmas client event's success, nothing could shake her upbeat mood, one that seemed as infectious as the coronavirus ravaging the country.

Friday's online interview, which focused mainly on more entertaining aspects of the couple, with a clear emphasis on the magazine's achievements, had been a resounding success. An extended version — something agreed upon with the Moresbys as a part of the arrangement — was being put together under the title *Celebrity Say What You Mean*, a hybrid of Marshall's usual show, and would air between Christmas and New Year. The magazine interview had been written long before and would be published during the week. All in all, Muriel had been so delighted with the results and the positive responses that she had promoted Beverley to Senior Events Manager on the spot. The fact that Evelyn, the previous events manager, had resigned the same morning had absolutely no bearing on the promotion, according to Muriel. On his part, Spencer had heard nothing about getting a bonus for suggesting the arrangement and, quite frankly, had given up caring. More important areas of his life had begun to take flight, a new optimism filling him with every waking morning.

By stark contrast, the rest of the country appeared to be in perpetual confusion about how seriously they should be taking the threat of the virus, with a government—like countless others across the globe—torn between keeping the economy from flatlining and protecting its citizens' health.

"Have you spoken to Muriel yet?" asked Bev quietly, while fiddling with his crystal paperweight. "About the new job?"

The formal offer had been waiting for him on his doormat as he had arrived home from work on Tuesday. That very morning he had phoned precisely two people. Six hours ahead of UTC—one-thirty in the afternoon in his time zone—Marshall had been having lunch with his crew in their hotel in Kryszytonia. He had answered after only two rings, and they had chatted for the whole of Spencer's fifteen-minute walk to the Tube station. Once settled at work, and as promised, he'd phoned Madeleine to tell her the good news.

"You must be clairvoyant. I received the offer last night but she isn't in today. Alice says she might be in tomorrow or Friday. I've asked her to book me a meeting both days."

"And what's the offer like? A good package?"

"It is. From what I can tell."

"What did Marshall say?"

"I haven't had a chance to talk through the details with him. Just the basics. But we're both sure it's fine."

"Do you want me to look, Squirrel? Make sure there are no glaring omissions? You know contracts are one of my things, don't you?"

"Would you do that?"

"As if you need to ask. You're my bestie. Besides, after being rushed off my feet last week, I need something to do right now. Talking of Marshall, how is lover boy?"

"I could ask you the same question about Prince," said Spencer, grinning. "And just for your information, Marshall is most definitely *not* a boy. Not in any sense of the meaning."

"I'll take your word for that. Have you heard from him today?"

"He kept me company over the phone on my walk to the station this morning. But he'll be offline for the rest of the day attending a private function. And Friday's the day of the inauguration ceremony. But he's back at the weekend."

"Bet you can't wait."

He really couldn't. The official event was taking place at midday on Friday, followed straight afterwards by a grand state dinner to which Marshall had been honoured with an invitation. He vowed to fly back Saturday morning, or late Friday night if he could snag a last-minute scheduled flight. Strings of voice messages — Marshall had defaulted to quick and sexy voice snippets from his text app — had kept Spencer on cloud nine, as well as confirming their plans for Marshall to stay at Spencer's flat over the weekend again. They had said goodbye to each other properly in Marshall's apartment as a van waited downstairs to whisk him and his crew off to the airport, and Spencer had almost spoken the words he had been aching to say all weekend. Once again, he'd relented, deciding he needed Marshall's full attention in case things didn't go as expected.

"Are you going to join us for drinks today?" asked Bev, bringing him out of his reverie.

"What? Where? Everything is closed."

"Prince drove his Saab to work today. And he needs cheering up. They cancelled their production of *Treasure Island*, so he has his nights free. Nile phoned him at lunchtime and said he'd found a gay club-pub in St Albans called Smugglers. They're doing this midweek special on house cocktails until ten. St Albans is still in tier one for now and on medium alert. Nobody's around, so we're going to leave at three and meet him there around four for an hour or three. Prince will only drink non-alcoholic drinks, and he's already agreed to drop you back at the Tube station on our way home, if you want to come."

"*Our* way home?"

Bev beamed, pleased with herself.

"You don't miss a trick, do you? I'm staying at Prince's place tonight. You're not the only one loved-up at the moment. So are you in or not?"

Spencer stared at his desk. He had completed most of his work, and any outstanding pieces awaited colleagues' attention before he could finalise them. With Marshall away for the week, what else did he have to do? Head home and feed the cat? Big whoop. Moreover, if Prince had already offered to drop him off, he had no real excuse.

"When do we leave?"

* * * *

Nile met them deep in the Smugglers' club interior, a long room at the back of the main pub. Unlike the few gay clubs Spencer had frequented, the oak-beamed pub in St Albans came across as steadfastly traditional, and Spencer rightly guessed that on most days, when the government allowed, the establishment served anyone who happened to enter through the doors. Only the back hall, with a bouncer on the door collecting a nominal fee and stamping the back of each entrant's hand with a red ink skull and crossbones, separated the main public bar from the well-ordered gay friendly gathering.

Nile had bagged a round table for six near the bar. Togged out in his combination of stylish silk shirt in black and gold, tight-fitting skinny jeans with the legs stopping short to show off his bare ankles, and expensive-looking brown leather loafers, he looked entirely at ease, despite being ogled at by a couple of older men propping up the bar.

"Mate of mine put me onto this place," he said, his grin wide as he greeted each of them, as each removed his or her mask and took a seat. "Good to get out of the house."

"Don't hold your breath," said Prince. "They're already talking about bringing in tighter measures nearer Christmas."

Spencer moved to the seat beside Nile and tried to get the attention of a waiter. Having been included in the little adventure, he felt it only right that he should buy them all a round or two. Prince needed the restroom, so Bev gave Spencer their orders then volunteered to accompany Prince, most likely to make sure some random guy didn't try to accost him.

"Have you spoken to Tommy?" asked Spencer as yet another waiter blanked him.

"Saturday. We talked for two hours. He's missing me badly, and truth is, I'm missing him just as much.

Even sent me dick pics. I tell you, once all this shit is over and he comes back home, we're going to give things another try."

"Finally, Nile comes to his senses."

"Shut up and get me a drink."

"You think I'm not trying? Feels like I'm wearing an invisibility cloak." Spencer noticed Nile flash a smile at one of the servers and nod towards Spencer, which appeared to do the trick. "What are you doing in a gay bar, then, Nile? Shouldn't you be playing the role of the dutiful boyfriend, sitting at home sexting your man?"

"First of all, my phone is in my back pocket, so I can do that from anywhere. Secondly, I'm going batshit crazy stuck indoors. As for the gay bar, there's no harm in window shopping, is there? Hey, don't panic, Spence, but I think your scumbag ex is here."

"Blake?" said Spencer. "Where?"

"I think I saw him getting messy drunk down the end of the bar."

"Oh," said Spencer with a shrug of indifference. "Whatever."

"Okay," said Nile, leaning back and scrutinising Spencer. "Not the reaction I was expecting. What's going on with you?"

"Nothing."

"Liar."

Right on cue, the waiter finally appeared in front of Spencer, who fired off an order of drinks and hot snacks.

"Has Prince told you anything?" asked Spencer once the man had left.

"About you? No. Like what?"

Spencer considered the improbability of Bev saying nothing to Prince about Marshall, so maybe he had been sworn to secrecy. And when a person made Bev a promise, they broke it on pain of death. But Spencer realised he didn't mind people knowing.

"Remember asking if I'd ever kissed someone who made my insides turn to jelly? Like Tommy did for you?"

"You said it was complicated."

"Yes, well. Not so much, anymore. We're seeing each other now."

"Fuck, Spence. Where is he then? Why didn't you bring him with you?"

"He's out of the country right now, on location in Kryszytonia, in Eastern Europe," said Spencer as a tray of drinks appeared in front of them. "Not sure you'd know him, he works as a news correspondent. Marshall High—"

"*Shut the front door!*" said Nile, his mouth dropping open. "Marshall Highlander is your fella?"

"Oh," said Spencer, sliding a bright blue cocktail in front of Nile. "You know who he is, then?"

"Marshall frigging Highlander? Hottest daddy in the northern hemisphere? Do I know who he is?" said Nile, before slapping a palm on the tabletop. "Whoa, Spence, man, you are one dark horse. What's he like? I bet he's really sexy, isn't he? Have you two done the deed? Wait, what am I saying? Of course you have. It's plastered all over your boat race."

"Yes, we're intimate and, yes, he's amazing," said Spencer, who couldn't do anything about the grin that had steadfastly fixed itself onto his face. "If that's what you're asking."

Spencer paid for the drinks then took a swig from his bottle of Pilsner. Openly talking about Marshall with Nile had left him feeling light and giddy.

"You know what?" said Nile, smirking curiously. "I'm beyond impressed, but strangely not surprised. Good on you, mate. Bet your ex, that brother-sucker Blake, is beside himself knowing you've moved on."

"I'm not sure he knows. And honestly, I don't really care."

Nile lifted his glass in the air in a toast with Spencer, who clinked his bottle against the cocktail glass.

"Here's to us both, Spence," said Nile. "Next year is already looking promising."

Spencer couldn't agree more. Not only would he see in the new year looking forward to starting a new job, but he would have Marshall in his life. When Prince and Bev returned from the toilet, Bev looked distinctly pissed off. Spencer handed over her pint of cider, and while she downed a good half, a smirking Prince explained what had happened.

"While she was waiting outside the loo for me — they're really modern and clean, by the way — some bloke came up and asked her if she was my fag hag."

"Do people still use that term?" asked a disgusted Nile. "It's a bit last millennium, isn't it? I thought it had gone out with cargo pants."

"And Crocs," said Spencer, joining in.

"Well, this drunken idiot did. I almost slapped him," said Bev, glaring at Prince. "No offence, darling, but if I was going to be anyone's fag hag — which I am not — then Squirrel would have first refusal."

After laughing together, they sat around chatting amiably. Spencer could almost believe the world outside had returned to normal. He only regretted not having Marshall with them, wondering if his friends would be relaxed around him, but then remembering

Bev meeting him and being completely at ease. At some point, he wanted them all to meet.

Eventually, as they decided on their last round, Spencer excused himself to use the restroom. Prince had been right. Unlike other gay bars he had been to in the past, the toilets were mercifully plush, clean and well-tended. He noted that one upside to the virus was that public places had increased the thoroughness and regularity of cleaning and disinfecting communal areas.

Washing up and pushing his way out of the toilet, he found Blake leaning against a wall outside, the remains of a pint of something amber cradled against his chest. Unusual for him, he appeared a little dishevelled, his gaze as dark as ever but very slightly unhinged.

"There you are," he said, as Spencer approached.

For a moment, Spencer considered walking past and ignoring him. But to do so might seem petty. Besides, Blake had lost any power he previously held over him.

"Here I am. Have you been waiting for me?"

"Maybe." Blake's shoulder slipped slightly on the smooth wall surface.

"Are you drunk?"

"On the contrary. I'm perfectly fine. Better than ever."

If he had been drinking, Blake's speech betrayed no hint of slurring. However, at odds with his words, his usually immaculate hair appeared ruffled, and he had left a collar tip of his blue cotton shirt turned up.

"You look a mess, Blake. I hope someone's taking you home."

"You offering?"

"We've been there and done that, remember? Why don't you call Ambika?"

Blake's face screwed up into a scowl.

"Bitch dumped me."

Spencer nodded and turned his gaze away, not particularly surprised. But he did wonder if anything he'd said to Ambika had influenced her decision.

"Have you ever wondered why I stopped seeing you, Spencer?"

Spencer looked back, surprised by the question.

"Not really."

"Sure you have. Come on, let me have it. I'm a big boy."

Spencer didn't want to have the conversation. When he had talked about water under the bridge, he had meant every word. Spencer had truly moved on.

"I suppose because you got bored."

"You see? Wrong. You have things entirely the wrong way around. The real reason is because I knew you would eventually get bored with me. Even in our short time together, you kept dropping small hints about going out for meals or meeting up with your friends or family. Eventually you would have started suggesting we move in together, build a home together. Maybe even start a family. In that way, you're not unlike Ambika."

"And what's so wrong with that?"

"Nothing!" said Blake, angry and miserable. "There's absolutely nothing wrong with that, not if that's what you want, and something you're confident and unashamed about. And you, Spencer, seem sure about everything. You hide nothing. But I can't live like that. I don't want to be known as the other half of a gay couple—or any couple, come to that. In three years' time my mother will retire and I'll become the face of the Blackmore Group. I'll be the one in demand, getting interviewed on television and having people answer to me. I won't just be Muriel Moresby's son anymore, as I am right now. And when that happens, Spencer, I'll be able to have anything or anyone I want. If and when I do decide to choose someone to stand beside me, it will be a real somebody — well-known, a good-looking face, a social equal. Everything that happens up until that moment is just time passing."

"You can't be serious?"

"Why not? That's when I'll finally get to call the shots."

Spencer lowered his head in disbelief. In all the time they had known each other, those had been the most insightful words Blake had ever spoken. But then, Blake had rarely opened up. To hear that he only cared about himself and the power trip he would inherit from his mother fitted perfectly with the image Spencer had built up of the man. But the truth made Spencer feel sad for him, sorry that even with somebody by his side, Blake would probably live his life with nobody he cared about, and nobody who cared about him.

"Not that you need to worry. Now that you're finally moving on from Blackmore," said Blake, grabbing Spencer's attention.

"Who told you?" asked Spencer, wondering who had betrayed his trust. The last thing he needed was to have Blake bleating to his mother before he'd had a chance to speak to her.

"I have my sources. And don't worry, I've not breathed a word to my mother, or Ms Salvatore over there. Or anyone else, come to that. Your secret's safe. Killian's husband, who is a good friend of mine, told me. I'm the one who got Killian onboard to write the column for *Collective*. Not sure how much you know about him, but although he's a naturally gifted, eloquent vlogger, he's not only mildly dyslexic, but his eyesight's failing. Cameron, his better half, who works as an editor for Tandem House publishers, helps ghostwrite his column. Cameron is the one who reads aloud your comments and suggested edits to Killian. They both adore you, by the way and, without my approval, Cameron went behind my back and recommended you to Ed Coleman at the *Herald*, the one who told me after the deed that you were wasted at Blackmore."

Spencer nodded slowly. Killian's partner, someone Spencer had never met, had seen enough in his work to recommend him to Ed. The thought left him feeling stunned but grateful for the good people in the world.

"In the meantime," continued Blake, pushing away from the wall, "I need a refill. I won't offer you one, because I imagine you need to get back to your nutjobs."

"Are we going to see you in the office tomorrow?"

"Mother asked the same thing. She'll be in. Offered me a lift. "

"And?"

"Maybe," said Blake, his back to Spencer. "Maybe not."

Perhaps he should despise Blake more, but all he could feel at that moment, watching him stumble unsteadily away, was pity. Spencer returned to his group, where he noted Nile several feet away ordering drinks and chatting to a bartender at the bar. Prince sat almost sullenly by Bev's side while she spoke to someone standing over them, a stranger who had his back to Spencer. Only as he got closer did he recognise the profile of Joey Hollingbroke. Prince's eyes landed on Spencer and widened, and he shook his head slightly. Joey, who had clearly noticed, turned around at that moment, an unpleasant smirk on his face.

"Here he is," said Joey, giving Spencer a dismissive once-over. "The man of the moment. Your ears must be burning."

"Joey," said Spencer, deciding he would not be intimidated. "To what do we owe this unexpected pleasure?"

"Saw you over here earlier. Thought you'd like me to come over and say hello."

"Hollingbroke's been telling us all about himself," said Prince, the disdain in his voice plain. "Even though we didn't ask. He seems to have a very high opinion of himself."

Of course, thought Spencer. Bev would have told Prince all about Joey's stunt at the Bangladeshi restaurant and shown him the freebie newspaper's news article about him. Prince would be firmly in Spencer's corner.

"Prince, behave," said Bev, smiling and nudging him, before addressing Joey. "Sorry. My boyfriend never watched your old show, not even the re-runs."

Joey appeared happy to dismiss Bev and Prince and turned his full attention to Spencer.

"How are things going with my Marshall?"

Spencer wanted to tell him that not only was it was none of his business, but Marshall was not his. Prince would have probably done precisely that. Bev even rolled her eyes. Spencer would not give Joey the satisfaction of reacting.

"Things are going extremely well."

"In which case, why is he not here?"

"He has an overseas assignment. We'll see each other Saturday when he gets back."

Joey's gaze hardened. Something in Spencer's last statement had ruffled his feathers, maybe because he was no longer in the loop on Marshall's life and whereabouts.

"I'd watch your back if I were you, mate. Associating with someone like him."

A little voice in Spencer's head wanted to tell Joey not to call him his mate.

"This should be good," said Prince, folding his arms. "Why does my friend need to watch his back around a national treasure like Marshall Highlander?"

"I bet Marshall never told you," said Joey, his attention still on Spencer. "He has a price on his head? You want to be careful you don't end up being collateral damage."

"What?" said Prince, followed by a barked laugh.

"Of course he told me, Joe," said Spencer, straight-faced, deciding not to let Joey get to him. "Along with the traumatising story about his alien abduction, and the time he was almost run over by the ghost of John Wayne on a Harley-Davidson."

Prince tilted his head back and laughed loudly again, this time making Bev and those sitting at nearby tables laugh along, much to Joey's irritation.

"Yeah, I didn't think so," said an unsmiling Joey. "Why don't you ask that useless bitch Darcy if you don't believe me? Marshall has interviewed a number of dodgy personalities during his career, including businessman Roberto Fiorelli, back in 2018, who was alleged to be associated with the mafia and supplying drugs to various European nations. Marshall did his usual job of putting the man on the spot, and stupidly backed him into a corner on live television. Afterwards Fiorelli went apeshit and, if rumours are true, threatened to put a hit out on Marshall. You should be careful getting into any cars with him, or being seen out anywhere in public. Otherwise, as I say, you might end up being caught in the crossfire."

"I'll take my chances."

"Really? You don't come across as a toughie. The bow tie and specs don't exactly scream street smarts."

"Like you, you mean?" said Prince. "Someone who's spent his whole life pretending to be other people? You wouldn't know street smarts if they bit you on the arse."

Spencer noticed Bev pull her glass to her mouth, trying to suppress a laugh, something Joey noticed too and that irritated him even more. Once again he attempted to ignore them and keep his attention fixed on Spencer.

"Don't say you haven't been warned—"

Joey had been about to step into Spencer's space, but Prince sprang up from the table in between them and almost snarled.

"Why don't you fuck off and play with the traffic, has-been."

"Prince!" said Bev, grabbing Prince's arm, shocked but grinning. The words had been enough, though. Joey backed off slowly before turning and heading into the crowded bar.

Spencer had noticed Nile remaining a few feet away, his eyes glued on them, eavesdropping on their conversation. As soon as Joey left, he moved back, handed out drinks and took his seat.

"That guy is such an asshole," said Prince, shaking his head as he glowered at Joey heading off. "Sorry, team, this has to be the last one. Enough excitement for one afternoon. I'm ready to drive back to civilisation."

"*That* was Joey Hollingbroke? Aka Donkey?" said Nile, also watching him go. "False advertising, by all accounts. Rumour has it he's hung like a squirrel. No offence, Spence."

Bev finally burst into fits of giggles she had clearly been holding in. No doubt the alcohol helped, but she seemed to be enjoying the show.

"None taken," said Spencer, grinning at Nile. "How did that nickname come about, anyway? I never watched the series."

"*Waterloo Lane?*" said Bev, getting herself under control. "They had him kitted out in a donkey jacket no matter the weather. In the beginning they wrote him as a simpleminded lad, shouted at by his dad, pushed around by his brothers. Audiences really sympathised and grew to love him — well, the character. And eventually he got to shine with his own monologues. I almost hate to say it, but he wasn't half bad back in the day."

"Now let me get this right, honey." said Nile, his hand on Spencer's shoulder. "Because this is just too delicious not to pass comment on. In one afternoon, you've faced off with the entitled prick, Blake — yes I saw you outside the loo. And now you've been confronted by Donkey, who is your new man's ex?"

"That's about it, yes."

"And they're both dickheads?"

"That is something I can now definitely verify," chipped in Prince.

"Spence, honey, you do know some interesting people, don't you?"

"Strictly speaking, I don't really know Joey," said Spencer, grinning at the gentle ribbing. "But I know what you mean. In my defence, though, I think I'm doing a lot better lately, don't you? In my choice of friends?"

"If you mean us, then *hell* yes," said Prince.

"Fuck, yeah," said Nile, at the same time.

"Come on," said Prince, finishing his cola. "If you want the designated driver to give you a lift home, drink up while I head to the john."

"In which case, we'll both meet you all out front," said Nile. "I also need to use the designer washroom one last time before we head off."

Outside in the car park, Bev and Spencer stood huddled together. Initially the chill evening air provided a refreshing contrast to the bar's muggy warmth, the wind whipping around their legs and promising a night of frost. But in very little time, coldness began to seep into Spencer's bones.

Even after meeting Blake then Joey, Spencer felt in an upbeat mood, the drinks and aimless chatter having relaxed and warmed him through. Before entering the bar, he had texted Marshall to let him know his plan. When he checked now, he had received a simple soundbite in response, requesting he enjoy himself and behave. Somewhat cryptically, Marshall had also quipped about them needing to sit down once he got back and have a chat about a brilliant idea he'd had. His tone sounded upbeat and endearing, nothing to worry about. Spencer thought about calling him once Prince had dropped him back at the Tube station, but realised with the time zone difference, that Marshall would likely be sleeping.

"Thanks for the invite," said Spencer, nudging Bev's shoulder, after noticing her look back at the bar doorway. "I was going to head home for a night in with Tiger. Even with the unscheduled entertainment, I'm so pleased I came out to play with you guys."

"That Joey Hollingbroke truly is a piece of work, isn't he?" she said, with a scowl. "Thinks he's God's gift. I honestly thought Prince was going to lose his temper at one point. What on earth did Marshall see in him?"

"It's a long story best told by Marshall. But let's just say he's a friend of the family."

"Okay, I'll take your word for that. At least Marshall's come to his senses now."

"I think we both lucked out there, Bev. Like you and Prince."

"Yes, he's amazing, you know. We're going to miss having you around at work."

Spencer remembered something that Blake had said.

"And on that note, Muriel's coming into the office tomorrow. Looks like Thursday might be D-Day."

"Well, if you need a coffee afterwards, you know where to find me," said Bev, before staring past Spencer and looking relieved. "Oh, here they are. *Finally.*"

Spencer turned to see Nile and Prince strolling towards them together, a conspiratorial smirk on each of their faces. Funnily enough, the way they moved and grinned, Spencer could see the family resemblance as clear as day.

"Where on earth have you two been?" said Bev, stamping her feet in the tarmac of the car park. "We were about to send in a search party."

"Sorry, boys and girls," said Nile. "My fault. Your Auntie Nile has just been doing a little bit of troublemaking, otherwise known as matchmaking. Don't know about you, but I noticed Blake looked a little lonely, and thought that he and Joey would make the perfect match. So I went over and hooked them up."

"You did not!" said Spencer, his mouth falling open.

"He bloody did," said Prince, impressed and chuckling. "As we left, I peered down the bar and saw the two of them chatting together."

"A match made in hell," said Nile.

"Nile, darling," said Bev, kissing him on the cheek, "you are officially a legend."

"And don't you forget it. Today's lesson, people, is that you do not ever mess with my friends. Let's go."

Chapter Twenty-One

Spencer sat at his desk, staring at his email inbox, picking at small items of work to keep him occupied and psyching himself up for his meeting with Muriel. He knew he ought to be feeling something akin to relief, but anxiousness weighed on the pit of his stomach like too much pepperoni pizza.

The night before, he'd signed and posted the employment contract back to the *Herald* recruitment team. That very morning he had brought a copy of the agreement into work with him, together with the covering offer letter. As soon as he had logged on, he had written, printed, and signed a resignation letter ready to hand to Muriel. The good-luck soundbite he had picked up from Marshall — Spencer had naturally texted him about his impending meeting with Muriel — telling him to be brave, then going into lurid detail about how he planned to reward him on his return, had made Spencer smile all the way to the station. By nine o'clock, he'd had everything ready to go, but he had to hang around until he heard from the woman herself.

Clicking through news channels to pass the time, he came upon a site showing preparations for the presidential inauguratior. in Kryszytonia. The whole square in front of the parliament building had been sectioned off. Three banks of empty seats around rows of seating on the ground faced the stage where the new president wculd be sworn in. Regimented rows of the national flag in blue, gold and ochre hung at regular intervals. Another site showed an ornate hall in the presidential palace where the formal dinner would be held, with an impressively long table of silverware, crystal glasses and elaborate flower arrangements in the national colours, the event catering for at least a sixty.

Right then, Spencer's desk phone rang.

"Morning, Spencer," came Alice's voice. "Muriel asked me to call you about your ten o'clock appointment. She wants to know if it's urgent. Told me to tell you she's extremely busy today. Between you and me, Spencer, I believe she thinks you want to see her about the staff Christmas party."

"It's not about that, Alice. This is about me?"

"I see. And — um — anything you can share?"

"Not really. This matter is personal and a little delicate, if you know what I mean?"

"Of course. Yes. No, I see. Sorry, you know what she's like. Asked me to try and find out before you got here. And she's in one of *those* moods this morning, I'm afraid. Okay, sorry, I'll let her know. Come over just before ten."

Almost exactly a month to the day, Spencer found himself once again seated opposite Muriel, in the chair that sank lower as he sat there. On the last occasion, he had been hoodwinked into taking on Clarissa's responsibilities. Digging his fingernails into the fleshy part of his thighs above each knee, he made sure he would stay focused this time.

"Can we make this quick, Spencer?" said Muriel, snapping down the lid of her laptop. "I've a lot on my plate today and I need to get cracking."

Spencer smiled, settled back and decided to wade in gently.

"The client party went rather well, don't you think? I know it was only last Friday, but I've already heard a lot of positive noises from clients. Particularly about the interview with you and Lord Moresby."

Muriel appeared to relax. No doubt she had heard many good things, but Spencer figured that dishing out a few compliments of his own couldn't do any harm and might even soften the news of his resignation.

"Have you?" she replied, looking out of the window. "That's good to hear. Yes, I've had some lovely messages. I was extremely pleased with the outcome, considering everything. Ms Salvatore did a sterling job. As did Prince, given the amount of time they had to bring everything together."

Spencer didn't expect to get any credit from Muriel but thought someone else ought to.

"Marshall Highlander recommended the company, you know? VIP? Don't you think his involvement not only helped to save the day but took the event to a whole new level?"

Muriel's gaze swung back then. In true Muriel style, she straightened up, pursed her lips and folded her arms.

"Mr Highlander did a very competent job. Apart from asking a few unscheduled and frankly inappropriate questions. Now what is it you wanted, Spencer?"

The moment of truth. He pulled the offer sheet from his inside jacket pocket and passed the paper across the desk. Muriel hesitated a moment before scooping up the letter and reading the contents.

"I'm here to hand in my resignation, Muriel. The *National Herald* has offered me a position at their newspaper. Starting as an assistant reporter."

"I see," she said in her usual haughty, waspish way. Without looking at him, she continued to read the letter. "And you consider this a good career move, do you? Why on earth would you want to jump into the lion's den with these people?"

"Because that's where my passion lies. And where I feel my talents might be recognised and appreciated."

"They will eat you alive," she said, passing the letter back across the desk to him. "Well, if that's your decision, so be it. But I'm afraid you're going to have to work out the full three months' notice —"

"One month."

Finally he managed to get her attention. She glowered at him as though he had just slapped her across the face.

"I beg your pardon?"

"My notice period is one month."

"I think you'll find you're mistaken. The senior editing manager role carries a notice period of —"

"That may well be the case. But, contractually, I don't have that role. I am *acting* senior editing manager. You never elevated me officially or got me to sign anything, although you did offer a small compensation for — what is it you called it — oh yes, *caretaking* the role. I agreed to take on the duties out of a sense of duty.

Anyway, I've already checked with the Human Resources department and, contractually, I am still a junior editor. My notice period is one month from today. With the twelve days annual leave I have outstanding, that allows me to leave here at the end of the year and take up my new position at the *Herald* on the fourth of January. I've done my homework, Muriel, and if nothing else, you must know by now that I am thorough."

The blood had drained from her face. Bev had suggested bringing in his mobile phone to videotape the meeting covertly, and he was beginning to regret not having done so.

"That's going to put me and the rest of the staff — your colleagues — in a very difficult position at one of our busiest times of the year. Do you consider that's fair, Spencer, after everything we've done for you?"

Had she simply accepted his resignation and left things there, he might have gone quietly. But to dare play a sympathy card pushed him well and truly over the edge.

"Fair? How can you preach to me about fairness? And what the hell have you done for me? Lumbered me with menial tasks, left me to clean up other people's messes, given me an insult of a financial incentive to assume a managerial role, and worse still, given me no credit for doing a damn good job since I did take over. And where is the promised bonus for me landing the final interview for *Collective*? Don't even think about lecturing me about fairness, when you have never shown me any."

"I see. Well, if that's the way you feel — "

"It is. And for the remaining days, I'll be reverting to my junior editor duties. Don't worry. I don't expect you to pay me the one per cent bonus incentive you promised at the beginning of November when I took on the additional duties. But I do recommend you get someone to step into the manager role as a matter of urgency. Have you considered calling Madeleine Morrison from Peerpoint?"

"I think I know more than enough about this industry to manage without a third-rate recruitment agency. Thank you, anyway. If that's all, Spencer, may I suggest you get back to work and allow me to return to mine."

But Spencer hadn't finished. Muriel had begun to reach the lid of her laptop.

"And that's it?" he asked.

"That's what?" asked Muriel. "I thought you'd made your position perfectly clear?"

"Two years, I've worked for you. Can I ask you something, Muriel?"

"I can hardly stop you now, can I?"

"Why have you never liked me?"

Muriel snapped the laptop lid back down. She leant back in her chair, her hands together beneath her chin, the trademark moue forming.

"Until you came along, my son had been completely focused and driven. And then somehow or another, not a few weeks after you joined, all he seemed to be able to talk about was this new junior recruit, who openly flaunted his sexuality around the office. And when you eventually foisted yourself upon him —"

"Is that what he told you?

"He didn't need to. I know my son. He changed a few months after we took you on —"

"If you had bothered to ask him — and if he'd been in the rare mood to tell the truth — he would have confessed that *he* propositioned *me*. Not the other way around — "

"My son would never waste his time and energy — " A red-faced Muriel had come the closest Spencer had ever seen to losing her temper. Instead, she caught herself and drew in a breath before continuing. "After that, I sensed you might be trouble. I should have listened to my instincts before you infected those around you. But I left things too late and was strongly advised against ridding myself of you by an employment law specialist — yes, I did consult one. Had I known the trouble you would cause, I would have terminated you during your three-month probationary period."

Spencer had heard enough. He pushed away from the table and stood up.

"I never stood a chance, did I? My mother said as much. You were never going to acknowledge my worth. What an absolute waste of my life, you dreadful woman."

"Be careful what you say, Spencer. Have you never heard about burning bridges? I've no doubt you will be expecting a favourable reference from the magazine."

"Muriel, if I received a favourable reference from you, Ed Coleman would probably withdraw my offer of employment. And a good friend once told me that every now and again a person has to burn a few bridges in order to stop the undesirables from following. I think that applies perfectly in this case."

"And I think you should tidy your desk and leave."

Spencer had to take a moment to let the words sink in.

"You want me to leave right away?"

"If you're not prepared to help with the transition of a senior editor, I would rather not have you in my office. We'll pay you until your official departure date, but I think it would be for the best for everyone if you leave today, don't you?"

"Suits me fine."

Muriel lifted the lid of her laptop and began typing, her attention back on the screen. Her voice came across annoyingly calm.

"Human Resources will be in touch with you regarding your final salary and other details. I trust I won't need to call security, trust you know how to find your way safely out of the building."

After staring in disbelief for a moment, Spencer turned and marched out of Muriel's office. On the way back to his desk, he snatched up an empty box from the floor. Hardly anyone was around to witness him. First of all, he stood over his desk and replied to a couple of emails before shutting down the computer. Fuming still, he began throwing things into the box, a bulky thesaurus paperback his father had bought him that he rarely used, photos of his family, a couple more textbooks, pens and a paperweight—barely enough to fill half the box. Two years' worth of his working life.

"I'm guessing things didn't go so well?" came Bev's voice. She had appeared at the end of his desk without him noticing.

"Depends," said Spencer, still seething. "If you're asking whether she kicked me out of the office, then the answer is yes."

"She can't do that," said Bev quietly.

"Well, guess what?" said Spencer. "She just did."

"Without pay?"

"Well, no. I'll still get paid until my official leaving date."

"You're on garden leave, then? You lucky thing. Any chance we could swap places?"

Spencer stopped what he was doing and peered quizzically at Bev, processing what she had just said. She was right. Despite what Muriel had said, he would have been prepared to come in and work until his last day, to help train up the new person and hand over tasks. But now he had been given a couple of weeks' extra leave on full pay. With a sigh, he collapsed into his seat and swivelled towards her.

"You're right. I'm just pissed off at not getting any credit for anything I've done."

"Which is perfectly natural, Squirrel," said Bev. "Come on. Let me take you to my local cafe haunt and get you a coffee and a muffin. I want to hear everything and I'm guessing you need to let off steam."

Spencer stood back up, pulling his coat on from the back of the chair.

"I'll need to hand my security pass to Kim on the way out."

Once he had lifted the cardboard box from his desk, he turned back to Bev. He found her staring at the container, then at him, shocked.

"You have to go straight away? You can't leave at the end of the day?"

"I asked her if she wanted me to go straight away and she said yes. Honestly, Bev, I need to get out of this place. Before I do something I regret."

"You don't even get to say goodbye to people? How is that fair?"

"For a start, there aren't many people around today. But don't worry, we'll sort something out. Come on, let's get out of here."

* * * *

Forty-five minutes, a large mug of coffee and a chocolate chip muffin later, Spencer felt as though a huge weight had been lifted from his shoulders.

Bev listened patiently to the retelling of his meeting. Like a good friend, she nodded or shook her head in all the right places. When Spencer explained how Muriel claimed he had foisted himself upon Blake and how she had tried to find a way to get rid of him, Bev finally lost her cool. She insisted he phone the Human Resources department and report her behaviour. He would not though, because, even in the short time since the interview, he knew he had moved on. Besides, he told her, with no record of the meeting, a grievance would come down to Spencer's word against Muriel's — and any fool could guess whose side people would take. Ultimately, he wanted to put his time at Blackmore Magazine Group behind him and concentrate on the future.

"Honestly, Bev," he said, hoping to put her concerns to rest, "Muriel's constant scrutiny and badgering has worked in my favour to give me the push I needed to move on."

"I think you should talk to Marshall," said Bev, her arms crossed.

As though on cue, his ringtone sounded. He pulled the phone from the inside jacket pocket, stared at the display and chuckled.

"Not Marshall," said Spencer, showing Bev the name on the display. "My mother. I swear she's psychic."

He pushed the accept button and thrust the phone to his ear, rolling his eyes at Bev.

"Hello, Mum. Let me guess? You're checking to see if I'm still coming for Christmas?"

Garrett could never be relied upon to keep a secret, like the one about Spencer bringing a friend — Marshall — home with him and must have spilt the beans.

"Spencer," said his mother. From the strained tone of her voice, Spencer knew something was wrong. "Garrett's been in a road accident. Came off that blasted motorcycle of his. I told him not to go out in this weather, but he never did listen to me. The policeman your father spoke to said he hit a patch of black ice somewhere outside Branksome — "

"Oh my God, Mum. Slow down. Is he okay?"

Bev, noticing his anxious tone, reached across and held onto his free hand.

"No, no. Yes, I mean, he's fine. Well, he's not *fine*, of course, he's in the hospital. His right leg is broken in two places — the femur and the tibia — and he managed to fracture his wrist in the fall, a Colles fracture and, from what they tell me, not serious. When they got to him, he was unconscious. Thank heavens he always wears that helmet, otherwise I don't want to think what might have happened. He's awake now, though, and seems alert. I spoke to him over the phone an hour ago. It all happened early this morning."

"Was Dad with him?"

"No, he was alone. Thankfully, a police car was coming from the other direction and saw the accident happen. Called an ambulance and everything. They said he was lucky to get off so lightly."

"I'll come back this weekend."

Bev, who was clearly trying to pick up the gist of the conversation, nodded her agreement. Spencer knew Marshall would understand.

"No, don't come home, Spencer. I'm only calling to let you know. There's little point coming back. He's at Bournemouth General but nobody's allowed to go and see him at the moment, because of health restrictions. They'll be keeping him in for at least three days. Your father and Peony are in touch with the hospital and getting updates from the doctors. But the ward is closed to visitors, to guard against anyone infecting patients with the virus."

"Is there anything I can do?"

"Not really, love. Sorry, I didn't want to worry you, but I thought you ought to hear the news from me. No doubt when you're back in a couple of weeks, he'll still be on crutches."

"Soaking up the sympathy. Playing it for all it's worth. Can't wait to see that."

"I know," said his mother, chuckling half-heartedly. "He's going to be a handful. Hopefully, he'll rethink the bike once he's better, especially after Peony gives him a piece of her mind. Anyway, son. How are you? Are things going well? Garrett says you're bringing someone home for Christmas. Did he get that right?"

Spencer considered telling her his news — all of it — but decided she had enough to worry about with her eldest son laid up in hospital.

"Everything's fine, Mum. And yes, I'm hoping to bring someone back. But I'll let you know more later.

Send everyone my best and tell my brother he's a jerk. Love you."

After ringing off, they headed back to the office, while Spencer gave Bev the full download about his brother. They stopped outside the main doors to the office block, Spencer still lugging his box. He felt strange, standing outside a place that had been his second home for the past two years, somewhere he was no longer welcome.

"Better get back to work," said Bev. "And you'd better go home and put your feet up. Have you got anything to keep you busy?"

"Not really. Although maybe I should start my search for a new flat."

"There you go. Give yourself a project. You've got all the time in the world now."

"Feels weird, having no real work. Don't think it's really sunk in yet."

"Enjoy it while you can, Squirrel. You'll soon be rushed off your feet at the *Herald*."

Uncharacteristically, she stepped forward and pulled him into a tight hug.

"I'm going to miss having you around," she said, squeezing hard before letting him go. "It's not going to be the same. Promise me we'll stay in touch?"

"Promise."

* * * *

Spencer woke at the usual hour on Friday morning, and only after he had showered, picked out his daily outfit, slipped on his shoes and jacket, and had already hurried down the stairs to brave the cold morning, did he realise he had no office to go to. Outside on the street, with the front door closed behind him, he giggled at his stupidity, into the sunny but frosty morning air and checked his watch — eight o'clock.

Fortunately, a couple of pings on his phone alerted him to messages that had arrived overnight, so he decided to head to the coffee shop along the arcade. After getting a morning takeaway fix — the largest coffee they made in a cardboard cup together with a cream cheese bagel — he strolled to the local park, putting in his earbuds and playing Marshall's message.

"Hello, sexy," came Marshall's hushed, but warmly familiar voice. "Just thinking about you. You're probably still asleep, so I won't call and wake you. I've had to sneak away to record this, because the ceremony is about to start. Probably means I'm going to be tied up until after the dinner. I hope you're listening to this privately, and not where anyone else can hear, because I had this amazing sex dream about you last night. Baby, you were on fire, taking charge and riding me cowboy style, wearing only your pink-and-black polka dot bow tie. Hot doesn't even begin to describe it. Fuck, Spence, when I woke up I'd messed my pyjama bottoms, if you know what I mean? I kid you not. Don't think I've had a nocturnal emission like that since the age of fifteen. Look what you do to me? We're definitely going to have to act that particular fantasy out, baby. Ooh, and by the way, I managed to book the red-eye out of here tonight at midnight. There'll be a short layover in Amsterdam, so I won't land in London until midnight local time. I'll text you first to see if you're still awake. If not, I'll bring over breakfast at seven. Hope that sounds okay. Take care, Spencer. I hope you realise how much I love you. See you Saturday."

Between finishing the bagel and checking other messages — one containing a photo of his toothy smiling brother with his arm in a sling and his leg in plaster, probably taken by a nurse — Spencer played the recording back repeatedly. Each time, his heart tugged at hearing how Marshall felt about him — the same way he felt about Marshall.

Coffee in hand, he sauntered along the pavement, taking the detour into the public gardens and plonking himself down on an empty bench. Despite the chill and residual frost, the air felt wonderfully clean. Commuters on their way to work hurried by, their heads down. Relaxed and feeling an extraordinary lightness, he stretched out his legs and tilted his face to the sun. Warmth bathed his skin, and a smile bloomed on his face. Of all the things that had happened to him in the past month, having Marshall in his life had been the best

Deciding to keep moving, he got to his feet and began strolling across the park, enjoying letting people hurry past. Interrupting his thoughts, the phone in his hand started ringing and, for a second, he wondered if Marshall might be calling from abroad, even though the caller ID came up as unknown.

"Spencer Wyrrell," he answered.

"Spencer. Thank fuck you're answering. Where are you?" Darcy's usually confident voice sounded on edge.

"I'm in the park near my flat. Why are you calling, Darcy? Has something happened?"

"Listen. You mustn't freak out, okay?"

Why was she telling him not to freak out? She had to be calling about Marshall. For some reason, his thoughts went straight to Joey having done something stupid.

"Darcy! What the hell's happened?"

"Look, I'm calling now because this is going to be all over the news in the next few hours. During the inauguration ceremony in Kryszytonia, someone made an attempt on the president's life. A suicide bomber managed to get past security and infiltrate the section in front of the presidential stage. A bomb went off. Horrific, by all accounts. The president's been rushed to hospital and it's thought he survived, although we don't yet know the extent of his injuries. The point is, Spence, that cordoned-off section housed the press corps and—"

Spencer heard no more. He stopped walking, feeling unable or unwilling to breathe. He knew Marshall had been honoured to be in the presence of the new president,, to be near him during the ceremony. Did he imagine the sudden cold wind that swept across the park? For a crazy moment, he wanted Darcy to tell him not to worry, that everything was fine. But instinctively, he knew. By a sheer effort of will, he managed to croak out one word.

"Marshall?"

"That's why I'm calling. They don't know much yet, except that the explosion caused significant damage. Communication is flaky at best while the emergency services are doing what they can. Reports are that some of the president's entourage were injured, but those are yet unconfirmed. As I say, the real damage occurred within the press enclosure in front of the stage. Someone described the scene as carnage. The bomber detonated in the very heart of the section. Spencer, I think we need to prepare ourselves for the worst—"

Spencer had stopped by a lamppost in the park. Just in time, too, because the ground beneath him suddenly shifted and became unstable, the motion making him nauseous. With the phone still clutched to his ear, he bent over and threw up his breakfast. As he remained there, one ice-cold hand clutching the solid metal post as though stopping him from being swept away, a masked couple passing him on the pavement glared with disgust. The woman said something he could not discern, her tone one of contempt.

"Spencer, are you there?" came a distant voice.

A single thought kept running through his brain, over and over, as though on a loop.

"Spencer!"

He had never told Marshall how much he loved him.

"Go back home Right now. I'll call Beverley and tell her what's happened. Tell her to let them know that you're not coming to work today. Then I'm driving over."

And now he had lost the chance.

Chapter Twenty-Two

Spencer lost count of how many times he had paced the length of his flat. Even Tiger, who followed him up and down occasionally weaving between his legs, seemed to sense his distress. Before putting his key in the lock, he had tried to phone Marshall's mobile number, but not unexpectedly, the call had gone straight to messaging.

Darcy had been right. As soon as he switched on the television, every news channel replayed the breaking news footage of the incident. One minute the president stood making a speech behind a transparent screen of what appeared to be glass or Perspex — probably a teleprompter — the next, an orange and red explosion followed by a vast cloud of grey smoke engulfed the stage and obscured the view. Somewhat ghoulishly, cameras in the upper stand at the back of the make-do stadium had kept rolling, silhouetting figures running out of the smoke, screams punctuating the general shouts and confusion.

"All we can confirm right now is that the new president, Tobias Karimov, has been injured, but survived an assassination attempt on his life during his first presidential address. How seriously he was injured is unknown, but he has been rushed to the main municipal hospital here in the capital of Kryszytonia. We have also been told that at least four of his cabinet members were caught in the blast, as were members of the world's press, including our own British media. In spite of rigorous security precautions, sources have confirmed this as the act of a single suicide bomber. An anonymous message received by a national network claimed the bomber carried out the attack on behalf of the Traditional Nationalist Party, outspoken opponents of the new president's proposed reforms. The TNP chairman has rejected any association to the bomber and has denounced this as a senseless and cowardly act of terrorism. As we speak, armed security teams together with emergency services are scouring the area, checking for any further threats, but also recovering bodies and tending to the wounded. We will bring you more as the story unfolds. Back to the studio now, where we revisit the unparalleled rise to power of Tobias Karimov."

Eventually Spencer muted the television before he continued to stride up and down the room. When his doorbell finally buzzed, he took a moment to compose himself, told himself to haul in his emotions in front of Darcy.

As soon as he opened the door and saw the concern in her eyes, he lost his composure. Two steps into the entryway, she ripped off her mask and pulled him into a hug.

"Come on, Spencer," she said, holding him awkwardly and patting him on the back. She smelled of expensive flowery perfume and fabric softener. "Don't make me fucking cry. I've only just slapped on this very expensive makeup. And remember the old saying? No news is good news? Well, I've heard nothing more, and I have friends everywhere in the press. As soon as they hear anything, they'll let me know. Right now, I need you to go up and grab a coat. You're coming to my place. Your ball of fluff can take care of itself for now, but we need to be somewhere more practical than this offline mancave."

Within minutes they sat quietly in the back of her car, while Spencer stared out at the bright morning. In his pocket, his silenced phone suddenly came to life, buzzing urgently with messages. Holding his breath, he pulled out the device but immediately saw that none came from Marshall. They were mainly from Bev, Nile and Prince—friends who knew about him and Marshall, and he decided to deal with them later. Sat next to him, Darcy tapped a long fingernail on her screen before turning to him.

"What's this Beverley told me about you not working out your notice?"

"Muriel released me early. On full pay."

"What the fuck did you do? Drop your pants and flash your junk at her?"

Despite himself, Spencer managed a laugh. Maybe that had been Darcy's intention, but he found telling her about his final meeting with Muriel helped to ground him. Except, similar to Bev but more vocal, his retelling of the tale had her spitting expletives.

"That fucking bitch needs hauling in."

Before she could continue, Spencer went on to tell Darcy about his brief history with Blake, stories about their short time together, then about his friend hooking Blake and Joey up at the gay bar. Finally, Darcy tipped her head back and laughed aloud.

"Karma truly is a bitch. Has Marshall met this friend of yours?"

"Not yet. I was hoping to—"

Spencer turned his head away, unsure of how to continue. Only a couple of days ago, he had mused about that very scenario, wondering how his old and new friends would get along with Marshall. They had also made plans to spend Christmas together and meet his family in Bournemouth. Now, he had no idea if he would ever get the chance.

"Listen, Spencer," said Darcy, correctly interpreting his silence, reaching across and squeezing his hand. "Of all the people I've known in my life, Marshall is one of the most resilient and resourceful. He's been in a lot of sticky situations the world over, and managed to pull through. You need to stay strong for him, to stay positive."

Spencer knew what she meant, but he had never been one for inaction in times of crisis.

"Isn't there something more we can do? Call someone at the British Consulate in Kryszytonia? Surely being on the ground they're going to know more than anyone in the press is saying? Or maybe we could look into getting a scheduled flight or, with Marshall's contacts, hire a private jet—"

"Okay, Spencer. Enough. You are going to have to learn to be patient. Are you a religious person?"

"Not particularly."

"Well, now might be a good time to reconsider. In the meantime, you're coming to my place, where I have high-speed internet, working phones, and televisions in every room including the bathroom. And I know you probably feel the last thing you need is food, but I'm going to stand over you if I have to and force you to eat something when lunch is delivered. You're no good to Marshall or anyone starving yourself. I'm also going to open a couple of bottles of wine I've been saving up for Christmas and tell you stories about your man that he has only ever told me."

Darcy's Chelsea apartment could not have been more different to the one Marshall lived in. Set in a pretty tree-lined square in the heart of the exclusive area, her residence felt like an extension of her personality — clean and sleek modernist artwork with a distinctive Japanese theme, perfectly complemented but subdued colours for her stylish but comfortable couches, Asian-themed sculptures in silver or limestone, and what appeared to be items of metallic junk, all staged beneath artfully placed spotlights.

Spencer had been to Darcy's apartment in happier times, for the post-interview party. Back then, he hadn't seen much of the place, had spent most of the time watching and waiting for Marshall to arrive.

Darcy settled him in the main living area. She took great pains to make sure he got comfortable, seating him on the sectional couch in front of the enormous flatscreen with the remote control within easy reach, and, without even asking, fetching him a large mug of freshly made latte. Once satisfied, and with the television volume on low, she set about completing other chores while Spencer made a call.

"Squirrel, I am so sorry," said Bev, as soon as she answered. "Do you have any news?"

"Nothing at all. But I'm at Darcy's place, and if anyone's going to hear first, it's her. Are you at work?"

"I am. Oh, and Squirrel. Your conspicuous absence is the talk of the office this morning. I know you probably don't want to hear this, but I was in the kitchen getting a drink when Blake wandered in with a couple of his people. Before I had a chance to speak, Kimberley stood up in front of everyone and asked him what his mother was thinking, dismissing you. Said that you were one of the nicest employees in the place, and at least deserved the opportunity to say goodbye to your colleagues. She asked if that was the way people were going to be treated in future and said she didn't want to work in a place with a family who treated employees like shit. She said the word 'shit', Squirrel. Out loud. And about four or five people chipped in and agreed with her. Blake stood there speechless. You should have seen his face, as white as a sheet. Priceless. He's probably gone to mummy dearest to report Kimberley. The way Muriel's going, by Christmas there'll be nobody left working for her."

At any other time, Spencer might have been pleased to hear the story. All he could think about was what was happening across the world. He signed off with Beverley, promising to contact her with any news. After that, he went through his phone and answered messages from Prince, and another from Nile.

Eventually Darcy stopped rushing about, doing things like checking messages and making calls, then brought her post and joined him on the sofa. Spencer watched, mesmerised, the way she ripped open letters, read quickly and either tore the thing up or placed pages in a pile for action. Eventually, she settled back and took a sip from her bone china mug.

"How are you feeling?" she asked.

"Pretty useless."

"Yeah, I know. Okay, I think you need a distraction. I'm going to tell you things about Marshall that few people know. But, Spencer, I honestly believe you're the closest he has ever gotten to a genuine relationship, which is why I'm trusting you. I'm not sure how much he's told you about his childhood, but he was a lonely kid. Having a famous mother and father didn't help, especially when they were either away or in the headlines for all the wrong reasons. Making long-lasting friends at school was almost impossible with the family moving back and forth between London and LA for his father's business, and Marshall being shipped off to boarding school in Scotland and then Eton. Eventually the family settled back in London, but almost straight afterwards they divorced and his father moved to San Diego with his new girlfriend. Poor Marshall might have wanted for nothing, and some might even argue that his father's connections gave him a head start in the media business, but he knew very little about close relationships and friendship."

"What about Alex, Joey's brother?"

"He told you about him, did he? University was the closest he came to making any lasting friends. I still find it unbelievable that Alex and Joey are brothers. I know you've met Joey, and I'm sure you'll get to meet Alex one day."

"One day, maybe," said Spencer, with as much hope as he could muster. "I know Marshall's close to his mother, but he didn't say much about his father."

"They clashed. Still do. Almost came to blows one holiday, when Marshall was a teenager, and the old man tried to pick a fight with his mum. Highlander senior is in his eighties now and has kids from his second and third marriages. He's still worth a small fortune and has threatened to leave Marshall nothing. Which is fine by Marshall, because he's independently wealthy, money bequeathed to him by his grandparents. But, you know, even with all of that, he is a very humble, a very private person—

"I know—"

"—and terribly lonely most of the time. And he gives back so much to charities, not just in terms of his money, but also with his personal time and getting his hands dirty. And he's doing so because he genuinely cares, not for any kind of publicity like some celebrities—"

"The day of my interview, he was going to help out at a homeless charity, in the freezing cold morning, to load boxes into vans."

"Maybe I should have started by asking how much you already know. Sounds like he's really opened up to you. Let's play a game of things you know about him and we can tell each other whether it's something we already knew. I'm not a prude, exactly, but can you keep the bedroom shenanigans to yourself."

Spencer enjoyed the diversion. Most of what Spencer knew, Darcy knew, too. Darcy knew lots of things he had no idea about, and each gem of knowledge made Marshall more human. As they talked, he kept one eye on the flatscreen on Darcy's living room wall.

"Most of his clothes are chosen for him by his mother, or me," said Darcy. "He's pretty hopeless when it comes to putting an ensemble together, even though he looks amazing in the right outfit."

"And out," said Spencer, grinning. "But I totally agree. Okay, my turn. He cooks a mean steak dinner — "

"Wait, what? He cooked for you? In all the years I've known him, he has never prepared a meal for me. I didn't even know he *could* cook. Steak dinner, huh? Did he make dessert, too?"

"Um, he kind of *was* dessert."

"Okay, time out. Too much information."

At midday, a delivery of an eclectic array of hot and cold food arrived. Everything looked fresh and healthy. Assorted sushi, vegetarian moussaka, chicken wraps, wholemeal noodle concoctions — enough to feed a family of four. Darcy quickly explained that she would keep any leftovers for her dinner, but Spencer wondered if she did so in the event Marshall came back. When she opened a bottle of Chablis, at first Spencer declined. But after some gentle nudging, he relented. And he felt happy to have done so, the combination of food and wine taking the edge off, helping to relax him so much that later in the afternoon he managed to doze off on the couch.

* * * *

He was awoken at four-thirty, with Darcy's phone ringing. In her usual curt way, she answered the call. After placing her hand over the receiver, she hissed out a command.

"Spencer. Some of the British media crews have just landed back in the UK. It's on channel six right now. The remote is on the sofa. Push three-two-four."

On the television, the news showed a KriztoAir A320 landing at one of London's airports and coming painfully slowly to the gate. Crowded around the arrivals gate inside the terminal, reporters shouted as a trickle of passengers exited into the concourse, some dazed at the attention and probably on different flights.

Spencer stood close to the screen, studying each of the faces to see if one might be Marshall. After the first few appeared, crowds clustered around cameras, emerging media people interviewing fellow reporters on the ground, and coverage focused on them rather than any newly arriving travellers.

"Don't worry," said Darcy, still on the phone. "My contact is getting a copy of the passenger manifest. As soon as he does, he'll let me know if Marshall was on board."

By nine o'clock, with Darcy glued to her phone, they had still not heard anything. Eventually, after returning from the kitchen, she parked herself at the end of the couch. He could tell by her face that she had some news and braced himself for the worst.

"Marshall wasn't on the plane. And nobody's heard any news about him. But one of the survivors who landed earlier said they believe Colm O'Donnell, Marshall's cameraman, was killed in the blast. That's all they know."

Spencer's heart sank. He had met Colm in the studio and seen him in the van when Marshall's team had picked him up. A big bear of a man, he had seemed happy working alongside Marshall, happy to be a part of the team. Now Spencer wondered what loved ones Colm had at home—maybe his own family—and guessed they too were anxiously sitting by the phone, waiting for news from Kryszytonia. Not only that, he thought, but wouldn't Marshall have had the cameraman with him at all times, recording footage and providing his own commentary? As always, Darcy seemed to sense his dread.

"Look, I have three bedrooms here. You're more than welcome to stay. Do you want me to make up a bed for you?"

"No, it's okay, Darcy. You've been really kind today, but I think I need to go home."

Spencer needed his cave. Maybe he really ought to be around other people, but his nerves felt frazzled with each report coming in, and he wanted to be home. Darcy appeared to sense his resolve because she didn't try to argue.

"You're sure?"

"I am."

"In which case, I'll call you an Uber."

Chapter Twenty-Three

Spencer sat stiffly next to the entrance on the very last bench of the Chapel of Rest. A distinctive almost cloying scent of furniture polish filled the air, outmatching the various expensively perfumed bodies seated around. He stared unfocused at the backs of vaguely famous people either perched in front or moving slowly down the aisle towards the front.

Life would go on. Christmas with his family would still go ahead. Once again, he would turn up alone. Garrett would be on crutches, and the women would be fussing over him to make sure he was happy and comfortable. Nothing had really changed.

Except everything had.

Joey slouched forward on the front pew next to an older man and woman and a slightly older version of him — probably Alex and their parents. Even seeing Blake seated next to Joey, both wearing ugly matching silver shell suits, inappropriately laughing together at a shared joke, had not sparked even a flicker of emotion in him. He almost wished it had.

Darcy sat upright and poised on the adjacent bench, next to an older woman crying into a black handkerchief, her long red hair spilling down from beneath a black veil. Unable to see her face, he assumed her to be Marshall's mother, although something in the back of his mind niggled about her appearance. Had Darcy suggested Spencer sit with them? He couldn't remember. But he would have felt conspicuous in the spotlight, preferring to mourn privately from the back without being stared at or singled out. Even having Muriel and her husband in attendance had irked but not fazed him. On entering the chapel, she had glanced over but pointedly turned away from his stern gaze.

People needed others beside them during this challenging rite of passage, but Spencer wanted to get through alone. The important thing was to give friends and family some form of closure. And with that thought, he had to admit to feeling a little mystified and — if he was going to be honest — disappointed, at not having Bev and Prince somewhere nearby.

On an easel set atop a raised dais near the coffin sat an enormous portrait of Marshall. Spencer recognised the beautiful photograph from a men's fashion magazine cover, his face so familiar, so full of life and love and possibilities. Soft strains of George Michaels' *Waiting for That Day* played from the speakers, the irony of the lyrics almost undoing his barely held together composure.

And a thought kept coming back to him, that he should have told Marshall not to go, should have insisted he stay home and be with Spencer, even though he knew Marshall would never have agreed.

Despite sunlight spilling in through the frosted windows and the chapel doors standing wide open, he found he could barely breathe. How could he have come so close to perfect happiness only to have everything ripped away from him? When the gentle hum of subdued chatter subsided, replaced by nervous giggles and a few soft gasps of astonishment, he looked up to see a lone bird, a chaffinch, had flown into the hall and performed a couple of circuitous routes before flying back out through the main doors.

Once again murmured conversations started up and Spencer squeezed his eyes shut. From outside, somebody oblivious to the sacred ceremony going on in the chapel, drilled then hammered on wood — *bzzzz, thump, thump, thump, bzzz, bzzz, thump thump*. At first, Spencer had tried to ignore the intrusion, had tried to calm his mind. Eventually, his temper rose, and he readied himself to slip outside and give the workmen a piece of his mind. Except he found he could not move, his body pinned to the pew, his head and shoulders weighed down by an invisible force.

Bzzz, bzzz, bzzz.

Through a sheer effort of will, he managed to wrench his eyes open and found himself gazing up at the ceiling of a darkened room. His bedroom. Fully clothed still, he lay on the top of his bed with Tiger sitting on his chest, staring at him. This time he could have sworn the buzzing sound came from nearby, from somewhere in the room. Tiger jumped off and ran out of the bedroom. Finally he managed to raise his head, slip on his glasses, and squint at the clock next to the bed.

Five-past-four in the morning.

Heart pounding and gasping for breath, he sat up and listened carefully. Had someone been ringing his intercom, because the persistence seemed reminiscent of something Darcy might do? Clambering out of bed, he hurried to the intercom and pressed the button, but on the video display, the space directly outside his front door was empty. Had he missed the person? Or had the buzzing been a part of his dreams? Either way, he needed to know.

Quickly shrugging on his padded coat and carpet slippers, he clambered down the stairs and yanked open the front door. Turning a full one-eighty in the doorway, he scanned the road outside.

Empty and deserted. Four in the frosty morning and not a creature stirred. He was about to turn around and head back indoors when a sound caught his attention.

"Spencer! Spence!"

Was he dreaming still? Because the voice calling out sounded familiar. And suddenly there he was, tall and impossibly composed, unfolding beneath the streetlight from the driver's seat of a parked car Spencer hadn't noticed. Wrapped warmly against the frosty morning, he strode towards Spencer while yanking off a black woollen hat. No crutches, both arms and legs working, no visible bandaging — all the terrible things Spencer had imagined, the worst being losing him forever — had not happened. Marshall was alive and well and whole and unharmed.

Halfway to him, the expression on Marshall's face morphed into a broad smile as heartwarming as a sunrise.

And by that one simple act, smiling that beautiful smile, Spencer came unglued. Stood inside the entrance, his legs gave way from under him and he collapsed to his knees, his eyes flooding. He wanted to pray to any and every god that would hear him, to thank them for being there, for listening and answering. Only peripherally, through blurred vision, did he notice the figure begin rushing towards him, to scoop him up and pull him into a fierce embrace he never wanted to end. Without conscious thought, he clung on for dear life, arms and legs wrapping around his lover, a death grip that nothing could ever shake.

"I'm sorry, baby. I'm so sorry," came the warm voice. "My phone got wrecked and then it got too late—"

From deep inside of Spencer, a sobbing started up, his body shaking uncontrollably. In response, Marshall tightened his grip around him.

"I thought—thought I'd lost you. I had a nightmare—that I'd never see you again."

"Hey, hey. I'm here now, baby."

Spencer cried unashamedly, all the pent-up emotions of the past day finding release.

"And I never got the chance to tell you I love you. I love you so much, Marshall."

Marshall chuckled at that and nuzzled his nose into Spencer's ear.

"I know you do, Spence. I love you, too. Come on, let's get you upstairs. I think we both need a hot drink. And I have some explaining to do."

Tiger sat regally in the doorway at the top of the stairs, looking smug and steadfastly blocking their way. Marshall stepped carefully over her and carried Spencer into the flat. Once he had ushered Tiger in and used Spencer's back to close the door behind them, he kissed Spencer deeply, a long lingering kiss that finally soothed away the undercurrent of dread that had filled Spencer.

Back on his feet, Spencer led Marshall over to the couch and made him remove his jacket and sit down.

Keeping busy felt necessary, and Spencer started by preparing to make hot drinks.

"Have you slept at all?" he asked.

When he looked around, Tiger had already burrowed herself into Marshall's lap, pushing her head into his hand, purring loudly, demanding to be petted. Spencer could hardly blame her. Everyone had missed him.

"A little. On the plane. Someone laid on a private jet to fly us home."

Spencer pulled out two mugs and measured out teaspoons of instant coffee. No fancy coffee machines in his flat, but Marshall knew that.

"You must be exhausted."

"Funnily enough I was, but not now. After I stopped ringing your buzzer, I went back to the car, to wait until later when you might be awake. Darcy told me you were home. We really need to do something about this offline status of yours, Spence."

"I know, I know. Totally agree. I'm so sorry —"

"Having said that, being offline has had its advantages. It wasn't that long ago your flat felt like the safest place on the planet. Just you and me and nobody to touch us."

"And Tiger."

Marshall grinned down at the cat curled in his lap.

"And, of course, Tiger."

"And me being the perfect gentleman."

"Exactly," said Marshall, looking up. "Although you no longer need to be a perfect gentleman around me. I hope you know that?"

Marshall's voice had lowered, and Spencer felt the words reverberate in his groin. He almost abandoned the drinks, but then restrained himself, comforted by the certainty that he had Marshall back in his life.

"Tell me what happened."

Marshall pushed out a sigh, but then, in the flawless, effortless way he had of talking, relayed the story of them landing in Kryszytonia and his exclusive interview with Chairman Tobias Karimov the afternoon before his inauguration. They had been there to shoot a documentary surrounding the event, not to provide a live feed of the day, which is why other news channels — not his own — had broadcast the incident. If anything, his crew had viewed the day of the inauguration as routine because they knew they could always get archive footage for the official ceremony from other media sources.

Finally the kettle boiled and Spencer brought over mugs of steaming coffee. After watching Marshall make a big deal of sniffing the steaming drink then sipping with a frankly filthy moan, Spencer asked about his crew, especially about his cameraman.

"No, no. Colm is alive and well. In the resulting chaos, there was a lot of confusion and misunderstanding. Another cameraman, the same build as Colm, died in the explosion, the poor guy. I've been in war zones across the world, Spence, seen some horrific things, but the carnage that day will stay with me forever."

"Darcy and I watched the news coverage. Honestly, Marsh, although I didn't want to believe it, I didn't see how you could not have been affected, not without a miracle. They showed the press lined up at the front of the stage where the terrorist detonated the device. How did you manage to escape unscratched?"

"That's another story altogether. Come and sit down."

Marshall settled back and waited for Spencer to join him, an arm clamping around his shoulders, before beginning to tell Spencer about the day of the inauguration.

"Karimov's advisers wanted him to hold the event indoors, largely due to worries about the weather but also because of security concerns. But the man insisted, said his people should see their leader sworn in under open skies, not behind locked doors. That morning, we were given the choice of setting up at the front or next to the national network, on a gantry to one side of the square. As I said, we were there to film a documentary, and we knew we'd get more candid shots of the crowd from the side. When the president made his speech, we left Colm filming. Kerry-Anne and I took a camera to see if we could speak to any dignitaries or other notable persons. I'm not even sure what made me look, but as we were passing behind a stand near the front, a wooden stall was selling souvenirs. I only slowed to look for a second then carried on walking, but something caught my eye. Did you know Tobias Karimov's presidential mascot is a squirrel wearing a national flag waistcoat and bow tie? On one stall, they sold these two-foot-tall mascot toys. I had to stop and laugh, and told Kerry-Anne that if I didn't buy one, I would never be forgiven and probably never get laid again. As I was paying, the bomb went off. The blast threw me into the stall, which came crashing down around myself and the stall owner. We were knocked off our feet, had a few scratches and bruises, but both escaped unharmed."

"And Kerry-Anne?"

"She was less lucky, thrown against a concrete post and knocked out cold. I stayed with her until I could find a medic. She'd gained consciousness by then, and seemed okay, but they insisted on taking her away to a medical unit, to get her checked out. I remained behind to help the medical staff as best I could. Honestly, those guys deserve medals, the way they worked tirelessly to help the injured. A couple of times I wondered if I was in the way, but they seemed to appreciate my support Later on, I tried to return to the team, but by then, of course, the place was locked down, with roads cordoned off all around the square. Eventually I found my way to a police station, and after a couple of hours' wait, we were reunited. Kerry-Anne gave me an update on casualties. She also told me about some of the British teams being flown home."

"We saw the news. You have no idea how much I wanted you to be on that plane."

"Almost as much as I did. But by the time Kerry-Anne told us, those people would have landed here. It was well after midnight in Kryszytonia. They never told us why, but the security team confiscated our phones and computers, so we couldn't let people know we were fine. And then we spent a long time being questioned by one officer or another, as well having them go through the footage we'd shot. I'm guessing my friendship with Tobias paid off because they didn't keep us long. They were the ones who informed us that he'd survived the blast with minor injuries, thank heavens. And then, before we knew it, we were being bundled off to the airport, to a waiting jet. I still have no idea who laid that on for us. This would have been almost six in the morning local time, midnight here. After checking our documents, we were taken to a private lounge in the airport, given back our luggage and told to freshen up before the flight. None of us had changed our clothes since the morning. Both Kerry-Anne and I looked a sight, still covered in dust and debris and blood, so the shower and new clothes felt wonderful. As soon as we joined the others in the lounge, we were being ushered off to the waiting plane, taking off as the sun began to rise over Kryszytonia."

"And you came straight here?"

"Zipped through immigration in absolutely no time—the wonders of private air travel. I called Darcy first, because I figured you'd either be there or at home. She suggested I come straight here, said you'd been worried sick and probably hadn't slept. Somewhat cryptically, she also told me I owed her a home-cooked dinner."

"Ah. I might have mentioned that you cooked for me."

"Did you now? And what else did the pair of you discuss about me?"

"Mostly about how much we both love you," said Spencer, pecking Marshall on the lips. "Me more, naturally."

Marshall took Spencer's almost empty mug and placed it with his own on the table before gathering Spencer into his arms. Spencer melted into the kiss, savouring Marshall's unique smell and warmth. When Marshall pulled his head away to yawn, Spencer let out a soft chuckle.

"I hope you don't mind, Spence, but since sitting down the tiredness has caught up with me. Don't think I don't want you—you're all I could think about this past week—but if I don't get some shut-eye soon, I'll be good for nothing."

"Of course, you poor thing. Go on into the bedroom."

"Um, I was thinking you'd join me. Keep me company."

"It would be my honour."

Spencer helped Marshall out of his clothes, undressing him as a parent would undress a child. Marshall simply stood there grinning, not moving unless Spencer guided him to do so. Eventually, with Marshall wearing only his briefs, Spencer pulled back the covers and directed him into bed.

"I could get used to this," said Marshall, getting comfortable, as Spencer climbed in beside him, lining their bodies up facing each other.

"That's my master plan," said Spencer.

He closed the small gap and kissed Marshall, a long, measured kiss. He could afford long kisses now that his man was back safely. Something moved at the bottom of the bed, and Spencer saw Tiger making herself comfortable at their feet. Marshall's eyes had closed, and he appeared to be drifting off, but suddenly opened them.

"Hey, before I forget. Something else happened while I was away," he said.

"There's more?" asked Spencer, horrified.

"Don't worry, this is something good. At least, I hope so. My mother sent me an email. She owns a small apartment overlooking the Thames in Rotherhithe — got the place in the divorce settlement — with a terrace on the first floor, above the river footpath. The apartment is usually rented out to overseas professionals. But the last tenants were European and moved back home in June. She's had the unit refurbished but it's been sitting empty ever since.

Anyway, she wrote and asked if I wanted to move in. As luck would have it, my father's found a potential buyer for his South Ken apartment and he's asked me to move out. And then I got to thinking that Rotherhithe is barely twenty minutes by train into London Bridge, where you'll be working next year. I guess, what I'm trying to say is — "

"Yes!" said Spencer, rolling on top of Marshall, kissing him playfully. "If you're asking me if I want to come and live with you, then the answer is yes. Of course, yes."

Marshall's laughter rumbled through his chest.

"Do you think Her Royal Highness will be okay with only a terrace?"

"Only a terrace? Are you kidding me? She's a reluctant house cat right now. The number of times I've seen her sitting by the window, staring through the glass at birds and other cats, pining to be outside. If you think she likes you now, wait until we move in together. She'll never leave you alone."

Marshall's sigh came out deep and contented, and he shifted Spencer around to spoon him, an arm wrapped around his waist.

"Can I ask you one question?" asked Spencer. "And then I promise to let you sleep."

"Anything."

"What colour is your mother's hair?"

"Didn't I tell you? She's a platinum blonde. Naturally, too. It's always been her trademark. Even in her seventies now, her hair is amazing. She says it's her best feature, although I think she underestimates her many other qualities. I got Dad's gene there. My hair is the same colour as his."

"I see. And her hair's never been red?"

"Red? Good lord, no. She'd never dream of dying her hair. Besides, she's never been a fan of redheads," said Marshall, and gently elbowed Spencer. "Where on earth is all this coming from?"

"Nothing," said Spencer, smiling to himself. "But I'd really like to meet her one day."

Marshall kissed Spencer beneath the ear, then settled back into the pillow.

"I would love nothing more than to introduce you. And the weird thing is, I already know she'll warm to you. I bet you become the best of friends."

"In the meantime, after having walked out of another major incident unscathed, you're going to need to survive Christmas Day with my family."

Marshall chuckled, his body vibrating along Spencer's spine.

"Okay, Spence. Enough drama for one day. Now go to sleep."

"Goodnight, Marshall."

"Good morning, Spence."

Chapter Twenty-Four

Since Marshall's return, Spencer had agreed to install himself — and Tiger — into Marshall's South Kensington apartment. Amid all the new jargon dropping into everyday life, such as lateral flow and polymerase chain reaction — PCR — tests, new government regulations had meant people creating their own support bubbles and Marshall's fully functional and, more importantly, fully networked apartment made more sense. With little else to do, Spencer was finally able to answer calls or text messages as soon as they arrived, even confirming to his mother that he would still be bringing a guest home for Christmas.

On Christmas Eve they drove to Bournemouth, relieved to be out of the confines of the London flat, speeding south down the almost empty motorway. Marshall appeared in his element driving, and Spencer didn't offer to share the burden, because he knew Marshall would refuse. The journey in Marshall's comfortable sports car flew by all too quickly.

"You cannot be serious?" said Marshall, leaning forward, his mouth dropping open.

Marshall slowed his BMW to a crawl as they approached the spectacle. Next to him, Spencer had been pointing out his parent's bungalow. Not that he'd needed to bother.

"In all fairness, my brother did warn me," said Spencer. "I just didn't imagine..."

Who could have? Garrett — bored to tears at home — had phoned him the day before about their father, usually the more conservative of his parents where the festive season was concerned, going all-out this year to brighten up the exterior of their pink-fronted bungalow. In a fit of seasonal madness, according to Garrett, their father had decided to 'put a bit more effort in this year' as a trial run before the arrival of his grandchild. Nobody could have expected the result. Giant red- and white-striped candy canes decorated the pink facade, fake snow covering the whole front roof. In the garden, a full-sized smiling snowman and laughing Father Christmas stood side-by-side next to a sleigh and a fifteen-plus-foot decorated Christmas tree, with huge colourful foil-wrapped presents beneath. Every surface and window frame had been illuminated in various arrangements of Christmas lights, banishing any hope of a good night's sleep. And those were only the big-ticket items. Little touches here and there came to life as they approached. Snow White on the roof, directing the seven dwarfs, all in colourful outfits with sacks on their backs, climbing the drainpipes. A row of miniature reindeer standing next to the chimney stack, one with its nose replaced by an illuminated red bulb. Mickey and Minnie sitting together on the guttering, arms around each other. Too much, Spencer thought, when he initially saw the display.

Except the end effect did not come across as tacky at all but perfectly befitted the fairy-tale aura of the bungalow facade. Context, thought Spencer, everything in context.

Even as they parked up outside, a young family of four had stopped by the front gate, pointing with delight as they spotted one detail after another.

"That's one way to get the neighbours' attention," chuckled Marshall, and Spencer stilled. Maybe Marshall had been joking, but this kind of stunt was bound to get people nearby talking and, at some point in time, coming over to meet the neighbours they had previously snubbed. Had that been his father's intent? Or more likely his mother's. Spencer wouldn't put it past her. She had probably encouraged him with the front display while formulating a plan to discreetly shortlist potential babysitters.

Spencer got out first and collected his luggage and the cat carrier from the back seat before waiting by the front gate for Marshall to lock up, manage his carryall and the large bag of gifts. They wound their way up the garden path, to where a giant Christmas wreath the size of a ship's wheel hung on the front door. Spencer had keys, but he wanted to surprise his mother, so pushed the doorbell a couple of times and stood to one side.

Except his mother wasn't the one to answer.

"Fuck me!" said Garrett, on crutches, gaping like a guppy at seeing Marshall Highlander on his doorstep.

"From what Spencer tells me, I'm not sure I'm your type," said Marshall, smirking and going to hold out his hand but stopping. "And I would shake your hand, if you didn't already have them full. You must be Garrett."

Garrett leant a shoulder against the door frame to steady his balance and took Marshall's hand while looking over Marshall's shoulder and pulling a face at Spencer.

"You sneaky little bastard. You could have said something."

"And spoil the fun? Don't worry, I've warned him about Mum's cooking."

"Then he's going to be disappointed. Peony's giving Mum a hand this year. And by a hand, I mean she's taken over the cooking, using Mum as her *sous-chef*. You should see the two of them. I didn't tell you this, but Peony trained as a chef straight from school. So she knows her way around a kitchen."

"Bang goes another Wyrrell family tradition. Sorry, Marsh, looks like we're not going to need that wholesale family bumper pack of Tums after all."

"Mum," Garrett shouted out at the top of his voice, and for a moment, Spencer thought his brother was going to snitch on him. "Your presence is required. For the arrival of your second-favourite son. With his plus-one."

"Don't shout, Garrett, dear," said Spencer's mother, already entering the hallway, wiping her hands on a tea towel. Before noticing anyone else, she pulled Spencer into a customary hug. "Hello, love. My soon-to-be-famous reporter for the *Herald*. Oh, and you brought the cat for Garrett. Good boy. Glad you could make it. And who else did you bring us? Oh, hello, dear — My goodness. Has anyone ever told you, you are the absolute spitting image of —

"Tom Holland?" said Marshall, making Spencer burst into laughter. "Yes, I get that kind of thing all the time."

"Who's Tom Holland?" said his mother, puzzled. "I was going to say—"

"Mum, this is Marshall. Marshall Highlander. My boyfriend."

"He's Marshall? *The* Marshall? Marshall Highlander?" said his poor mother, completely confused, looking back and forth between Spencer and Marshall, before settling her gaze on Marshall. "And you're dating my son?"

"As long as I have your approval, Mrs Wyrrell."

"Please. Call me Coleen. And believe me, if you knew anything about my sons, you'd know neither of them ever seek my approval to do anything. Welcome to the family home. Come and meet the rest of the inmates."

Spencer felt a distinct sense of pleasure watching the surprised looks on the faces of his father and Peony, but even more at how quickly everything returned to normal. His mother had already let Tiger out. She had gone straight to Marshall, brushed herself up against his leg before heading over and swiping a paw at the bottom of one of Garrett's crutches. While his mother went to prepare hot drinks for everyone, his father dragged out a newspaper and began asking Marshall about his experience in Kryszytonia. Spencer took the opportunity to catch up with Peony. Only as he walked around the counter to hug her did he notice her very noticeable bump. Instead of the usual heavy-duty Wyrrell hug, he kissed her gently on each cheek—until she pulled him into a fierce hug that squeezed the breath out of him.

"See?" she whispered into his ear. "I told you one day you'd surprise the lot of us. Just didn't realise it would be so soon. He is an absolute dreamboat."

"He is," said Spencer, looking around and grinning at Marshall talking seriously to Garrett and his father. "I really lucked out there."

"I bet he says the same thing about you."

He turned back and smiled happily at her before his gaze dropped to her belly again.

"Enough about me. How are you doing? Tell me all about the joys of pregnancy."

"Don't. Twenty-three weeks and I look like a sumo, with huge boobs to match and swollen ankles, and I'm tired all the time. Insult to injury, I've developed an unhealthy obsession with Marmite and sugar sandwiches. Usually I hate the stuff, but for some reason it's become my go-to craving. On the plus side, your mother has been an absolute saint. She seems to know how I'm feeling almost before I do."

"Do we know the gender yet? Or are you going to be modern and opt for a non-gender-specific baby?"

While he was talking, the oven beeped. She opened the door and was about to bring out a tray of what looked like biscuits, but Spencer stepped in to help, placing them on the counter next to another two trays.

"Very funny. We had the ultrasound a couple of weeks ago, but Garrett wanted to tell you all tonight. I'll save the news for the proud dad-to-be."

"And can I assume his motorcycling days are over?"

"You know, Spence, I'm not going to tell him what to do. But I get a sense the accident woke him up a bit, especially with the little one on the way. Maybe he'll start up again in a few years, who knows? But did you notice your dad's bike is no longer there? He sold it to a friend for cash a few days after the accident. She might not tell you directly, but your mum's beyond relieved."

"And can I say for the record, I'm a little relieved myself to hear you're helping with the cooking this year."

Peony rolled her eyes.

"Let me guess? Garrett told you I was a trained chef?"

"Aren't you?"

"I worked in a gastro pub straight from college while I pondered what I wanted to do with my life. They sent me on a couple of cooking courses where I learnt the basics. The way he tells it, I was the top chef at the Ritz. And the men of this family are totally unfair about Coleen's cooking skills."

"Well, the way I see it, with the two of you on the case, things will be brilliant. What's with all the biscuits?"

"Cookies. Better ask your mum."

At that moment, Spencer's mum brought him a cup of coffee and a mug of something smelling of peppermint for Peony. Once she checked everyone had a drink, she clapped her hands together to get their attention.

"Right, everyone. Peony and I have been making Christmas cookies all afternoon, so you're going to be helping decorate them before we sit down for dinner. You too, Marshall."

"Christmas cookies? Is this some kind of cultural exchange programme you're involved in that I know nothing about? Since when did we become American?" asked Spencer.

"Since Dad constructed a mini replica of Christmas Disneyland in our front garden," said Garrett, rolling his eyes.

"What did you think, son?" asked his father, looking over at Spencer.

"He thinks you have too much time on your hands," said Garrett.

"Let your brother speak, Garrett," said their father.

Spencer laughed and shook his head at Marshall who was also laughing.

"I think it looks amazing."

"Anyway, eyes back to me," said Spencer's mother. "There are tubes of icing in lots of different colours, mini chocolate buttons in white, milk and plain flavours, and tubes of hundreds-and-thousands sprinkles — even little slices of dried fruit. A few of the neighbours are coming over on Boxing Day, only to the front gate. I already have the schedule. I'm going to give them each a gift bag of cookies and hot chocolate."

"Recruiting babysitters, Mum?" asked Spencer after raising his eyebrows to Marshall.

"I don't know what you mean. We're just being neighbourly. And as we can't attend midnight mass because of all the restrictions, I thought this might be a nice diversion."

By the time they had finished decorating — a pretty good job, if Spencer did say so himself — Peony and his mother had laid the table for a simple dinner of fish pie with a crunchy mash topping and steamed veggies. His mother had even set aside a small bowl for Tiger, who had made a new friend in Peony. While they served up the food, Spencer's father opened a couple of bottles of wine he had been saving up, discussing grapes and different types of wine with Marshall. Spencer had no idea whether Marshall knew about wine, but whenever he looked over, his man seemed to be doing just fine.

"Are you sure you won't have a glass, Peony?" asked Spencer's mother. "Just one can't do any harm. I had red wine every now and then when I was carrying Spencer."

"That explains a lot," said Garrett, which made Marshall laugh.

"I'm fine, Mum," said Peony. "Thanks, anyway."

"Mum?" Spencer mouthed to his mother.

"Yes, dear. I asked Peony to call me Mum. She's the daughter I was never blessed with. But if you do decide to marry my son, Marshall, I'd prefer you to keep calling me Coleen. Are you going to be here on Boxing Day?"

Either Marshall didn't hear or recovered quickly from the marriage remark, Spencer couldn't tell.

"We'll be here," said Marshall. "But we'll need to leave the day after. I have a couple of conference calls I need to take from home. We'll definitely be here all of Boxing Day."

"Excellent. The neighbours are coming over after lunch. I'll need you front and centre, Marshall. Can't wait to see their faces when they realise we have a celebrity in the family, when they see what they've been missing all this time."

"If Peony's calling our mother, Mum," asked Spencer to Garrett, in an attempt to save Marshall any more embarrassment, "does that mean you two are getting hitched? To make the endearment official?"

"That's always been the plan. But with the way things are at the moment, it might be a simple affair," said Garrett. "Before our daughter arrives."

"Quite right, too—" began Spencer's mum, before her gaze swung to Garrett. "Wait. What did you say?"

"You're going to have a granddaughter, Mum and Dad," said Garrett, beaming.

"A little girl?" said Spencer's mother to Peony, her eyes starting to well up.

"I was sworn to secrecy," said Peony, smiling fondly at Spencer's mum while stroking her tummy. "Garrett wanted to tell you when we were all together."

The rest of the evening was spent chatting and drinking, with the television left switched off. Even after Spencer loaded their presents beneath the Christmas tree, and after Tiger had rummaged around, they agreed to stick to the British tradition of opening gifts on Christmas morning.

Well before midnight, Spencer and Marshall snuggled together in the double bed in his bedroom. Both were a little drunk and, because of the restricted space in the bed and the noisy old bed frame, had decided against fooling around.

"Nice place. Although the walls are a bit thin. I think I can hear your father snoring."

"That's Mum."

Marshall's rumbled laughter vibrated along Spencer's spine.

"Your family's lovely."

"We're all mad. The lot of us. You don't know what you've gotten yourself into."

"Whatever it is, I'm more than happy to be here."

Spencer melted inside to hear Marshall's words. Turning his head, he kissed Marshall gently on the lips.

"And I'm happy to have you here," he said softly. "They absolutely love you, Marsh. And I'm not just saying that. Dad gave me a hug across the shoulders earlier when we were picking out wine, which he never does unless he's really impressed with me."

"My father used to throw money at me so he didn't have to hug me or verbalise his approval. I'm not sure we even shared a joke. Christmas wasn't a fun time in our house, so it's not a tradition I ever looked forward to."

"Well, you have a new family now, and a new tradition."

Marshall sighed deeply and squeezed his arms around Spencer.

"I know it's been a dreadful year for a lot of people, but I consider myself one of the lucky few —"

"If you're about to say you're lucky because you met me, then you need to change that to 'we'. We're the lucky ones, because we found each other. And I know we're not out of the woods yet, Marsh, but I can't help this feeling of optimism as we head to the new year."

"No wonder. New job, new apartment. New members joining the family —"

"Oh, you heard that, did you? About us getting married? I do apologise. Sometimes my mother jumps the gun and speaks before she thinks —"

"Actually, I was talking about Peony and your niece who's about to arrive. Although, yes, I did catch your mother's mention of us marrying. And just so you know, Spence, I would love nothing more. But how about we live together first, and then see how things go? I would hate to disappoint you."

"Marsh, you could never disappoint me. I love you, remember?"

"I — yes, I remember. God, now I feel like an ungrateful prick and a complete moron."

"Hey, don't call my boyfriend a moron. He's a pragmatist."

"Pragmatist? Yes, I suppose I am. Not particularly romantic, though, is it?"

Spencer turned over and faced Marshall.

"Marsh. I'm absolutely fine waiting. You're in my life now, and I'm in yours. We're going to be living together next year, which is an enormous step by anyone's standards. My parents paint a rosy picture of marriage, but I know things weren't so wonderful for yours. So let's take our time. I'm in no hurry, because I know I'll win you over in the end. After all, I've got Darcy on my side."

"I see. In which case, I might as well surrender now."

* * * *

Throughout Christmas Day, Spencer kept checking to see if Marshall needed saving from any of his family, but he seemed to wallow in the attention. As the men — except Garrett, who sat with his leg up, directing from the sofa — laid the table for lunch, Spencer noticed how Marshall had started to adopt his clever questioning. Layer by layer, he found out more about Garrett's company and his future plans, while inquiring about his father's lengthy experience in the force and what he thought about recent developments. Neither of them cottoned on, but his mother caught Spencer's eye a couple of times and smiled.

As he stood back from the table, waiting for his mother to give her final approval, Spencer's phone rang. They had already done a round of calls in the morning over breakfast, straight after opening presents, but this person — never an early riser — hadn't answered.

Immediately, he put Bev on speaker.

"Merry Christmas, Squirrel. To you and the family. Oh, and Tiger, too," she said, and the family all echoed her greeting. "Prince and his family are here with me. Sorry we missed your call earlier this morning, but we had a bit of a late one. Is Marshall there?"

"He is," said Marshall.

"And are you behaving yourself?"

"So far."

"And what did you buy my bestie?"

"I owed him a two-foot-tall soft toy Squirrel," said Marshall. "And I moved heaven and earth to get one sent over in time. It's back in London."

Marshall had surprised him with the present before they had set off, rather than lugging the toy all the way to Bournemouth. Because the family had no idea who he was bringing, they had arranged plain, generic presents for Marshall of men's toiletries and festive socks. The simple gesture had genuinely moved Marshall. Spencer had bought him a fitness watch — because they had both vowed to get fit in the new year — and a card with a voucher that had the words 'good for one autobiography ghostwriter, should the recipient ever need one.' The latter had been a joke, until Marshall looked up, shocked, and asked how Spencer knew a publisher had only just approached him.

"And he also bought me a new phone," added Spencer. "Because just after the new year we're moving into his Bermondsey pad, which has twenty-four-seven Wi-Fi connection."

"You're doing what?" asked his mother, frozen over a pot of something steaming.

"Uh — something I've yet to tell my parents," said Spencer, causing Prince's whole family to laugh out loud.

"What with starting the new job," said Marshall, "and having to hand back his flat, and noting his not-so-healthy eating habits, I thought it might be for the best."

Marshall spoke aloud but made sure he meant the words for Spencer's mother, who smiled and nodded.

"Well," said Bev, "I'm looking forward to an invite to the house-warming. In the meantime, I suppose you've heard about Blake?"

Spencer looked to Marshall, who shrugged.

"No. What's happened now?"

"He tested positive for Covid. They admitted him to the Royal London two days ago. From what Kim tells me, his symptoms are mild. Apparently, he demanded to be released, said he wanted to discharge himself. But nobody argues with those NHS specialists."

"Quite right, too," said Spencer's mum.

"He'll be monitored for at least a fortnight. Muriel's furious. Blake was supposed to manage the office over the Christmas holidays while she took a break. Now she's been running around the office like a headless chicken with the recent resignations."

"Who else has jumped ship?"

"Apart from you, me and Prince, you mean?"

"You've both resigned?" asked a shocked Spencer.

"The virtual events company are expanding and offered us jobs. Appears they were really impressed with how we managed our end of the Blackmore event, and asked if we'd consider coming on board. The future is virtual, Spence. Sweet deal, too, and we're going to be working with a great bunch of dynamic people."

"Muriel must be pulling her hair out."

"Alice said when she heard about our resignations, she threatened to throw herself out of her office window."

"I wouldn't worry, Bev," said Spencer, winking at Marshall. "As usual with Muriel, it's an empty threat. Yes, Blackmore is on the eighteenth floor, but not only are the windows of her office made from reinforced glass, none of them open."

This time the laughter came from both ends of the call.

"Anyway, Wyrrells and guests," said Bev. "We just wanted to phone and wish you all a wonderful Christmas."

"Same to you all. And a very happy new year."

Chapter Twenty-Five

Sunday morning, Spencer stood outside the Bermondsey apartment wearing a plain white towelling robe over his tee and pyjama bottoms. The concrete terrace, which overlooked the Thames, was adorned with lush evergreen plants and bushes in blue-and-white china pots and terracotta plant holders, not unlike Muriel Moresby's penthouse apartment. Spencer cradled a mug of steaming coffee against his chest, watching a barge inch down the Thames. Tiger sat stock-still beside him, watching vigilantly as sparrows chirped excitedly in the branches of a tree across the way. Behind him, a door slid open and shut.

"Bit fresh to be out, isn't it?" said Marshall, coming to stand beside him and putting a warm and comforting arm around his shoulders. Spencer noticed he had a matching towelling robe on, with a folded newspaper stuffed into one pocket. "Aren't you cold?"

"Her Royal Highness wanted to come out and do her business. And then forgot all about it when she spotted the party going on in the tree over there."

Built on a lower floor, the apartment looked directly onto treetops lining the river walkway. Marshall had told him they were cherry trees and would blossom spectacularly in spring. Something else on his long list of things to look forward to in the new year.

"She does love the terrace, doesn't she?"

"Of course she does. We both do. Her, because she finally has some open space."

"And you?"

"Because it's not too far from the ground. In case you ever feel the urge to step over the railing again."

"Arse," said Marshall, pushing his nose into Spencer's ear and nipping the lobe.

The moment he had walked over the threshold, Spencer had fallen in love with the flat, which felt far more like a home than Marshall's South Kensington space. All the furnishings had been chosen for comfort, not style, the cosy tan sectional settee with a place for two to lie next to each other while watching the television, giant cream cushions that could be used on the shag pile carpet, to sit upon. Once the authorities had lifted restrictions, he couldn't wait to get friends over for dinner and drinks. In the days leading up to the new year, when Marshall wasn't rushing into the studio to put the finishing touches to their Kryszytonia documentary, they had moved in together, with Spencer informing his landlord that he could have the flat back early to begin renovating.

"When you're finished, your ladyship," said Marshall, tilting his head down at Tiger, "I have some new gourmet canned food for you to try out."

Tiger blinked up at Marshall, and Spencer could almost believe she smiled at him before she moved over and sat between her new master's slippers.

"You're spoiling her."

Marshall crouched down and scratched her head, a manoeuvre he knew she would love. The two of them had bonded well, Tiger loving having the run of the apartment and, of course, the terrace.

"It's a new year's treat. Anyway, I have to make sure she's on my side, if I want to keep her owner happy."

"You really don't need to worry. Both of us couldn't be happier. I absolutely love this place. Apart from the sex-on-demand, it's bigger than my old gaff, has amazing views, modern kitchen, bathroom and bedroom, and, to top it all, is incredibly convenient. I can't believe we did the journey to my new office in less than thirty minutes yesterday."

"Over the weekend, too," added Marshall. "When the service is probably limited. How are you feeling about tomorrow? Nervous at all?"

Having sorted the apartment out during the week — Spencer had brought mainly clothes and Tiger's things — they'd had Saturday free, so Marshall had suggested they do a trial run using public transport ready for Monday, Spencer's first day on the new job. On their way back, they had shopped in a supermarket together, a simple domestic chore that had made Spencer's heart burst with pride. They were officially a couple.

"Not so much nervous, more excited."

"You're going to do just fine. And, by the way, I've got an online meeting with the publisher tomorrow. Are you going to need to clear your involvement with Ed?"

"I'll talk to him tomorrow. But I can't see it being an issue."

Rather than ghostwrite Marshall's autobiography, Spencer had suggested they write the book together. Marshall had taken some persuading, citing his busy work schedule, but Spencer had convinced him with the image of them both holding the finished hardback in their hands.

"Have you thought any more about what you want in the book? Key events that shaped your life and career? It's important to focus on exceptional things and anecdotes that are going to grab the attention of the reader, but in your line of work I'd expect there to be lots."

"What sort of things did you have in mind?"

"Oh, you know — special moments. Like having a drug lord put out a hit on you because they didn't like the interview you'd done with them."

Peripherally, Spencer noticed Marshall turn to him.

"You know about that?"

"Is it true, then? Joey said something that day I bumped into him at the bar, but I wrote the comment off as his usual brand of bullshit."

"No. I interviewed Fiorelli in 2018 and backed him into a corner. Not the smartest man on the planet, and not the first person I ever pissed off on screen. He did indeed threaten to end me himself. We had a roomful of witnesses, but I took it all as bluster."

"You weren't worried?"

"Not unduly. Comes with the job. Besides, six months after the interview aired, Fiorelli was involved in a family disagreement. His brother-in-law decided he could run the outfit better, went into a restaurant in downtown Boston with his gang of three for a confrontation. Only the restaurant staff walked out alive."

"That is *definitely* going into the book."

Marshall chuckled, and they fell into a comfortable silence for a few moments.

"By the way, have you read the paper this morning?" asked Marshall.

"Only the front cover. We've got all day."

Even in the coldness of the morning, just saying the words aloud filled Spencer with warmth. After a leisurely breakfast, he planned on taking Marshall back to bed. Maybe later he would finish the Sunday newspapers, or perhaps he could persuade Marshall to read aloud to him, a new and surprisingly effective form of foreplay.

"Thought you might be interested to see this."

Marshall pulled the newspaper out of his pocket and handed Spencer what looked to be a full-page advert.

"I don't have my glasses—"

"Here they are."

Marshall pulled them out of the same pocket and placed them on Spencer's face. When he focused on the top of the page, he screwed up his nose.

"Positions Vacant? Why would I be interested in— Oh, I see."

The full-page advertisement was for the award-winning Blackmore Magazine Group and contained no fewer than six positions vacant. Spencer skimmed them briefly, seeing his and Bev's former roles advertised.

"Hey, I meant to tell you," said Spencer, handing the paper back. "Blake sent me an email overnight. Probably from his hospital bed. Asked if I would consider coming back to Blackmore, to officially take over Clarissa's role, if the pay and incentives were right. I declined immediately. I want nothing more to do with him or their family."

"I would have been disappointed if you'd even considered the idea. You've made a good career move, Spence."

"Yes, I know. But I feel a little sorry for Blake. I think he can see the writing on the wall, and he's starting to get desperate. I'll bet you a blowjob he's contacted Bev and Prince, too."

"Even though that's a bet I don't mind losing, I'm guessing they would also have said no, if they have any sense. Don't waste your time feeling sorry for bad management, Spence. From everything you've told me, Muriel Moresby knew exactly what she was doing but has the emotional quotient of a Grinch. I've seen the same thing time and time again, bad business owners treating good staff appallingly, and then blaming everyone but themselves when things go belly up."

"Wow. Harsh, Marsh."

"That's because I know what you've been through. I love what you told Muriel about burning bridges. But now is not the time for looking back."

"I know what you're saying—"

"But a little part of you still wonders why you never got the credit you deserved. Am I right or wrong?"

"I spent two years of my life there, Marsh. I don't want to be there anymore, but neither do I want to see Blackmore fail."

"And that's what makes you the better person, Spence."

"You know," said Spencer, a thought coming to him, "I'm surprised Blake didn't get Muriel to phone you, get you to try and sway me, now she knows you and I are an item. Especially after you agreed to the client event interview."

"That's never going to happen, I'm afraid."

"You've spoken to her?"

"I don't need to. But once you see the final cut of my interview with her and Lord Moresby, you'll understand why. A number of my additional questions made her extremely uncomfortable — although his lordship was a good sport throughout. So, no, she won't be calling me anytime soon."

Spencer slipped his arm around Marshall's waist.

"Remind me never to get on your bad side."

Marshall draped his arm back across Spencer's shoulders and kissed his temple.

"Never going to happen."

"You know, I have Muriel to thank for something," said Spencer, after a few moments.

"Whatever could that be?"

"You. Unknowingly, she brought us together. At that charity event in her penthouse flat back in October. If it hadn't been for that, we might never have met."

"Was it only October?"

"I know, right?"

Right then, Spencer's tummy rumbled, and they both laughed.

"Come on, let's get you some breakfast. And then we need to shower and I need to have a conference call with Darcy. I know it's Sunday, but she's insisting. I'd like you to join, if that's okay? If you're there, she might keep it short and snappy."

"Of course. What's it about?"

"It's Darcy, Spence. Who the hell knows?"

Marshall and Spencer had already talked about divvying up chores around the place, with Spencer opting for the general household tasks. At the same time, Marshall confined himself to the run of the kitchen.

They had only just finished their breakfast of hot oatmeal, fresh fruit and honey — with the obligatory mugs of fresh coffee — when Darcy's call came through. Marshall had already rigged up the large flatscreen on the kitchen wall so they could take the meeting without getting up from the kitchen island.

The moment Marshall accepted the call, a full-screen version of Darcy appeared, her hair pinned up hastily on her head, no makeup, and wearing what appeared to be a Chinese silk dressing gown in scarlet with small golden dragonflies around the mandarin collar.

"Good morning, lovebirds," she said, grinning then sipping from a mug.

"Morning, Darcy." They spoke in unison.

"Is this going to take long? We've got some urgent things needing taken care of this morning." asked Marshall, as Spencer felt a warm hand land on his upper thigh

"Don't worry, I won't keep you long. Got some interesting updates for you."

First, Darcy talked about the book, their online meeting with the publisher and what to expect. He loved the way she worked, telling Marshall she would kick off proceedings and instructing him to steer away from any hint of money topics — advances or percentage royalties. She would take care of all that.

Eventually she got onto the Kryszytonia documentary and the post-production progress. Spencer knew President Karimov had called Marshall the week before, mainly as a social call. But Marshall had used the opportunity to ask him some follow-up questions about what had happened since the assassination attempt, his presidency plans, and to get permission from his advisers to use his answers in his documentary.

"They've come up with the working title. *Kryszytonia: Rise of the Squirrel and the Phoenix*. The squirrel relates to President Tobias Karimov and the phoenix represents the country, rising from the ashes of the past. As I say, it's a working title, so if you have any other suggestions, let Kerry-Anne know."

They went on to talk about the difficulty of getting everything into the forty-minute time slot. Colm had shot a wealth of extra material when he'd searched the rubble for Marshall, and while this was unique footage, they needed to provide a balance to add weight to the documentary.

"Now the big news. Although the producers still want a couple of tweaks made next week, the documentary will have a special screening at the end of January. There's a lot of excited buzz in the industry, Marshall, because your team was the only one there to record the historic event as a documentary. Please don't get your hopes up yet, but it's likely your little gem will be picked up for a number of best documentary award nominations. We're not sure what format each of the ceremonies will take, but they'll expect us all to be available. Hope you've got a tuxedo, Spence I want you looking your scrubbed-up best that night. And if Marshall wins anything, I expect no less than you planting a full-on kiss on his lips. Are we all on the same page?"

"We are, Darcy," said Spencer, laughing along with Marshall. "And you don't have to worry. If he wins anything, I'll be all over him like a lap dancer."

"Okay, I'll love you and leave you," said Darcy. "I'm sure you've got better things to do. It's going to be a good year, boys. I can feel it in my blood."

Darcy ended the call, and Spencer sighed before turning to Marshall.

"It already is a good year," he said, moving Marshall's hand farther up his thigh.

"Oh yeah?" said Marshall, his voice becoming deep and gruff.

"Oh yeah. Want me to show you how good?"

"Lead the way."

Want to see more from this author?
Here's a taster for you to enjoy!

Salvaging Christmas
Brian Lancaster

Excerpt

Trevor McTavish loved traditions.

Or, more to the point, new traditions built on old ones. After all, wasn't that what most of them were, a blend of old and new, built layer upon layer over time? They provided a foundation, something people could rely on, even when everything else around them broke down, or changed unexpectedly, or disappeared entirely from their lives—which seemed to happen to him all too often of late.

Traditions ensured continuity, and even with the few hiccups this year had brought, Trevor loved the Christmas tradition he and Cheryl had created for their friends.

As the sullen driver of the prepaid cab steered in silence through the early morning streets of London, Trevor rested his head against the ice-cold window. Gentle vibrations from the hybrid engine massaged his skull. Already the sky had begun transitioning from purest black as the night shift packed up and daylight took over. Fully alert despite the early hour, he looked for homes with their Christmas lights still burning and gardens or roofs decorated with seasonal figures. A part of him instinctively knew he would get along with the person who had gone to all the effort to put them up, most likely done to make other people smile.

Nothing could shake Trevor's upbeat mood as the cab turned into the familiar road where the Madison family lived. Since he'd packed last night, the sense of anticipation and excitement at the promise of a road trip with best friends had kept him pumped up and grinning like an inflatable snowman.

Six in the morning on that pre-dawn Friday in December, he climbed out of the overheated car and crunched down onto a pavement of overnight frost. After collecting his luggage from the boot, he pulled out a five-pound note from his wallet and tapped a fingernail on the driver's window. With a smile, he held up the banknote, ready to wish the man a heartfelt season's greetings. After all, if the poor guy had to drive a cab at this early hour, he obviously needed the money.

Without even bothering to acknowledge Trevor, the driver pulled away.

Left standing alone in the road, Trevor shrugged and put the fiver back. Perhaps the man had somewhere better to be. Not everyone shared his passion for all things festive.

Humming to himself, he manoeuvred his wheelie luggage up the broken-tiled garden path and prodded the front doorbell. Bing-bongs chimed from somewhere inside. Cheryl Madison's mother opened the door in her furry-hooded olive parka and mismatching navy Wellington boots. Further at odds with the ensemble, her pink floral nightie peeked out from beneath the jacket.

Trevor almost let cut a giggle.

Until he saw the expression on her face.

After a furtive glance at the staircase behind her, Mrs M nodded sharply towards the Volvo out front while handing him a small but deceptively heavy cardboard box. Hauling a larger one from the floor, she strode past him and he trailed after her, the wheels of his luggage clunking arrhythmically on the broken pavement. Only as she unlocked the hatchback and placed her carton inside did she reveal the predicament.

"Hannah's not coming. She broke up with Cheryl last night. Met someone at their Christmas office party on Tuesday night. Supposedly."

The way she articulated that final word said everything. Trevor dropped onto the tailgate — causing the car to bounce — and placed his container next to hers. Mrs M stood there studying him, arms folded appearing to wait for his response. Instinctively, he mirrored her body language and sighed. Of all their friends, he understood only too well the devastating effects of being dumped. Right before their long-anticipated Christmas trip, too. Hannah had always possessed a selfish streak, an immunity to the sensibilities of others. She had often manipulated Cheryl but he'd never thought she would stoop so low.

"Shit. Poor Cheryl. How's she coping?"

"You'll see in a minute. Putting on a brave front. I tried to sound surprised when she told me, but something's not been right for months. The important thing, Trevor, is that we're down by one more guest."

"Double shit," he said, staring down at the road between his legs.

"I'll let you think about that before I bring out any more boxes, and while I go and put the kettle on," she said, before heading back to the house.

So much for the *Yuletide Gay Club*.

They had started the group five years ago. Cheryl, his best friend since high school, could take credit for the idea and him for its successful implementation. Sick of hearing in January how many of their gay friends had spent the holiday season either alone or with families who barely tolerated them, they had created their own tradition.

Six couples shared the cost of renting a country cottage in rural Britain. Seven or eight days spent enjoying Christmas their own way, with their own people, in the countryside.

Far from the maddening crowds.

At first nobody had known whether bringing together couples who were occasional friends would work. That first time, the gathering in the six-bedroom farmhouse in Devon had turned out to be nothing short of a miracle. Everyone had gelled quickly and mucked in together, laughed and got drunk together, played games like Cards Against Humanity until sunrise and raved about the break well into the New Year. So good was the experience that Trevor had already had the next event booked up by February. The same thing had happened the following years, with the small group growing closer.

Except this year—the fifth—grim providence had made a personal appearance. Tragically, Mrs M's seventy-two-year-old Scottish girlfriend, Monica, the only other person allowed in the kitchen at Christmas and the life and soul of the party, had succumbed unexpectedly to a brain aneurism and passed away in late January.

Next up, at the beginning of March, they had received a cryptic email from regulars Johnny and Frank. Both having quit their jobs, they'd decided to take a hiatus from the rat race, managed to rent out their home, and set off on their travels. Finally free, they'd also committed to a technology-free tour of the world and their last handwritten postcard had been sent from somewhere in the Middle East.

As the year progressed, the casualties had continued to fall like autumn leaves until the usual company of twelve had dropped to five.

Then in April, Trevor's husband of two years, Karl, had not only announced his newly discovered heterosexuality, or bisexuality, or sexual fluidity—he had yet to settle on a label—but admitted that he had fallen in love with a woman. Four years together, and Trevor's spouse had woken one morning and realised he had been wrestling for the wrong tag team.

Which left four of them. Initially, they had considered cancelling the event. But without consulting any of them, Hannah had tactlessly filled one space with a new girl from her office, twenty-year-old Jessica, who, in turn, decided that bringing along a male colleague would be perfectly acceptable.

Could things get any worse?

Apparently, they could. After Trevor had signed the online divorce papers, there had followed a doorstep altercation with Karl about which artwork, pillows, bed linen, dishes and cutlery he was entitled to take in the divorce. Not thinking straight, Trevor had succumbed to all his demands. In addition, for their Christmas excursion, Karl had seen no reason why he should be ostracised, why he should not still be invited with his new partner. Maybe because of dwindling numbers, or more likely the result of a temporary lapse in sanity, Trevor had capitulated.

Cheryl had refused to speak to him for three weeks after he'd told her.

By the beginning of December, the promise of a seasonal sanctuary, which used to be the epitome of a cosy, warm and cuddly Christmas Hallmark movie, had morphed into the awkward, dysfunctional cast of characters befitting a Woody Allen feature.

"The question remains," came the voice of Mrs M. Lost in his thoughts, he jumped when she perched down beside him. "Is it too late to cancel?"

Trevor huffed out a steamy breath and searched for seasonal inspiration along the row of terraced houses. All year he had been looking forwards to their getaway. But this wasn't only about him.

"Technically, it isn't. But we won't get a refund, so we'll lose the full amount, deposit and all. I'll also need to ring around and let everyone know pretty swiftly before people set off tomorrow. And I'll try, but I'm not sure I can contact the owner. Apparently, she has her own family gathering abroad."

Two nights ago, he had received an email from Mrs Mortimer-King telling him that she would not be in Scotland to meet them, but would arrange for someone to hand the keys over and settle them in. Even though he'd never met her, he liked dealing with her, enjoyed her clear instructions, efficiency and her friendly communications.

"I had a long talk with Cheryl last night," said Mrs M. "She still wants to go. Doesn't want to spend Christmas at home sitting around moping."

"Understandable. How about you?"

Mrs M provided another smile before gazing wistfully to the heavens.

"No matter where I am, I'm going to miss having Mon by my side. She always made this time of the year special. Might as well be busy in Scotland as stuck here with too much time on my hands. Cheryl can help me in the kitchen. How about Karl?"

"Karl? What about him? He's going to be there."

"That's my point. How do you feel about that?"

"It's fine. I'll deal."

Total nonsense, of course. Privately, Trevor prayed his ex-husband would do the decent thing and not show up, or perhaps the new significant other would be better at talking him down from the ledge of his principles. Most of all, he dreaded the idea of seeing Karl fawning over a new partner. Over the years Trevor had grown to love the man, had looked to their life together. Karl suppressed his emotions well and had never been afraid to put on a front and fight for what he believed to be right. Trevor had never been a fighter. He had felt emotionally volatile during their doorstep argument. After Karl had gotten everything he came for, he'd promptly turned on his heel and headed back to the comfort of his newfound relationship. That evening, Trevor had curled up on his side of the double bed he had managed to keep, feeling so painfully alone and pathetic. All night he had lain awake, wondering why Karl had never fought for him the same way.

"In different ways, we've both lost someone this year, Trevor. But you know we'll be there for you, Cheryl and me, don't you?" said Mrs M, as though hearing his thoughts.

"And I really appreciate that, Mrs M. But if they do show up, promise me you won't let the break turn into an us-and-them fiasco. You know what Karl's like when he becomes militant."

"Wouldn't dream of doing so. But I'm also not standing quietly and letting him order anyone around. Like he usually does." She pushed a lock of grey hair from her face before turning to him. "He's still going to the SLAGO meetings. Turned up at the Christmas fundraiser. Did he tell you?"

Karl had said nothing, but Trevor was unsurprised. His ex might have woken up one day and realised he wasn't gay anymore, but he still loved a cause, a fight to champion. Hence his unfailing loyalty to the Surrey and London Association of Gay Organisations. After the break-up, Cheryl had mused somewhat unkindly whether Karl had ever really been gay, whether he had decided to call himself queer because he needed to wear a badge of honour, to fight on the side of something subversive and radical, become a member of the Great British LGBTQ Cause Club. Trevor knew different, because their relationship had not been a sham even if Karl had shunned affection outside the bedroom. Trevor accepted those things because they meant having someone to care for, to love and share a life with. And more than anything, even after everything that had transpired, Trevor still respected Karl as a person.

"What he does now is his own business. Lots of straight people go to those meetings," he offered. He didn't want an argument about Karl. "Helping young gay kids who are chucked out on the streets by their families, kids with nowhere to go. Karl's still supporting a worthy cause."

Mrs M didn't appear to want to listen. In some ways, she was just like her late partner.

"Lesbians that convert and cross over to the hetero side are labelled 'hasbians'. What do you call men who denounce their homosexual status?"

"He's not calling himself straight, if that's what you're asking. So I don't think he's entirely forfeited the title."

"Mon would have called him a *fecking wee Judas*."

Trevor let out an exasperated breath. Had she been alive, Monica would have probably gone round to see Karl and given him a piece of her mind, and would at the very least have withdrawn his invitation.

"Look, I know you're supporting me, Mrs M. But if we're going to get through this holiday, let's keep our thoughts to ourselves and try to struggle through with the minimum of casualties."

After a glance, she chuckled a steamy breath into the morning.

"You're really selling this holiday, aren't you? But I'm deadly serious, Trevor. If you want to back out now, we're with you all the way."

He stared into the distance and thought about something Cheryl had said recently to him Quoting the five stages of grief, she believed Trevor should be going through the anger stage by now, showing signs of betrayal or issuing threats of revenge. But that was never going to be his style. Others had made their thoughts and feelings known about Karl, but Trevor wasn't built that way. Yes, of course he had wallowed in self-pity at first, but he had also had nine months to use up those emotions and now felt wrung out, emotionally exhausted, and resigned to living out the rest of his days as a bachelor gay. And a holiday far away from the city smoke could be just what the therapist ordered — if he'd had one.

"Stuff it, no. Let's do it, Mrs M. If not for us, for Monica. She loved this time of year. And we're gathering in the land of her ancestors, the Caledonian Celts."

"Oh, baby," she said, putting her arm around his shoulders and hugging him tightly. "You have such a good heart. I promise never to mention this again for the duration of the holiday, but Karl was neither right nor good enough for you."

"You're obligated to say that. It's written into the mother charter under the 'Cheryl's best friend' subsection. So how many are we now?"

"You, me and Cheryl."

"Three."

"Karl and his new — is she his girlfriend?" asked Mrs M.

"Partner, I think."

"What's her name?"

"No idea. But that makes us five."

"Jessica and this guy she's bringing. From Hannah's office."

"Seven then. Are they a couple?"

"Not according to Hannah."

"How are they travelling there?"

"Train, I think. Not our problem, is it? They have the address."

"Are they even gay?"

"Don't think so."

"Heaven help us," Trevor said, shaking his head. "This keeps getting better and better. Seven of us in a seven-bedroom converted lakeside lodge — sorry, *lochside* lodge — that sleeps up to eighteen. Obscene, really. Mind you, the place looks amazing, especially the kitchen. Did Cheryl show you the latest website photos? Modernised, but they've still maintained its vintage charm, especially with that huge Aga cooker."

"Never trust photographs. Remember the Lake District? All mod cons, my foot. Just because they provided a four-slice toaster and a heated towel rack. And I've tried cooking on many an Aga, and recall what a temperamental pain in the backside they can be."

"That's your superpower, Mrs M. Wrestling temperamental pains in the backside. I suppose you've packed enough food to feed the whole village?"

"You might thank me if we're snowed in."

"The way the weather's been playing up, we're more likely to experience heat stroke."

At that very moment, Cheryl emerged from the house, juggling three mugs of something hot and steaming. Decked out in her faux-Versace beige-and-burgundy silk dressing gown and pink slippers, she came to a stop before the garden gate. With a mimed roar, she issued a steamy yawn into the morning.

"Trevor Oswald McTavish," came her familiar voice. She was the only person he would allow to use his full name. Sometimes his friends called him Mac, because nobody — *nobody* — ever referred to him as Trev. Not unless they wanted to be ghosted. Considering everything that had gone down over the past twenty-four hours, she did not look too bad. "Thought I heard your dulcet tones. Well, don't sit there like pigeons on a pole. One of you open the gate for poor, lonesome old me. Can't you see my hands are full?"

"Someone's cheered up," whispered her mother. "Must be hearing your voice, Trevor." Standing up from the tailgate, she went over and unlatched the access. "I thought you were showering. You told me we needed to be on the road early, to beat the traffic."

"I didn't know if you and Trevor had decided to pull the plug. But judging by your smiling faces, I guess not. And anyway, there's no rush now. I just checked the satnav app and listened to the latest traffic report." Cheryl handed a mug of deep brown tea to her mother, and a milkier version to Trevor. "Looks as though people stayed home. So we may as well do the M25,

M40 then hit the M6. If we leave by nine, with an hour's stop for lunch, we'll reach the lodge between eight and nine this evening."

"Perfect," said Mrs M, taking a sip from her mug and pulling a face. "Means we'll arrive in time for a quick shower and a bite to eat before bedtime. Then a whole day getting things ready before the others arrive."

Trevor studied Cheryl as Mrs M spoke. She seemed far too bright and perky considering everything. Either she was putting on a brave face or, more likely, the news had not been unexpected.

"So what's gonna be the theme this time, Martha Stewart?" Cheryl asked him.

Each year, Trevor had been tasked with decorating the venue in readiness for the rest of the troupe's arrival. If Cheryl's mum excelled in the kitchen, his forte was in decorating spaces. On the first trip he'd created a freedom rainbow theme, conceptually tricky but accomplished without making the place seem too tacky, or like a set from *My Little Pony*. In subsequent years, other people had pushed their choices — *Frozen's* pure white, and blue for Johnny and Frank, after their favourite Christmas song, *Blue Christmas*.

This season Trevor had consulted nobody. But he always remembered Monica's reaction whenever he unveiled one of his creations, a simple, '*Nice, Mac, but what's wrong with normal decorations?*' This year, he had decided to go with a conventional Christmas theme, fresh and natural, incorporating whatever he could find around the lodge. Hopefully this would entail a visual and fragrant display of branches of fir, evergreen and pine cones, items he could fix together and finish off with the red or tartan ribbons he had brought from home. No gaudy colours, no artificial paints or glitter this year, just earth colours and raw materials.

"Trade secret. But let's just say I'm not taking requests this year."

"Whatever you do," said Mrs M, patting him lightly on the shoulder, "I'm sure it will be lovely."

"Not sure anyone will notice," Trevor muttered to himself as she shuffled off, a move clearly meant to leave space for Cheryl and him to talk. As she managed the latch on the garden gate, Cheryl moved to take the place beside him. They sat for a few moments, each sipping their drinks, before either broke the silence — an honour given to Cheryl.

"Mum and I talked last night. As long as you were still on board, I'd be driving the first leg until Birmingham," she said, the ordinary topic surprising him. "Mum's insisting on doing her bit, but her eyesight's getting worse. So I suggested she take the second leg for a couple of hours until mid-afternoon before the light starts to fade. After that, you can take over."

"Fine by me."

"Told her you're the only one who's been to Scotland and knows back roads."

"I've been there once. To Edinburgh by train. When I was ten."

"She doesn't need to know that. Besides, we have my trusty satnav app."

They sat in comfortable silence again until he peered at her.

"Why didn't you call me last night? About Hannah?" he asked. Few of the people who knew Cheryl got to see the morning version — pale and makeup free and, quite honestly, looking like she needed a blood transfusion. She held her mug before her in both hands but refused to look at him as she took a big sigh and replied.

"She called at midnight. And I didn't want to bother you. You're still working through your own relationship aftermath." Cheryl smoothed an errant lock of her long mousy brown hair over her right ear, a trademark habit. "I'm angry, Mac, of course I am. But the truth is we've been drifting apart for months. Last night wasn't a knife to the heart so much as the final squeeze that stopped the heart from beating. Worst of all, everyone saw what was happening but me. Maybe because I'd hoped that if I didn't say anything, things might eventually turn themselves around. But everything makes sense now. I wanted us to marry, she didn't see the point. I wanted to move in together, she preferred her own space. Can't tell you how many times she voiced her dislike of kids, as though letting me know not to even dare ask. All the signs were there. I was just deaf and blind to them."

"Yeah, well, love can do that."

"I'm not even sure what we had was love. More like comfortable familiarity. This was my wake-up call, my epiphany, telling me it's time to grow up and move on."

Trevor reached across to squeeze Cheryl's hand.

"Must say, you're taking this like a trooper."

"Really? Right at this moment, I feel like standing up on the bonnet of this car, getting my Adele on and belting *Make You Feel My Love* into the morning at the top of my voice."

"Please, no. Think of the sleeping neighbours. Besides, no karaoke before midday."

Both chuckled, Cheryl bumping her shoulder with his, before she sighed deeply.

"I've no idea who she is," she said. "This girl she's supposed to have met at the work party. Not even sure there is anyone. If you want my guess, she needs time alone over Christmas, or at least the company of her own family."

"Could have picked better timing," said Trevor. "I'm not sure we'd have gotten a refund, though, if — "

"Doesn't matter. I paid her share," said Cheryl.

A heavy silence hung in the air between them.

"They say bad things come along in threes," said Trevor.

"Threes?"

"Monica, Karl and now Hannah. Although your mum's loss is hardly comparable to ours. How's she doing?"

"You know Mum. She tries not to let anything get to her, puts on a brave front for everyone. But I know she's hurting. I know she misses Monica terribly. A couple of times I've heard her talking to herself, in the bedroom or the bathroom. Until I realised she was actually talking to Monica."

Trevor breathed out a sigh and let the sadness sink in.

"Poor Mrs M. Our worries pale by comparison, don't they? I suppose things gets better, over time."

"So they say. Do you still miss Karl?" asked Cheryl.

Trevor stared at his feet. *Every day*, he almost blurted. For five of their six years together, they had lived under the same rented roof, shared the same bed, watched the same television shows, cooked and cared for each other — in sickness and in health. On the other hand, each had stuck with their own set of friends outside of their home and the two camps had rarely mixed. He and Karl had only ever showed up as a couple on the rare occasion, such as family gatherings or meetings with their support group friends.

When Karl left, Trevor had holed himself up, and the flat had become a tomb. Apart from visiting Cheryl's place on occasion, he hadn't felt brave enough to step out on his own.

"Sometimes," he lied. "But I'm finally comfortable with my own company. At least you didn't get married then get dragged through the gutters of divorce."

"True enough."

"All those years the gay community spent chasing marriage equality. And once we finally won the right, we totally forgot that marriage comes with that evil and twisted twin lurking in the shadows, waiting for an opportunity to pounce. We forgot that once you get the main prize, there in the wings like a vicious predator, hungry to get its fangs into anything you have and stamp on anything you ever felt, lies good old-fashioned divorce."

"And *finally* Trevor's anger raises its ugly head—"

"You think you know somebody until you're threatening to strangle each other over throw cushions, nylon quilt covers or placemats decorated with the heads of Lenin, Mao and Che Guevara. Even a novelty penis bottle opener. I'd love to know what my replacement has made of that little gem."

"What's her name, by the way? This new girlfriend."

Cheryl's mother had asked him the same thing.

"No idea. We'll find out tomorrow. Unless the pair of them come to their senses and decide not to show." Trevor stared at his mug and gently shook his head. "I'm twenty-eight, Cheryl. There's this guy the same age as me who works for one of my clients. He's married to another man and they have a kid he walks to school each morning."

"And your point is?"

"When am I going to grow up?"

"*We*, you mean. And to be honest, I hope we never do. At least you get to cross marriage off your list." Cheryl placed the mug against her cheek and sighed deeply. "Is this trip going to be a disaster?"

"Are you giving me permission to burst into *My Heart Will Go On*?"

Cheryl checked her wristwatch.

"Sorry, Mac, still morning. No karaoke. Your rule, not mine."

Once again, they grinned at each other, and Trevor felt his bravado swell through their shared humour and adversity.

"You know what, Cheryl? Your mum asked the same thing, and I'll tell you what I told her. We're doing this. We may not have the usual crowd, but your mum's still serving up her amazing Christmas fare, there are plenty of rooms for privacy, and we'll be in walking country. So if anyone starts to get on our nerves, we can find each other and go for a long walk in the glen. Or a hike to a local pub. Or go for a swim in the bloody loch for all I care."

"I am so not packing my swimwear," she said, horrified.

"Wimp," he said, nudging her shoulder.

"Bloody right. But I'll happily cheer you on as you cut a hole in the ice and dive in. I may even help you out, if you can find the hole again," she replied with a mischievous smile. "And I am going to eat and drink whatever I want, no calorie counting and no judgement."

"And no disagreement from me. I am with you one hundred percent."

"God," she said, breathing out a long sigh. "Maybe we should just get married to each other. If celebrities are alleged to be able to make marriages work, I'm sure we can. Sex isn't everything, is it?"

Trevor took the question to be rhetorical.

"Love you as I do, Cheryl, we would only ruin a perfect friendship. We'd end up killing each other over which TV programmes to watch, acceptable toilet seat etiquette, whose turn for the karaoke machine, duvet hogging — any number of things. Besides, not only am I never getting married again, I am never falling in love. And you can quote me on that."

"Oh, trust me, I will."

"Now, let's get our arses into gear. We've got a long road ahead. But just so you know, I'm not booking anything next year. Takes too much effort. This is definitely going to be the last."

"Last what?"

"Last Christmas. And no, that was *not* your cue for a song!"

About the Author

Brian Lancaster is an author of gay romantic fiction in multiple genres, including contemporary romance, paranormal, fantasy, crime, mystery, and anything else that tickles his muse's fancy. After living for over twenty years in Southeast Asia, he has now comfortably resettled in the sleepy south of England, where he shares a home with his husband and two of the laziest cats on the planet.

Brian loves to hear from readers. You can find his contact information, website details and author profile page at https://www.pride-publishing.com

PUBLISHING

Sign up for our newsletter and find out about all our
romance book releases, eBook sales and promotions,
sneak peeks and FREE romance books!